DRAGON'S WINTER

BOOKS BY
Elizabeth A. Lynn

THE CHRONICLES OF TORNOR:
WATCHTOWER
THE DANCERS OF ARUN
THE NORTHERN GIRL

A DIFFERENT LIGHT
THE SARDONYX NET
THE WOMAN WHO LOVED THE MOON
AND OTHER STORIES
DRAGON S WINTER

DRAGON'S WINTER

WINTER

Elizabeth A. Lynn

ACE BOOKS, NEW YORK

DRAGON S WINTER

An Ace Book
Published by The Berkley Publishing Group,
a member of Penguin Putnam Inc.,
200 Madison Avenue, New York, NY 10016
The Putnam Berkley World Wide Web site address is
http://www.berkley.com

First Edition: April 1998

Library of Congress Cataloging—in—Publication Data

Lynn, Elizabeth A.
    Dragon s winter / Elizabeth A. Lynn.
        p.   cm.
    ISBN 0-441-00502-0
    I. Title.
    PS35620Y443D73   1998
    813'.54 dc21   97-21543
                                          CIP

Printed in the United States of America

10   9   8   7   6   5   4   3   2   1

DRAGON'S WINTER

*O*ur country has wide borders; there is no man
    born has travelled round it. And it bears
    secrets in its bosom of which no man dreams.

*U*p here we live two different lives: in the summer,
    under the torch of the warm sun, and in the
    winter, under the lash of the north wind.

*A*nd when the long Darkness spreads itself over the
    country . . . men's thoughts move along devious
    paths . . . and many hidden things are revealed.

Blind Ambrosius

PROLOGUE

———◆———

THE WOMAN IN the bed was very weak. Sweat streamed from her: it was August, and the morning air was still and hot in the close stone chamber. The huge mound of her belly barely moved. She had been in labor for two days, long for one so small and delicate as she. The room smelled of sweat, blood, and herb-smoke.

"My sweet lady Hana, you must keep pushing," said Lirith Cordis, chief among the castle women. She wiped the narrow soaked face with a cool cloth. Lirith knew as much about birthing babies as anyone in the domain: she had borne three of her own, now grown, and had been present at the birth of Kojiro Atani, lord of the castle. She kept all anxiety from her voice, but it could be seen, briefly, on her face. Hana Atani, eyes closed, did not see it, but she did not need to. It filled the room, like the smoke. The birth was early by nearly a month, and the babies — two of them, merciful Mother! — were big, and Hana was fine-boned, with little hips, and young . . . She was only seventeen.

But she was a warrior's wife, and a warrior's daughter. Gasping for air, she gathered her exhausted spirit and pushed as she had been bidden. A blinding pain knotted her insides. She thrust her head back like a wounded horse and screamed. The sentries sweating on the battlements heard it through the tall, narrow windows; the young ones winced, and those whose wives or lovers had borne children counted the hours in their minds, and shook their heads. A few glanced furtively at Lorimir Ness. The young Averran warrior stood apart from them, face turned south into the sunlight, elbows leaning on the stone.

"Lirith," Hana whispered. "It hurts."

"I know, my heart," Lirith said. "That is the way of it. Be brave. The pain will end."

But it did not, though at times it eased slightly. The women did their best to make the struggling mother comfortable, with hot cloths, and sweets to give her strength. Hana Diamori Atani thrashed weakly, and whispered a name. Lirith said harshly to young Bryony, who had come with clean water from the kitchen, "You did not hear that." Hana Atani moaned in her bed, and thrice more called the name of a man who was not her husband.

The end, when it finally came, came quickly. Within the soaked, twisted bedclothes, Hana cried out hoarsely. Her fists clenched on the sheets. Blood gushed from between her legs, and with the blood came a red-skinned, slimy child, its huge head covered with light golden hair. Aum, the under-steward, wiped the infant lightly with a cloth, while Lirith cut the cord with a steady hand. "Why is she bleeding so?" said Bryony nervously.

"She is torn, inside. Be quiet, and press here," said Lirith. "How is the babe?"

Aum said, "A boy. Strong. Well-formed. Eyes like blue gems." The baby wailed vigorously. "Strong lungs."

"The Mother be praised. Hana, little one, sweetheart. Hana! Julia, pass the herb-stick under her nose. There is a baby yet to come."

Aum said suddenly, "Oh, merciful Sedi."

Lirith let her gaze turn from Hana. "What is it?" There was near-panic in Aum's usually level voice. Aum never panicked.

For answer, Aum captured the boy-child's flailing angry

fist and held it for Lirith to see. It was a surprisingly big fist. At the very tips of the fingers were small, sharp, curving claws.

"A dragon-child," said Lirith. She gazed into the baby's gleaming azure eyes, unable to keep pride from her voice. "The dragon-blood runs true. Ah, the darling. Thou art thy father's son, right enough. They will slough off. We will have to bind them, so that he does not prick himself, or Tessa." Tessa was the wet-nurse from Chingura, who waited in the kitchen. "Here, Nella. Bathe him and put him in his cradle."

"Lirith, the lady Hana is not breathing!" Bryony cried.

"Prop her up," ordered Lirith. "Hold the smoke close. Wash her with cold water, cold as it can be."

But there was no cold water in the stifling August dawn. As the red sun drove upwards from out the eastern sea, Hana Diamori Atani died. Lirith pulled the second boy-child from her belly. His hair, like his brother's, was gilt, but his fingers were soft-tipped, clawless. Lirith dangled him head downward, and slapped his backside to make him breathe. He gasped, but did not cry.

A hot wind sighed through the close stone chamber, and the harsh hard clamor of dagger hilts pounding shields came from the battlements. A rushing, thunderous murmur shook the Keep. "At last! The dragon-lord is home," Aum said. She straightened the frail body. It looked very small in death. "Bryony, go, quickly, and bring clean linen. Hurry! He will come at any moment. We cannot let him see her like this."

Bryony hurried. Wearily, for she had had little sleep over two days and nights, Lirith laid the second infant into Julia's outstretched arms. "Bathe him, and cover him well. He looks to be more delicate than the other." Blood slimed his slender frame, and welled from shallow wounds on his right cheekbone and hip. "Poor little one. It was cramped in thy mother's womb, and thy older brother was impatient to be free. They will heal, I promise thee." The silent child stared at her, not moving under her bloodstained hands.

Booted footsteps pounded along the stone hallway. The door opened; the women fell quickly back. Kojiro Atani halted in the doorway. He was a young man, lithe and strong, with hair the color of yellow flame, and he moved like flame, graceful, silent, inexorable.

"Well?" he said.

Lirith said, "My lord, you have two beautiful sons."

She lifted the eldest boy from the nest of linens. Kojiro Atani cupped his huge warm hands. Lirith laid the infant into them.

"A dragon-child," the man whispered. He bent his head. "Be welcome, little golden one. Thy name is Karadur." The name meant *Fire-bringer*. His fair face glowed with prideful wonder. "He looks well."

"He is well, my lord." Lirith lifted the second boy from Julia's arms. "And this is his womb-brother."

Kojiro Atani gazed at the second boy. "He is so small . . ." A jagged line of blood marred the silent child's fair face. "He is torn. Who has bloodied him?"

"His older brother was in a hurry," Aum said softly.

"Ah." The big man nuzzled Karadur's rose petal–soft cheek. "Little eager one. That is no way to treat thy brother!" The dragon-child gazed blankly upward, and waved one aimless fist. "Lirith, he stares right at me! Can he see me?"

"Not really. He is too young, my lord," Lirith said.

With great tenderness, Kojiro Atani laid his eldest son into Aum the steward's arms. Then he cupped a light hand beneath his second son's fuzzy head. "Little one, thy name is Tenjiro." It meant *Heaven's hope*. He frowned. "He is very still, this one. Is he healthy?"

Lirith felt for the boy's heartbeat, and was reassured by the strong, clear pulse. "He is well, my lord."

"Be certain that he stays so," Kojiro Atani said softly. "For if aught should happen to him, or to the elder—others also have sons." For an instant, white-gold dragonfire scorched the sultry air, and the promise of immeasurable savagery shimmered in the dragon-lord's eyes. The girl Julia and Aum Nialsdatter, the under-steward, both flinched. But Lirith Cordis had served the Crimson Dragon, Atalaya Atani, this man's mother, and she knew that the quality the dragon-kin most prized, after loyalty, was courage. She faced him squarely.

"No harm will befall your children, my lord."

"And—my wife?"

Lirith moved, so that he could see the bed, and the woman on it. They had cleared the bloodstained linens, wrapped her in rose silk, and combed her fine dark hair over her pillow until it shone like spun glass. Her delicate, ivory-colored face was smooth as moonlight. Around her slim neck they had fastened the amber and topaz necklace which had belonged to Atalaya Atani.

He moved to the side of the bed. Lifting his dead wife's hand, he held it in his own. "She was so young," he said. "So far from home."

Lirith said, "My lord, we did all we could to save her."

"I know . . ." He turned. "The house will keep vigil for her tonight. Aum, you were her friend. Will you see to it? Tomorrow we will make a place for her to lie."

Aum said, "You will not send her home?"

"No. Averra is too far. I will let her family know, of course. But her spirit should rest near her children, to protect them."

The women looked at one another. "But where—" There were no burial mounds or cairns near the dark walls of Atani Castle. The dragon-kin did not lie in earth.

Kojiro Atani frowned, impatient. "What difference can it make! She is dead." He laid the limp hand down. "Let it be a place where her sons may honor her," he said in a gentler tone. He left them then. Aum laid Karadur Atani into his cradle.

"Lirith, I must leave you," she said softly. "I have been absent so long, Azil will be hunting for me . . ." Azil was her own little son, three years old. "I will tell Tessa to make ready. Is there aught you need?"

Lirith shook her head. Aum and Julia left the sad, hot chamber. Lirith sat on a corner of the bed. She was a big-boned, heavy woman, and her legs ached. She hummed. The infant Tenjiro lay motionless in her arms.

"Lirith," a man's voice said softly. Startled, Lirith's arms tightened defensively. Lorimir Ness stood in the doorway. "May I see her?"

Lirith rose. "You shouldn't be here."

"I know." The man's square-bearded face was rigid with grief. He crossed to the bed. Briefly he lifted Hana Diamori Atani's small cooling hand to his lips. "When will they bury her?"

"Tomorrow."

"Do you know where they will put her? It should be somewhere green. She loved gardens." His voice broke, and then steadied. Tears gleamed in his beard. He glanced at the silent baby in Lirith's arms. "Is that the dragon-child?"

"No. This is his younger brother, Tenjiro. Lorimir, go now, before you are seen."

"I go," the warrior said, and left.

A slow breeze, blowing through the tall window, nudged the curtain aside. Sunlight trickled across Tenjiro Atani's bloodied cheek. He stirred, whimpering, and his paper-thin eyelids tightened. "Poor motherless one. All will be well," Lirith crooned, rocking him. "*Bird sleeps, insect creeps, Sunshine goes a-walking, Starlight find, quiet mind, Hear the night a-talking . . .*" The boy in her arms lay very still, eyes clenched against the searching light.

PART
ONE

1

HIS NAME WAS Karadur Atani. His brother called him Kaji; the officers of his household and garrison called him, to his face, *my lord*, and privately, among and to themselves, *Dragon*.

His home, Atani Castle, in Ippa, was known as Dragon Keep. The black-walled castle was ancient and solid, strong as the northern hills against which it had been raised. Unlike most of its neighbor castles, Dragon Keep had never been stormed or besieged or taken by an enemy.

On a blue September morning, the man his soldiers named Dragon, accompanied by his best friend, his twin brother, and half the garrison, rode across the ridge of dry brown hillside below the Keep. He was hunting a wild boar. It had blundered out of the forest north of Chingura into a farmer's cornfield, and, pursued by the enraged farmer and half a dozen of her neighbors, it had been brought inexpertly to bay at the river. Armed with rakes and hoes, the farmers had scored its sides, and taken its left eye. Pain-maddened, the boar had trampled one man, gored another, and charged north.

The twins rode side by side: Karadur on Smoke, his big black gelding, Tenjiro, to his right, on a bay mare. The brothers' faces were alike, except that the bones in Karadur's face showed harder and more prominent, and Tenjiro bore a clot of white scars along the line of his left cheek. Karadur Atani wore unadorned black, and his sun-gilt hair gleamed like thick silk rope in the sunlight. Tenjiro's hands and clothing sparkled with jewels, and his hair was sleek as a greyhound's coat. He was an elegant and graceful man: pretty, some called him, who looked no deeper than the surface. He had been absent from the Keep for nearly a year, and returned barely a month ago. He had been studying, he said, though he had refused to name his teacher, or even to say what the subject of his study had been.

Azil Aumson rode on Karadur's left hand. He was a reserved, dark-haired man, slender, of no notable comeliness, except for the grace and sensitivity of his long, musician's fingers, and the resonant beauty of his voice.

"The dogs have the scent," said Tenjiro. "Do you want to follow further?" As he spoke, the clamor of the hounds and the sound of the pursuing horses grew close. The black boar burst up the hillside toward them. Murgain, the club-footed archery master, yelled orders, and the men divided, making a wide circle around the snorting, bleeding animal. Half the men dismounted, spears in their hands. The razor-sharp edges scattered rainbow light against the thick dry grass. The bowmen nocked the heavy steel-headed arrows to their bows. Winded and angry, the boar tossed its head at them, and turned in savage dancing rushes, trying to see them all with one good eye.

Tossing Smoke's reins to his friend Azil Aumson, Karadur slid to the ground. The dragon-lord flexed his big fingers. The boar made a rush at the circle. The men shouted, waving their arms, and it retreated.

The dragon-lord glided into the circle. Recognizing an adversary, the boar snorted and pawed the ground like a bull.

"My lord?" said Murgain. He held out the heavy boar-spear.

Karadur waved it away. He strolled toward the enraged animal. Feigning a charge, it hooked its tusk toward his belly. He slipped easily away. The dogs, held fast, and furious about it, set up a frenzied barking.

Walking directly to the rank, sweating boar, the dragon-lord caught its tusk at the base with his left hand. Squealing in rage, it tried to swing its head. But Karadur Atani's extraordinary strength held it motionless. He made a fist of his right hand, and brought it down like a hammer between the animal's eyes.

The boar folded, and dropped. The soldiers shouted. Karadur caught the reins of his horse from Azil. Mounting, he wheeled his shaggy black horse, and rode on alone toward the castle.

The soldiers hung back, glancing at one another in unease. The dragon temper was famous throughout Ippa, and Karadur Atani had his share of it. Finally, talking softly, they moved in to disjoint and quarter the great beast. Tenjiro, holding his horse in place, was watching his brother ride along the edge of the hill.

Azil checked his own horse. Not looking at him, Tenjiro said, "Well, he *is* in a temper."

Azil said diffidently, "He was—not happy last night. He would not say what was disturbing him. I thought you and he might have had a disagreement."

"He has not told you? I thought he kept no secrets from you."

The singer said quietly, "What is said between the two of you stays so, Tenjiro. It has always been so. You know that." The dogs, released, charged uphill, splitting to either side of them in a brindled river. The horses danced a little.

"How diplomatic of him," said the younger man. Then his ill-humor seemed to vanish. "Sorry. None of this is your fault. We did have a disagreement. He told me that he means to change. To take the form."

The singer said, "That I knew. He has been planning it all summer. He wanted only to wait until you came back, so that you could be here."

"So he told me, last night. I told him he should wait. He did not want to hear it."

Azil's face grew thoughtful. "Why did you tell him that?" he asked.

Tenjiro said, "I thought it would be obvious. He has no children."

"I don't understand."

Tenjiro frowned. "Azil, think! It is perilous to assume the dragon-nature. You know how our father died."

Azil had a child's memory of Kojiro Atani: a huge man, bright as fire, before whom all other men seemed diminished. "Of course I know." Everyone in the Atani domains knew how, four years after the birth of his twin sons, Kojiro the Black Dragon had flown ungoverned and enraptured over Ippa, burning forests and villages with his fiery breath, until, wild beyond recalling, he threatened the city of Mako, and the sorcerer Senmet crippled his great wings with a spell, and sent him tumbling to his death. "You think Karadur is in danger—of that?" The singer drew a long breath. "I do not believe it. Forgive me, Tenjiro, but your father, may his soul find peace, was—" He hesitated.

"A savage and undisciplined man," said Tenjiro Atani. "But our father at least had a son. Kaji has no one."

"He has you."

Tenjiro Atani smiled. There was no kindness in that smile, for the man with whom he spoke, nor for himself. "He has me. But *I* am not Dragon, my blood carries none of it. He needs children, to protect the transmission."

"Whom would you have him marry?"

"Gods, I don't care."

Azil said thoughtfully, "Reo Unamira offered Kaji his granddaughter last year."

Surprised, Tenjiro gave a shout of laughter. "Reo Unamira? I didn't know the old pimp had a granddaughter. How old is the little sow—eight, ten?"

"Twelve, I believe. Her name's Maia."

"What did Kaji say?"

"He said he wasn't ready to marry."

"Well, of course. No, I would not have him wed that brigand's spawn. Let him do as did our father: find some respectable family with empty coffers and an overabundance of girl-children. There must be a dozen of them between here and Nakase."

Azil said, "Truly he does not want to." He colored. "Not for the reason you might think."

"Oh, I know," Tenjiro said. "He explained it last night, most emphatically. He does not want some innocent girl to suffer our mother's fate." Abruptly Tenjiro urged his horse into motion. Azil followed him. They halted at the edge of the field. A gust of wind swept downhill at them, rustling the autumn grass. The banner over Dragon Keep snapped like a sail. It bore the Atani family sigil: the golden dragon, wings spread, on a white field.

Tenjiro said softly, "Imagine what it feels like, to be Dragon: to fly, to summon dragonfire, to be impervious to heat, cold, darkness . . ." A painful longing twisted his taut mouth, and roughened his usually self-possessed voice. The scars on his face darkened. For a moment he looked very like Karadur. "A power beyond price. But there is only one Dragon. It was not always so, the records say. But over the centuries our blood has grown thin."

Azil said, "But you do have power. You are wizard."

Tenjiro's glance was sharp as a boar-spear. "Is that what common talk is saying?"

The singer smiled. "It depends whom you talk to. Until you returned last month, half the domain believed that you and Kaji quarreled, and that you transformed yourself into a basilisk and flew into the mountains, or went looking for the treasure of Telmarniya in the center of the Crystal Lake. The other half believed you simply rode to Mako, and waited until his temper cooled before returning home."

"What do you believe?"

Azil said simply, "I know you are not afraid of Kaji's temper."

"You think I found the treasure of Telmarniya?"

"I think you found a teacher."

"Now, why would you think that? I have no interest in the mumblings of some hedge-witch. And there are no wizards, no true wizards, in Ryoka. Not since the Mage Wars."

Azil said, "Senmet of Mako was a true wizard."

"Yes. But she is dead. She was the last of them."

"Then what are you? A warlock? A sorcerer?"

Tenjiro moved his long fingers. Suddenly a cold mist seemed to rise from the ground, thickening and thickening until it seemed the two men stood isolated and imprisoned in a chill grey-white cloud. Azil's horse whinnied in fright. The cloud swept castle, hillside, even his companion from his sight. "Tenjiro?" An ominous, wordless gabble filled his ears. "Tenjiro?"

Slowly, grudgingly, the chill mist blew away. Tenjiro Atani's eyes seemed darkened, and there was an expression in them that Azil had not seen before. "Sorcerer will do. You may call me that. Only say it softly."

"That was—unexpected," Azil said. He was thankful for the steady sunlight bathing his shoulders. "I was right, then. You did find a teacher."

"You could say that. I went south, and east, through Nakase and Kameni, and finally to Nalantira Island, to the ruins of a castle where a great wizard once lived. It is said he was of dragon-kin. Later another wizard came to live there, and he must be buried in that place: no one lives there now, save goats and little monkeys, and madmen hunting for buried treasure. But the castle still exists. And inside the castle, hidden by magic spells, is the old wizard's library, which holds all the books of magic that ever were in the world. It's a big room, with shelves from floor to ceiling, holding books and scrolls and scraps of vellum and paper . . . It would take a lifetime to master them all. But I found what I needed."

"Does Kaji know of this?"

Tenjiro shrugged. "What is magic to Dragon? *He* does not require it. His attention is on his own desire; a desire whose fulfillment will change him utterly, in ways that you and I cannot even imagine. He is your friend, and you think: *I know him. He cannot change so much that I will not know him.* But I tell you, Azil, he *can.* The changeling-folk are different from the rest of us, and none more so than dragon. Kojiro Atani and Erin diMako were good friends, close friends; but the Black Dragon burned the city of Mako to ash. *That* is the dragon-kind's true nature. Karadur will change, and you will not know him, nor he you." Tejiro's soft, elegant voice roughened. "We are a violent lineage, we Atani. You're a singer: you know the stories."

Azil said evenly, "I know them." He felt cold all over again, as if the magic mist wrapped him invisibly round. "You cannot keep him from his destiny, Tenjiro."

"That is not my wish. I want only to safeguard the line. Before he takes form, let Kaji do as did our father, and marry, and sire children. Then it will matter less when he sloughs his human nature, and vanishes into air, as did our grandmother, the Crimson Dragon, or flies into the sun."

They were alone on the field below the castle. Azil's brown horse, catching his rider's disturbed mood, sidled and pulled against the reins. Stumbling a little over the words, the singer said, "I know that you and Kaji are not— not friends. It was always so. But you are all he has of family. If you think it dangerous for him to take the form, you must say so, and keep saying it until he hears you."

Tenjiro snorted. "I tried; he will not listen. He's stubborn as a Nakase ox. What else would you have me do?"

"I don't know. Can your magic help?"

"Ah," said Tenjiro. Something dark and smoky moved behind his pale blue eyes. He cocked his head. "Possibly."

His voice caressed the word. "What do you know of changeling magic?"

"I know what everyone knows," Azil said. "Tukalina made changelings at the same time She made beasts and men."

"Stories," Tenjiro said disdainfully. "That is not what I meant."

"What do you mean?"

"The power to change, like the gift of wizardry, cannot truly be taught. It is indwelling, in heart, bone, blood. Wizards use instruments to channel power. Language is an instrument, and even a village hedge-witch can scry in a mirror. Changelings direct power through a talisman. It is a device through which the changeling may concentrate his gift. Before he can assume the form, Karadur must make a talisman. He will need privacy, silence, a place where he can be alone, undisturbed, where no one, not even an animal, could blunder in to interrupt his work. Where would he go?"

"The tower," Azil said. "The old signal tower. He had it rebuilt this summer. New floor, new roof, new chimney, new shutters. No one goes up there. He told Aum to tell the servants not to touch it, even to clean."

"And does he invite folk to visit it often?"

"No. Never."

"Have you been there?"

"Once."

"Does he go there often?"

"Occasionally. Not often. He never stays long."

"The next time he goes to the tower, if you know, tell me. Especially if it is late at night."

✣   ✣   ✣

THAT EVENING, AS was his custom three nights every week, Karadur ate in the guards' hall. Those who had been on the previous morning's hunt recounted it, with some embroidery, to those who had not. The boar's head appeared, on a plate, with a cooked duck egg neatly substituting for the missing eye, and was admired, and eaten.

After the meal, the tables were drawn back, and the young men challenged each other to wrestle. "Sing something," Karadur suggested lazily to Azil. The two men sat side by side, shoulders brushing, near the fire. A decanter of red wine stood near them, with one cup. A rosewood harp lay propped against Azil's knee.

Azil brought his harp onto his lap. "What would you hear?"

"Whatever you like."

Azil plucked the melody of 'The Red Boar of Aidu.' *"The red boar came from the forest; the red boar came to the hills; his tusks were iron and his breath was fire and his bellow toppled the castle spire; O the red boar, the red boar of Aidu."* The firelight pulsed in time to his strokes. His low voice was clear and strong. The soldiers pounded on the tabletops, and sang the chorus.

Karadur did not sing, but when the song ended, he touched the musician's shoulder a moment. "Sing another."

"Sing 'The Ballad of Ewain and Mariela,' " called someone.

The others groaned derisively. "Don't listen to him, he's lovesick," yelled Devlin. "Give us 'Dorian's Ride!' "

Azil said, "I need to retune for that." He bent over the pegs. A string snapped, lashing upward. "Damn. I'll get another."

"No matter," Karadur said. "Let it go." His strong fingers caught the singer's wrist. A torch flared as one of the doors opened.

Lorimir Ness, the garrison's swordmaster and senior captain, stood framed momentarily in the doorway. Karadur beckoned to him. The captain crossed the hall to his side. "My lord."

"How serious were the injuries in Chingura today?"

"Nothing too bad, my lord. A shoulder gored, and a broken leg. Macallan rode to treat them." Macallan was the Keep's physician.

"Good." Karadur's face grew thoughtful. "Lorimir, set a guard at the foot of the tower stairs tonight. Someone unimaginative."

"Lennart," Lorimir said. "He has no imagination whatsoever."

"No one comes to the tower chamber without my explicit permission." Karadur glanced into the leaping shadows. "I don't see my brother tonight. Is something wrong?"

"Not that I know of, my lord. Do you want me to send to find him?"

"No, let it be," Karadur said. With a slight bow, Lorimir left him. The young men, still eager and noisy, had begun to tease each other into an archery contest. He watched them for a while. Then: "Come," he said abruptly to Azil.

Giving his harp into Ferlin's care, Azil rose and followed his friend from the hall and across the courtyard. The sky beyond the castle walls was a deep dark blue. The autumn stars glittered in Karadur's hair.

Later, well past midnight, the dragon-lord rose from the bed they shared. He dressed in the quiet darkness. As he turned toward the door, Azil lifted his head from the pillow. The room smelled faintly of applewood. Drowsily he said, "Kaji? Is all well?"

"It is. Lie still." The dragon-lord trailed warm fingers across the recumbent man's chest. "I am going to the tower. Don't follow me." He closed the door behind him.

Azil rose on an elbow.

Ferlin the page curled on his pallet in the hall, snoring softly. Lennart, the guard at the foot of the tower stairs, bowed as Karadur passed. He climbed the narrow stairs to the octagonal chamber. Within, he stood a moment. The little room was dark, though moonlight through unshuttered windows touched the floor planks with silver. A lamp

on a low table flared at his glance. Tapestries threaded with
gold decorated the chamber walls. Wood for a fire lay neatly
crossed in the hearth.

A rectangular table in front of the unlit fire held three
items: a lump of gold, a shallow bowl, and a knife. The
dragon-lord crossed to the table. Lifting the knife, he tested
its edge against his thumb. The blade was razor-sharp.

He set it down again. A shadow fell over the light. Dark
wings emerged slowly out of polished stone. A dragon-shape
arched against the ceiling beams. It was a presence he
knew: he had seen it all his life, though as far as he knew,
no one else had ever seen it, save Azil Aumson, and once or
twice, Tenjiro. "Father?" he said softly.

But the shadow, as always, did not respond. Drawing a
long breath, Karadur looked at the hearth. Yellow flames
burst along the edges of the wood.

In the bedroom, Azil groped swiftly for his shoes. Then,
with care not to disturb the sleeping page, he hurried along
the corridor to another chamber. The door opened before
his hand touched the wood, and Tenjiro slipped out to face
him. Despite the lateness of the hour, he was fully dressed.

"He's gone to the tower. He told me not to follow," Azil
said. "And he told Lorimir to set a guard on the tower stairs
tonight. Someone unimaginative."

"He said that?" Tenjiro closed the door. "Good. Follow
me."

"Where are we going?"

But Tenjiro did not answer, only hastened along the corridor to the rear stairs.

In the tower, the air was brilliant, bright and hot as the
heart of a fire. Within it, as in the still center of a mael-
strom, Karadur gripped the lump of gold. Fire ran along his
big frame like water down a sluice. It poured in a controlled
stream into his fingers. Slowly the lump took the shape of

an armband fashioned like a dragon, fanged, bat-winged, jaws open, talons extended.

In a small chamber in the deepest cellar of the castle, Tenjiro and Azil sat across from each other at a square table. A torch flared fitfully from a wall sconce, but despite the smoky heat it gave, the room was cold. Tenjiro leaned his head against the chair back. His long, ringed hands moved slowly, weaving a complex pattern into the smoky air.

"You will help me, Azil. I will make a little box, a little magic box. You are his friend, you love him. I need that love. Give me your love, your loyalty, your fidelity, so that I may feed it to the box, my little dark box . . ." The soft, light words, like an incantation, wound about Azil's mind. He slumped boneless to the table. Cold spilled into the chamber. Merciless, it licked his bare skin, kissed his eyes, entered his lungs. Darkness closed about him like an imprisoning fist.

Karadur set the armband on the table. It pulsed with fire; beneath it, the thick oak began to char. Positioning his left arm over the bowl, Karadur took the knife and sliced his forearm. Blood dripped into the bowl. He scooped the band from the scarred table and dropped it into the bowl. The blood spat and frothed.

Churning, bubbling, the darkness flowed through Azil. As it left him, it took form, acquired edges, shape, weight. A small black box rested on the table in the cellar. Tenjiro's hands stilled. Then, changing the pitch of his voice, he began to chant. A deep hum seemed to rise from the earth. It spiraled up the stairway to the courtyard, the kitchens, the stables. The dogs in their cages began to snore. Horses slept in the stable. Chickens slept in their pens. Sentries nodded at their posts. Lennart's knees buckled; with a soft snore, he slid to his knees and then to his side.

On the rampart overlooking the main gate, Lorimir nodded and woke and nodded again, until, infuriated by a weakness he could neither explain nor control, he set the point of his dagger against his rib, so that the flare of pain would wake him if he slept again.

The hum crept upstairs, to the tower chamber. The fire died. The alabaster lamp sputtered, went out. The sorcerous murmur intensified. It closed Karadur's eyes and buckled his knees. He fell, boneless as the boar. His hand opened; the armband tumbled from his grip.

Tenjiro, rising, put a hand on Azil's shoulder. "Azil. Get up."

Azil opened his eyes. His body ached as if he had been running, or fighting. Tenjiro bent over him. Tenjiro had done something . . . some magic. A terrible lassitude held him immobile. "Up!" came a soft, irresistible command. He struggled to his feet.

"Listen to me," said that light, clear voice. "We will go to Karadur's chamber now. We will take his talisman from him. You shall take it; I need every fiber of concentration to maintain the sleeping spell. If Kaji wakes before the talisman is in the box, he will burn the castle to ash around us. Once the talisman is in the box, you will go. The grooms are asleep; you'll have no trouble getting horses. The binding spell will hold for an hour or two." Tenjiro's long hands moved irresistibly as he spoke. "It's time. Bring the box."

Azil's head was thick and muzzy, as if he had taken a dose of the sleeping potion Macallan kept to treat the sick or wounded. Obediently he lifted the black box.

"It's cold," he said, meaning the box. "Why is it so cold?"

"It is made of void. It eats light."

The two men climbed the long stairs from cellar to kitchens to the upstairs chambers. Servants lay sleeping in hallways and chambers. The cook lay prone like a worshipper before his stockpot. One of the scullery boys snored at his feet. Old Lirith, chief of the castle women, a huge woman, massive and elegant, lay sprawled in utter indignity at the foot of the main stairs. Blood pooled in a pocket below her white hair.

Tenjiro halted. He reached a hand out. Then, drawing back, he moved past her. The somnolence that enveloped Dragon Keep from foundation to flagpole grew stronger as they moved. It lay heaviest at Karadur's door. Tenjiro whispered a word.

The chamber door opened. They went in. Karadur lay motionless on the floor. Against the dark cloth of his shirt, a small golden circle flashed bright as a star.

"Open the box," Tenjiro whispered. Azil tipped up the lid of the black box. Inside was lightlessness, absence, a chill blackness that sucked light out of the air and devoured it. "There is the talisman. Take it," Tenjiro said. "Put it in the box."

Azil walked to Karadur, and knelt. He lifted the shimmering band with both hands, wincing as he did so, put it in the box, and shut the lid. Karadur's eyelids opened. With a harsh sound, he tried to sit upright. "Go!" Tenjiro said. Azil went out the door. Tenjiro said two words. Karadur tensed. A look of strain crossed his face.

Tenjiro said softly, "Farewell, dear brother. No, you cannot move, Kaji, so don't trouble to resist. Or, no, go ahead, fight! Struggle with all your force. It will tire you out."

"Tenjiro, what are you doing?"

"Leaving, dear brother. You cannot pretend to care. You think I don't know how you hate me?" He touched the scar lines on his cheek. "In our mother's womb you tried to destroy me even before our birth, just as you killed our mother. When you could not, you took what should have been mine."

Muscles stood out like ridges through Karadur's shirt. "Tenjiro, you cannot believe that. A child in the womb makes no choices. I did not choose to be eldest. And by all the gods, I did not desire our mother's death!"

"So you say," said Tenjiro contemptuously. "I do not believe it. I have never believed it. *I* should have been the changeling child. I should have been eldest. I would have been dragon and wizard, both. Can you feel the chill, the weakness in your heart, Kaji? Do you like my little box? I made it especially for your little dragon. It will eat your little dragon, Kaji. It will eat your heart."

"Tenjiro, don't do this."

"It's done. By darkness and by ice, I bind your power." Below, in the Keep's deserted courtyard, a horse whinnied. Karadur closed his eyes. His muscular body tightened with effort. The lamp began to glow. The wood in the hearth burst into flame. Tenjiro's face whitened with surprise and sudden terror. He said a string of sibilant words, very fast. Karadur gasped, and slumped. The lamplight vanished; the fire hissed, and died as if doused in water. Tenjiro Atani laughed malignantly, and stretched his spine like an athlete too long confined. "Ah, I have you! Struggle as you will, Kaji. I learned my lessons well, this year."

The door to the chamber opened. Azil stuck his head through. He said tonelessly, "Tenjiro, the horses are ready, we can leave."

Karadur lifted his head. "Azil?" He closed his eyes, then opened them again. "Azil, don't go with him. I don't know what he has told you, but whatever it is, it is not as you think."

"Shut up, Kaji!" Tenjiro said. "I don't want you to speak to him." His supple hands wove swiftly. "There, now you can't. Azil, wait for me in the courtyard." Without looking at the man on the floor, Azil left the room. "It's too late, Karadur. What, do you love him? He betrayed you. He is mine, now. Don't worry; I will punish him for you. I will care for him with the exact tenderness that you have used toward me." His face no longer resembled his brother's. His eyes were wide and black. "Unfortunately, I suspect I cannot kill you, just as you could not butcher me in our mother's womb as you desired. But I can take everything you care for, and I will. Let us see who shall be Dragon! Fare ill, brother mine!"

Karadur Atani, trembling, strained to speak, to move. But his frozen muscles would not unlock. He lay paralyzed, while the tower room lightened with the dawn. At last, fire flared in the hearth. Grimacing with pain, Karadur pushed to his knees, to his feet, took an unsteady step, another. Tears, like droplets of blue flame, ran down his face.

2

WINTER CAME HARD to eastern Ippa that year. Snow lay deep on the roads. Trappers returned to their villages telling of snowdrifts higher than trees, and a thick fog that drifted down the mountain trails, sending goats and deer and a few tired hunters to their death.

Inside Dragon Keep, the mood was grim. All autumn, since the September morning that nobody could quite remember, the morning Tenjiro Atani and Azil Aumson vanished from the Keep, Karadur Atani had kept to himself. His soldiers watched him silently, unhappily. Only Lorimir Ness, who had watched, frozen and helpless, from the rampart as Tenjiro Atani and the harpist left the dormant Keep and rode slowly north, dared to speak of it. The glare Karadur turned on him sent him to the floor as if he had been clubbed. It took some time before he could stand.

Early in March the following year, a yellow-eyed, soft-voiced stranger appeared in Sleeth village. He came from Ujo, in Nakase, and had been born in a village named Nyo, he said, which lay south, at the border between Nakase and Issho, where the Estre River poured into the Crystal Lake.

The folk of Sleeth who heard these names shrugged, for few of them had ever been south of the domain. They were courteous, but wary, fearing that the stranger would turn out to be a ne'er-do-well, or even an outlaw banished from his home village.

But the yellow-eyed traveler seemed to be neither of these. His name was long and foreign. "Hard to pronounce," he agreed. "Most people call me Wolf." He touched his hair, which was thick and dark and tipped with silver.

He asked at the smithy if anyone needed help, especially with wood. "I am handy with an ax," he said, "and was counted a good carpenter in Ujo." Ono the smith, who had little use for braggarts, and though he was over sixty, still had forearms the size of hams, handed him a blunted ax head and told him to put an edge on it, for a man who could not mend his own tools would not survive in the mountains. Wolf put a neat edge on the ax head. Within a week, he had a bed next to the forge and work aplenty, mending and building, for old Gerain, who had been the village carpenter for fifty-odd years, had started to get stiff in his hands, and none of his three sons could tell birch from maple.

Wolf was a lean, quiet man, not old, despite his silver-tipped hair. The village men liked him: he could drink, and seemed to enjoy sitting in the common room at the Red Oak, listening to village tales, and occasionally telling one of his own. He told excellent stories. He had served the Lemininkai, in Ujo, and lived in Skyeggo, in far-off Kameni, beside the unimaginable ocean. He had sailed on a ship around the Gate of Winds to Chuyo, and even gone raiding with the men of Issho across the wastelands into Isoj. The girls guessed his age, giggling, and made up their own tales about him. The women found his yellow eyes attractive, and wondered why he had come north alone. He lived all spring in the back room of the smithy, and seemed content with it. Rain, Ono's wife, was happy to set a third place at the table, but neither she nor Ono asked questions, and Wolf was free to come and go.

One day in early June he was sitting outside the smithy in the sunlight, knife in hand, when Thea, daughter of Serret the ale-maker, stopped to watch him work. Wolf knew who she was. She was apprenticed to Ferrell the weaver; he had once carved a new leg for her loom. He had asked Ono about her, for she seemed gentle and thoughtful, and she was clearly a woman, near twenty, well old enough to be wed.

"Did you see her face?" the smith asked. He splayed a hand across his right cheek. "She is marked; a birth scar. We call them dragon scars."

"So?"

Ono explained that people so marked rarely wed, for it was feared that their children might be deformed. Instead, they were early apprenticed, and taught some trade. "A pity," the old man said. "She's a fine woman."

But Thea did not pity herself. She enjoyed weaving: it gave her pleasure to know that she had a skill that was her own, and she treasured the solitude it gave her. She had long grown used to the notion that she would not be wed. It did not trouble her, save sometimes, when she watched boys and girls tease each other in spring, and saw how sometimes a boy would gaze at a girl a certain way, as if he might cease to breathe if she did not look at him. She liked the stranger from the south. He was neat-handed, as she was, and quiet, and he greeted her by name, respectfully, as he might have greeted Rain or Serret, her mother, who was also Rain's sister.

"May I watch?" she asked. He nodded and did not halt his work. Wood curls dropped to the ground. She stood silently for a while, enjoying the sun on her hair, the movement of Wolf's hands, and the smell of the fresh wood shavings.

Finally she said, "What are you making?"

"A toy for Lisbe." Lisbe was Gerain's youngest grandchild; she was four. He rotated it and she saw the forked tail, the neck, the rearing proud head.

"It's a dragon." She was delighted. "Where are its wings?"

"I will carve them separately, and joint them on, so they can move." He mimed with one hand the slow powerful beat of a dragon's wings.

"Have you ever seen one?"

"No." He moved on the bench so that she could sit beside him. "Have you?" The irregular purplish scar traced across her upper cheek like lace, and ran up her temple into her black hair. She wore her hair loose, tied back with a strand of azure wool. It fell to her waist. Her eyes were hazel.

"They say I have. My uncle held me on his shoulder one day when Kojiro the Black Dragon, the lord Karadur's father, flew over the village. But I was only two, and do not remember. No one has ever seen our lord Karadur take dragon form."

"Why not, I wonder?" Wolf asked. It had come up before, but only in the kind of conversation that did not admit questions.

Thea said cautiously, "I don't *know*. But they say our lord's brother was a sorcerer, and when he left the castle last year, it was in anger. Tallis, my cousin Nora's husband, is a guard at the Keep; he says that Tenjiro Atani laid a curse on his brother. Lirith died that day, and no one who was at the Keep remembers how, or knows where Tenjiro Atani is."

"Who was Lirith?"

"Lirith Cordis. She was eldest of all the castle women. She birthed the brothers. She was like a mother to Karadur and Tenjiro."

They sat in companionable silence for a while. Then Thea recollected her errand, a visit to Felicia, her sister, for whom she was making a baby blanket, and she left.

Three days later Thea was seated at her loom when someone knocked at her door. She crossed to the door and opened it. Wolf stood in the doorway, holding a delicate wooden comb, such as a woman might wear in her hair for decoration. On its crown, above the narrow tines, romped a dragon with a gleaming seashell eye. "For you," he said, and laid it her palm.

She wore it through the village streets the next day. A

week later Wolf returned from a day's work at the mill, where he had rebuilt a rotten stair, to find a cloak on his bed. It was soft and warm, of a fine thick wool that he knew to be the best that one could find in Castria Market. It was grey, with red threads running through it like the red grain of yew heartwood. He stroked it, smiling.

That night, sitting alone with a candle, he wrote a letter to his friend Terrill Chernico, called Hawk, who lived south, in Nakase county, in the city of Ujo:

> *I seem to have made a place for myself in Sleeth. There is work to do, and I have a home, of sorts, with the blacksmith and his wife. They are kind people. The village reminds me of Nyo, except that it is not so big, and I am not forever falling over brothers and sisters and cousins. It is not at all like Ujo.*
>
> *As you know, they call this Dragon's Country. The lord of this region is Karadur Atani. He is indeed changeling, as we thought, and liege to the villages near it and to the lands south of the mountains by half a hundred miles. There's mystery here: they tell me he has never taken dragon-form, and I have heard a story that his estranged brother, who is reputed to be a sorcerer, laid a curse on him. His father, Kojiro the Black Dragon, who was famous for his rages, burned the city of Mako. I have heard a dozen stories of Kojiro Atani's temper, and none at all of the son's. In fact, they rarely talk about him.*
>
> *The hunting is good. You would like it. The ale is good, too—excellent, in fact. The brewer is a woman named Serret. She has a daughter, Thea the weaver, with whom I am somewhat friendly.*
>
> *If you see our friend Bear, give him my love.*

After a while it became not uncommon for Wolf the carpenter and Thea the weaver to be seen together in Sleeth, walking, or sitting in the Red Oak, side by side, while the younger men drank and told hunting stories and wrestled. When summer turned hot, Wolf left Sleeth for a while, and not even Ono and Rain knew where he had gone. Then word came back that he had gone into the hills north of the village, and found a sheltered spring-fed meadow between Sleeth and Chingura, and was felling trees to build a house. The men from Sleeth whose homes or barns or workshops he had built or repaired went to help him. When asked, he explained that he was no farmer, but he had done some fur-trapping once upon a time, and thought he might like to try that life again, if he had a house to come home to.

The morning after midsummer festival, Wolf returned to Sleeth, and asked Thea to go walking with him. She left her loom with its work unfinished, and took her cloak from its peg. It was a half day's climb to the hollow, but Thea was a mountain woman, and she had roamed these hills all her life. They took the slow way round, dawdling by the river, and came to the house at sunset. It was small and neat, built in northern fashion, with common room and kitchen below, and sleeping chambers above. There was a pen for sheep, a pantry, and a little room off the pantry with a window that looked west, across the meadow, and a room upstairs that was not a sleeping loft. It had a window. Thea pictured her loom into it, and herself sitting at it, looking at the meadow, and a hawk flying.

"It's a fine house," she said.

They went outside, and Wolf showed her the spring, and the root cellar, and the berry bushes near it, and the path he had cleared between spring and house. "Next month I'll dig a well."

"That's good," she said.

"In spring the meadow is covered with yellow flowers."

Thea nodded, trying not to smile, for she knew he was having trouble with the words.

"There is something else," he said.

And suddenly, with a shimmer in the air like silver smoke, the man who stood across from her, with silver-tipped hair and dark eyes and long, elegant hands, was gone. She stood six feet from a lean black wolf. It gazed at her coldly from amber-yellow eyes. The shimmer came again, and Wolf was standing where the wolf had stood.

He was waiting for her to move, so she did. She walked to him and fitted her hand to his. "If we have children," she said, "will they be wolves or human?"

She felt him breathe then, and his fingers tightened on hers. "They may be neither. Or both."

They were wed that September, a week after harvest moon. The morning of the wedding, after breakfast, during which Rain had cried, Wolf walked with Ono to the forge. He said, a little formally, "I have not thanked you for your welcome of me. Many men would not have been so friendly to a stranger."

"Most strangers are not so handy with an ax."

"If ever you need me, for any reason, or no reason at all, I will come. I am not so far away that word cannot be sent. Anyway, my work will bring me here. You will see me often enough."

Ono nodded. They went into the smithy. Corwin was working the bellows. He was fifteen, a strong lad, Ono's brother's son, and the pallet that had been Wolf's was now his. Ono went to the rear of the smithy. When he came out again, he held a leather-sheathed sword. He handed it to Wolf. Wolf unsheathed it. It came easily, with only a little initial resistance. The blade gleamed in the light. It was a short tough blade, well-balanced, with a wicked edge. Wolf laid a thumb against the steel. "It's good metal," he said respectfully.

"From Chuyo." Chuyo steel was the finest in Ryoka. "Niall Cooley made the sheath." Wolf ran his hand along the fine smooth leather. It was unadorned, with bronze rivets. Niall Cooley, from Chingura, was principal leather-worker for Dragon Keep. "There are odd folk in the hills sometimes. You may need it, when you go trapping."

"Yes."

"Thea is my niece," Ono said. "When she was little, she came often to the house. She was a happy child. Rain thinks of her as a daughter."

"As long as I live, no hurt will touch her," said Wolf.

At the wedding, which was held in the little temple on the hillside, there was much laughter and drinking. Ono got drunk on Serret's best red ale, and sang a song. The priestess Sirany said the words and lit the incense in front of the smoke-blackened statue of the Maker Goddess, Tukalina. Wolf and Thea drank thrice from the bowl, and Serret cried, from joy, mostly. After an appropriate time, Wolf and Thea slid from the building and were ceremoniously pursued by the young men, laughing and carrying torches. But Thea and Wolf had a head start, and Nevis, Thea's brother, and Dai, Gerain's youngest son, got into a less-than-ceremonious tussle, and Dai twisted an ankle in the tricky moonlight and had to be carried to the inn. So the lovers climbed the hill path in the moonlight, and had anyone been there to see—but no one was—they would have seen a marvel, as Thea Serretsdatter Dahranni crossed the mountain meadow to her new home with one hand triumphantly gripping the silver-tipped fur of a lean black wolf.

❦   ❦   ❦

THAT YEAR, WINTER came early and stayed late. The trappers were happy, for the bitter cold drove fox, lynx, and rabbits south out of the steppe in great numbers, but when they came in from their journeys to trade their pelts in the markets and drink at the inns, they told alarming stories, of huge, high snow banks, frozen streams, and an icy mist that rolled down the mountain paths, obscuring dangerous rocks. A trapper from Castria was lost in it. They found him three days later in the crags above Dragon Keep, mad as a skunk, declaring that he had heard the voices of little children crying in the fog.

Later that winter a hunter from Mitligund came to Castria Market and described moonlit ice moving so fast that it would outstrip a man walking, and a freezing fog in which evil voices called.

"A demon has entered that country," he said flatly. "We do not stay." All winter, frightened families from Mitligund and Unik and Hornlund trickled south with their belongings on sleds, or tied to their backs. Others went west, into the Nakase highlands. They told strange tales, tales of ice and fog, of voices in mist, and of armed warriors on pale horses who moved and spoke like men, except that they were made of ice. This no one believed, especially when Tuvak of Hornlund claimed to have killed one with his spear, but insisted that when he tried to strip the armor from the man, horse and rider melted into the snow.

No imaginary warriors troubled Thea or Wolf. The bitter cold surprised them, but the well did not freeze, they had plenty of wood—birch mostly, for the east side of the meadow was fringed with birch and aspen—and the house was solid and sound. While Wolf trudged through the snow, checking his traps, Thea wove rugs and wall coverings and blankets. The path between Sleeth and the meadow was snowbound for a while. Then it thawed: the snow melted from the trees in one day, and the river ran high.

Early in January they had a visitor. Thea greeted him with pleasure, for it was Tallis, of the castle guard, who had married her cousin Nora and taken her from Sleeth to live in Chingura, under the Keep walls. They brought him in and fed him warm ale, and invited him to take off his boots and get dry. He drank the ale, but kept his boots on. "I can only stay a moment."

"Are you well? And Nora?" Thea asked. "What are you doing away from the castle?"

"Nora's well. Dragon sent us. We are ordered to visit every household between Dragon's Eye and Castria, and if any are hungry or destitute, to bring them whatever they need. We hunt all the time; we have cartloads of meat at the castle." He grinned. "Dragon took us out hunting last week. We brought down four moose."

"Hunting bows?" Wolf asked. "Triple-barbed arrows?"

"For three of them, yes. He brought the fourth down with his hands. It was a big one, not the biggest, though." Tallis grinned again, and stretched his hands toward the fire. "That's good."

"With his hands? A moose? That's not possible," Wolf said.

"You'd think not, but it happened; I saw it. The hounds encircled it, like a deer brought to bay in a field, and Dragon wrestled it to the ground and snapped its neck."

Thea said, "He must be strong."

"He is. Quick, too. He can pluck an arrow out of the air. I saw him do it."

"Someone shot at him?" Wolf asked.

"A mistake. One of Rogys's arrows went wide. He can't shoot, not at all. I thought Murgain would burst apart. He's the archery instructor."

"What did the lord do?" Thea asked.

"To Rogys? Nothing. But he skulked in the stable for a week anyway." Tallis drained the ale mug. "I can't blame him. I'd not want Dragon irked at me."

"What is he like?" Wolf asked.

"You've not met him?" Wolf shook his head. "That's not an easy question." Tallis turned the mug in his hands. "He loves courage, in beasts or men. He is exacting. No drunkenness on duty, weapons cleaned and oiled, and if you trouble one of the girls, or mistreat a dog, or horse, watch out."

"Is he brutal?" Wolf asked bluntly.

"I would not say so. Not like his father. He can punish, though. You want to watch his temper: used to be if you could make him laugh, you could breathe easy, but he doesn't laugh much now. And gods help you if you lie to him. He hates it, and he always knows. Ah, I must go, or they'll think I fell over a cliff and come looking for me." He clasped Wolf's hand, kissed Thea's cheek, wished them joy, and marched off in his high boots and thick fur hood.

✢ ✢ ✢

IT WAS HARD for Thea, being alone that winter. She had not expected it to be so: she had liked to weave in solitude, preferring it to the giggling and gaggling of company, but she had not realized how alone she would be in the mountains. In Sleeth, even when she sat alone with her loom, there had been familiar sounds, well-known voices, the rustle of cart wheels, the hoot of animals, the laughter of children. Here, locked in snow, while Wolf was trapping or hunting, she was by herself, four and five days at a time. She was not afraid: no wild beast would approach the house, and no human marauders would climb this high. But it was hard. She wove. She cleaned a lot, and sang to herself, old songs, children's tunes. She braided her hair, experimenting, seeking new ways to pin it to her head. Once she tried to make a magic mirror. She poured water in a bowl, and let it sit all night where moonlight could fall upon it. In the morning she took it where no sunlight could touch it, and let the ice which had formed over the surface thaw. Then she leaned over it, saying the finding rhyme which all children in the domain know:

"*Sleeping, waking, moonlight eye, find the one for whom I cry . . .*"

But though she thought as hard as she could about Wolf, no image of man nor wolf appeared in the clear water.

Then Wolf returned, tired, cold, his sled piled with frozen bodies of rabbit, marten, white fox, beaver. Thea cut meat from bones, wrapped it, and stored it on the high rack behind the house, where it froze. Wolf cleaned and stretched the pelts. They talked little, taking time to grow used to each other again.

They talked more at night, lying naked against each other in the bed Wolf had made, warm under heavy quilts. In bed, Thea heard the names of places and people from a part of her husband's life she did not know. It did not trouble her that he was older than she, that he knew so much more, that he had lived in so many places. She loved the stories.

"Tell about Skyeggo," she said, and Wolf described a huge shining city on a tall hill, and white-sailed ships dancing over the sea, and ferocious storms that sometimes broke upon the coast, driving ships back to land, and the great sea monsters that appeared off the coast after a storm, lifting their flat scaly heads from the water, breathing out fire and steam.

"Like dragons," Thea whispered, eyes shining.

"They are cousins," Wolf agreed.

"Tell about Bear."

Wolf told her about his changeling friend Bear, with whom he traveled, sometimes, and beside whom he had fought.

"No one ever knows where Bear is," he said. "Guarding someone, loving someone, hunting someone, looking for a fight . . . If ever you see a man walking up our road, a big man with red-brown hair and beard, carrying a long thick staff, that will be Bear, come to visit."

"Tell about Hawk."

And Wolf told of his friend Hawk, who lived in Ujo. "She is one of the Red Hawks of Ippa. They are changelings, all sisters. She and I served together, in the Lemininkai's war band. She was Kalni Leminin's archery master. Now she makes bows. She has more books than anyone I know. Her workroom at the shop has one wall filled with them. I believe she has read them all."

"Is she a scholar, too?"

"She has many talents. She tells stories."

"Like you."

"Better than me. She will come to visit us, someday, and you will see."

They were together for nearly a month, this time. Then Wolf loaded the sled with fresh snares. He kissed her, and she moved her body hard against him. He groaned and pushed her away. "I love you," she said, after the door closed.

❦   ❦   ❦

FAR TO THE north, beneath the mound of ice, the darkness talked to itself.

It was weak, dependent on the human mind and form that had wakened it and brought it to this place. Centuries before it had lost its original human form and nature. It no longer desired light, warmth, food, comfort; indeed, it hated those things with a passion, because their presence reminded the darkness that it had relinquished them. Its sustenance now was hatred, pain, cruelty, fear, destruction. It delighted in those. It craved those with a desperate, consuming hunger.

Its human host, although a sorcerer, was unaware of its existence. Human beings were singularly stupid about themselves. This sorcerer was very young, and swollen with envy and anger. Coiled in the recesses of the sorcerer's mind, the darkness fed on these emotions, and subtly nourished them, as the fires of the earth, nourished by hidden fuel, are left to burn unexposed, undisclosed, deep underground. Carefully, it allowed the oblivious sorcerer access to small bits of its own power, in such a way that the sorcerer would mistake this borrowed power for his own. This was perilous, for that borrowed power was absolutely corrupting. To wield it would inevitably destroy the human being who tried. That destruction was its goal and also its punishment. It had tried for centuries to break free of its enchanted prison, so that it might manifest as once it had, unfettered by human limitations. But the dead mages who made those secret walls had done their work well.

But despite this restraint, the darkness was still capable of great mischief. It was strong enough to summon the ice warriors; strong enough to lift its old stronghold out of the center of the earth. Its host, the little wizard whose life it drank, believed that *he* had created the ice warriors, and raised the ancient castle. Let him think so. He would learn. *Too late, he would learn.* Under the ice, twisted like an invisible filament around the mind of its human host, the darkness contemplated the betrayals to come, and whispered softly, unceasingly, to itself.

3

For the first time in twenty years, there was no feast in Sleeth village to celebrate the New Year's Moon. It was too cold.

As late as March, heavy snow fell over Sleeth and Chingura, and blocked the mountain passes. At last the thaw came. Ice melted in the Estre River. Snow melted from the spruce boughs. Birds returned from their winter homes in Nakase and Issho, and began to forage, leaving tiny sparse tracks like writing on the near-translucent snow.

In late March, when the road between Sleeth and the meadow grew passable, Wolf and Thea went to the village. Wolf hauled the large sled, piled with skins to be sold at the market, and Thea pulled the smaller one, which held four large wool blankets. Three of them would go to Ferrell, to be sold. One was a gift for her mother.

It was slow going; the snow was still high in spots. In the village, they separated. Thea went to her mother's house. Wolf pulled the big sled as far as the smithy. Ono was bent over some metal, hammering at it, while Corwin held it steady with the tongs. The boy had put muscle on over the winter. Ono looked unchanged. He laid the hammer down.

"What brings you into town?" he said.

"I've skins to sell," Wolf said. "Thea wanted to see her mother."

"She's all right?"

"She's fine. We're both fine."

They ate that evening at Serret's house, which was filled with the people who lived there: Serret, her youngest daughter, Martia; her mother, Aea; Felicia and Merrit her husband, and their son, Kevin, born at end of summer. Merrit brought him from the cradle and paraded him boisterously around the room for everyone to admire, as if he were a prize pig. Kevin was passive and placid and slept through the fuss.

After the meal, they crossed the market square to the Red Oak, where Serret made sure that Egain the innkeeper served the best red ale. People moved in and out, stopping to greet Wolf and Thea and say the same things: *Good to see you, long winter, late thaw, you look well, strange what's happening in the north, what news do you hear from the castle, long winter.* After months of solitude and silence, a big room filled with voices and so many faces was a little hard on the nerves. Wolf found it easier to deal with than Thea did. He drained his cup, and pressed Thea's thigh under the table.

On the other side of the room, a group of five men and one tired-looking woman sat sullenly. The men were drinking; the woman was filling their glasses. One of them, a brawny, bearded man with a scar down his face and gold rings winking on his fingers, seemed to do most of the talking.

The look of them made Wolf uneasy. When Egain stopped by the table to ask if they wanted more ale, Wolf inquired softly, "The men at that table near the door: who are they?"

"The weasely-looking youth is Tuar; he's the son of Bryony and Nirrin Maw. Nirrin died four years ago, but Bryony is chief laundress at the Keep. The big one calls himself Rand. He's from someplace in Nakase. The woman's Luvia; she lives with Tuar. They have a little girl. Tuar does bits of metalwork, the kind of mending Ono hates to do. He's not bad at it; he's mended some of my pots."

"And Rand—what's his trade?"

Egain pulled a face. "Mischief and mayhem, likely. He claims to be a trapper, but I've never seen him with pelts."

The scar-faced man rose, and at his barked command the others drained their glasses and followed him. Tuar and Luvia were last out the door. Merrit fed his son a taste of ale. The babe gurgled happily, and then began to hiccup.

Felicia whisked the boy from his arms. "Enough! It's mother's milk he needs, not ale. To bed he goes, now."

Wolf rose, drawing Thea with him. "We'll come with you."

The night was cold and dry, with no threat of snow. A quarter-moon dipped in and out of the scudding clouds. They crossed the square to Serret's house. Felicia sang softly to Kevin. Merrit lagged behind. Suddenly a stocky figure in trapper's furs staggered toward them, almost falling into Thea. She cried out in surprise. Wolf stepped swiftly in front of her. He glimpsed a dark knotted face, anguished dark eyes. The man staggered into the wall of a shed, slid down, and lay flat on his face.

Merrit had come quickly up to them at Thea's cry.

Wolf said, "Who is he?"

"That's Chary. He's a trapper from Ashavik." They stood looking down at the man. "He came out of the ice this winter, and stayed." Merrit did not lower his voice. The man on the ground seemed not to hear it.

Felicia said, "Am I walking by myself?"

They caught up with her. Thea said, "Is he drunk? He didn't smell drunk."

"No," Merrit said, "he's mad. He saw something on the ice, who knows what, and now he won't go back, and he can't sleep."

"What did he see?" Wolf asked. An owl called from a rooftop. Felicia crooned to the baby, who had stopped hiccuping.

Merrit said uneasily, "Oh, it's nonsense. A tale."

"Tell us."

"He claims that he and his friend were trapping, when a huge beast with fangs and claws and red eyes sprang on them from a rock. It killed his friend. He beat it away with a brand, but when he tried to stab it, his knife broke. He tried to bring his friend's body back, but the sled stuck in the ice. When he got back to Ashavik, he found the village burned, and his family gone. He hunted for them but could not find them." There was a question in Merrit's voice, and he looked at Wolf as if Wolf knew the answer to it, though he had not voiced it.

Wolf said, "That's an evil story."

They stayed three days in the village. They slept at Serret's, sharing the sleeping room with Serret and Aea and Martia. Thea went to the temple and visited with Felicia. Wolf bargained in the market, trading furs for supplies. When he could, Wolf spent his time with Ono, even taking Corwin's place at the forge. The third night, the clouds blew wholly away, bringing a night brilliant with stars and a waxing moon. It grew very cold. Under the quilts that night, Thea whispered, "Husband, let's go home."

The next night, as they lay leg to leg in their own bed, with only night sounds about them, she told him she was pregnant. "Sirany says it's a boy," she said into the darkness. "A sturdy little wolf cub."

Wolf laid a palm on her smooth, rounded belly, trying to feel the difference. "When?"

"October."

The delayed spring came with a rush. All the snow melted in three days, leaving the ground soggy. Fireweed and rhubarb shot first through the earth. The birds returned in an explosion of song, hanging off the birches and alden trees and quarreling over choice nest sites in the spruce. The river rose, and the fish began to crowd it, so that a net thrust into rushing water filled itself. Wolf turned the soil in back of the meadow for a garden. One afternoon he smelled smoke. Following his nose north, to the small meadow above his own, he found a makeshift, ramshackle hut. Near it, a shaggy-coated dun mule ate meadow grass.

Tuar the tinker sat outside the hut beside a coal-filled brazier. A drying rack next to the house held clothes, and a blanket. Some of the clothes were child-sized. "Hoy," Wolf called.

Tuar jerked his head up, and stood, peering suspiciously. He came quickly toward his visitor, leaving a glint of metal in the dirt.

"Who are you?"

"My name is Wolf. My wife and I live in the meadow below you."

"What do you want?" The hut door opened. A woman, the same tired-looking woman Wolf had seen at the inn, looked out. "Get inside," the tinker snarled at her.

Wolf said, "I smelled your smoke. I came to see who it was."

"Well, now you see," the young man said sullenly. He went back to his place in the dirt, and hunched over the brazier.

Wolf returned to his own house to tell Thea about their neighbors. "That poor girl," Thea said thoughtfully. "Did you see aught of the child?"

"Clothes on a line."

"I knew Tuar as a child. He was a pinched-faced little boy. Always whining."

Wolf said, "I can't say I like them being so close." But except for the smoke, Tuar and Luvia and their daughter might as well have been invisible. Occasionally Wolf saw other men, one or two, or three, striding toward the upper meadow, and once he recognized Rand. He never saw Tuar with bow or snare or net.

He said to Thea, "I wonder what they're eating."

"I don't know," she said, pushing the hair off her face. "I know what we're eating. Would you bring me some onions?"

As summer moved toward autumn, Wolf left the meadow to build. Half a dozen people needed such work. Thea was seven months on; her back hurt. He made certain that she had sufficient wood, and that the well pulley was well-greased. She laughed at him and told him not to be a fool, she was fine. He built a storage shed for Ferrell, and new shelves for the wine cellar at the Red Oak. Egain was unhappy; someone had been stealing from his guests. "Most of it is small stuff, coins and trinkets, but one man lost a Chuyo dagger with a small ruby in the hilt, *he* claims. If word gets around I have a thief, no one will rent my rooms!"

When Wolf next went home, he found Felicia, the baby Kevin, and Martia in possession of the sleeping room. They giggled and fussed, and made it clear there was no place for him upstairs. He slept downstairs, rolled in a blanket. In the night he would wake, missing Thea's steady breathing beside him, and look at the ceiling.

A month or so before the baby was to be born, Thea ceased speaking to him. Her beautiful hair grew straggly and her face grew almost gaunt, though her belly was huge. She would barely look at him. "A mood. It will pass. Leave her alone," Felicia said, but it frightened him. He tried to talk to her, and she turned from him. He brought her toys, a cradle which he had carved for their son, and she would not look at them, or him. He shouted at her, once, in the garden, and Felicia came storming from the house and told him to get out, that he was doing her no good.

He went fishing, but the Estre trout hid from him. He went hunting, and brought back a fat badger. He built a fire in the meadow and laid the beast on it.

Felicia came from the house. "Thea says the smell makes her sick."

He said, "Let her tell me herself."

She glared at him from the other side of the fire, hands on her hips. In the warm dusk she looked like Thea. "This happens. You have to be patient. It will end when the baby is born."

"My wife will not talk to me, and you tell me to be patient." He turned the badger with a stick. The fat dripped from the hide and made flame. "Tell me what is happening."

The shifting smoke blew her way. She came and stood next to him. "She is frightened."

"Of having a baby?"

"Of having *your* baby." Felicia looked obliquely at him. "She told us. Mother, and I. Not Merrit. She told us that you are changeling."

"What do you think?"

With some asperity, she said, "What am I supposed to think? No one in our family married a wolf before."

"It's common, in *my* family."

He had meant it as a jest, but Felicia responded with anger, "You are not from this country, you don't know—"

"Then, in the Goddess's name, tell me what I don't know!"

She did not want to tell him. She hunched her body against the words.

"When Dragon, the lord Karadur, was born, they say he came from his mother not a human baby, but a dragon, with claws and teeth. His mother died, and his womb-brother, Tenjiro, was torn, and *he* nearly died. Thea is afraid that your baby will come from her a wolf, with teeth and claws."

"Imarru's balls. Why didn't you tell me?" Wolf tossed the stick away and went into the house. He thundered into the bedroom. Thea was in bed, on her side. Her face was sunken. Martia hissed at him like a cat. "Get out," he said. She scurried away. Wolf knelt by the bed. Thea turned her face to the wall. "Dear heart," he said, "love, listen to me. My mother birthed six children, four changelings, and every one came from her womb pink and butter-soft and human. My little changeling sister Calli, twelve years younger than I, I saw her ten minutes after the birth. She was born human as you and I, and she squalled just like Kevin. Our son will be pink and fat and toothless as he should be. I promise you, Thea, I swear it." Holding her against him, Wolf stroked her hair, saying it again. Thea said nothing, but she let him hold her, and did not pull away.

That night, after they had all gone to sleep, she came slowly down from the sleeping room, and sat beside him in the darkness, her shoulder against his. "What name do you want him to bear?" she said.

"Anything you like. I don't care."

"I want to call him Shem." It meant *fearless.*

Three days later Felicia sent Martia to Sleeth. The next night Rain, accompanied by Sirany the priestess, appeared at the house.

"Go away," Rain said. She patted his shoulder. "Go to the village. Don't worry, between us we have birthed a hundred babies. Thea is strong and young. Go away."

He did not want to go to the village, to sit with the men at the Red Oak. He went into the mountains. Snow made a light white dust across the hills. He climbed in the rocks above the Keep, staying well out of sight of sentries, who would raise the alarm if they saw a wolf so close to the castle. He hunted white grouse and rabbits. He slept in a cave which had been some bear's den.

He stayed wolf for three days. The evening of the third day he went home. Sirany and Rain were gone; Felicia was sleeping downstairs. The sleeping room smelled of milk. Thea drowsed in a nest of blankets. She turned a corner of the blanket to show him a pink flat face, tiny petaled hands.

His son's head seemed very wrinkled, and much too big. It was covered with fine dark hair. "Was it bad?" he asked.

"Not so bad."

He kissed her eyelids, and touched the baby's cheek with one finger, marveling at the delicacy and softness of the flesh. Somehow they had made this marvel, his son. His own hand seemed huge, grotesque, hard as horn.

Winter roared in. Snow flung itself at the mountains, blocking the roads. Wolf stayed home. There was work to be done: mending snares and nets, carving fish hooks. They had meat and fish on the rack, potatoes and apples in the cellar. They had wood. The snow brought silence, except when the wind blew, or the baby cried.

"His lungs are like Ono's bellows," Thea said, walking up and down, jiggling a red-faced infant in her arms.

After February's dark moon, new snow ceased to fall. The old snow crust froze hard. Wolf took Shem outside. Thea had bundled the infant securely; he was rigid as a bolster, and twice his true size. He watched everything: the sky, the snow, the chimney-smoke. His wide gaze was intimate and intense.

At the height of the freeze, two men drove a mule-pulled wagon into the meadow. One was young: he looked as if he had just left the farm. The older man had the confident step and ease of a professional soldier.

"Dragon sent us," he said. "Do you need anything? We have meat, wood, flour."

"We could use some flour," Wolf said. Thea had warned that they had little flour left, and that soon there would be no bread. The younger man shouldered two sacks into the pantry. "Would you like ale?"

"We would indeed," said the older man. His boots were stiff with mud. "But we can't stop, if we are to reach the Keep before dark. I've heard of you: you're Wolf the carpenter, who married the weaver. My wife has one of her blankets. I'm Marek Gavrinson. This useless sprout is Toby." The young soldier grinned. Marek clucked at Shem. "He's a big one. How old is he?"

"Three and a half months," Wolf said. "He's not that big, he's just well-wrapped."

"Ah. Hello, youngling. Do you like the world?" Marek bent over Shem. The baby gurgled, and reached exploring fingers towards his square black beard. "I have two of these, older. They live at the Keep with their mother."

Wolf said, "Do you know about the folk in the meadow above us? There are three of them: the tinker, his wife, and their child." He felt derelict that he had not visited them: he had no good opinion of Tuar's hunting skills.

Marek said, "We'll look in on them. Farewell, youngling. I must go."

Two weeks later, at sunset, on his way home from the river with a string of new-caught fish, Wolf smelled smoke. The small hairs lifted on his neck. He sniffed, letting his keener wolf sense work. The strong smell was blowing from the northwest, from the meadow where Tuar and his family had their hut. He ran home, and by the time he got there he could see it, a column of dark smoke rising above the trees. He handed Thea the fish. "It's the tinker's house, I think. Pray he hasn't set the wood on fire. I'm going up there."

She touched his face with her hand, like a kiss. "Go."

Under the trees, he changed. In wolf form he raced through the trees and along the snow-crusted ground to the small meadow. Under the flat black shadows of the spruce boughs he regained his human form and walked into the clearing. The tinker's hut was a bonfire burning into the sunset. It was ringed with Dragon Keep's soldiers. They held Tuar and four other men, one of them Rand. Luvia crouched nearby, a little girl in her arms. The child, terrified by it all, sobbed helplessly.

Next to Luvia lay a heap of blankets, pots, clothing, a

fishing net, and a smaller pile of shiny objects: rings, pins, a scabbard with gold fittings, a dagger with a red jewel in its hilt. A fair-haired man in a black cloak was standing in front of the hut, head thrown back, watching it burn. The fire gleamed redly on his skin. He wore a long sword across his back, cavalry-style. His face was youthful, but merciless, hard, like steel that can take a blow, and bend, and never crack: a warrior's face. His hands, despite the cold, were bare.

Wolf moved quietly closer. The man in black said, "Tuar Maw, you are a fool. You were a tinker. Now you are a thief. You know the penalty for thievery in my domains." His voice was very deep. "You will be taken to my castle, and chained by your wrists to the wall."

Luvia struggled to her feet. Her clothes were threadbare, and her feet were wrapped in rags, as were the child's. "No. It's winter. He'll die." She stepped forward. "My lord, I beg you. He thought to sell the things he took, to buy food for us."

The man in black glanced at her. Wolf thought he saw a softness in the ruthless gaze. "Do you plead for him? He beats you."

She said, "He is my child's father. He is not evil, lord, only weak, and easily led. He listened to that man's talk—" She pointed at Rand. The big man cursed, calling her whore and bitch. One of the soldiers holding him struck him in the face. He thrashed, almost breaking free of their grip.

"I see." The man in black frowned. "Very well. I will spare his life." Tuar's head lifted. "But punishment there must be. Tuar Maw! Which arm will you lose?" The color went from Tuar's face. "Choose, or I choose for you." But Tuar could not speak. The man in black drew his sword. It glowed red, like fire. "The left. Stretch him out." Four men wrestled the tinker down. One of them, Wolf saw, was Marek. A soldier tied a rope to Tuar's left wrist, and pulled it taut. Luvia covered her child's eyes and averted her head. The sword swept down, and sliced cleanly through the arm at the elbow. The man in black held the blade against the cut limb. Tuar screamed and slumped onto the snow. There was a stink of burnt flesh.

The man knelt, cleansed the sword in snow, and wiped it with a cloth. Rising, he said softly to Luvia, "If you come to the castle, you can have food, and a bed. You need not stay with him." But she shuddered, courage spent, and clutched the little girl tight, and did not answer.

Suddenly he looked up, directly at Wolf . . . *The snow was on fire. There was blue flame all around him, sweeping toward the trees, he was helpless, trapped, he could not escape . . .* Then there were soldiers on either side of him, holding him still, and the tip of the sword was inches from his throat. He could not look away.

Dragon.

"My lord," Wolf said, in a whisper.

A deep voice said thoughtfully, "Who are you to call me *lord*? I never took your oath." The bright hot gaze was like a vise on his mind. Wolf could not have moved had he wanted to.

He said, throat tight, "My lord, I am Illemar Dahranni, called Wolf. I came from Ujo. I served the Lemininkai for nine years. Kalni Leminin released me from his service two years ago. I live in the meadow below this one with my wife, Thea the weaver."

"What are you doing here?"

"I thought the hut was burning," Wolf said simply. "I came to help."

The raking blue stare broke the sweat out on Wolf's face. "Release him," Karadur said. He sheathed his sword. The hands clamped on Wolf's arms opened. "Bring *them*." He turned, a shadow moving over snow. The soldiers dragged the four men in his wake.

When they were well gone, Wolf went forward. Tuar was

moaning, but no blood seeped from the stump: Karadur's sword had seared it cleanly as a physician's knife. Luvia looked mutely at Wolf. Her eyes were hollow with shock. She was younger than he had thought; he guessed her to be little more than twenty, and his heart wrung with pity for her.

"Come to my house," he said gently. "All of you. You may sleep there tonight."

She shook her head. "He would not like that." She meant, he realized, Tuar.

"You and the child need shelter. It will be dark soon."

She was stubborn with grief. "We stay with him." He tried to persuade her otherwise, but she refused to move. The child hid its head in her lap.

The next day, Wolf wrote a thoughtful letter to Hawk.

> *I have met the Dragon of Chingura. We met by acci-dent; he nearly put a sword through my throat. He has hair like the sun and eyes like blue fire, and a grip, so I'm told, that can crack stone. He deals harsh justice. But he is dragon; I touched his mind, and I am as certain of it as I am of my own nature, or Bear's, or yours.*

A month later, visiting Sleeth, he told Ono what he had seen.

"Aye, I heard about that. Kojiro the Black would have had them all stripped naked and chained on the castle wall for the mountain crows to pick," the smith said calmly. "But I saw that woman a few days ago, I think it was the same one, at the Red Oak. When are you bringing Thea and the boy to visit us?"

Wolf inquired at the Red Oak. Egain said, "I've got her scrubbing pots."

"And Tuar?"

"He's working in my stable. He's not bad with horses, and they don't care what his arm looks like."

"That's kind of you, considering."

"What mischief can a one-handed groom do? Besides, I know his mother."

"Do you know what happened to Rand, and the others?"

"The lord did as his father would have done: he put them on the walls. They died."

❧   ❧   ❧

IN A FAR, cold place, in a cage made of ice, a naked man lay shivering. A soft, malevolent voice spoke to him; it seemed to come from everywhere: the air, the ice, his mind; it was inescapable as the cold.

"*. . . You can never leave,*" it said. "*You believe you can. You imagine that you are free, free of snow and ice, free of torment, free of nightmare . . .*" The voice laughed, like ice melting, and cold sweat sluiced down the trembling man's sides.

"*You are not free, traitor. You are in a cage. Your skin sticks to the bars. Your flesh rips each time you move. You freeze, and you beg, and no one comes to open the door. You cannot get out. You will never get out. The ice runs in your veins, in your heart.*

"*You will never be free. You will never be warm . . .*"

4

THAT JULY, AS the blistering sunlight settled across neatly planted fields, a dark-haired, plain-faced stranger appeared on foot at Sleeth's south gate. She bore a dagger at her hip, and a quiver of arrows slung across her back. She carried an Isojai hunting bow.

She was Terrill Chernico, called Hawk, she told the gate guards; she was from Ujo, and had come north to visit a friend. "Is there a tavern nearby where I can get a meal?" she asked. "I hear the beer is excellent in Sleeth."

The chief guard looked pleased. "Down this street and to the left: the Red Oak. You can't miss it. Tell them Bjorn Skalson at the gate sent you."

In the Red Oak, the tables were filled with traders from the south, farmers in town for supplies, and craftsmen taking their midday break. At a table beside the door, three men hunched over a keph board. There was an empty chair beside one of them; Hawk sat in it. She was served red ale and a bowl of lamb stew. It was excellent, flavored with onions and dill.

Across the room a chair tipped with a bang as an argument broke out between two flushed youths. A man with a sandy-red beard and no hair on the top of his head hurried from the kitchen, calmed the combatants, and competently eased them both out the door. Hawk lifted a hand to attract his attention.

When he came to the table, she said, "My respects to your cook, and to whomever makes your red ale."

His experienced appraisal took in the quality of her boots and the silver inlay on her dagger's hilt. "Thank you," he said. "We like our customers to be satisfied."

"I came from Ujo. I am friend to Illemar Dahranni, whom most people call Wolf. I've not seen him since he left Ujo. But I know he came north to live, that he married a woman of Sleeth, and that they have a son. Can you tell me, are he and his family well?"

"A friend of Wolf's! Luvia! A fresh glass of ale for this customer. My name's Egain," the innkeeper said. "That ale you're drinking was brewed by Serret, Thea's mother. As far as I know, they're both well. Of course, it's been a while since I've seen them; at least a month: it was a bad winter, which tends to keep folks inside, and then what with planting, and the traders coming—" He waved a hand at the crowded room.

"How do I find them?"

"Follow the river. They live north of here, in a meadow above Sleeth. Wolf built the house himself. You'll see a stand of birches, and a well. Are you on foot? I can lend you a horse from my stable."

"Thank you, but I need none," Hawk said.

The meadow was not hard to find. A neat house squatted beside white-trunked birches. A hill sheltered it from the bite of the northern wind. To the east, beyond a dark outline of trees, the river, high now with snow melted from the mountain passes, sang a distant song. As she spiraled down into the small clearing, Hawk smelled woodsmoke—apple wood, by the scent—and heard the sound of an ax. To the rear of the house, a man was chopping wood, and laying it neatly on a woodpile. His black hair was tipped with silver, and he swung the ax in a way that she knew. She saw his face lift to follow her flight.

She landed, and changed. They looked at one another.

"It's summertime. So you came," Wolf said. He brought her into the house. "Thea. Here's someone I want you to meet." Thea came from the kitchen. "Thea, this is my friend Terrill, called Hawk, from Ujo. This is Thea Serretsdatter Dahranni, my wife."

The two women gazed gravely at each other. Thea said, "Welcome to the north, Hawk of Ujo. My husband has spoken to me of you."

"And he has written to me of you," Hawk said, "and of your son. May I see him?"

Thea brought the visitor to the cradle beside the hearth. Shem lay on his back, strong legs kicking. He was singing softly. "This is Shem," Thea said. She lifted him from the cradle. He gurgled, and swung a hand at her face. The fine dark hair that had covered his head at birth had fallen off, to be replaced by thicker dark hair. His eyes were wide and light, with eyebrows that swept across his face like wings: Thea's eyes, Thea's brows.

Hawk laid her smallest finger against his fingers. "He has a wolf's grip," she said, as the infant's hand curled tightly. He nestled against his mother's cheek. His questing eyes moved from her familiar face to the face of the stranger. Then he smiled, and reached for a strand of her long dark hair, and held it firmly.

Hawk stayed with Thea and Wolf three days. She slept beside the hearth, on a pallet made of Thea's softest blankets. For two days, she joined Wolf to weed and water the garden; she piled wood; she fished in the river; she sat with Thea in the upper chamber, silent and companionable, while the shuttle sped whispering across the threads on the loom.

In the evening, by hearth and lamplight, the three of them sat together beside the apple-scented fire. Thea sang Shem a lullaby. *"Bird sleeps, insect creeps, sunshine goes a-walking, Starlight find, quiet mind, hear the night a-talking . . ."* Wolf brought knives and a wood block from his workroom. Firelight sparked off the blade of his small knife. The block took rudimentary shape: four long legs, a lean arching neck and long-nosed head, a fluid tail.

"What is it?" Thea asked. "Not a dragon this time." They shared a private smile. "It's a horse," Wolf said. "For when he's older."

The third day, Wolf and Hawk went hunting in the hills above Dragon Keep. Hawk soared in the tricky currents over the mountains, while Wolf ran, silent, deadly, through the steep-sided crags and dark, dense, shadowed woods. They flushed, and ignored, grouse, two quarrelsome weasels, and a vixen desperate to protect her month-old cubs.

The hunting is sparse today, my brother, Hawk said.

So it has been. Do you want to turn back?

Not I.

Late in the afternoon they surprised a tribe of long-legged goats, who bounded in panic from the wolf-scent. Wolf leaped upon a straggling kid, and tore out its throat. In the slanting light, they cooked the meat, and ate, and dressed the kill to bring back to the house. Wolf cut a pole, and they hung the meat from it. Carrying it between them, they made the slow, tricky journey down the trails to the meadow. On the way, they passed the bear cave in which Wolf had slept while Shem was born. The summer stars gleamed overhead; so bright, they seemed close enough to touch.

Hawk said, "This land reminds me of the country I was born in. I miss it, sometimes. What do they name that mountain, the one that is taller than the others?"

Wolf said, "They call it Dragon's Eye."

The dark blocks of Dragon Keep were indistinguishable from the outlines of the mountain. Then lights flared, as guards on the Keep ramparts lit the torches.

"For what do they watch?" Hawk asked. "Does Dragon's country have enemies?"

"There are bandits," Wolf said. "Reo Unamira, up on

Coll's Ridge, reputedly gives them shelter. They prey on merchants, and on the outlying farms."

"Ah. Careful, here." They picked a path across a stretch of slippery shale. At the foot of the slope, they halted to rest. "You know, I've heard some strange talk in Ujo, these past few months. The traders say a tribe of demon beasts has risen in the north, and that they hunt men."

Wolf said, "I have also heard such stories, and others. But if there are demons, they have stayed well north of Dragon's Eye." He leaned against the rock. "I am tired. I must be getting lazy."

"You are," Hawk said gravely. "Lazy, and also fat."

Wolf, who had not gained a pound in twenty years, shook his head mournfully. "It is so. You will have to visit us often, to keep me from such a fate. We'll go hunting. Sometime, some summer, when Shem is older, we shall go to Balas Bay, you and I. I would like to be the one to show you the cliffs at Gate-of-Winds. Such a journey will keep us both from getting flabby!"

"I," said Hawk austerely, "am not flabby." She smiled. "Agreed."

Thea met them at the door, a cup of spiced red ale in her hand. "Ah, you must both be wearied to the bone! I was worried for you." She exclaimed over the meat, and took what she needed. Wolf gathered the rest and hauled it outside to the smokehouse. Later, when the meal was done, and Shem lay sleeping on the hearthstones with his head in Thea's lap, Thea said, "Hawk, tell us a story." She refilled Hawk's cup with warm spicy ale. "My husband says you have more books in your house in Ujo than are in the whole of Sleeth, and that you have read them all. Surely one of them must hold a story."

Hawk reached for the cup. "I know some stories. What kind of story would you like?"

"Tell a story about a dragon. If you know one."

"I know one. Do not they tell stories of dragons, here in Dragon's country?"

"Yes. But tell one anyway," Thea said.

"Do you know the story of Morrim?" Thea shook her head. Wolf rose quietly and put another log on the fire. "No? I will tell it, then.

"Morrim was a prince out of the south, who traveled out of his own country to a remote and desolate northern region. The story never says how he came to be there. Being as he was from a green and placid country of flat fields, lakes, and pleasant, rolling hills, Prince Morrim was unused to mountains. He was riding over a mountain pass when his horse was frightened by an immense shadow. It reared, and threw him. He fell over a cliff.

"He grabbed a tree root as he fell, and managed to save himself from smashing on the rocks, only to find himself trapped on a ledge below a precipice. The winds whipped about him. He could go neither up nor down. Trapped, he could see nothing else to do but to call for help, and hope that someone heard him. He called, and called.

"Suddenly he was answered, not in words but in flame, and he was lifted between huge claws, and brought to safety by a black dragon with scarlet wings. Though terrified, Morrim kept his head. With all courtesy, he thanked his rescuer, and begged to know to whom he owed his life, that he might make suitable recompense.

" 'I am Lyr,' the dragon said. 'I am king of this country.'

"Now, Morrim did not know that he was traveling in a country ruled by a dragon. And when he heard this, his heart sank. For dragons, he knew, love gold, and covet it above all things. But Morrim's country, though pleasant and fruitful, was not rich.

"Nevertheless he put a brave face on. 'We are well met,' Morrim said, 'for I am ruler of my own land, and I would thank you for my life as one ruler thanks another.'

" 'Indeed?' said the dragon. 'And how would that be?'

" 'I would offer you the most precious thing in my kingdom: my beautiful and beloved only daughter, Alisandre, to
be your wife and bear your sons.' And in offering this, Morrim was holding in his heart an unworthy thought: that Lyr
the Dragon-king might be already wed, and thus have no
need of a wife.

"But dragons, as all men know, can see into the hearts of
men, and moreover Lyr the dragon-king was not married.
Therefore, to Morrim's chagrin and pain—for he did indeed love his daughter, and had no wish to be parted from
her, not yet, anyway—he accepted the offer. 'Tell your
daughter I will come for her,' he said. And then he sprang
into the air, and was gone like a black and scarlet arrow in
the sunset, leaving Morrim to turn about and plod south,
with the feeling on him that he had made a terrible mistake.

"So Morrim reached his home. Reluctantly, he told his
family and his advisors, and particularly his daughter, Alisandre, what had happened to him during his unfortunate
visit to the north, and what he had said, and what he had
done. His councilors sighed.

" 'O Prince,' they said, 'forgive us for pointing this out,
but Alisandre is your only daughter, and you have no sons.
You have given the inheritance of your kingdom to a
dragon!'

"Morrim had completely forgotten this. 'Is that so bad?'
he asked humbly.

" 'I doubt your people will accept it,' his advisors said.

" 'What shall I do?' Morrim asked.

"And his advisors hemmed and hawed, and finally said,
'O Prince, we think you should, in the absence of a further
heir, will the rulership of your land to Prince Amyas, who
lives east of here. He is a gentle lord, and will guard your
people well.'

"Morrim did not want to do this, but he could see no
choice. All the folk of his realm that he spoke to said that

they did not wish to be ruled by a dragon. Therefore he wrote out a great document, and signed it in the presence of all his advisors, to state and attest that in the absence of any other lawful heir, his realm should pass into the keeping of Prince Amyas, whose kingdom lay east of his own.

" 'Perhaps the dragon will not come,' his wife said.

"But of course, or there would be no story, the dragon did come. He came flying out of the north on a great wind, and strode into Morrim's hall, not in dragon-form but walking as a man strides, save that his eyes were the color of flame, and where he stepped in the great stone hall, his bootprints left the mark of fire. He stood before Morrim's throne, and said, 'I have come for my bride.'

"Morrim wriggled uncomfortably. His throne had never felt so hard. 'You know,' he said, 'maybe we can talk about this. I have some very fine horses in my stable, and some excellent wine in barrels in my cellar, and I breed some of the best hunting dogs.'

"But Lyr had a dragon's temper. 'Do not play with me,' he said. 'I have come for my bride, the princess Alisandre. Do the princes of this land not keep the promises they make? If not, they do not deserve to be princes!' He stretched his hands out. Flames shot from his fingers. 'If I do not receive what was promised to me, I will burn this castle and all in it to the ground!'

"At this, Morrim shrank into his throne. Then a woman, small and soft, and dressed in green like a flower, moved from her place to kneel before the angry dragon. It was Alisandre, the princess. And Alisandre looked at the fiery-eyed warrior, and his eyes softened, and changed, and became human. And it seemed to her that she could learn to love him.

"She said, 'O my lord dragon, I am Alisandre, daughter of Morrim, who was promised to you. I will marry you. Only, promise me that I may, sometimes, now and then, return to my father's kingdom. For I love the lakes and fields of my own country, and I am told it is cold, in the north.'

"And the dragon-king Lyr reached a hand to Alisandre the daughter of Morrim. 'I promise,' he said.

"He took her to his castle, and they married. And each year, in the summer, Alisandre returned to the country of her father. Each year, her mother asked her, 'Are you happy, my daughter? Is your husband kind to you?' For it is well known that the dragon-kind are capricious, and cruel, even to those they love. And Alisandre assured her mother that she was indeed content to be the wife of the dragon-king. And in the course of time, Alisandre bore the dragon-king two sons. The eldest son, Sedrim, was dragon, but the younger son, Cerdic, was not.

"Then Alisandre came to her dragon-husband. 'O my husband,' she said, 'I have been a good wife to you. I have given you sons. I beg you, let me go home to my father's country. I miss the fields and lakes I grew up with. For I am cold, in this hard land, surrounded by mountains.'

"But the dragon-king only looked at her with fiery eyes. 'No,' said Lyr. 'Your place is with your sons.' Over and over Alisandre begged to be allowed to return to her father's country. Lyr grew weary of her pleas. Finally, enraged, and believing that her words revealed a deep and subtle disloyalty, the dragon-king imprisoned his wife in a tower, and would not permit her to leave it, nor would he permit anyone to see her, save the servants that brought her food. Alone, silenced, hopeless, the daughter of Morrim ceased to speak, and eventually, to eat. Soon after, her attendants found her broken body at the foot of the tower.

"The children grew to manhood. Sedrim was like his father: hot-tempered, impulsive, tenacious, fierce and proud. Cerdic was quiet, reserved, and given to study. But deep inside he hated his father for having treated his mother so cruelly. Of his grandfather to the south he knew little, for Lyr had ordered that no couriers or travelers from Morrim's kingdom be permitted to pass the borders of his domain.

"But nothing can be kept secret forever. Over the years Cerdic learned that his mother's father's name was Morrim, and that he ruled a kingdom near a lake. Not being a fool, he knew well that he could not withstand his father's will, and so he hid his rage behind indifference. He waited until a day when Lyr and Sedrim were both gone from the castle. Telling the folk of the castle that he was going for a ride, he took his favorite horse, and headed south. But he did not stop at the borders. He kept going, and as he traveled through this or that country he asked the name of the king. But none of them was Morrim.

"Finally he came to a pleasant green country and a great lake, and beside it a tall castle.

"Cerdic asked the people who tilled the fields beside the castle whose it was. 'That is the castle of Prince Morrim,' the people told him. And Cerdic knew that he had found his grandfather's lands.

" 'You seem sad,' Cerdic said. 'Is his rule harsh, that you live in misery?'

" 'No,' they answered. 'He is a good lord. We are sad because he is ill, perhaps dying, without an heir.'

" 'Indeed,' Cerdic said softly. 'What will happen to his kingdom?'

" 'By our law, the land will pass into the hands of Prince Amyas, who rules to the east of us.'

"Then Cerdic went to the castle. The story doesn't say how he managed to get inside to see the dying prince, but he must have been a most persuasive young man: not only did he speak to the prince, but he managed to convince him and all his advisors that he, Cerdic, the son of Alisandre and the dragon-king Lyr, was the rightful heir of that realm. So Morrim proclaimed Cerdic his heir, and the people rejoiced. The only person unhappy with that arrangement was the prince to the east, whose kingdom had nearly been so neatly expanded.

"But Cerdic had not forgotten his mother, and her dreadful fate. Though he was not dragon, still dragon blood was in him, and with startling ferocity he abandoned the scholarly pursuits of his youth. He studied war, until he became a great and feared warrior, and on a day in high summer, he assembled his war band and led them north to the Dragon-king's domains. There he surrounded the castle, and sent a herald with a challenge, inviting the lord of the Keep to meet him in single combat.

"The herald asked him what name he should tell the Dragon-king. 'Tell him: the son of the daughter of Morrim,' Cerdic replied.

"And his challenge was answered. A black dragon with scarlet wings came from the castle. They fought. The fight went on half a day. I know. You do not believe it. No man can stand against a dragon in battle. But according to the chronicle, when the dragon agreed to the battle, he agreed to lay aside his most potent weapon, that of fire. They fought spear against talons, from the hour of noon until the sunset. At last Cerdic maneuvered the dragon so that the setting sun fell fully into his eyes, blinding him. And at that very instant, Cerdic killed him with a thrown spear.

"As the dying dragon tumbled to earth, he changed. Cerdic advanced to look upon his father's face.

"But the slain dragon was not the Dragon-king, but Cerdic's eldest brother, Sedrim. Lyr was traveling, in dragon-form, far from his domains. And as Cerdic knelt by his brother's body, a tall woman came from the castle, and she carried a child.

" 'Who are you that has slain the dragon's son?' she challenged.

"And Cerdic rose. 'I am the son of the daughter of Morrim. Who are you?'

"She said, 'I am Elinor, the wife of Sedrim. And this is Har, his son.' And Cerdic looked at the child in Elinor's arms, and saw the dragonfire in his eyes.

" 'Kill him,' whispered the leaders of his war band. 'Kill the babe, lest he grow to manhood, and in turn come seeking you, or your children. At least take him hostage, against the old dragon's wrath.'

"But Cerdic shook his head. 'That I will not. For this child has not harmed me, nor my kingdom, nor anyone in it. I do not kill children. Tell my father,' he said to the Dragon-king's courtiers, and to the woman, 'that I have taken vengeance for my mother's death.'

"It was barely a day later that Lyr returned, to find his kingdom in turmoil, and his dragon-son dead. With tears of fire streaming down his face, the old dragon buried his son. What was the name, he demanded of his councilors, of the warrior-king who had overcome his son.

"Shaking in terror of his anger, they told him, 'Lord, the warrior said only that he was the son of the daughter of Morrim. And he said to us, and especially to the lady Elinor, "Tell my father that I have taken vengeance for my mother's death." '

"Then Lyr perceived that the killer of his son Sedrim was in fact his son Cerdic, Sedrim's younger brother. Wild with grief and remorse, he flung himself into the sky, and disappeared like a winged shadow into the blaze of the summer sun. Har, the son of Sedrim the son of Lyr, inherited his father's kingdom. And the moral of the story is, at least as it was told to me: Do not lose yourself in Dragon's country! For it is perilous for humans to know and love the dragon-kind."

The fire shifted and hissed into the darkness. Shem, limp in Thea's arms, stretched suddenly, and sneezed without waking, boneless as a sleeping cat. "That is a fine story," Thea said softly, with great delight. "Thank you, Hawk." She rose. Her hair, left long, framed her face like wings.

"The cradle for you, my heartling." She brushed Wolf's hair with one hand, and smiled at Hawk. "Good night, my guest."

Hawk left the next morning with a guest-gift—a length of soft silver-grey wool, Thea's finest weave—in her pack, and the memory of Shem's gurgling laughter.

⚜   ⚜   ⚜

IN THE COLD damp darkness of the tunnels, a slender man walked slowly down an endless corridor. The tunnel walls glowed, a spectral, greenish-white glow that pulsed and moved as though it were alive. The man muttered softly as he staggered from one icy wall to the other. An observer might have guessed him drunk, but he was not. The jewels on his once-elegant clothes were muddy and dim.

"They will see. They will all see. *He* will see. I will bring him here, and he will see that I am strong. He always hated me. He always wanted my power, my power. It was my power. I should have been the one to have it; I should have been Dragon."

You shall be Dragon. He always hated you. A metallic whisper shivered through his mind. *His power shall be yours. It was meant to be yours.*

"It was meant to be mine. I should have been the one to have it. I will have it. It is mine, I have it now, in my little box, my cold little box." He laughed, a terrible soulless cackle. His pale face was thin and lifeless. Only his eyes burned, with a black, hungry stare that was not human.

Suddenly his face changed. Color flooded into it; his thin mouth softened. The black horror in his eyes diminished. In a child's voice, he said, into the chill, "Lirith? Are you—is it you? Please don't be angry. I never meant to hurt you." Then his features grew rigid. The black stare blazed out of them. He straightened. With light, firm steps, he walked down the corridor and stepped into a high cold chamber filled with cages. A man in tattered furs crouched near the door. He cringed as the other man passed him.

Most of the cages were empty. In one, a man lay moaning weakly. His back and chest were bloody and marked with weals from a recent beating. A woman with long blond hair sprawled in another. As the man went by her cage, she lunged upward, throwing herself against the icy bars with a cracked, demented roar.

The man in the last cage was naked, slimed with his own waste, and very thin. He lay on his side, knees drawn up. A crust of bread lay at his feet. His sides were scarred with whip-marks. "Azil," the standing man said, "I know you're awake. Look at me." The captive opened his eyes. "I'm sure you missed my company. It must be lonely here. Are you bored with the silence yet?" The man in the cage did not answer. "You know, you could be warm. Even the slaves have coal fires, and fur. That would feel good, so good, the warmth and softness of fur against your bruised skin. You have been cold for so long. Cold hurts. Tell me it hurts. Say it."

Resolutely, despairingly, the caged man shook his head, and was silent.

"Traitor," purred the man outside the cage. "Damn your stubborn soul! You will speak, you know." He picked up a short-thonged leather whip. He ran the three tails through his fingers. "Get him out," he snarled at the man beside the door. The cage door swung open by itself. Gingerly the slave dragged the unresisting prisoner through the narrow entrance, and backed away. The man with the whip snaked the thongs very lightly, caressingly, across the other's battered ribs. Then he brought it down hard. Azil gasped. "That's better," Tenjiro Atani whispered. His eyes were hollow with the darkness. "Sing, traitor."

PART
TWO

5

IN THE CITY of Mako a woman gazed into a puddle of water as if looking into a mirror.

She saw: a small child curled in a dirty blanket, sleeping; a man, dark hair tipped with silver, lying mortally wounded; a red hawk flying in a mist; a man with shattered hands shivering in a snow bank; an icy field, strewn with bodies of the wounded living and the broken dead.

Last she saw a man. He was fair-skinned, fair-haired, with eyes that should have blazed blue in a young and vital face. But the face was haggard, aged beyond its natural time, and the eyes were deep, deep black, welling with a destructive and malevolent darkness.

She slapped at the image, and it shattered. Water filmed her hand.

She rolled to sit, clenching her teeth against the ache in her joints. Even with the heavy blanket she had wrapped around her like a winding sheet, the August nights were ridiculously cold. She wiped her wet hand on the dirty wool. The sky was thick with clouds, but beyond the clouds lay darkness. Her stomach growled. She was hungry, though she had eaten meat that night, the bottom round of a merchant's dinner, thrown out as scraps for the dogs. No one in the fine house on Aspen Street had seen a beggar woman crouched near the back gate, and no dog living could cow her; they had not even barked, only slunk aside whining, and the bitch had licked her hand.

The streets were stirring; a wagon creaked along the road, pulled by a balky mule. Haggard features slid stealthily into her mind, between clip and clop, heartbeat and heartbeat. Ignoring them, the beggar woman rolled her blanket, tied it with heavy twine kept for the purpose, and slung it on her back. Pulling her black stick from its place against the wall, she levered herself to her feet.

At the House of White Flowers on Plumeria Street, two doors down from the Temple of the Moon, the girls were still asleep, but the cooks were up, grumbling over their pots. She banged on the door till it opened.

Kira the head cook brought her half a loaf and honey in a crock.

"A cold night," Kira said. "A bad night to be sleeping on the street. It's been strange weather for August. Did you eat last evening?"

She grunted assent. As she lifted the bread, the crust warm in her hands, she saw a dead woman lying in snow. Beside her lay the man with silver-tipped hair, his red belly ragged and wet. She growled like a dog at the image. It vanished.

Kira said, "What is it?"

Shaking her head, she bit into the loaf. A picture slid into her mind: two dragons, one black, one gold, locked in lethal combat in a brilliant blue sky. Deep within her mind she heard the cold laughter of the darkness. She snarled, and the laughter ceased.

Kira chattered at her: house gossip; this or that girl was sick, or having a birthday. This one was in love, or sulking, or pregnant. The torrent of words broke over her head like a wave. She finished the bread.

"Here." Kira slid her a wedge of hard cheese. "For later." She thrust it under her cloak.

Kira hovered over her. Kira was always kind to her. It entered her mind to wonder why.

"Thank you," she said. The words came slowly, as if her mouth had no memory of such sounds.

Because she was looking at the floor, she did not see the wonder that fell across Kira's round face. Rising, she shouldered her bundle, and left the kitchen, leaning on her black staff. The temple cats, as always, came to twirl around her ankles. She bent, crooning to them, and then went on. Kira watched the silver-haired figure until it rounded the corner. "Watch the oven," she said to Lena the under-cook. Then, drying her hands, she sped from the warm kitchen up the brothel stairs and scratched on Sicha the madam's door.

After a long while, Sicha herself opened it. She had obviously been wakened from sleep: her hair lay loose and straggly over the shoulders of her cerulean silk robe, and her fine narrow feet were bare. Green malachite stained her face above the high curve of her cheek. The room smelled of jasmine. The bedcovers were soft fleece, and the lamp was fine silver, with a bronze base.

Kira said, her voice shaking, "She spoke. The Silent One spoke."

"What did she say?"

"She said, *Thank you.* For the bread and cheese. Every day for ten years I have given her bread and cheese, and never has she done more than grunt."

Sicha said, and her voice, too, shook, "Was there more?"

"No. That was all."

"It doesn't matter." Sicha sat, then. The smell of baking bread drifted upward from the kitchen. "I will have to go to the castle." She glanced sharply at Kira. "You know you must not speak of it."

Kira said, with dignity, "I shall not speak of it. I never have."

That afternoon the beggar crouched in her place against the temple wall. It was raining, a hard, dismal rain; it pounded on the cobblestones and ran in rivulets along the muddy streets. Only the beggar's heavy blanket and the jutting overhang of the temple roof kept her from the wet.

A passing cartwheel splattered her. She glared from the tent of her blanket at the oblivious driver. A rear wheel wobbled and dropped from the cart, which lurched, and juddered to a stop. The driver leaped swearing to the ground. He scoured the street for the pin, which had unaccountably come loose. Borrowing a hammer from the bakery across the alleyway, he banged it back into place.

You did that. The words leaped accusingly from the depths of her mind.

"No." She did not realize at first that she had said the word aloud. The sound skipped from her like a pebble from a child's hand. "No," she whispered.

Sleeping, waking, moonlit eye, find the one for whom I cry . . . The words, a country witch's rhyme, came unbidden out of the jumble of her mind. She felt for her staff. Shivering, she stood. Her blanket slithered unheeded to the street. She saw again the man with silver-tipped hair lying in the snow. The dead woman was his. The living child was his. He would die, too, and she could not save him.

"Go away!" she cried aloud.

The words, abrupt and flinty as stones, hurtled from her and spun into the rain-wet day. The rain stopped abruptly. The clouds drew apart. Sun lit the puddles and sparkled off the cobblestones. A fierce warm wind blew down the wide street. The staff in her right hand was vibrant with life. An image slid across her mind. She cupped her left palm.

"Fruit," she said aloud. A large yellow peach appeared in her hand. She rubbed its fuzzy skin against her cheek; smelled it, touched her tongue to it. She bit into it. Sweet juice ran down her chin. She ate it, and dropped the ridged pit into a crack in the cobblestones.

"Cloak." The folds of a cloak settled on her shoulders. It was thick and warm, a soft dark red, lined with black fur. It seemed to draw the sunlight into her tired bones. She tucked her hands beneath it.

When she looked up, two soldiers with badges on their vests stood watching her. "What?" she said to them.

The older man, whose scabbard and sword belt were well-worn with the mark of battles, said respectfully, "My lady, I bear you greetings from the lord Erin diMako. He asks if you would come to the castle and speak to him. He sent us to escort you."

The castle: that was the grand white building on the hill, where the great horse banner waved in the sun, where the soldiers lived. She stroked the fur of her cloak. That was not a place for her; she was a beggar.

Go *with them*, said the whisper in her mind. It had been years since she had been inside such a building. The street was her home: this district, this wall, this eave.

"No," she answered and wondered if they would yell at her, and draw their swords.

But they only looked unhappy. The older man nodded. "As my lady wishes," he said, in excellent imitation of a courtier, and did not move. She reached for her staff, and saw the young one flinch. His fear made her want to comfort him. She handed him a peach, twin to the one she had eaten. He handled it as though it were venomous.

"Good," she said to him simply. "Eat it." He lifted the peach to his face, sniffed, and took a bite. She watched him eat it. He was not hungry, she knew, but he had eaten it to please her.

How do I know that? she wondered. I would not have known it yesterday. She touched the soft lining of the cloak. Nor did I have this yesterday. Bare, horn-hard feet poked out from beneath the cloak's bottom hem. The juxtaposition made her smile, and the curve of her lips felt strange. She touched her mouth. How long had it been since she had smiled, or spoken, or slept in a bed? She gazed wonderingly at the tough, weathered skin of her hands. She did not remember their aging.

The rest of the day she roamed the city. The soldiers followed her. She walked across the bridges where the river cut through the city like a silver band. She went to the market, weaving through the bustle, staring at the piled goods, cloth and rope and kettles, and the horses in their stalls, and at the tall heaped baskets of apples and pears and sweet white corn, for the early harvest was in. She stopped at a stall hung with mirrors, and gazed at them. Her skin was darker than that of those around her: they were pale; she was bronze. She saw a toy in a peddler's cart: a rude carved dragon, with painted leather wings and a stubby tail. She held it a long time before returning it to the peddler. Wherever she went she felt people watching her. Once a tall man in elegant clothes tried to speak to her. The soldiers shouldered quickly between them, and the older one spoke urgently to the tall man. The man had tears in his eyes.

The pictures returned, small and far away, as if they retreated into the past she could barely remember. But others replaced them, bright, colorful, and clear: a black dragon with a scarlet crest soaring over the city, and a silver rain falling onto the roofs and burning, and steam boiling white from the river.

At the end of the day, under the soft blue summer sky, she turned to the patient soldiers. "Now," she said.

They guided her to the castle, up white marble steps that gleamed red in the hazy sunset. They led her through shining hallways floored with polished wood that was slippery to her feet, and ushered her into a room in which a lordly man sat waiting.

"My lord," said the older soldier, "we have brought her." Both men bowed and left. Light shone through tall uncurtained windows, warming the wood, filling the room with the scent of new oak and oil. Sunlight gilded the floorboards.

The man rose from his high-backed chair. He had a spade-shaped black beard in which bits of grey curled like ash. His face was weathered with sun and wind. He wore blue and amber silk, and carved riding boots, and his sword belt was worn with handling in the way the older soldier's was. "My lady wizard," he said gravely. "Welcome to Mako Castle. Do you know me?"

She searched her memory: found a face like this man's, but older, grey and fierce, with white unseeing eyes. She said, "Erin diMako. You look like your father."

She saw him catch his breath. Then, moving to the wide oak table, he filled two cups from a silver pitcher, and brought her one of them. The wine was light and sweet and flavored with honey. "There's food, if you are hungry." He pointed to a platter that held slices of fruit and small pies filled with meat and mushrooms. A wind slid in and out the windows. A bluejay chattered from its perch on the coping. Soldiers paced the ramparts in measured steps.

When she had eaten her fill, she sat in the second chair. Erin diMako sat opposite her.

After a while, she said, into the silence, "Tell me."

"It's been a long time," he said quietly. "We thought you might never wake."

"We?"

"The physicians. The lesser magicians and hedge-witches to whom we spoke. All of us—the whole city—" He waved a hand toward the city scattered below the castle. "They found you in the street, unconscious, locked in profound slumber. No one could wake you. They brought you here, silent, sleeping, limp as a gillyflower. We would have kept you always in honor and comfort, here in the castle, but when at last you woke, you would not stay, and we could not persuade you, or restrain you—gods, we would have given you all the gold in the city for your guerdon, except that you would not take it!" He halted, and then resumed. "You vanished into the streets. You wore rags, and slept in alleys. You fought with the dogs for your dinner. You would take nothing from anyone, and you never, never would speak."

"I was hurt," she said. She touched her head. "Hurt, here."

"The physicians said that you were injured in some deep and hidden place, and that if you were to heal, you would have to find the way to it yourself; they could not help. They counseled us to let you be."

"Your father—does he still live?"

"He is dead," said the lord. "But he lived long enough after the burning to know the rebirth of the city. We rebuilt it from the ashes, as you see. I inherited his place seventeen years ago. I married Nianne of Averra a year later. We have four daughters. No sons."

"The city thrives."

"I do what I can. Kalni Leminin is my overlord. My daughter Perdita married his brother's second son. I am friend to the Talvelai, and to Danae Isheverin of Chuyo, and to Karadur Atani."

"Karadur Atani." The name resonated slowly through her mind. "The dragon's son."

"Yes. He is Dragon Keep's lord, now. I think you will not have known him. He was only four when his father died."

Black dragon battled golden dragon across a cobalt sky. "What manner of man is he?" she asked.

"Hard to say," Erin diMako said. "Strong. Quick. Proud. At twelve, he had the strength and size of one near grown. He rode in my war band for two years, and I made him one of my captains. He has the habit of command, as did his father. There is no quarrel between us." He leaned forward. "My lady, what woke you?"

"Ankoku." The name was like ash on her tongue.

Erin diMako looked puzzled. "I beg your pardon?"

"The darkness," she explained. But she could see he did not understand, and she did not have the energy to say more: speech was hard for her. She rose. So did he.

"Home," she said. Her staff slid into her hand. "Plumeria Street."

"My soldiers will escort you," Erin diMako said promptly. Then he stretched a hand to her. "My lady— Lady Senmet—you are more than welcome to stay here. You do not have to sleep in the streets, or beg for bread in a brothel. Or if not here, any place of comfort. The city begs to do you honor."

She shook her head. "Home."

The soldiers came. She let them follow her through the streets of the twilit city, through marketplace and alleyway, to a familiar doorway. A scented oil lamp burned beside the gateway. The girls were giggling upstairs. She went into the kitchen. Kira glanced at her shyly.

"Hungry," Senmet said, although she was not. She let the cloak slip from her shoulders, and sat at the table. "Bread?"

Beaming, Kira set a huge slice of cake in front of her. "There's orange bits in it," she said happily. "I made it for Anastasia; the sweetheart, it's her fourteenth birthday. The girls held a party for her this noon, and Sicha gave her an emerald, a real emerald!"

Senmet shut the sounds out. Pictures slipped into her mind: a massive black castle looming out of the snow; a red-haired soldier standing in a circle of fire; a small child crouching, a chain around its galled neck.

In the north, in the cold, the darkness crowed its vengeful laughter.

6

JUST BEFORE SHEM'S first birthday, Wolf went north into the steppe-lands to set his traps.

Thea had suggested it, back in August. Wolf demurred, troubled that she and Shem would be alone. Since Shem's birth, he had stayed close to home. "What if you run out of wood? What if you get sick?"

She laughed at him. "You worry too much. I am never sick."

She said it again after the first frost. The morning was bright, cold as a knife-blade. They lay in bed, while a squirming, singing Shem navigated happily over their bodies. At intervals he halted, to thump the quilts and harangue his parents in no known language. "There is food, and wood enough in the woodpile for two months, let alone a week. Go set your snares. We will be fine."

He left on a bright chilly morning. His sled, piled with snares, bumped at his heels. Just below Dragon Keep, warned by the jingle, he stepped from the path to let a small troop of soldiers trot past on their way to Chingura. He recognized Toby, and waved.

"Hoy!" the boy called. "Where are you off to, hunter?"

"North!" he shouted back. "Some of us work for a living!"

The path through the mountains was steep, but clearly marked. Past Dragon Keep, the weather changed. Snow began to fall, clogging the path with drifts. Stubbornly he persisted, dragging his sled with its burden of snares behind him.

A freeze that night forced him into wolf form. He lay all night on the lee side of a rock, thick brushy tail curled over mouth and nose. Dawn of the next day was cold. The sun hid behind a wall of cloud. Resuming human form, Wolf built a fire and ate some meat which he had brought with him. He was troubled. Something had changed. Two winters ago these hills had teemed with fox, lynx, marten, deer, and hare. In three days he had seen nothing living, save owls, field mice, and one mournful grey goose.

That afternoon he climbed the last ridge. As he reached the top, he halted, expecting to see, as he had two years back, a wide grassy sweep of land, clumped with small trees and grey-brown hillocks. Instead, he found ice.

At first he thought it a mirage. It spread before him, milk-white, under a milk-white sky in which there was no trace of blue. His breath crackled between his teeth. The landscape was silent: not the silence of rest and sleep, but the silence of death. The steppe was empty; the land plundered.

Shaken, wondering what had happened, he retraced his steps south.

Three nights after Wolf returned from the ice, a storm howled in across the mountains: no snow, just wind, a cold rage of wind. In midafternoon the light was so dim that it felt like night had come. Wind pounded clenched fists on the cottage, finding chinks in the house planks that it had not found before. The bed was the warmest place in the house: Thea took Shem under the blankets. Wolf fed the fire with logs, and put bricks in the warming pan.

He felt—something.

He knelt by the fire, unsure for a moment. He felt it again. Inside his head, a mind was crying, like a dream half-remembered. It came again, a fingernail scratching at a closed door, the sound of a spider web being spun. He banged the warming pan on the hearth tiles, cracking one. "Go away," he said aloud. But it was still there.

He went to bed, burrowed in the covers beside Thea and the child.

The cry was there. *Help me. I am here.*

He kissed the soft nape of Thea's neck, and rose. She murmured his name. "I'll be back," he said softly, and dressed, and went out into the slashing wind.

Wolf-shaped, he followed the cry. It led him toward the Keep. He gave himself up to it, trusting his wolf nature to keep him from killing himself on the spiny rocks. The wind howled as if it wanted to snatch him from the crags and send him spinning to his death. In his mind, the cry continued: wordless, desperate, alone.

At last, below the bear's den in which he had slept while Thea was giving birth, he found a near-naked man sprawled on the stony ground. *Help me,* he whispered soundlessly.

Wolf changed, and laid a hand on the man's left shoulder. The man was breathing, but his eyes were tight shut, and his pale skin was icy cold. His face was obscured by a tangle of beard and mud-caked hair.

"Hey," Wolf said.

The man did not answer. He did not seem to hear. But inside Wolf's mind, the terrible whispering stilled.

Wolf stood a moment, considering. The Keep loomed overhead. Lights flickered from windows and battlements: promising warmth, food, a bed. But it would be hard, and harder, especially this night, in the rampaging wind, to climb up than to go down. Crouching, Wolf gathered the stranger into his arms. The man weighed less than Thea. Steadily, calling on his wolf senses—balance, vision, strength—Wolf brought his burden down the mountain and into the meadow. He kicked the door.

Thea opened it. The wind whipped at her hair. Wolf carried the man inside, and laid him by the fire. "Who is he?" Thea asked.

"I don't know."

"What happened to him?"

"I don't know that either. I found him in the rocks." He threw a log on the fire. Thea lit a candle, and brought a cloth from the kitchen. Wolf leaned lightly forward, and laid his ear against the stranger's bare chest. The man breathed steadily, without the clotted sound that warned of infection in the lungs. Wolf felt his legs and feet. They were cold, but not, he thought, the frozen ice-like cold that means that the limbs have died.

"It's going to hurt when he wakes," he said. "If he wakes."

"There's blood on his legs," Thea said. She made an odd noise. A blotchy patchwork of scars covered the man's skin. His ribs were skeletal. "Oh, goddess. Look at his hands." His fingers were knotted, broken, gnarled with red scars. Thea laid a gentle hand on the man's cheek. "You're safe now," she said. "Can you hear me?" The long frame did not move. The closed eyes did not flicker. Thea ran upstairs, and came down with arms filled with her thickest blankets. "Help me," she said, and Wolf helped her arrange the blankets around the sleeping man.

In the dark morning, before dawn, Wolf went barefoot downstairs. He was thirsty. He crossed to the pantry and found the stone jug of ale sitting where Thea kept it, in the cool spot. The ale went down easy. He listened for the wind; it was still. The storm had passed. He drank another trickle of ale.

The fire was nearly gone. Wolf walked to the long shadow on the floor. The man had turned himself: he lay on his side, face turned away from the hearth. Kneeling, Wolf gazed into the grim gaunt face. The eyes were open. Wolf said gently, "Can you hear me? Who are you?"

The dark eyes did not change. Whatever they looked at so fixedly was not in the room.

*   *   *

In the morning, the stranger was awake. His legs and feet were warm, but however much it had hurt as blood returned to them, he had said nothing. He said nothing when they spoke to him. But he drank the water they brought him.

Thea said, "What's the matter with him?"

Wolf said, "He's been starved, and tortured."

Thea said, "Well, he ought not to be lying naked on the floor like a beast. Give him some clothes, and put him into the rocking chair."

"He may not have the strength to sit," Wolf said. But he found some warm clothes, and awkwardly tucked and pulled them over the stranger, and lifted him into the chair.

Dawn seeped through the window shutters and drew straight lines on the floor. Thea made wheat cakes and poured honey on them. She sat down in front of the man and held a piece of wheat cake to his mouth. She said, "Whatever happened to you, you lived through it. You are safe. Whatever hurt you is not here. You must eat."

The dark eyes looked at her. The man opened his mouth, accepting the cake. Wolf found that he was holding his breath. He released it. He had once met a man whose tongue had been cut out. But this man had a tongue. Thea fed the stranger, and gave him water. Then she brought comb and scissors, and combed and clipped the tangled hair and beard. As she finished, the man's head drooped, and he slept. Thea fixed a pallet on the floor, and Wolf lifted him from the chair and put him into it. He slept as if he had not done so in weeks.

That morning, Wolf went to the Keep. The day was fair, almost warm, as if the night's storm had been some wizard's illusion. Branches snapped from birch trees littered the dark ground. A group of soldiers outside the walls were shooting at a straw target with longbows. Sunlight shone on the castle walls and roofs. Wolf told the sentries who he was. "I need to see the physician," he said.

In a little while, the man himself came to the gate. He was a small, neat, sandy-haired man, not young. In Sleeth they said of him that he was good with wounds and broken bones. Wolf introduced himself, and explained why he had come. Macallan looked curious. "You're sure he's not some poor trapper who's been wandering lost on the ice? Those folk go blind, and their minds grow strange."

"I don't think so," Wolf said. "Of course, if you're busy—"

"No, I'll come. It sounds interesting. This way." He led the way to the stables. They rode double to the clearing. "That was a hell of a wind we had last night," Macallan commented. "The trees are in shreds. Odd, that it should blow out so swiftly."

Thea had seen them coming from the upstairs window. She met them at the door with an ale jug, and two cups. Macallan grinned. "Milady weaver, my deepest thanks. Riding always makes me thirsty. Ah, that's good." Shem's pen sat in the middle of the room. Macallan leaned over it. Shem lay on his back, snoring softly. "Ah, that's a fine-looking boy. Now, where's this stray of yours?" He was being polite; there was no way he could not have noticed the long body bundled in blankets by the hearth. Thea brought him to it.

The stranger was asleep, his breathing steady. Macallan looked at him, and went very still.

"You know him," Thea said immediately. "Who is he?"

Macallan reached blindly for the cup. Thea filled it. He drank it off, still staring at the sleeping man. "I don't know who he is now. His name's Azil. He's son to Aum Nialsdatter, steward of Dragon Keep. He lived at the Keep. He vanished in autumn, three years ago."

Thea said softly, "That is when the lord's brother left."

"Yes," Macallan said.

"Wherever he went, they were not kind to him," Wolf

said. "He's been starved, and he's badly scarred. His hands—"

"I saw."

"What could do that?"

"Fire," the physician said bluntly. "Someone hated him, that's certain. He played the harp. He'll never do that again." He crouched to look into the stranger's face. "Has he opened his eyes?"

"Yes. He even ate a little this morning," Thea answered. "But he's not spoken. I'm not sure he can."

In his pen, Shem started to bang on the bars, informing his parents he was awake and wanted their attention. Thea picked him up. He grinned at her. "Ma," he said lovingly.

Macallan looked benignly at him. Shem reached for the physician's black beard. "A lovely boy," Macallan said, but his attention clearly was absent. He turned away. Shem screwed his face up, ready to argue with the universe. Thea bounced him on her hip, and he squirmed, his hands in fists.

"Would you let him stay with you a while longer?" Macallan said. "It will not be for long."

"Of course," Thea said.

Wolf walked with the physician to the meadow, where they had tied the mare. When he returned, Thea had taken Shem upstairs. He went up to her. She was sitting at the loom. She had dragged the baskets filled with wool thread around her in a circle. Wolf leaned in the doorway. He could feel her unhappiness.

"Would you open the shutter?" she asked. He muscled open the shutter, which had stuck. Sunlight and cold air streamed in together.

"He is empty," she said, speaking of the stranger. She picked up the shuttle, and reached for a skein of thread. "Whatever he was before, he is not that man. He is a hollowed gourd, a bell with no clapper."

Downstairs, the stranger slept. Wolf went to his workroom. He patched his favorite salmon net, and carved fish hooks from the antlers of a deer for which he had traded two white mink pelts in Chingura Market. When the sounds of hoofbeats and wheels and harness jingling came through the window shutter, he laid his knife down and went into the front room.

Someone tapped softly on the door. He opened it. Karadur Atani, in black, stood on the step. Leashed power radiated from his body; it was like standing beside Ono's forge.

Wolf backed up. "My lord," he said. *Dragon*, said his mind.

Karadur's face was unreadable as stone. "I'm told you have something here of mine."

Wolf pointed to the long-legged man sleeping beside the hearth. Karadur crossed the room, and knelt. For a moment he only looked. Then he laid a hand on the stranger's shoulder.

"Azil."

The sleeper's eyes opened. He gazed up into Karadur's face. His dark eyes seemed to grow darker, brimming with supplication and a profound, defenseless, desperate shame. Whatever strength was left to him at that moment, he was spending it all so as to not move his head. Wolf turned away instead, because he did not have the right to see more. Karadur said something deep and too soft to hear. Then he left, and Wolf heard him giving orders. Two men came in.

"Gently!" their lord said, and very gently they lifted the stranger in his blankets and took him from the house, and brought the blankets in again.

"My thanks; I am in your debt," said the lord of Dragon Keep. "You have done me a service. How did you find him?"

Wolf said, "My lord, I heard him calling."

Karadur frowned. "Macallan told me that he does not speak."

"He has not. I heard no words, my lord. His need was

very great: it reached from his mind. I heard it, inside my head."

That answer brought, for the first time, the dragon-lord's full attention. "You have that gift?" he asked. "To touch another mind? You were trained to it?"

Wolf answered truthfully, "I had some teaching."

"It is magic? Are you a sorcerer? A wizard?" Karadur's eyes went hard, blue-white, bright as diamond. A hot wind seemed to blaze through the room. Wolf felt white fire grip his mind.

"No," he said. Sweat ran down his sides. "I'm sorry, my lord, I thought you knew. I am of the wolf tribe. I am changeling."

The searing wind died away. The grip on his mind eased. "Are you indeed," the dragon-lord said. "Then we are cousins." Stooping, Karadur drew a narrow-bladed dagger from his boot. The leather-wrapped hilt was set with a pattern of jewels, like stars. "This is yours."

"My lord—"

"Be quiet." He laid the dagger on the cracked hearth tile. "Is your wife home? I would thank her."

"She is upstairs," Wolf said. But she was not; she had come down and stood now at the foot of the stairs, Shem in her arms. She wore an old apron, and she smelled like lambswool. She had pinned her hair high on her head with the dragon comb that Wolf had carved for her. The red scar on her face showed dark against her smooth cheek. She stood very straight, like a queen.

"My lord," she said, as if it was a greeting she made every day, "welcome to our house."

"Thank you, Thea of Sleeth," Karadur said. He inclined his head; it was almost a bow. "And thanks also for your kindness."

"I would be kind to a beaten dog, my lord," Thea said.

"So would I." Their eyes met. Thea's shoulders lost some of their rigidity. "You need not fear to leave your refugee in my hands." He nodded at the baby. "I was told you had a son. Felicitations. May I see him?"

Wolf crossed the room and took Shem from Thea's arms. Shem's small round face clenched mutinously, but Wolf crooned to him, and he quieted. He brought Shem to Karadur. The fair-haired man and the black-haired child gazed curiously at each other.

"What is he called?" Karadur asked.

"His name is Shem."

Karadur held out his big hands. "Give him to me." Wolf put his child into the outstretched palms. Bright blue flame spurted along Karadur's fingers and ran along his arms, and along Shem's tubby body. Thea gasped in terror, and crossed the room in three strides. Wolf caught her before she could snatch the child away.

"It's safe," he said quickly. "Thea, it's harmless." She quivered in his arms. The cool fire danced, and Shem crowed at it with wonder and delight.

"Fearless," Dragon said.

Wolf said, "My lord. You reminded me when we first met that I swore you no oath. But my son will, when he is old enough, if you will accept it."

Karadur looked at him a long moment. "I do accept." The benign fire went away. He put Shem into Thea's arms. "You must visit *my* house," he said to her. "This spring, when the snow melts." He touched the plump baby cheek with a fingertip, and left the house. Thea was feeling Shem all over. Shem, irritated because the wondrous blue light had vanished, kicked, and yelled.

That night, with Shem nestled between them, Thea said, "Why did you do that?"

Wolf did not pretend to misunderstand her. He lifted Shem into the blankets which lined the crib beside the bed, and pulled Thea against his side. "Let me tell you a story," he said.

"Is this an answer to my question?"

"Yes, it is. My mother, Naika, told me this story, when I was young. I was very full of myself. I thought because I would someday transform into a wolf, that made me better than the children I played with who would never be wolves.

"She told me that when Tukalina the Mother Goddess made the world, She filled it with four different kinds of beings, Monsters, Beasts, Changelings, and Men. And during that time when the world was new, She told each to gather among themselves and name from among themselves a lord, a king: otherwise, She warned them, there would always be disputes and disagreements and battles and wars. So the monsters went to the east, and the beasts to the south, the men to the west, and changelings to the north, and each gathering of beings attempted to choose a lord.

"And the monsters snarled and clawed at one another, and refused to give any one of them lordship over the others, and they fell to fighting among themselves, and that is why there are so few monsters in the world, because they killed each other at the very beginning, when the world was new.

"And the beasts talked and talked, and chose Elephant, but Elephant refused, and said, 'No, I will not be lord.' So the beasts gathered again, and talked and talked, and chose Lion. So Lion is king of beasts, except that Lion will always yield to Elephant, because Elephant was chosen first.

"And the men talked and talked, and some of them chose this one, and some of them chose that one, and others chose yet a third, and then they all drew apart and began making weapons, and killing each other over who was to be lord. And Tukalina was sad, and angry at them, seeing that their choices came out so ill.

"But the changelings could not choose. For there were very few of them, and each one of them felt that she or he had the qualities and abilities to be king, and none would yield. And at last they came to Tukalina and said, 'Mother, we cannot choose.' And Tukalina was angry at their pride, and they hid from Her wrath, and were ashamed. But they were filled with self-love, and they remained stubborn.

"And Tukalina took pity on them, for She saw how few of them there were, and feared that in their pride they would kill each other, like the monsters and the men, and She did not desire that, because She loved them. So She spread Her wings, and made a wind into the Void, and the Void at that time was empty, except for the stars. So great was that wind that a star tore loose from the night, as a leaf is torn from a tree. It tumbled toward the world, and Tukalina caught it. It burned in Her hands. She blew on it, and cooled it, and then She shaped it, and gave it wings and a tail and a great proud head, and talons mightier than any eagle, and She named it Dragon. She said to Dragon, 'Go to the north, and find your people.'

"Dragon flew north, and found the changelings, and flew to them. And the changelings were filled with wonder, and it seemed to each of them that here was one more puissant than any of them, and worthy of all honor. And each changeling bowed to Dragon in turn.

"And Tukalina was well pleased. She gave Dragon a home in the north, and She said, 'You shall live here. And there will always be only a few of you, for many of you would be dangerous: you are changeling now, but at times you may forget this form, and remember only that once you were a star. When you do that, you will wreak great misery on men, and they will kill you. But if you live, you will live long, and the other changelings will bow before you, and obey you.'

"That is why I did it."

"Hmm," Thea murmured. She kissed his bare shoulder. "Because Dragon is lord."

"Because Dragon is lord. And because that is a powerful man, and it cannot hurt Shem to be under his eye and his protection."

"And you are a clever man," Thea said. "Very clever." She twined her bare legs with his. "Now tell me a different kind of story, husband."

"What kind of story shall that be, wife?"

"One with no words."

7

⎯⎯⎯⎯◆⎯⎯⎯⎯

"... So the pigs all ran away into the snow, and Lorimir made the young soldiers go to round them up because it was their fault that the pigs had gotten loose, you see, and not the fault of the pig-boys, and now the soldiers are all hunting pigs on the mountainside, and Lorimir and my lord Dragon are sitting in the courtyard counting pigs and pretending to be very stern, except that Lorimir let out this big caw of laughter when three of the men brought back a sow tangled in a salmon net, and I saw Dragon's shoulders shake, I swear it . . ."

The girl came to stand in front of him. She was young, with a round face, and black hair cut in a cap around her head. She had a pleasant voice, though not as tuneful as that of the woman in the little house, the one with the child, the one who had fed him.

"I hope you don't mind that I talk a lot," she said. "They told me you could not talk, and I thought maybe it was because you had forgotten how and you needed to hear the words to remind you. My grandmother had a fit, just a little one; it made her leg and mouth go numb, and it made her forget words for months, but we talked to her, and the words came back, mostly. Perhaps yours will, too. Is the fire big enough? Dragon said we had to keep you warm." She had built the fire hot: it blazed in the hearth, yellow and blue and red. He nodded.

"Good. My name is Kiala. My brother Torik will be here in a little while to bathe you, and help you put on your clothes. Oh, and I am to tell you that Macallan will be in to see you. Would you like some water?" She brought it to him in a dipper, clear cold water. He drank with gratitude. He knew she was talking because he frightened her, and he wanted to tell her not to fear him, but then she left, leaving him alone with the fire.

People were shouting and laughing outside the window. He remembered what the girl had said, that someone had left a gate open, and the pigs had gotten loose. He supposed the shouting was the noise of the soldiers, whooping at pigs, and probably the cooks and pig-boys whooping at soldiers. There had been no pigs or pig-boys in the ice, no bright colors, no warmth. There had been laughter, though, and the memory of that cold, soft laughter made him start to shake. He gathered his will and made the trembling stop. He was not in the ice. He was free of the cage. *I will take you home*, his lord had said. Home. He held to that word, as a man holds to a rope in a raging sea.

He heard a flute. Someone was playing "The Ballad of Ewain and Mariela," not very well. There had been no music on the ice.

Macallan came in. "Well," the physician said, "you look better."

Probably he did. He had slept. He was warm. He shut his eyes as Macallan drew back the covers. He knew well enough what had been done to him; he did not need to see it. Macallan prodded his right leg. "Broken?" He nodded. It had snapped in a fall during his first escape attempt. He had splinted it himself, and gone on, but they had found him, and brought him back, and put him back in the cage.

"Didn't feed you very well, did they?" Macallan put an ear to his chest, and thumped on him. "Lungs seem clear." He drew the covers back. "Did they take your tongue?" His voice was matter-of-fact. Azil shook his head. "Good. You have to eat, and to move, so that your body can start to make muscle. I will send Torik to help you dress and bring you food. Let me see your hands." He took hold of Azil's curled fingers, and opened them gently, drawing his breath in when he saw the deformities, and the terrible red scars. "Can you move your fingers?" Azil slowly closed his fingers, and opened them again. "Your arms?"

He lifted his arms from the covers. They moved perhaps six inches. After his first escape Gorthas had ordered him bound: they had tied his arms behind his back with leather thongs around his wrists and elbows. They threw food into the cage, and he ate by putting his face to the floor. When they cut the thongs, his arms and hands had flapped as if the strings of his shoulders had been cut by a knife.

Macallan said, "It will improve. But I do not know how the hell you got here."

He said the same thing, later, to the lord of the Keep. They sat side by side on a bench in the courtyard. The yard was quiet; the soldiers had retrieved most of the wayward pigs. "I have seen the result of worse torment. Though he is still in pain. But to have traveled alone in the north, over rocks and snow, starving, half-frozen, and to still be alive—" He shook his head in amazement. "Most men could not have done it."

"Will he—can he speak?"

"I don't know. He has the means. I would guess that he was forbidden to speak, punished if he did."

"He might be under a spell," Karadur said.

Macallan glanced sideways at his lord's unrevealing profile. He knew that Azil had left the Keep in the company of Tenjiro, the lord's twin brother. Rumor in the Keep then had said that Tenjiro Atani was a magician. For two years, tales had drifted with the hunters out of the north woods, tales of warriors of ice, and hideous fanged beasts, and fogs that no wind could dissipate.

"He might be. But spells fade far from their maker, or at least, so it is said."

"I need him to speak," Karadur said. "I need to know what he knows."

Macallan said, "It will happen, or it will not. There's nothing I can do for it. And even if he regains his speech, he may not be able to tell you what you need to know."

"Will he otherwise recover?"

"Will his body recover? Probably. He may limp on one leg. His hands—something very brutal was done to his hands. Broken, burned—I don't know what. Wasn't he a musician? He'll never hold harp or flute again, or a pen, or any fine instrument. Will his mind and his heart recover? I don't know. He is not what he was. I do not know what he is; I doubt that he knows what he is. He has been emptied."

"Then he must be filled," Karadur said, and rose. He went into the castle, to the room in which they had put Azil. Torik, sitting on the bed, was helping the man close his fingers around a spoon.

Karadur said, "Go outside." Torik went. Karadur sat where Torik had been sitting. He brought the spoon handle to Azil's right hand, and waited for him to tighten his fingers around it, and then closed his own fingers lightly around Azil's shattered ones. The meal was simple, a child's meal, porridge with bits of meat in it. "Eat," he said. "I want you strong." Beneath his hand, Azil struggled to clench his fingers and to lift the spoon. Bit by bit, slowly, the dragon-lord fed Azil the meal, and then brought him water, and helped him drink.

"Can you say my name?"

Azil swallowed, and shook his head.

"Can you say *his* name?"

Azil's whole body went rigid.

"You will. I need you strong, and I need you to speak." He cupped Azil's face in one hand. There was no flesh on the man; it was like holding a skull. Under his grip, Azil was trembling. Karadur let him go, and stood, and made his voice gentle. "I will send Torik to you. Find a way to tell him what you need."

He went out, and gestured Torik to go in. Inside his head, he condemned his twin to all the hells that all the gods of all the universes had ever made. The fire was moving in him, glowing and pulsing beneath his skin. Light flickered on his hands, and those of his house who needed to go to the other end of the hall hesitated, and found a different path, rather than pass that formidable burning presence leaning on the tapestried wall.

The next morning, the steward of Dragon Keep, Aum Nialsdatter, who was also Azil's mother, went to see him. Whatever she said was not anywhere recorded, and what Azil, still wordless, responded, no one knew but those two alone. That night, Azil was able to feed himself, though slowly. Three days later, he could dress himself.

Six days later, in the evening, Karadur sat at a table in the castle library, studying a map. Books, most of them old, and worn, and powdered with decades of dust, made a rickety tower at his elbow. The door swung open; Azil limped in. Torik followed him.

The boy said, "My lord, I couldn't stop him."

Karadur said, "Why should you stop him? He can go anywhere he wants to. Get that chair." Torik scrambled across the room and struggled with the big chair. He brought it to the table. Azil sat. His dark eyes gleamed with triumph, and his face was less gaunt. "Torik, get him a glass." Torik brought a glass from the cabinet by the wall. "Thank you. You may go now." He saw anxiety in the boy's face. "What is it?"

"Lord, he's never walked so far before —"

"I'll care for him. Go on." The boy bowed, and obeyed. Karadur poured wine into the second glass, filling it nearly to the brim.

Azil lifted it to his lips with his deformed right hand. His wrist trembled slightly, but he did not drop the glass or spill the wine. He drank, and set it down.

"Good," Karadur said. "You are getting stronger. Say my name."

Azil tried. And could not. He slammed both hands on the table. His face whitened at the jolting pain.

"Don't do that," Karadur said sharply. "Look at this." Turning the map around, he slid it across the table to Azil, and moved the candelabrum so that light fell on the thin old paper. "This library is full of maps. Old maps. Some are hundred of years old, and have been in this library nearly that long. There are maps of every county and city in Ryoka, from every time, so that if you set them side by side, you can see how a city has changed. There are maps of Isoj, with the invasion paths marked. There are maps of sea currents, star maps, even a map of the desert. There are maps of lands I have never heard of. And this one. It is the best map of the north I can find. Here is Hornlund. Unik. Ashavik. Tolnik. Mitligund.

"I have spoken with the northern hunters and with people who fled the north with their possessions on sleds. They tell me their villages are burned, broken, gone. A huge black fortress, larger than Dragon Keep, has appeared just north of Mitligund. That is *his* castle, is it not? Show me where it is."

Azil drank a little, and the color came back to his face. He drew a line with his right forefinger along the map. Karadur reached for the quill beside his right hand, and daubed a mark on the map. "Good." He reached his huge left hand out suddenly, and trapped Azil's right hand against the table. "But not sufficient. What did he do to you, that destroyed your hands?" Azil tried to free himself, and could not. Karadur seized his chin with his other hand. "Tell me." Azil caught his breath, unable to look away from that fiery blue gaze. Blue fire stroked his skin. Then Karadur released him.

"He makes himself a kingdom on the ice." He put a hand on the tower of books. "Can you guess what *these* are? Old histories, old legends. They speak of another castle: the Black Citadel, they name it. It was the stronghold of the Dark Mage, during the time of the Mage Wars. Is it the same castle? The hunters tell of hideous fanged beasts that leap on them from the mist. Do you know where they come from? Are they illusion or real?" The candle flames flared like torches. Karadur glared at them, and they retreated. "You were with him for two and a half years. You must know. I need you to speak. Say my name. Say it!"

Azil was silent.

Karadur rose over him. "Say my name!"

The candlelight flared as if a wind had caught the flames. Toothy shadows leaped across the table and the map. Azil looked despairingly, painfully, courageously at him, as he might have looked at an avalanche, or a firestorm. Karadur strode from the chamber. Torik sat cross-legged on the floor, playing a game with colored stones.

"My lord," he said, sweeping the stones into his pocket, and leaping to his feet. "Is he—should I—"

"Help him to his room."

For four days Karadur kept his distance from Azil. Five days after their encounter in the library, he was talking to Lorimir in the guards' hall when the spatter and clatter of noise in the room died to a pregnant rustle. Azil crossed the long space. He stopped four feet from them, and drew a deep, steadying breath. The men scattered about the dark stone hall drew back into shadow, watching avidly, all trying to pretend that nothing untoward was happening.

"My lord," he whispered, and took another breath. "Dragon."

⚜   ⚜   ⚜

FROM THEN ON, Azil Aumson was most often to be found in the company of the Keep's master. When the Keep's officers mounted to the tower room to receive orders or to report, they soon grew accustomed to the silent, scarred man in the second chair. Thrice each week, Karadur ate dinner in the guards' hall. Azil sat near him, and the servers grew used to keeping the quiet man's wineglass filled. When the dragon-lord joined his men to shoot or race or ride or wrestle, the dark-haired man stood aside and watched.

The younger soldiers nicknamed him Dragon's Hound, and as much through self-interest as through compassion or respect or delicacy, let him alone. One night, Finle Haraldsen, addled by too much beer, teased Azil lightly on his lameness. The next evening, in the flaring torchlight of the guard hall, he found himself facing the master of the Keep in the wrestling ring. Fifteen bruising minutes later, he was grateful to be permitted to withdraw with a dislocated shoulder.

Late at night, though not every night, in the tower room, with a fire blazing in the hearth and a jug of red wine at his elbow, Azil talked. It was not easy; the words came slowly. But wine helped, and warmth, and Karadur's methodical questions.

He did not ask, *Why did you betray me.*

"Tell me about the ride north. Did you know he meant to go there?"

"No. He said we would have to leave Ippa. I thought we might ride east, to Kameni. But we went over the mountains. Tenjiro seemed to know where he was going. The weather stayed fine for us, clear and windless. There was plenty of game."

He did not ask, *What did he say, what did he promise, to make you leave.*

"He made the mist at Hornlund. It was cold and thick, and voices howled and cried inside it. The ice warriors rode out of it, tall pale warriors on skeletal horses. The villagers fled, and those that did not, or could not, the children, the old, he killed. Once the villagers were gone, he destroyed their houses. When I questioned him, he told me to be quiet. When I would not, he made it so that I could not speak. He did that at all the villages, Ashavik, Narrovik, Unik, others whose names I never knew, all the way to Mitligund. Then he summoned the castle."

"Tell me about the castle."

"He calls it by that name you said: the Black Citadel. He said it had been there for centuries, waiting for its master." Azil shivered, and was still. "It seems very strong: walls thick as mountains, iron gates, spires taller than Dragon's Eye. Inside it is laced with tunnels and caves, like a giant wormhole. One room in it is filled with cages. He put me in there, after I tried to leave. There was a woman in a cage near me: she was very tall, with golden hair. He had a whip . . . He thought it funny that I had believed him, trusted him. He would come to speak with me, and laugh."

"What did he speak of?"

"Magic. He claimed to have unearthed a magic, terrible and wonderful, that had been unknown for centuries. He talked about power, and about darkness. The dark," he halted, and then continued, "darkness has become his god. There is no sunlight in the Citadel, no natural light, and only coal fires. He hates fire. Only Gorthas uses it, for torment."

"Who is Gorthas? How did Tenjiro find him?"

"He was there, sleeping in the ice. He is a warg-changeling. Tenjiro woke him when he raised the castle, and Gorthas bowed to him, and called him master, and swore to serve him."

"Tell me about the wargs."

"They look like wolves, but they have scales, not fur, and red eyes. They don't eat, or sleep. They smell like graves." Azil stared through his half-filled wineglass into the leaping fire. "I don't know where they came from. Perhaps he made them. Perhaps they came out of the ice, like Gorthas."

"Does Tenjiro have human servants?"

"Yes. Not all the folk of the northern lands fled south. Some chose to stay. He promised them gold, great riches, if they would serve him. They hunt for him, and guard the Citadel, and dig the ground for gold and jewels. Some are slaves." Azil drained his glass, and refilled it. A log shifted. The fire woke crackling in the hearth. Karadur glanced toward it; like a cowed dog, the flames stilled.

"How did you escape the first time?"

"I smashed the cage and found my way through the tunnels. I fell into a hole, and broke my leg. I splinted it, and went on, but the wargs hunted me and brought me back."

"How did you escape the second time?"

"I pretended to be mad. Perhaps I was a little mad. Gorthas came to see what was amiss, and when they dragged me from the cage, I attacked him. I had a stone . . . I was very weak, though. I didn't get far that time."

"What does he plan to do? Will he try to spread darkness across Ippa? Will he bring an army of ice warriors to storm the Keep?"

Azil said, "I don't know."

"Tell me what happened to your hands."

Azil closed his eyes. His face lost color. He drank more wine. "No."

That night, Azil dreamed. He was in the cage. He was naked, frozen to the hard ice floor. He tried to move; ice ripped his skin, burning against his flesh. An icy voice, barren as the heart of winter, wrapped itself around his mind. *You cannot get out. You will never get out.*

Beside him, in another cage, a naked woman lay trapped as he was. Her hair, which had once been pale gold, was long and white. Elsewhere in the still room an unseen man was sobbing. A figure walked toward his cage. It was Tenjiro

Atani, triple-thonged whip in hand. His eyes were hollow as night.

Azil woke, then, and heard the noises he was making. The next night, he drank so heavily that Torik had to guide him from the tower room down the unreliable stairs to his own chamber. The following night he took the jug to his room. In the morning, he could not rise. Kiala called Macallan, who came, and took one look, and twitched the jug from under the bed.

"Fool," he said, not unkindly. "If you must drink, at least water it. This swill will poison your gut and rot your mind."

"Don't tell him," Azil whispered.

But Macallan only shook his head, and walked out whistling. Shamed and sick, Azil was sober by midafternoon. That evening, when he went to join his lord for dinner in the tower room, he found Ferlin posted at the foot of the stair, with orders not to let him pass.

At the riding yard the next day Karadur neither looked at him nor spoke to him. In the guards' mess that night, he was invisible.

In the guards' hall, drunkenness on duty was punished by a flogging, public, professionally applied, and over quickly. Finle, who when he was not drinking was neither stupid nor insensitive, watched Azil's face through the meal. After both men had left the table, he leaned to mutter to the redheaded Rogys, "Imarru's eyes, I think I'd prefer the whip."

"So would he," Rogys said softly.

In that he was wrong; Azil knew his limitations well enough. That night the voice and the dreams returned: thrice he woke screaming into his pillow, with cold sweat coating him like oil.

The second night, he did not sleep.

The third morning, no guard barred his way to the tower. As he climbed the stair, his spine and the muscles of his damaged right leg crawled with tension. Herugin was inside; he could hear the lieutenant's voice, detailing the sentry assignments. He went in. Karadur glanced at him impassively, and pointed to his usual chair. The table beside it held, as it always did, a partially filled wine jug and a glass. Azil carried the jug into the hallway, where Derry, the tow-headed page, kicked his heels against the wall.

"Take this away," he said. "Bring water instead."

8

THAT WINTER, THE wargs came over the mountains.

It was early morning, the day after New Year's Moon. A cold mist trickled along the snow-capped rocks above the Keep. Clouds laced the sky, and the bright moon slid slyly between them. Moonlight flickered on the stony path. Crouched amid the rocks, the fanged beasts trembled and snarled, drawn by the smell of blood and flesh.

Their master cuffed them to silence. *Go,* he told them.

Flowing with a foul and lethal grace around the walls of the Keep, they sped south toward Chingura. Eyes gleaming crimson through the darkness, he watched their passage until they were out of sight.

At dawn, the watch on the Keep's wall changed. Finle Haraldson, coming late to relieve his friend Garin, who had the post on the west wall, found it deserted. Untroubled, he strolled along the wall to the protected space behind the kitchen chimney, expecting to find Garin curled against the warm brick, asleep. Though it was forbidden, on cold nights the man assigned to the west wall sometimes tucked himself into that warm corner, out of the blowing wind.

He found Garin in shreds, his intestines ripped open, his eyeless face a chewed ruin, his legs shattered. The first man to hear Finle's shouts went racing down the stairs to find Lorimir. The second sped toward the lord's bedchamber. When Lorimir reached the wall, Finle was slumped against the blood-splashed wall, sobbing. Azil, who had been awake most of the night, was dressing when he heard Finle's shouts. His limp slowed him on the stair.

In the chimney corner, Karadur knelt beside the dying soldier. His face held no more expression than the unyielding stone. He spoke gently to the stricken man. "Garin, do you hear me?" Garin's ravaged face stared blindly into the rising sun. His wheat-colored hair was red with blood. He breathed in long, agonized drags. Blood trickled in a steady stream from his smashed mouth.

Macallan puffed up the stairway. The merciless light, strengthening, limned Garin's injuries. Macallan knelt. In a moment, he met Karadur's eyes, and shook his head.

Karadur said softly to Garin, "The litter will be here soon. Lie easy." Sunlight glinted off the dagger in his right hand. Azil looked away.

When he turned back, Karadur had thrown his cloak over Garin's face. The dragon-lord's right hand and sleeve were bloody. Methodically, he cleaned the dagger on his shirt. Men with a litter between them were negotiating the stairs. Herugin, below them, issued terse orders.

A guard approached Karadur, holding a notched sword. "Lord, I found this behind the chimney stack. It's Garin's. Is he —?"

"He's dead," Karadur said. Lorimir took the sword from the guard. The soldiers lifted their friend's body onto the litter. Finle shivered, still slumped against the wall.

"I thought he was asleep," he whispered hoarsely. "Oh gods. I thought he was asleep."

Lorimir said, "Finle, go down. You're off duty."

"I'll take him," said Herugin. He turned Finle about and drew him to the stairs.

Karadur said, "Macallan, what do you think made such injuries?"

The physician said, "Nothing human, my lord."

"Cat?" suggested Lorimir. "Bear?"

Macallan frowned. "No cat or bear would be so vilely selective."

"Warg," said Azil. Lorimir and the physician both looked at him in puzzlement. "My lord, they hunt in packs."

Karadur said, "Lorimir, double the watch. No man stands sentry alone. Make sure one of each pair is a decent bowman, and that both have bows, and arrows with heads that can stop a moose. Arrange for Garin's body to go to his family for burial. Where is he from?"

"Castria, my lord. His family has a farm just outside town."

In the tower room, the maids had built the fire, and brought pork sausage and fish and brown spiced bread for breakfast. Derry stood by the door. His eyes went wide at the smell and sight of blood. "Go get a towel and basin," Azil said quietly to him.

Boots stamped in the hallway. Lorimir came through the doorway, with Larys, one of the Keep's guards. The captain pushed the young man forward. "My lord, you need to listen to this."

The soldier was breathing hard, and his boots and clothes were mud-spattered. Karadur filled a glass with wine and extended it to him. "Drink." Larys gulped the wine, choked, and recovered. "Larys, is it not? Stand easy, man. What have you to tell me?"

"I was on the road to Sleeth, my lord, coming from Chingura. I had just passed Rometh, when a beast with red eyes and four clawed feet sprang from behind a tree and knocked him down. It had a wolf's head and body, but instead of fur or hide, it had scales, I think, like fish scales, only thick as plate. I shot at it, but my arrows bounced off its side. Its nostrils smoked, not like smoke from a fire but something foul. Rometh—after it knocked him down it tore his throat out." Tears ran down the side of Larys's nose. "I'm sorry, my lord."

Karadur said gently, "You did well to try to kill it, and well to come back. Go downstairs, now."

Larys left the room. Reaching back one-handed, Lorimir shut the door. Under his beard, the swordsman's face was pale. "My lord, what is that thing?"

"A warg," Karadur said shortly. "It is a creature of magic: a vicious, evil beast, sent to rend and kill. We shall have to alert the villages. I want armed messengers in pairs riding to each village, with orders to the Councils. Neighbors should arrange with neighbors to act as guards for one another. Men must be dispatched to every outlying farm, every shepherd's bothy, every wood-chopper's hut or hunter's cabin. Garin and Rometh may not be the only dead."

Lorimir looked shaken. "How many of these wargs are there? Do we face a single hunting pack, or an army?"

Karadur looked at Azil. The maimed man said, "I do not know, now. Four months ago there were six of them, and Gorthas."

"Who directs them?"

"My brother," the dragon-lord said. His skin had lost all color; the hard planes of his face made it resemble a sculpture carved in ice. A table beneath the window held a keph board, its pieces carved from ivory and jade. Karadur reached out one finger, and slid the fragile figure of the Winter Warrior down two squares. "Is this what wizards teach their apprentices? Someone trained Tenjiro to conjure those monsters, and set them to hunt human prey. What malevolent sorcerer would impart such skills?"

He splayed his hand against the window. The thick whorled glass misted, blotting out the view. "He said to me, that morning, *Let us see who shall be Dragon.* He kills my people to challenge me. Gods, what *is* my brother? What has he become?" The window glass cracked. Bits of glass peeled downward and shattered on the rocks. A scorching wind swept violently through the chamber, extinguishing all the candles, sending papers and lists blowing into corners. The fire roared ferociously in the hearth. A tapestry smoldered, and burst into flame.

Lorimir seized Azil's upper arm. "Out!" He drew the younger man out of the chamber. The door slammed behind them.

☙ ☙ ☙

TWENTY DAYS LATER, at the House of White Flowers on Plumeria Street, Kira opened the front door to an insistent knock, to find a stocky man with a grey-streaked beard standing on the doorstep. He was holding the reins of a tall roan horse, and was accompanied by an alarming number of soldiers.

At first she thought it was some absent-minded, though noble, idiot, come to visit one of the girls, though none of them would even be gowned yet. It was early: the sun had barely cleared the horizon. Kira opened her mouth to utter something scathing. Then she recognized him. She staggered, and would have knelt, except that he caught her elbow firmly, and urged her back from the step.

"You must forgive me," he said gravely, "for coming unannounced. You know whom I wish to see."

Then she came to her senses. "Of course, my lord. Will you—will you wait here? Or would you prefer the parlor?" The parlor was more elegant, but it smelled of scent, and there were all the mirrors . . .

"This is acceptable." Standing there in the kitchen, he seemed amused, and quite at home. Beth the maid, marching from the laundry with clean sheets in her arms, stared at him open-mouthed, and fled. The calico cat jumped on the table. The lord of the city patted it with a gloved hand. "You go," he said. "Tell her I'm here."

Kira hastened up the stair, heedless of the giggling whisperers hanging out their doorways: *Kira, who is it? Is he rich?* She scratched on Sicha's door. Sicha looked out. Her normally pale face was pink. "I saw," she said. "Out the window . . ." She had put her gown on inside out, and her ring-less hands were trembling.

"He wants to see *her*." Kira motioned toward the door at the end of the hall. They had given Senmet the corner room. It was the best room, after Sicha's, but the money Erin diMako sent to the house every month more than covered the loss they took by not using it for trade. "I didn't—gods, Sicha, he's just standing in the kitchen!"

At that moment the door to the corner room opened. Senmet stepped barefoot into the hallway. "Ask him to come up," she said.

In the end, Sicha herself dressed and escorted Erin diMako up to the corner room. His steady gaze took in the furnishings: a simple chest, two chairs, a table, a shelf filled with books, two tall oil lamps, a brazier for warmth, and an immense, pillowed, perfumed, ruffled, silk-curtained bed. The bed hangings were pink. So were the lamps.

His mage stood at the unshuttered window, gazing over the city. At his step, she turned. She wore a high-throated copper-colored gown. Its sleeves were trimmed with lace. Her hair fanned smoothly over her shoulders.

"Come in, my lord," she said. "There is wine on the table."

"So I see." Stripping off his gloves, he sat, and filled the cups. The rich aroma eddied through the opulent room. He raised his glass, saluting her. "You look different."

"I am warm, well-fed, and excellently clothed." She touched the dull flame of the gown. "The gown was a gift from the girls."

"Are you recovered from your injury?"

She did not immediately answer him. A white-breasted magpie, landing on the windowsill, croaked imperiously at her. "Not now, little sister," she told it. "There is a cricket in the next room, go and find it." It flicked its long tapered tail at her, and flew away. Shuttering the window, she drew the heavy velveteen curtain across the slats of wood. "Not entirely, my lord," she said.

"But you will recover."

"I do not know that." She smiled crookedly. "How odd to hear myself say that. Magery is knowledge. Yet I cannot remember my mother's face, nor the name of the Abbess of the Temple of the Moon, though I have heard it a thousand thousand times in twenty years, nor the spell which calms the winds: a spell which any village hedge-witch knows, as she knows the number of fingers on her own hands. But you did not come to hear me talk about myself, my lord." Senmet walked to the table, and sat in the second chair. "Tell me what has brought the lord of Mako to consult his mage."

He set the wineglass on the table. "A visitor arrived at my castle yesterday, lady. Once he was in my service, but when Karadur Atani left this city to assume rulership of his domain, he took with him six of my best horses and Herugin Dol, to be his cavalry master. Oh, it was fairly done: it was Herugin's right to go, he was not oath-bound . . . Ah well. Herugin brought me an urgent message from his lord. Dragon Keep desires to purchase twenty of my stable's hardiest warhorses, all trained, all at least four years old, and preferably of full northern lineage." He leaned forward. "That is no small request, you understand. Twenty trained warhorses represents one third of my stock. When I asked him what Dragon Keep would pay for my horses, he emptied two saddlebags on the table. They were packed solid with gold: gold nobles from Ujo, coronas from Lienor, even a string of golden bracelets like the ones Chuyo troubadors wear. I asked what had spawned this lust for horses. Herugin answered, *Dragon Keep rides to war.* I asked, *Who is your enemy?* He would not say. I asked, *Do you need troops? Shall I strengthen the watch on my northern border? No need,* he assured me. *Only send the horses.*

"I will send Karadur Atani his horses. But I come to my wizard for counsel. Does Karadur Atani's enemy threaten my city? Is Mako in danger? If it is, I need to know. I watched Kojiro Atani turn this city into a pyre; that is sufficient havoc for my lifetime."

Two doors down, Ani, the smaller of the two temple bells, chimed the half hour into the morning. Senmet gazed thoughtfully into the ruby depths of her glass. *Sleeping, waking, moonlit eye, find the one for whom I cry . . .* Going to the chest, she lifted the lid, and felt within the cavity until her fingers touched glass. She pulled out the glass, and brought it wrapped to the table. "I do not know, my lord," she said. "Let us see."

Erin diMako sat quietly, watching as she moved the decanter and glasses to the floor beside the bed. She unfurled the fine linen, baring the glass to the day. It was oval, the size of two spread hands, set in a plain wood frame. The polished surface was black as a cave. Senmet lit a candle, and passed the flame above the surface. No reflection glittered in the mirror.

"How can it do that?" Erin diMako muttered.

Beyond the pink room, the house was waking. On the other side of the door, a woman laughed. The mirror showed her: young and lissome, with skin white as apple blossoms, and hair like a fall of fine red silk. Arching her back, she rolled amid the bedclothes, and stretched her arms toward the ceiling. Erin diMako moved abruptly in his chair.

"Her name is Anastasia. She is fourteen," Senmet said. She passed one hand over the mirror. Anastasia's image vanished. "So. The question you wish to ask is: *Is Mako in danger?* My lord, have you your dagger? Hold your left hand over the mirror." He stretched his broad fingers above the glass.

"When I speak the word *Now*, nick your hand with the dagger, and let the blood fall to the surface of the mirror. It must be at least three drops. Staunch the bleeding, and do not speak. Is that clear?"

"Yes."

Softly she chanted the required words. Her skin prickled to the touch of a thousand tiny needles. "*Now*," she said.

His right hand moved. The poniard slipped across his palm. Blood welled in the cut, gathered, and fell to the mirror, which swallowed it. A second drop fell, and a third . . .

Brightness blossomed in the heart of the mirror. The surface shimmered silver, rose, blue, a radiant cobalt blue. Sharp-peaked mountains thrust upward into that luminous day. Against the tallest mountain, a castle gleamed darkly. A banner on a pole glinted white and gold in the sun. Below the castle spread tilled fields: a placid dreaming countryside. She saw a brown ribbon of road, a white bird flying, the blue sparkle of a river amid trees. Horses grazed in a pasture. A boy loped through a flower-laden meadow.

Like a secret river, a dank grey fog blew inexorably across the mountainside. The castle disappeared, devoured by shadow. The horses bugled in terror. A high mad laughter bubbled in her mind. Deep in her bones, she felt the malice of the darkness as it poured across the hills.

Then the image in the mirror faded. The mirror darkened. Nothing showed in the glass: no stain, no streak of color, no light. The laughter died.

Erin diMako pressed a cloth against the cut on his palm. His blood-streaked dagger gleamed on the table. "Well?" he said. "What answer can you make to my question? Is Mako in danger?"

Senmet rewrapped the mirror in its cloth, then returned the decanter and wineglasses to the table. Finally she said, "The obvious answer is No."

"And the true one?"

"The speculum always shows two responses: the direct and the abstruse. It is not necessary to choose between them. The indirect answer is: Dragon Keep falls to its enemy, Mako will be imperiled."

"Then I did well to agree to Karadur Atani's request."

"I think you did."

The bleeding had stopped. Erin diMako cleaned his dagger and returned the slender blade to its sheath. "Why blood?" he asked.

For the first time since their conversation began, the wizard lifted the glass to her lips. "Magic requires sacrifice," she said shortly.

He nodded. Then he said, "My lady, what is Ankoku?"

Surprised, she set the wineglass down hard on the table. "Why do you ask that?"

"You spoke that word the day you first awoke, standing in the hall of my castle. And just now, as you looked into the mirror, you said it again."

"Did I? Ankoku is not a *what*. It is a *who*. It is a name. In a very old tongue, it means the Hollow One. It is the name borne by the Dark Mage."

"The Dark Mage?" He grinned. "Is that the same wicked wizard my grandmother promised me would carry me off if I did not leave off playing and go to sleep upon the instant?"

"Is that what the folk of Mako believe? The history of the Mage Wars is older than this city. The Dark Mage lived, my lord. Battles were fought, and brave men died, when your city was little more than a cow patch."

"I will take your word for it, my lady. But the wizards who fought those wars are long dead, surely."

"They are, all save one. Khelen Arayo is dead, and Myrdis Uliyef, who spoke, it is said, all the languages of men, and Danio Nellikos, the Shapechanger of Nakase, and Hedruen Imorin, who was the most powerful mage Ryoka has ever seen. All, all are dead." The melodious names trembled in the air, music from a distant country.

He leaned back in his chair. "You do not name the one you call the Dark Mage. Ankoku."

"Ankoku is not dead, my lord. His conquerors did not kill

him. Perhaps they could not. But he was defeated, bound, and imprisoned in some unimaginable place."

"Then why does his name trouble your thoughts?"

A woman's high sweet voice called down the corridor beyond the chamber. Senmet said, "All you have said troubles me, my lord. The smell of the wind troubles me, and the hue of the winter light as it lies across the northern hills; my long sleep troubles me, and the circumstances of my waking." Rising, she walked to the window, pulled back the heavy curtain, and thrust at the shutters. Light streamed in, and the sounds of the street: the rumble of wagon wheels, the clip-clop of horses' hooves on stone, the voices of the street vendors, crying their wares. "I can say no more than that."

The sonorous voice of Edo, the big temple bell, tolled through the room. Erin diMako rose. "My lady, I thank you for your counsel," he said.

She bowed her head. "I am at your service, my lord."

He left. She heard his steps on the stairs, and a man's crisp voice, not his, raised in command. A wind sprang suddenly through the chamber. It fluttered the bed hangings. The flame of the candle flickered, and went out. Senmet walked back to the table. The wind had teased the silk from the mirror. The keeper of the stall at which she had found the glass had refused to let her pay for it. He had begged her to take a larger mirror, near as tall as she, with an ornate gold-leaf frame, and had been disappointed when she assured him that all she needed was a plain glass, nothing fancy.

Seradis Ishaya, her teacher, had taught her the spell to turn an ordinary mirror into a diviner's speculum. *Be careful what you ask*, Seradis had cautioned. *The mirror will answer what you ask of it, but it will also respond to that which you do not voice.* A restless warning prickled along Senmet's skin. She leaned over the glass. The surface rippled like a windblown pond, then cleared. She saw a vast room; it was filled with rows of tall shelves laden with books. A fair-haired man in elegant clothes sat at a table, reading. His youthful face was lean and pale, as if he had been out of reach of sunlight for many months.

"Who are you?" Senmet whispered. But he did not answer: he did not see her. The scene shifted. She saw a mountain lifting into a cobalt sky, and below it a glittering blue sea. A white eagle flew in slow circles around the mountain. She knew the place, though she had never been there: Nalantira Island, where the dragon-mage Seramir had built his castle, and gathered the greatest collection of books of magery the world had ever seen. The castle was gone, but the library, Seradis had told her, still survived, hidden beneath a veil of spells. Turgos lived there: Turgos Archimenedes, who had been Seradis's teacher.

The scene changed again. She was standing halfway up a hill. It was a rounded hill, but barren and wild, not a place she knew. There was light, a soft pale light like the light of dawn. By it she saw a man, young, fair, with straight black hair that fell to his shoulders. Silently he turned from her, and walked over the crown of the hill. Others followed him: a woman with bright blue eyes and fire-red hair; a wiry, fierce-eyed youth; a warrior in a plain black helm, who held a drawn sword. They marched up the hill, and vanished into darkness.

Then the light brightened. It came from the moon, she saw: a great full moon that rose like a lamp into a starless sky. Within that circle of brightness she saw another man. He raised his hands: fire streamed from his fingers, pouring into the starless night. A voice called across the tor:

> "*Riven hill; sundered stone; darkness sleeping all alone,*
>
> "*Castle summoned from the ice; Dragon's children sacrificed:*
>
> "*Wizard rises, dragons fly; Three shall live, one must die . . .*"

Then the wind came up, driving the words before it. There was more, she *knew* there was more. She strained to hear it, but the words were lost in the rising, tempestuous wind.

"*Remember!*" the voice cried. The man in the moon flung wide his hands.

Then man, moon, and hill shriveled in flames.

9

———◆◆◆———

SHE FLEW TO Nalantira Island on a storm wind.

It poured out of the north like a giant's icy breath, and she rode it down the length of Nakase into Kameni. From there she flew east, across rolling hills and fields, now brown in winter, to the great port of Skyeggo.

The ocean, grey and cool and limitless, dreamed in its bed. A few fisher boats plied the currents near the shore, dragging for herring and cod. The big ships sat in winter dry dock, while men caulked and painted and scraped barnacles off their hulls. East of Skyeggo the black basalt cone of Nalantira Island rose from its rock. It was dawn when Senmet arrived at the island. Resuming human form, she sat on a stone, to rest, and to reacquaint herself with hands and feet and upright spine. The warm air was misty, thick with moisture; it reminded her of Laith, where she had been born. Senmet wondered if anyone in that tiny town would recall a skinny long-legged girl who roamed the dunes, collecting black stones and crescent-shaped shells, and talking to the gulls as if she thought they might answer. . . .

A lizard crept onto the stone on which she sat. It blinked at her with huge moon-shaped eyes.

"Turgos Archimenedes," she said into the mist. "Magister, I am Senmet Antok. I was Seradis Ishaya's student. I need your help." A white and brown spotted goat with bud-like horns gazed at her, then wandered away. High in the treetops, a single monkey gabbled, and was answered by a shrill hoot.

By midday, she had walked the whole west curve of the island. She had not found Turgos, nor his library, nor any sign that there were any human beings on the island. Goats browsed the stony slopes, and golden-eyed monkeys clambered over the vine-wreathed stones. There were spells to make visible that which is hidden: she recited them, but the monkeys only chittered at her, and the goats continued their incurious chewing. The mist had burned away. She sat on a stone. A dust-brown monkey dropped from its treetop refuge and sat opposite her. Its bright, alien eyes watched her curiously. Three more leaped from their nests, calling challenge, imprecations, mockeries. They played a dizzying game of tag around the massive granite blocks, racing from one to the other, yipping, following some path she could not see.

Suddenly, in mid-leap, the pursued monkey vanished. Thirty seconds later it reappeared twenty feet behind its pursuers. It shrieked joyfully at its friends. They whirled, screaming, and began to chase it, flinging themselves into invisibility and out again.

"Let all objects and beings seen and unseen now manifest and be made visible . . ."

As she spoke the spell, the jungle faded, to be replaced by a wide room filled with shelves, which were themselves piled with every kind of book: books in boxes, books in covers, loose sheets, scrolls . . . Senmet lifted one at random. Its pages crumbled as she turned them: she put it hastily back.

A plump woman with coal-black hair, wearing a long indigo robe, glided soundlessly by her. "Excuse me. Can you tell me where to find Turgos?" The woman did not respond. A tall man with a tilting walk like that of a crane stalked by. "Excuse me—" Senmet said, and caught her breath, realizing that he had not seen her, and would not see her. Other phantoms appeared: grave old men and women with studious faces, young ones with bright and burning eyes.

At a small table under a window, a white-haired man in a shabby grey robe sat reading a book. More books lay in neat piles on and beneath the table. She studied him, uncertain, until she noticed the tiny monkey curled on his knees, sucking its thumb.

After a while he lifted his head. "Who are you?" he said. He had a fierce, bony face

"Magister, I am Senmet Antok. I was Seradis Ishaya's student."

"Senmet of Mako. Senmet of Mako. I know of Senmet of Neruda, who spoke only to birds, Senmet the Faithless . . . Ah. I remember. You are Senmet of Laith, who was called the Last Mage. You killed the Black Dragon." He marked his place with a strip of yellow cloth, and, to the irritation of the monkey, which flounced away chittering, he levered himself from his chair. He was thin as a stick, and very tall. He walked to a shelf and returned with a manuscript.

"Here," he said, thrusting it at her. "Read."

The words were in a language she did not know, but even as she stared at the page, the looping script shifted so that she could read it. . . . *And the youthful wizard caused an illusion of a golden dragon to appear in the cloudless sky. But the Black Dragon, perceiving an enemy or rival, flew at the apparition and shriveled it with his fiery breath. . . .*

"Who wrote this?" she asked.

The old man frowned. "You should ask, *Who will write that?* The answer is: a woman named Lyass of Mako, putting down the words of her grandmother, Dorcas Niro." He lifted the manuscript from her hand. "An observant woman, Dorcas. I have not read this in many years."

A phantom glided past the table: a regal, grey-haired man with skin like ivory, and smoky black eyes in which a deep red flame seemed to burn. His black robe was embroidered with small silver stars.

"Magister," Senmet said softly, "who is the man with stars on his gown?"

"That is the shade of Seramir, the Firelord. This library existed in his castle, until Shea Sea-lord destroyed it." He nodded to a man seated in a phantom armchair, head bent over a book. His right arm ended at the wrist. "That is Hedruen Imorin, Prince of Lienor, master of us all." The shade of Hedruen Imorin glanced up from his book. He was not old, as she had always pictured him: he was young, fair, with straight black hair that brushed his collar. His eyes were a keen, pale grey. He seemed so present, it was hard for her to accept that he was not flesh and blood.

She wondered who the man who walked like a crane might be. She turned to ask Turgos, but he had picked up his book again. His concentration was so acute that it was nearly audible. Amber light sifted through tall arched windows. The phantoms ignored her. If there was order to the placement of books, she could not see it. If there was a key which might help an ignorant traveler find what she was looking for—assuming she knew what she was looking for—Senmet could not imagine it.

She wandered among the shelves, letting intuition steer her. At random she unfurled a dusty scroll. Its spidery letters read: *A spell to make gold; to ensure the potency of this spell it is first necessary to obtain a basilisk's skin . . .* Near it she spied a basket of smoky-crystal globes, some small as her thumbnail, some large enough to hold in two hands. She cupped one in her palm. It was light, warm to the touch, and vibrating slightly. Hastily she put it back.

Then she heard the laughter. It raised the hairs on her neck. Silently, she chased it, hunting through the aisles until she could go no farther. The monkeys shrieked at her as she edged into a narrow space formed by two looming shelves, and out again into a tiny chamber. Its walls were lined with shelves. A shade sat at a table, a pile of manuscripts and scrolls at his elbow. The man was young, pleasant-faced in a nondescript way. But his eyes were wrong. They gleamed with a barren, dreadful darkness. Careful not to touch him, she slid behind him, and peered over his shoulder at the text. It contained a dispassionate, detailed description of death by drowning.

The pleasant-faced man, uninterested in the agonies of the drowned, set that scroll aside and unfurled another.

Let one who would make a warg first seek out a place of death and despair. Recommended is a battlefield, an executioner's ground, or a chamber in which men suffer torture . . .
Senmet's skin crawled. Wargs were the Dark Mage's creatures, fashioned from the rot of corpses and the despair of dying souls, and animated by foul spells.

Turgos said, "His name is Henrik Lum."

The old man stood under the arch of shelves, leaning on a pale grey staff. Over his head, in the jungle of the shelves, the monkeys gabbled warningly.

"Who is he? What is wrong with him?"

"He was a sorcerer; he lived in Chuyo, in Namyrie, a small town east of Dorry. Fifty years ago darkness fell over Namyrie; a frightening icy darkness, in which voices called from the mist. Your teacher, Seradis, finally found the device which made the darkness: a tiny box, cold and lightless as the Void. *He* had made it. They discovered him barricaded in his house, dying of starvation, tormented by demons which he saw, though no one else did."

Turgos's eyes glittered through the oddly shifting shadows. "Ninety-two years ago, in Merigny, in Nakase, the daughter of the sorceror Ydrial Diamanti died of a fever. They found Diamanti mad, and the undecayed, unburied body of her child walking the streets of the city, kept animate by a spell not heard in Nakase since before the Binding."

"What happened?"

"A wizard happened to be passing by the town. He knew the spell which freed the sorceress from her madness. When she realized what she had wrought, she killed herself. Her daughter's body fell at once into dust."

"Is she here, too?"

"If you stay long enough, you will see her."

Like a cold wind, distant laughter blew through the cul-de-sac. The amber light dimmed. The shadows thickened, and seemed to wriggle forward. Turgos snapped a phrase, and they retreated.

"Why would anyone choose such a path?"

"Grief," Turgos answered. "Fear. Love. Hatred. Envy. Hunger for power."

"Do they always die?"

"The ones who call the darkness? Always. The Hollow One has no life of his own to give them. He makes them into monsters, and devours them."

"I don't understand," Senmet said. Her mouth was unaccountably dry. "My teacher told me: Ankoku is bound."

"Ankoku is bound," Turgos said gravely. "I know it. I was present at the Binding." His voice strengthened. "We stood on the Hill of Anor, in Kameni, in the circle of stones. Imorin called four of us to guard the hill: north, south, east, west. The south side was mine to guard. Genarra of the White Spear held the east, and Danio Shapechanger the west. Sorvio Ulief, Myrdis Ulief's brother, held the north, the place of danger. He was not a mage, but he was an experienced, deadly warrior, and he swore that he and his company could hold hill against any assault."

"Why was there need for a guard?"

"Even there, amid the terrible carnage and triumph of that momentous day, some of his creatures remained loyal to the Hollow One. Imorin feared they might attempt to free him, and indeed, they tried. But we repelled them, we Guardians." The old man lifted his staff, and for a moment Senmet saw him, not as he was, but as he had been:

wreathed in spells like armor, young and prideful, fierce as a lion.

"Imorin and Myrdis Ulief wove the spells to bind the Hollow One. Ankoku sleeps, unable to act, until he is summoned by a human mind. *But when he is summoned, he wakes.* And when they die, he sleeps again." The shadows had begun to slither forward again. The old wizard pointed his staff. They hissed, and fell back. "Come, child. This is not a good place."

Edging around the table, she followed him through the shadowy tunnel, and out into the hall. The change made her lungs hurt, as if she had come up too quickly from the depths of the sea. The shade of Hedruen Imorin had left his chair. Senmet glanced at Turgos. The old man shook his head. "They go where they will. I do not govern them." He nodded at the chair. "Sit. You must be weary." He laughed at her expression. "It is a real chair. Go on."

She was weary: the white eagle had neither slept nor eaten on its journey. The pillows were soft and welcoming. Amber light blazed like a blessing through the tall windows. Neither its intensity nor its slant had changed since she had first entered the library. Time moved differently here. The whole great hall was magical; aloof, mysterious, sheltered in ways she could not see. It must have other rooms, she thought dreamily, an attic, a cellar, annexes, other hidden corners like the one in which she had found the shade of Henrik Lum. One could spend a lifetime here, studying, observing the shades who glided back and forth through the aisles, ferreting out the library's secrets . . .

"Magister. Excuse me." Turgos glanced up from his book. "Do you recognize this man?" She framed the pale-skinned, fair-haired image in the air.

"The dragon's son," he said promptly.

"*Karadur Atani?*"

For answer, he rose, disappeared among the shelves, and

returned with a large, heavy book. It was finely bound in red leather. "Try chapter seven."

The title of the volume was *Annals of the North*. It was filled with lists and names and descriptions of princes whose realms and reigns she had never heard of. She opened to chapter seven. It appeared to contain only genealogical charts. One was labeled "Atani." It went on for several pages. She turned to the last page. *Kojiro Atani*, it said, *born Year one thousand seventy, married Hana Diamori Year one thousand eighty-seven. Year one thousand eighty-nine, the year of her death, Hana Diamori Atani had birthed twin sons, Karadur and Tenjiro.* "What does the gold lettering indicate?" Senmet asked.

"It marks the dragon-kindred," Turgos said. A golden-eyed monkey swung down to chatter at him. He soothed it absently. "Karadur Atani is dragon, and his brother is not. I remember him."

"He was here?" Turgos nodded. "Is he a sorcerer?"

"He has a gift. That is not so unusual. There have been other dragon-mages. The changeling power itself is a kind of magery. Although he cannot call upon it as his older brother can, still, power runs in his blood. But had he possessed ten times the talent he does have, it would not have been enough to assuage his need. He did not want to be wizard, or warrior, or scholar, or anything he could have been."

"What did he want?"

"He wanted to be Dragon." The old man stroked the monkey's fur. "Oh, yes, I remember him, although he never saw me. A neat lad, elegant, soft-spoken, glittery as a sunflower. And when he left, the darkness followed at his heels, grinning like a dog."

☘   ☘   ☘

WER-LIGHT LIT AN empty, high-ceilinged chamber. A nearly naked man crouched on the seat of an immense chair. The remnants of elegant clothing dangled like a beggar's rags from his thin frame. A voice whispered in his mind: *You are the son of a dragon, the brother of a dragon. You have his power. Try again.* A dark shadow rippled along the man's coiled body; he writhed as if in pain.

The compelling, commanding whisper said: *Fire is mutable; fire can be quenched. Your body shall be fashioned out of cold itself. Try. All you desire is within your grasp.*

The man's fingers clenched on the chair arms. He shuddered, and groaned. Sweat stood out in great drops on his pale fair face. "I can't do it!"

You can do it, the murmur in his head urged. *Let go of fear, let go of your body, that puny human thing; you have no more need of it. You shall have a new body, greater even than his. It will not need to eat, nor to sleep. It shall be immutable, indestructible. You shall have a new form, a new name . . .*

The man in the chair screamed. A pallid slime oozed out of his skin. His tattered clothes fell into the mud. His body contracted, and then arched in agony as the glistening muck slowly dripped to cover him, forming a scaly integument. His arms and legs vanished beneath it, and it stretched, becoming thick and serpentine. It grew until it filled the chair with its coils.

The whisperer said, *Hail to Koriuji, the Cold Serpent, ruler of the north, emperor of winter. Welcome, Koriuji!*

A human head rose grotesquely from the serpent's body. It opened its mouth, displaying a viper's fangs and a red, forked, flickering tongue. In its leprous-white face, its human eyes were black, staring, and mad. "Koriuji," said the serpent, and its human-like mouth dilated in what might have been a smile. "Koriuji." It giggled, and coiled languorously on its chair.

PART
THREE

10

THE SNOWDRIFTS WERE still high on frozen roads when the supply wains started rolling toward Dragon Keep. They came from Mako, from Ujo, from Lake Urai, from Derrinhold, from Averra, and from every cranny and corner of Dragon's domain. They carried lumber, leather, canvas, and furs. They carried food for men and fodder for horses and mules. They carried timber for building, and timber for burning. They carried blankets, horse tack, rope, cedar for arrows, and behind the laden wagons came horses, from Erin diMako's stables, from Mathol Ragnarin, and even from Ydo Talvela, across the border in far-off Issho. Word had gone out across Ippa to Nakase and Kameni and Issho: *Dragon Keep is buying horses. Dragon Keep rides to war in the spring.*

Dragon Keep's soldiers were everywhere that winter, watching for wargs, and keeping the roads clear for the wagons. Every able-bodied man was given a shovel. More than once, during the long winter, Wolf found himself working side by side with men from Sleeth and Chingura and from the Keep itself, shoveling the snow back from the frozen roadway, while down in the market square stolid oxen waited to resume their journey. Only the old and sick were spared the effort.

He wrote to Hawk:

Winter has been hard, with many storms. The wargs have killed nineteen people, but Dragon's bowmen patrol the roads and fields, and have beaten back four attacks, maybe more. I have told Thea that we would be more than welcome in my mother's house, but she refuses to consider it. To tell the truth, I would rather stay.

Dragon Keep rides to war in spring. The levy has gone out across the countryside, for men and horses, and since the last full moon, the wagons have not ceased to roll. Dragon has not named his enemy, but the talk across the domain says that Tenjiro Atani, Dragon's wizard brother, has taken up residence in the north, and that it is he who is responsible for the wargs, and indeed, for all the miseries visited upon the domain since his disappearance, including the fierce weather, and poor hunting, and Gerain Jorgenson's piles. Despite the whispers, I am sure that when Dragon takes his soldiers north this spring, their need will be not for magicians but for experienced warriors, and especially archers. Could you see your way clear to leave your shop, I know you would be very welcome.

At the beginning of March, when the snow finally started to melt, and the ice on the Estre to break, Tallis appeared at Wolf and Thea's door. "Dragon sent me. He told me to tell you, now that the worst of the storms are past and the road is clear, he hopes to see you at the Keep." He stretched his boots to the fire, grinning over his mug of steaming wine. They knew it was a command.

A week later, they set out for the Keep. A late snow had fallen that night; a dust of it lay still on unplowed fields, but the morning was clear and cloudless, with shadows sharp-edged as a sword's point. They each bore a light pack. Thea's held her heavy cloak, and food for Shem. Wolf's held a tinderbox, some rope, and, well-wrapped, the dagger which had been Karadur Atani's gift. It still needed a sheath, and on their way through Chingura, Wolf suggested, they could stop at Niall Cooley's shop.

Shem, riding his father's shoulders, was rapturous. To celebrate this day, Thea had dressed him in a pair of soft blue pants which fell to his ankles, and a shirt with blue embroidery and long bloused sleeves. He looked older than his years. His development startled Thea, but Wolf had reassured her. "Changeling children grow more quickly than other children." Indeed, at sixteen months he had the size and quickness of a child of two. He walked everywhere, in a truculent stumbling run. Wolf wrote to Hawk:

> *Shem's mobility is astonishing. He is always underfoot. He climbs: stairs, my leg, the woodpile. He is, as his name says, fearless, and has nearly tumbled into the river twice, in pursuit of sunlight on the water, or a half-glimpsed fish.*

They passed a tall birch. Stripped of leaves, it swayed in the sunshine. Shem reached for it. "Boof!" he exclaimed. It was his favorite word. According to Thea, it meant beautiful. Bouncing joyfully, he wound his fists in Wolf's hair.

"Ouch." Reaching up, Wolf attempted to unwind his son's pudgy fingers. It was useless. Thea giggled.

"Boof!" Shem shouted at the blazing sky.

Chingura Market was crowded. Traders, travelers, carts and mules, were crammed into the little square. Keep soldiers armed with longbows stood in wary clumps, looking grim. Wolf hooked a box from a nearby stall. "Something's happened. Sit. I'll find out what it is." He waved. "Toby!" One of the soldiers turned at the call.

Shem, enchanted by the confusion, wriggled in Thea's arms. "Shem get down."

"No," Thea said. "You can't get down, there are too many people."

Shem's small face screwed into a dangerous knot. "Shem get down," he repeated.

Wolf returned to Thea's side. "Three wargs were seen yesterday morning, circling the village walls. The soldiers charged them and drove them off, but the merchants are nervous. Dragon sent extra men to reassure them."

Thea said, "Do you think the wargs are still—"

"No," Wolf said firmly. "I think they are long gone." He reached to pat his son's head. "Why the red face?"

"He wants to get down."

A wagon, laden with barrels filled with fish, halted beside them. Two men emerged from an alley, and started to unload the barrels. One tipped; a torrent of silver-scaled trout cascaded into the street. Distracted, Shem reached greedy hands toward the silver-scaled fish.

"Ish!" He started to sing, a soft dissonant composition with which he had lately begun to mark moments of particular joy. Entranced, Wolf watched his son.

Thea said softly, "Husband—do you still wish to stop at the leather-maker's? If so, we should go. We mustn't tarry."

"No." But it took a moment before he could take his attention from that small blissful countenance. Niall's shop was on a side street. Outside, in the crowded street, three men were loading hides onto a wagon harnessed with two stolid-looking mules. Within the shop, Niall was talking to an apprentice.

"I know you," he said to Thea. "You're Ono's niece, the weaver. You're the southerner who married her. That's a big fine lad you've got there. Here, youngling, play with this." He produced a pliable scrap of bright red leather, which Shem seized in both hands.

"Down?" the boy said hopefully. Thea let him slide to the floor.

Niall said, "You live above Sleeth, don't you? What

brings you into town?" His gaze sharpened. "I made the sheath for that sword you're wearing."

"I know," said Wolf. "We're on our way to Dragon Keep. But I need a belt and sheath for this." He took the dagger Karadur Atani had given him from his pack and unwrapped it. "Not for me. For her."

Thea said, "But it's yours!"

Wolf brushed her cheek with the back of his hand. "I have a sword, my love. And it was you who mostly cared for our refugee, not I."

Niall held the narrow, elegant blade to the light. "This is fine, this work. Those are sapphires." His eyes narrowed. "You know, I've seen this weapon before. In a boot."

"It was a gift," Wolf said.

"Ah," said Niall, enlightened. "You're the man found the steward's son. I heard about that. All right, milady weaver, let's see what your waist span needs. Stand here, please." With a remarkably impersonal grip he turned Thea to be measured, as if she were a calf or a pig. "Calfskin for the belt, and red leather for the sheath. I will have it for you as soon as I can. It may be a while: I've got more work than I can handle. I've got a wagon out front with hides going to the Keep as soon as it's loaded, and two journeymen on permanent loan at the castle, fitting saddles and harnesses and making packs and boots—"

Thea interrupted him. "A wagon? Going to the Keep now?" She glanced at Wolf, who nodded. "Do you suppose we might ride in it?"

"No reason why not, if there's room," Niall said. "Jonno, go see if the wagon's left yet, and if it hasn't, tell Berris to wait, and to make some room among the hides. He's got passengers. Aye, and you can do me a favor, if you would." He rummaged beneath a counter, and brought out a pair of brown leather riding gloves. "These need to go to Azil Aumson."

The gloves were oddly thick, the fingers padded and

curled. Wolf stuffed them in his pack. "What will we owe you for the work?" he asked.

The leather-worker shrugged. "I could use a warm blanket."

"Done," Thea said.

"I thank you." Niall glanced at his feet. "You planning to leave the boy?"

Shem had vanished. Thea squeaked. Wolf caught her wrist. "Listen," he said equably. She lifted her head, and heard Shem's peculiar crooning emanating from the rear of the shop.

Niall beckoned them through a curtain. Their son was seated beside a box in which six piebald puppies squirmed. A bowl of warm milk and meal teetered on a crate nearby. Niall said, "The bitch died, and I'm trying to keep them alive with milk porridge." He crouched, and guided Shem's fat hand to stroke a puppy's thistledown fur. For a moment the dark bent head was absolutely still, absorbed in the delicate sensation.

"Puppy," Niall said.

"Boppy," repeated Shem.

The ride to the Keep was swift. Wolf sat on the box with Berris. Lulled by the steady plod of the mules, Shem fell asleep against a pile of soft calfskins. Thea sat upright in the wagon, watching the road as it wound up and up through a rocky defile, and then out into mud-brown fields. Beyond the fields the mountains towered, peaks she had known all her life, Brambletor and Whitethorn and the jagged majesty of Dragon's Eye. And hard against the grey wall of rock rose the castle, black and old and solid as the stone out of which it had been hewed.

Within a very short time, they were within its gates.

The courtyard teemed with mules, wagons, and men. Along one wall, a chain of men lifted slabs of frozen meat and lengths of roughly finished red-gold wood from two large wagons. Horses, mostly geldings and mares, paraded back and forth, and then stood, while a lean, dark-haired man ran his hands along their legs and looked at their teeth and hooves.

Shem, waking, gazed upward at the great stone walls. "House," he commented. "Big house."

"Yes," Thea said. She scrambled from the wagon. "This is Dragon's house."

Wolf, descending the box, took his son in one arm and put the other reassuringly around Thea's shoulders. "Look," he said softly. Thea followed his gaze. Azil Aumson stood in the shade, contemplating the parading horses. As they approached him, he took a step to meet them. He had put on weight; his face was lean but no longer starved.

"He told me he had sent for you," he said. He spoke with an odd hesitation before each word, as if he had to think of it before he could pronounce it. "Thea and Wolf of Sleeth. Welcome to Dragon Keep. It's good to see you."

"And you," Thea said warmly. "You look well."

"Yes." He nodded at Shem. "I have forgotten your son's name."

"This is Shem," Thea said. Shem grinned, a ridiculous, gap-toothed grin.

"He has grown," said the scarred man. His maimed hands hung quiescent at his sides. "Please, come and sit." He led them to a stone bench. Thea sat. Wolf slid the pack off his back. The smell of baking bread eddied tantalizingly through the courtyard. The steady sound of a smith's hammer chimed counterpoint to the shouts of men and the stamping of horses and the rumble of wagon wheels. "I must tell you, the lord of the Keep is not here. Three wargs circled Chingura yesterday morning, and then ran north over the rocks. They were seen. My lord took a party of soldiers and hunting dogs in pursuit."

Wolf said, "You are busy here."

The scarred man's voice was grim. "We are preparing for a war."

"When?" It was the question all the folk of the domain were asking.

Azil said, "He has not told us. But it will be soon."

"Before I forget," Wolf said, digging into his pack. "I brought you these." He handed Azil the gloves. Azil stuffed them into his belt.

"And I brought you this," Thea said. She drew a length of scarlet wool from her pack. "It's a scarf. You were so cold when you came to us . . ." She refolded the soft fine cloth into a square and laid it across his twisted palms.

On the ramparts, a sentry shouted. A horn blew twice. Shem wriggled imperiously in Wolf's arms. "Down," he commanded. Wolf loosened his grip so that the little boy might slide to his feet. He landed swaying, triumphant, fingers clutching Wolf's leggings.

"Shem, stay here," Wolf warned.

The horn blew again, closer. "Get those wagons out of the way!" someone shouted. The wagoners grabbed the reins of their mules and tugged. In the pens, the dogs started barking. Men ran to the big gates, and swung them back. A man bearing the dragon standard rode first through the gate. Abruptly, the courtyard brimmed with dogs and armed men on horseback. Boys ran to seize the horses' reins as riders swung from their saddles. A pack of perhaps fifteen hunting dogs milled about the meat wagon's wheels. Unleashed, they growled and snapped at each other.

The lean man slid among the horses to catch the reins of a limping grey gelding. The grey's rider, dismounting, waved his hands, answering a question. "Who's that?" Thea whispered into Wolf's ear, pointing at the lean man.

"I don't know. At a guess, I'd say the cavalry master."

"It is. Herugin Dol is his name," said Azil softly. But he

did not turn his head; he was watching the bright-haired, dark-cloaked man in the middle of it all.

Shem's face glowed. "Boppy!" he declaimed, releasing his grip on Wolf's leg. In a toddler's headlong rush, he marched boldly across the courtyard, right into the middle of the irritable, hungry dogs.

The hunting pack snarled. Savage, the pack's leader, shouldered forward, growling. Thea screamed. A shimmer of light seemed to hang in the air. A black wolf with silver-tipped fur streaked across the courtyard and knocked the boy off his feet. Baffled, buffeted, and frightened, Shem let out a roar. Straddling the child, the wolf faced the dogs, thick fur raised, yellow eyes blazing danger. The pack broke into frenzied, guttural barking.

Silently, Savage's huge brown head lowered. Baring his fangs, he crouched to spring. In three strides, Karadur crossed the yard. One big arm scooped the yelling child from the ground. The other cuffed the massive pack leader and sent him head over heels across the stone. The other dogs crouched on their bellies, whining.

Wolf changed. The dragon-lord bounced Shem casually on his forearm.

"Hush, wolfling," he said. "Be still. Naught has hurt thee." Cool blue flames flickered along his hands and arms.

Shem forgot his tears, and snatched rapturously at the teasing blue patterns. "Boof!"

A redheaded soldier appeared at Karadur's elbow. "My lord, I'm sorry. The dogs were in my charge." He was breathing hard.

Karadur looked at him. "Rogys. Is this how you usually obey my orders?" The redhead swallowed. Freckles stood out darkly on his ashen face. His shoulders braced. "We will speak of this later. Get those beasts to kennel." The redhead and two other guards grabbed for the dogs' leather collars. The man named Herugin came up on Karadur's left shoulder.

"My lord, Hern Amdur's here. He's brought a string of seven cavalry-trained horses from his father's stables: three geldings, four mares."

"Hern? Good." Karadur flung Shem into the air, and caught him. Shem crowed aloud. Karadur surveyed him, and handed him to Wolf. "Illemar Dahranni, my wolf cousin. Welcome to my house."

Thea was trembling at his side. Wolf put an arm around her shoulders. He had never gone on his knees to any man, and would not now, but he chose his words as carefully as ever he had made a choice.

"Lord, thanks are too small for what I want to say to you. There is nothing I own, or could borrow, build, or steal, that is not yours if you want it. And if you have, now or ever, the least use for a threadbare, forty-year-old wolfskin, I think I could find you one."

That brought a near-smile to Karadur's hard face. "What makes you think I would prefer you with your skin off? Let you and your family be free of the house, until I am able to greet you properly. My household will be pleased to make you welcome. Will you rest the night?"

"My lord, we would be happy to."

"Rogys!" The redhead snapped to attention. "Make your amends by showing my guests around the Keep."

Karadur strode toward a stairway, Azil on his heels. Rogys exhaled deep and long. "Gods." He hovered. "Do you want food, beer, wine? I'll send for it."

"We're fine," Wolf said. Shem, wedged peacefully into the crook of his father's arm, made a bubbling, humming sound.

Thea said, between her teeth, "I would like a club. With nails in it, long sharp ones." She lifted Wolf's free hand in hers, brought it tenderly to her lips, and bit his thumb, hard.

Rogys escorted them around the castle, as proud of the place as if he had built it himself. The bakery steamed with transcendent smells. The forge was dark and hot as a troll's cave. At the stable, looking down the row of equine heads poking curiously from stalls, Thea said, "I have never seen so many horses in one place."

Rogys grinned. "Aye. Herugin says we've stripped the north of horses."

"How many?" Wolf asked.

"Eighty, and fifteen mules. Twenty of them—the ones with the red and gold bridles—came from Erin diMako," Rogys said. He rubbed the nose of the nearest horse, a blazoned bay mare. "Hey, Star. Art bored? I have no sugar with me, bright one."

He led them next to the carpenter's shop. At the doorway, Thea lifted Shem from Wolf's arms. "I will see you later," she said to her husband. She smiled sweetly at Rogys. "I think you should take me to the kitchens."

The wood smell was strong as wine. Lengths of yew and cedar were stacked against a wall. There were bows everywhere, in various stages of completion. Wolf ran a surreptitious finger along one that appeared finished. The oiled wood was satiny. A man about ten years his senior was planing a yew stave. Wolf introduced himself.

"Liam Dubhain," said the bowsmith. His hands maintained their steady stroking movements with the plane. "I've heard of you. You work with wood."

"Rough carpentry, mostly," Wolf said. "Walls, roofs, shelves. I have a friend in Ujo who makes bows. Terrill Chernico is her name. Her shop's in Lantern Street."

"We've never met, but I know of her."

Wolf ate that night in the guard hall. It brought back memories of his own service to Kalni Leminin. The Lemininkai castle and garrison were twice the size of this one. But the appetites were the same, and the noise, and the spirit. Rogys, taking his escort duties seriously, brought him to meet the cavalry master, Herugin, and the archery master, Murgain.

"That's Captain Lorimir," the redhead said softly, pointing to a broad-shouldered, bearded older man. "He's originally from Nakase, but he's been here thirty years. He served the Black Dragon, our lord's father."

After dinner the men shoved the tables aside. In the antechamber, the dogs whined to be let in, and at Lorimir's nod the doors were opened. The younger men initiated a contest involving throwing-knives and the carcass of a pig. Wolf moved hastily from the line of fire, and found himself standing between Herugin and a young, slender, fair-haired man.

"Hern Amdur," the young man said. He held out a jug. "Want some?"

Wolf lifted the jug to his lips. The mellow taste of wine warmed his mouth. He passed the jug to Herugin. "There's a free bench," the cavalryman said softly. The bench was empty, and the jug, though small, was full. The three men sat. Wolf stretched his heels contentedly. His stomach was full of roast glazed ham. Before the meal, he and Rogys had visited the kitchen. Thea, deep in conversation with the cooks, had pretended not to see him. Shem, wrapped in a bright yellow blanket, lay fast asleep in the well of a copper cauldron.

Herugin and Hern talked cheerfully of horses. Suddenly Herugin turned the jug upside down. "Empty. How did that happen?"

"I'll do it," said Hern. He rose, and strolled toward the kitchen.

Wolf said, "You seem to know each other well."

"Well enough. His father, Thorin, was cavalry master here when I arrived. He retired about a year later. Thorin and his wife Mellia breed horses. Their farm is north and east of here, just this side of Coll's Ridge."

"Where did you come from?"

"Mako. But I was born in Selidor, in Kameni. My father was a traveling horse doctor. We moved to Merigny when I was small, and then up the river to Ujo, and finally to Mako. I served four years in the city guard. So did Hern. That was where we met."

"How is it you are here?" Wolf asked.

"Dragon was a captain in the Mako garrison for two years. When he left, I followed him."

Wolf said, "That must have been odd. After all, his father nearly destroyed the city. Did the men know who he was?"

"He called himself Kani Diamori. He was careful. Some of the men never knew."

Hern returned with a jug beneath his elbow. "This stuff's weaker than the last batch."

"It better be," Herugin said.

Without announcement, Karadur entered the rear of the hall. Quietly, stopping briefly on his way to speak to this man and that, he moved through the long room. He angled toward the bench. The men rose. He gestured them to sit. "Herugin, how is Arnor?"

"I sent him to Macallan, my lord. His shoulder's no better."

Karadur nodded. "His horse fell on the ice," he said to Hern and Wolf. "He was thrown. And the gelding?"

"Improved. The boys are poulticing his leg every four hours." Herugin offered the jug. "Wine, my lord?"

"Thank you, no." He surveyed Wolf. "You look comfortable enough."

"I am, my lord. Thank you."

"Where is your son?"

"With my wife, in the kitchen."

The dragon-lord nodded. "Hern, it's good to see you."

"Sir. Thank you."

"How are your parents?"

"They're fine, my lord."

"I am grateful for the horses. Tell them so. What do you hear from Dennis?"

Hern said, "He's well. My lord—they say you ride north next month."

"It's true," the dragon-lord said.

Hern said tightly, "I would give anything to join you."

Karadur said gently, "I know you can fight, Hern. But if every rider and archer and swordsman in the domain were to come north with me, the land would empty. I need men I can trust to guard my back. With the war band gone, half the thieves and outlaws in Ryoka will be heading this way, hoping to catch the villages unaware and undefended. What if Reo Unamira's boys were to take a sudden notion to come over the ridge and raid your stock?"

Hern snorted. "That foul-mouthed, sheep-stealing old drunk. He wouldn't dare." He flushed suddenly. "I'm sorry, my lord. I shouldn't have said it."

"No need to be sorry," Karadur said. "I know what he is."

In the middle of the hall, a group of men had left the pig carcass and were practicing their grappling techniques near the fire. A stocky man, who had clearly had an ample portion of drink, challenged Rogys to wrestle. "Come on, Red. Two falls out of three. Loser to shave his head to the bone and clean the winner's boots for a week."

"You'll lose," Rogys said comfortably. Karadur, soft-footed as a cat, moved to stand in the shadow of the hearth.

"Try me."

"Who's he?" Wolf whispered to Herugin.

"Orm Jensen. He's an archer. He's good, but Rogys is better."

Orm pulled his shirt off. Under it his muscles bulged. Rogys imitated him: he was leaner, wiry, but with the clear advantage of height. They moved into the circle. Orm lunged, laughing, for Rogys's legs.

"You would never know," Wolf said to Herugin, "that half these men just spent two days riding through a mountain pass and over snow-fields."

"They're good boys," Herugin said austerely. "They work hard."

A cheer rose from the middle of the room. Orm was on his back. Rogys spun toward the hearth, arms raised in triumph. "My lord," he said, "will you wrestle?" It was put half-seriously, out of sheer bravado, and it drew a chorus of laughter and catcalls.

Karadur undid the lacings of his shirt and pulled it over his head. "Surely." He sauntered into the ring. "What stakes?"

Silence fell over the hall. Clearly Rogys had not expected to have his challenge accepted. He swallowed. "Whatever you like."

"No stakes," the bigger man said. "Call it a practice bout." The candlelight ricocheted off two bare torsos, two bent heads, one fair, one red. Shadows played along their backs and arms as they moved, feinting and testing. Rogys moved first, diving for his opponent's legs, a technique to shake the larger man's balance. He was countered, by a smooth twist and a scissoring grip that broke the hold and turned him on his back. He twisted, trapped the other man's knee with his heel, and came upright. They circled, and closed again. Rogys tried for an armlock; Dragon whirled and pulled free with a powerful jerk. The circle of men whooped. Even the kitchen staff had crowded into the hall to watch.

Wolf said, "The boy's fast. Does he have any chance at all?"

Herugin shook his head. "To hold Dragon?" said Hern. "Not in this lifetime."

They circled again. Rogys swept his leg at his opponent. Dragon fell. Rogys sprang forward. But as he sprang to pin, Dragon moved. There was a flurry of movement, too fast for Wolf to see. Suddenly Rogys was down, with Dragon's pressed knee firmly against his spine, and both arms twisted up behind his back. Someone pounded on the table. The dogs barked wildly.

Dragon's swift, rare grin gleamed through the shadows. He pulled Rogys up in one weightless motion. "Well done."

The servers, obedient to Lorimir's signal, began to snuff the candles. The dog-boys called the dogs. The soldiers, talking softly, strolled to bed. "My lord," Azil said, moving from the shadows. He was holding Karadur's shirt. Karadur took it from him. His skin was flushed and gleaming. He worked the shirt on and pulled it down, freeing his head. Their eyes met. Karadur reached to touch the scarred man lightly on the cheek.

"Ah, well," Herugin said. He rose. "Time for bed. Wolf, your wife is probably wondering where you are. Gods be thanked, Murgain drew the night watch. Hern, you know your way." The young horseman nodded. Herugin hailed a pageboy. "Torik! This is Wolf, Dragon's guest. You know where he is to sleep?"

Wolf followed the boy's flickering candle along one corridor and up a flight of stairs to another corridor. It was a long ways from the guard hall. Thea was sitting upright in the bed. Her hair fell like silk around her pale shoulders. Shem, his breathing soft and even, lay near her, nested in furs. His round face was soft and innocent as a flower. The tapestries on the stone walls were faded, lines indistinct, colors muted.

Under the quilts, Thea was warm and naked. Wolf undressed, and slid beside her. He could not tell if she was angry. He brushed his lips against her shoulder.

"I'm sorry," he said.

She said softly, "I thought you would both be torn to pieces."

He decided not to tell her how close it had been. "I know." He kissed her again. Her skin tasted of flowers. "Did you enjoy the evening?" He felt her nod. "Whom did you talk to?"

"I met Marek's wife, Beryl. She is the Keep's chief

seamstress. She lives here, with her sons. I met the head cook, Borys, and the steward and Bryony, Tuar's mother. The bake oven in the kitchen is so big you can walk into it."

"What did they talk about?"

"They gossiped about the captains." She turned her head slightly. Her grin made him uneasy. "What did you do in the guard hall, besides eat and drink?"

"I did nothing," Wolf said virtuously. "The soldiers threw knives at the pig bones, for money."

"I know." She giggled suddenly. "Borys was mad enough to spit when the servers brought the tray back. He wanted to make a stock with the leavings. Whom did *you* talk to?"

"Mostly Herugin."

"Was Dragon there?"

"He was there." Wolf extinguished the candle. Coals glowed redly in the hearth. "Did they gossip about Dragon, too?"

"What would they say?"

"Gods, I don't know. What he likes, what he hates, who he sleeps with."

Thea said, "Dragon sleeps alone."

Her certainty startled him. "They said that?" She shook her head. "How do you know, then? I thought—Azil—"

"No. Once, perhaps. But Azil Aumson left him, and whatever drew him away still lies between them."

He did not doubt her knowledge. A log slipped in the hearth. Shem murmured in his sleep. He smelled of spice and soap.

"His parents are dead," Wolf mused. "He has no lover, no friend, no kin, save a brother who hates him. Gods, he must be lonely." A deep, pleasurable ache stirred his body. The chamber was shadowy as a cave. "My wise woman." He drew her on top of him. "My wise, beautiful, wondrous woman. Come here. How did I survive, before I met you?"

She laughed, deep in her throat, and nipped his ear. "You have friends."

11

They woke to the scent of bread baking, and Shem's soft unmelodic crooning.

Wolf sat up, confused by the angles and colors of the room. Then he remembered where they were. Thea's dark hair fanned like a peacock's tail over counterpane and pillow. Gazing along the capacious bed, Wolf looked for his singing son.

He found Shem naked, as close to the fire screen as he could get. The ashes were cold, but the red bricks that lipped the fireplace had retained their warmth, and Shem sat happily upon them, playing with what Wolf took to be wood chips, until he lifted one and found that it was assuredly not wood. Clay? "What've you got there?" he inquired.

Shem nudged the little shapeless chunks with his fingers. "Orse," he explained blithely. "At. Boppy."

Upon closer examination, Wolf agreed that the largest of the three bits—he realized they were made of bread dough—could conceivably be said to resemble a horse, and the smallest a cat, and the middle one a dog.

"How did you get down from the bed?"

"Shem get down."

"I know that," Wolf said patiently. "How did you get down?" He lifted the smooth shell-pink child and deposited him in the center of the bed. "Show me."

Shem chortled. His hazel eyes were the exact shade of Thea's. With a practiced motion, he crawled to the edge of the bed, stuck his legs straight out in front of him, arched his back, and slid, letting his legs fold as soon as he touched the floor. Landing in a frog-squat, he grinned at his father. "Shem get down."

"We have birthed an acrobat," Wolf informed his wife. Going to the window, he pushed the heavy rich curtains aside and opened the shutters. Light and cold air streamed in. Thea snatched for her clothing. Shem, seeming oblivious to cold, crouched on the brick beside his toys.

They ate fresh-baked bread and cold ham in the kitchen. Thea kept Shem close; the breakfast cooks, though indulgent, were busy, and the pots and trays the servers slung with such skill were heavy and hot. A black dog nosed through the scraps.

"Boppy," Shem said happily. "Shem get down."

"Shem stay here." Thea caught him as he moved to slide from her lap. Shem reddened. "He is going to yell in a minute. Come, my treasure, we are leaving, don't cry. We are going home. Shem go home."

They went into the courtyard. The warm wind held a touch of moisture. The sky was grey-white with cloud. As Wolf slung the pack over his shoulder and buckled on his sword belt, a fair-haired child tugged at his elbow.

"Sir? Dragon sent me. He wants to see you."

Wolf kissed Thea's cheek. "I won't be long," he promised. "Lead on," he said to the page. They climbed a stairway, strolled along a tapestried corridor, and climbed a second, narrower staircase. At the top of the second stairway, a thick wooden door lay partly open. The windowed room was bright and hot. A tapestry on a wall showed a city with flags flying, and a light-filled sky, and in the middle of that sky, a black dragon.

Karadur Atani sat in a high-backed chair behind a desk.

Papers lay in piles on a long table, along with wine and plates, the food on them half-eaten.

Wolf stood in the doorway. "My lord. You wanted to see me."

"Come in." Karadur pointed to a chair. "Sit. Be comfortable."

"Thank you, my lord."

Azil Aumson moved from the corner in which he had been standing to fill a glass with wine, and set it at Wolf's elbow. The dragon-lord leaned back in his chair. Wolf felt the heat of him across the plank of the desktop.

"How is the boy?"

"My lord, he is fine."

"He is a brave child. He was well-named. Did my people treat you well?"

"We were entertained like princes."

Karadur nodded. "Good." His tone changed. "You know that we prepare for war." Wolf nodded. "Do you know who our enemy is?"

"I have heard rumors, my lord."

"I am sure you have. What do they say?"

It was direct as the prick of a sword point against his bare skin. Wolf said, "The rumors speak of a quarrel between you and your brother, Tenjiro."

"Yes," the dragon-lord said. Something moved behind the controlled lines of his face. "Have you a brother?"

"I have four brothers, my lord," Wolf answered. "Three sisters."

"Are they all changeling?"

"No, my lord."

"And is there dissension between the changeling kin and their siblings who lack their powers?"

It was not an easy question to answer. Wolf said honestly, "We are not all friends."

"But there are many of you," the dragon-lord said. "If an

enemy army were to attack the place of your birth, would you set your animosities aside, and stand together?"

An army in Nyo . . . For a moment Wolf saw the low sprawling buildings of his family's manor surrounded by leaping flames. "My lord, I believe we would."

Rising, the dragon-lord walked to the window. Looking toward the towering black silhouette of Dragon's Eye, he said pensively, "You have lived in my domain how long? Three years? You must know I have never taken form."

"I have heard so."

"And do those who speak of it say why?"

"They say different things."

Karadur whirled, his eyes suddenly blazing. "Answer what I ask you, man!"

It was like facing a firestorm. Nerves thrumming like harp strings in a wind, Wolf said, "They speak of sorcery, and of a curse."

"Yes." Karadur lifted his hands to his face a moment. When he dropped them, the hard, disciplined detachment had returned. "Three and a half years ago, on a quiet September night, a month after my twentieth birthday, I made my talisman. I had no parent living to tell me how, so I guessed what to do and how to do it. I made it out of gold, shaped it in dragonfire, and tempered it with blood." He pushed the sleeve from his arm, exposing a white scar on the underside of his left forearm. "My brother, Tenjiro, took it from me, and locked it in a box that he made, a box that eats fire." Azil Aumson, in the corner, made a sudden movement. Karadur did not look at him. "He has it now, somewhere in the northern ice, hidden in a fortress he has made for himself." The Dragon-lord extended his fingers. Blue flames flickered from wrist root to tips. "I have, as I have had since childhood, some dragon powers. I have a physical strength that far outstrips the men who serve me. I can call fire, the blue illusion fire that does not burn, and true fire.

But I no longer summon dragonfire, and I cannot take the form." He nodded toward the tapestry on the wall. "That was Dragon. I am not Dragon." The slow, painful words were more harrowing because the deep voice did not change. "Four people know of this. Three of them are in this room." He almost smiled. "I hope you can forgive me for telling you."

Wolf said softly, "My lord, I am honored." The back of his tunic was soaked with sweat.

Karadur leaned forward, just a little. "Would you show me your talisman?"

Wolf had not expected that request. He fumbled for the silver chain around his neck. Drawing it over his head, he cupped the rude little silver wolf in the hollow of his palm.

Karadur touched it lightly with one huge finger. "How old were you when you made it?"

"I was fourteen."

"Did someone help you? Tell you what to do, and how?"

"My mother Naika."

"Your father is dead?"

"He was alive, my lord. He is dead now: he died four years ago. He was much older than my mother. But my father was not changeling."

"Before you made your talisman, did you know you had a wolf inside you?"

"I knew. My family told me, and also, I had some of the wolf-gifts. I could hear, and I could smell."

"But you could not change. You were not—Wolf." Karadur's hands closed hard on each other. He gazed again at the dark bulk of the mountain, as if it held some secret, or a promise. Wolf remembered the savage silence of the plundered ice.

I do not want you to go, Thea had said to him, when word of the levy came to them. *I need you. Shem needs you. Say you will not.*

I will not, he had said then. *I have fought my battles.*
Across the room, Azil Aumson was watching him.

When he came into the courtyard, he found Rogys standing at Thea's elbow.

"I'm to escort you home. Dragon's orders." A stableboy trotted up, leading his grey mare. She was shaggy, like the horses the Isojai raiders rode, but bigger, a cross between an Isojai pony and the larger southern breeds. The Lemininkai stables had been full of her kind.

Shem bounced in Thea's arms. "Orse!"

"Hush," Thea said. "You may stroke her nose, but you must be quiet." She steered Shem's fingers to touch the long velvet nose.

"Shem quiet," her son whispered.

"You must both be tired," she said to Rogys. "You just came back from the ice."

Rogys shrugged. "I'm all right. And Silk can go longer than I can."

The big gates were open. Men on horseback were filing through, riding in pairs. All were armed with swords; most carried longbows, with a quiver of trefoil-barbed arrows.

"Where are they going?" Thea asked. Her hand brushed Wolf's. He put his arm around her waist.

"Patrol," Rogys said. "That's Forgon's company, from Castria. That's Olav," he said, pointing to a huge blond man, walking beside a dun horse. He bore a bright ax across his shoulder. "He heard there was a war, and came all the way from Serrenhold to fight. That's Irok, on the horse. He's a northerner, from Hornlund." Irok was small and dark, and carried an Isojai bow. The two men were deep in conversation. "When they came here, neither could speak the other's language, and now they're the best of friends."

Thea said softly, "Husband, are you well?" Wolf nodded, and brushed her hair with his lips. He would have to tell her.

He did not want to tell her. He glanced upwards to the tower. The castle was a maze, and at its heart a fire lay burning.

Halfway down the hill from the castle gate, Rogys said to Thea, "You want to ride?"

"Yes!" Thea said. Wolf unwound his arm. Rogys put his cupped hands under her foot and swung her into the saddle.

Shem crowed in excitement, "Shem up now!" he commanded. Wolf handed Shem to Thea. Wide-eyed, he gripped the pommel in both mittened hands. The sky stayed grey. Flakes of snow circled teasingly on the warm wind.

They halted briefly in Chingura to eat: bread and meat from the Keep's kitchen, generously portioned, and cold porridge for Shem.

South of Chingura it grew warmer. The clouds stirred, and separated: sunlight blazed through grey in a bright circle of glory. It was noon when they reached the meadow. Shem slept, head on Wolf's shoulder.

Wolf put a hand on Silk's rough-coated neck. "Our thanks. Will you come in for a moment, and get warm?"

Rogys demurred. "Why would you want a stranger at your homecoming? I think it's going to snow. I'd like to get Silk back before the light goes." He patted Shem's cheek. "Goodbye, little wolf."

"Another time," Thea said firmly. "You must stay another time."

"I will." The redhead raised a hand in farewell.

Shem muttered, and then sneezed abruptly, and woke. "Orse!" he complained.

"The horse went home to its stable, my heartling," Thea said. She took him from Wolf's arms. The house was cold. Wolf knelt beside the hearth. The pile of straw and twigs in the arched fireplace sat as he had left it. He struck flint, and lit the kindling. Thea brought the angry Shem to the fire.

The sight of the flames soothed him; he stopped crying, hiccuped, and then stilled.

"Boof," he said contentedly. He reached his hands toward the warmth. "Fire hot."

"That is fire," Thea said. "True fire. Very, very hot. Shem take care."

Wolf said, "Thea. We need to talk." Someone banged on the house door. Thea put Shem into Wolf's arms.

"Who can that be?" She opened the door.

Cold air swirled in. A grinning, hairless man holding a naked sword took two strides into the house. Tearing Thea's cloak from her shoulders, he laid the sword tip against her naked breast. Shem, feeling the tension race through his father's frame like fire through straw, gasped for breath, and yelled.

"Come outside," said the man with the sword, "or I'll kill her." His voice rasped like iron dragged over stone. His eyes were blood-red. With the point of the sword, he prodded Thea through the door.

Helplessly Wolf followed. Four red-eyed wargs stood growling in the meadow.

Wolf said, "Who are you?"

"My name is Gorthas. Put the boy down," said the hairless man.

"No."

The sword point moved to Thea's throat. "Then watch her die."

Wolf knelt, and set his son on the snow. Long-armed, the man seized Shem by the nape of the neck and ripped his shirt, exposing Shem's soft belly to the air. He laid the cold steel across the child's bare skin. A trickle of blood ran into Shem's pants. The wargs licked their lips.

"I wonder," said that hideous voice, "which you will choose to do: save your wife, or your child? If you move to help her, I will gut him like a fish."

He laughed, and spoke in a tongue Wolf did not know.

Thea called his name. Wolf cried out, his muscles locked and shaking. The wargs bore Thea to the ground. Wolf shut his eyes. Shem was screaming.

"No!" said Gorthas in his ear. "You will watch. Or your son dies." Wolf opened his eyes. Thea was on the ground, bloodied, torn. Her hazel eyes fixed on his face.

I love you, he said to her, with all the vital power of his mind. *Go quickly, my love.*

He saw her face change, and the life leave it, like water spilled from a jar. In Gorthas's grip, Shem screamed and struggled in an agony of revulsion and terror. The wargs lifted from Thea's lifeless side, their jaws bloodied, and grinned.

Wolf crouched. Leaning forward, Gorthas ripped the sword and sword belt from his waist. "If you change," he said, "I will kill your son."

He fought them with his hands. But they clawed and tore at him, and the strength drained from him with his blood. His collarbone and both legs were broken, his right arm nearly out of its socket, most of his ribs cracked, his left eye gone. As he lay helpless on the cold snow-covered ground, they ripped his abdomen open. A hand tore the silver talisman from his throat.

"You'll not need this again, changeling. Thank you for the sport. Your son will live—until dinner." He smiled, and kicked Wolf in the torn intestines. The explosion of pain took his senses. When he regained consciousness, he was alone with the body of his wife.

He was shivering. The carrion stench of his attackers contaminated the spot like a loathsome fog. Something rustled, to his right. He glimpsed behind a rock a sleek pale form, a glittering eye: a young lynx, hungry, but wary. It knew he lived.

Wait a little longer, cousin . . .

A fat flake of snow wandered desultorily to kiss his cheek.

He shivered fiercely, uncontrollably. The snow was falling faster now, and the light was fading. He barely felt the wound in his belly. The retreat of pain meant that his nervous system, like the rest of his body, was dying. He did not mind, because Thea was dead, and he had not saved her. He tried, with all his strength, to roll toward her, but his body was frozen, save for the uncontrollable shivering. Her dark hair fanned across the snow, looking much as it had that morning, spread across the pillow in sleep. He tried to touch it, but his right arm would not respond to his will.

Shem . . . The name was a blade, sharper than fang or claw, more bitter than his own death, which waited for him now behind the rock. Prayer had never been his habit, but he stared at the white sky and prayed, *If he must die, merciful gods, let it be swift, with no further fear and torment.* He had no confidence that the silent gods would hear him.

Hawk would be so angry at him. He wondered if she would ever see the letter he had written to her . . .

A raven called, somewhere amid the stripped birches. It, too, was hungry. Behind the rock, the impatient lynx stirred. Then it lunged. Its hot jaws closed on his exposed throat.

⚜   ⚜   ⚜

THE WARGS TRAVELED quickly over the ice.

From Dragon Keep to Mitligund was an eight-day journey for a man. It took the wargs four days. The beasts had no need of sleep or rest or food, and Gorthas could put sleep behind him at will, though he did need to eat.

The man he served, though not his master, had given him clear instructions.

"Kill the father and mother however you wish. Bring me the child unharmed. Keep it fed, clean, and dry. If it is hurt, I will put you in the cage with the bear."

Since it was his master's will that he obey this little sorcerer, Gorthas did so. There was nothing in him of compassion or sympathy, but intelligence told him to bring the woman's fur-lined cloak, and wrap the child in it, for warmth, and for the quieting comfort of the smell. He made a pouch of the cloak and slung the child across his back. The boy ceased to scream after a while, and simply sobbed. They halted as necessary to clean and to feed him. The first day the boy closed his lips, and refused to eat the little bits of raw meat that the man held to his mouth. Gorthas considered forcing the food down his throat, but reasoned that if that were done, he might choke, or struggle, and hurt himself. He did force water into the soft angry mouth. The child made fists, and tried to strike him, which amused him.

The second day the boy was weaker, and ate.

The fourth day they reached Mitligund. The Black Citadel gleamed in the cold white light. Ice warriors on their ice horses galloped to meet him, but Gorthas ignored them, knowing them to be illusion. The great black gate yawned like a toothless mouth. As his wargs trotted through it, their three fellows, who had led the soldiers on their fruitless chase, rose to greet them. The sentry at the inner door was human, one of those whom the wizard had bought with gold, and held with terror. The wargs eyed the living man hungrily.

Grinning at the man's fear, Gorthas ducked into the spiral maze of tunnels. The wargs trotted at his heels. Wer-light glowed from the icy walls. Doors off the corridor led to sleeping rooms, places for humans to eat, and to the room with the cages. But at the heart of the castle lay a hole, a great open chamber. It was empty, except for a huge chair made of blocks and shards and streamers of ice.

Here the wer-light was stronger. An arching ceiling rose into darkness. The chamber was cold, which troubled Gorthas not at all, but the child on his back began to shiver. Plucking the boy from the pouch, Gorthas wrapped him more securely in a second fold of cloak. He approached the occupied chair, and put a knee on the frozen ground.

"My lord Koriuji," he said. "I have the child."

The great white worm that coiled on and around the

chair lifted its head. A human face, pale as a leper's skin, gazed coldly at man and boy. Its black eyes were shot through with blue lights. It hissed, and licked its human lips with a flickering, forked snake's tongue. "Well done. Did you kill the mother and father?"

"We did, my lord."

The worm rose higher in the chair. The coils of its body were thick as a grown man's trunk. "Let me see it." Gorthas unwrapped his captive. The worm slid from the chair. Hollow-eyed, Shem watched the monster come closer to him. As it loomed nearer, he shrieked, a thin hoarse cry, and struggled in Gorthas's hard cold hands.

"A restive little wolfling," said the worm. "We will bring it to heel soon. Send for Takumik."

Gorthas spoke to one of the wargs in the language it understood. It sped away. The worm crawled silkily back to its throne. The warg returned, a human being at its heels. He entered the chamber, limping heavily on his left leg, and fell full-length to the ground.

"Get up," the worm said.

Takumik stood. He was from Hornlund. The wargs had killed his wife and his three sons. With the beasts slavering over him, the sinews of his leg in strips, Gorthas had given him a choice: to die hideously beside his family, or to live, and serve Koriuji for a period of five years. He had chosen to live.

"Give him the child."

Automatically, Takumik put his arms out.

"You will care for this child," Koriuji said. "Keep it alive and reasonably healthy. If it dies, I will give you to Gorthas. Tell the hunters what food you need for it. Go."

Takumik bowed and backed from the chamber. Taking the boy to the cavelike, ice-walled room that he shared with two more of Koriuji's human servants, he built up the small fire, and laid the boy near it. What he had seen and, indeed, done, in the worm's service had drained him of the softer emotions, but the child's silent misery woke the little pity that was left to him, and with gentle fingers he washed the boy clean of grime and filth and laid him on a blanket. This was not a child of his people: this one was straight-nosed, and his skin pale, and his eyes the wrong color. He was, Takumik judged, something over a year old, sturdy, well-muscled, and beloved.

"What is thy name?" he asked, in his own language.

The wide light eyes stared at him without understanding. He repeated it in the tongue of the men who lived in the southern villages, in wooden houses. The child stared dumbly. Perhaps it had understood, perhaps not. Takumik wondered what was planned for it, and shut that thought off quickly: it did not matter. He could not allow it to matter. He stirred the stew in a pot near the fire, and spooned some into a bowl, and sat to coax it into the mute child. It took some time. But that he had, and patience, and eventually the boy ate, and lay still by the fire, not weeping, its strange light eyes fixed on nowhere.

Later, the men who shared this sleeping space came in, worn from hunting—game was sparse—and apprehensive, since Gorthas had returned, and his particular inventive cruelty was much feared. Takumik told them that if the child were injured, they would all die. It was not true, but these men served Koriuji willingly, for gold, and he had no trust in them. One made a coarse joke, and they lost interest, and left him and the boy alone.

Takumik did not rest well that night. He dreamed of his children: not of their deaths—that would have been unbearable—but of them alive. Once he rose, and stumbling along the corridor to the pit where the men relieved themselves, he pissed into the fetid hole.

Coming back, he peered at the child, who lay knees to chest, silent and unmoving. He thought its eyes were open. "Go to sleep," he said gently, in his own tongue.

Toward dawn, the boy stirred. Takumik was asleep, or he would have seen Shem uncurl and sit up. Crying, he had learned, brought no attention, and so he did not cry. The fur he was still wrapped in smelled of himself, and Gorthas, and faintly, still, of his mother. He did not know she was dead; he knew only that he had been hurt, and that he was cold, and in a strange place. He was frightened. The fire had gone out and it was dark. Near him, twitching in the grip of an evil dream, lay the man who had fed him and had spoken kindly to him.

"Go home," he whispered, to the chill, uncaring darkness. "Shem go home?"

But there was no answer.

12

INEXORABLE AS NIGHT, a fast-paced storm blew over the northern mountains.

Snow fell for four days. The fifth day, the storm broke: the sun rose, to sit blazing in a cloudless March sky like a lamp hung on a pole. In Chingura, Castria, and Sleeth, men weary with winter once more cleared the drifts from roads. In Dragon Keep, stableboys released the impatient horses from the stables and set about raking out the stalls. Lorimir went to bed at dawn, having led half the men in the garrison on a three-day march over the pass and back, through the storm. Despite bone-deep exhaustion, he was pleased with their endurance. He said as much to Dragon. They could march all night, sleep where they stood, and kill anything he pointed them at. They were almost ready for a war.

☽ ☽ ☽

IN THE WORKROOM of her shop in Lantern Street, in Ujo, Terrill Chernico, called Hawk, sat cross-legged on a cushion, planing a stave.

The room was bright. Even though it was the middle of the morning, candles burned in the wall sconces. Bows of all sizes and weights, some in cases, others not, were horizontally mounted on the east and west walls. Shelves stacked with book rolls and bound books and folios lined the long north wall.

In the front room, Tiko, her apprentice, was singing the latest love song.

> "*I cannot number all the ways I love you; They are numberless as the fishes in the sea,*
> "*In the sunlight, in the moonlight, in the starlight, I lie contented when you come to me.*"

"Tiko," Hawk called.

"Mistress?" Tiko pushed the curtain aside.

"Sing something else. Every fishmonger in Ujo is singing that song."

He grinned, rubbed his mustache—he had only been growing it a week, and it was still sparse—and vanished, whistling 'The Riddle Song.' He had a tuneful whistle. Smiling, Hawk bent over her work.

The stave in her hand was hazelwood. The bow would be a child's bow, ceremonial rather than useful; a gift, she thought, from the scion of one noble house—the Lemininkai, once her employers, now her patron—to another. It was not the kind of commission she preferred, but she never turned down a commission from the Lemininkai. The little bow would have rosewood insets and a deer-horn plate; in its own way, it would be lovely. She ran a thumb along the smooth amber wood. The grain was clear and straight. If you looked closely, you could see strands of silver threaded through the amber.

Then the candles in the chamber went out, one after another. Hawk froze, senses alert, eyes huge in the precipitate darkness. The curtain had not moved. There had been no breath of air. Tiko's song faded, as if the darkness were absorbing it. The workroom grew bitterly cold. A pale blue-white light, like moonlight on snow, glimmered over the polished floorboards. Caught within the light stood the figure of a man. His head was bowed, but she did not need to see his face: she knew the lean poised body, the black hair tipped with silver, the strong, skilled, familiar hands . . . The pale light strengthened, and she saw the appalling wounds, open, bleeding, fatal, that marked his body. He lifted his bowed head. His left eye was gone; his right eye and his mouth were racked with fathomless sorrow.

"Wolf!" she cried; but there was no knowledge or recognition in the ghostly face. "Wolf, wait!" But the apparition faded. Sound returned: Tiko's whistling, a hawker crying in the street. One by one, the candles relit.

Hawk rose. "Tiko," she said. Her voice was not quite steady.

"Mistress?" Her apprentice's head poked through the curtain. "Did you call me?"

"Did you notice anything odd just now?"

"Odd?"

"Out of the ordinary. A chill in the air, perhaps."

"No, mistress. Was there—did something happen?"

"Never mind," Hawk said. "Thank you. Go back to your work."

⚜　⚜　⚜

IN THE GOLDEN Cup Inn in Sogda, two hours north of Mako, Bear sprawled on a mound of tangled blankets in a warm, dry room, snoring softly.

A pine log burned in the hearth. Curled into the crook of his arm, a large naked woman slept, her dark hair fanning gracefully over the pillow. A stack of gold coins lay on the table, payment for five days travel through rain-soaked hills, guiding a nervous man who had not wanted to hire a conspicuous troop of men to guard him, but did not want to walk unescorted on lonely roads. Bear had no idea what the man had carried from Yarrow to Mako, except that it was small. Three men had followed them at one point, tough, hard-faced men, ex-soldiers turned outlaw from the look of them, but one or more of them had recognized the red-bearded giant who strode so lightly beside the merchant's brown mule.

Fifteen, even ten years ago, he would have turned, swinging his iron-tipped cudgel, and taunted them into battle for the sheer joy of it. But these days he was older, wiser, and usually lazier, content simply to earn the gold which paid for food, drink, sex.

A sharp wind raked its claws across the window shutter. Ariana shivered, touched by chill, or nightmare. Wakeful as a cat, Bear's eyes opened, glittering amber in the darkness. He turned his head from side to side. The wind huffed again, moaning like a man in pain. Untroubled, Bear drew his companion close, and closed his eyes.

Bear was finishing the last of his breakfast when Ariana came in. She wore red, and the pearl earrings he had brought her from Skyeggo. "There's a woman here to see you." She pouted at him. "She says it's business."

"Is she alone?"

"As far as I can tell."

Bear frowned into the remnants of his steak. "Bring her in."

Ariana glared at him, hands on her waist. "You've barely arrived. Is this all I am to have of you—three nights?" She sashayed from the room, swinging her wide hips in a way that stirred his blood. In a very short while she was back. "She says, Do you come out."

It was Bear's turn to glare. "Out where? Into the road?"

"Round the back of the house, under the red oak, beside the stable." She cocked her hip at him. Irritated, but curious, Bear seized his great iron-tipped cudgel and followed her. He strode through the common room, ignoring stares, and marched to the great-branched oak.

A shadow moved, became a plain-faced warrior woman wearing silver-grey, who bore an Isojai hunting bow. She thrust the hood from her face, and he saw the crevices of weariness and grief around her eyes and mouth. "What is it?" he said.

"Wolf is dead."

His breath stopped.

"I saw him. He was wounded, torn open, broken." Her hand circled unconsciously across her abdomen. "I suppose it was his ghost. He—it—didn't see me. I said his name—"

"Who killed him?"

"I don't know."

"When did it happen?"

"I don't know. The ghost appeared two days ago."

"Two *days*? The trail will be ice-cold! What in the gods' names kept you? In four days you could fly to Gate-of-Winds and back!"

Her voice stayed level. "A snowstorm held me back. And it took me a little time to find you. Nelli at the Street of Painted Fans insisted you were somewhere in Kameni, but then Joab the Purse told me that he'd met you in a bar in Yarrow, and that you said you were coming here."

"I'll get my pack." Ariana was in the common room. "I have to go," he said to her. "I'll come back when I'm finished." He went up the stairs at a dead run. He left half the gold on the table. When he left the room, Ariana was standing in the hallway, holding a wineskin. He took it, and felt her hands slide across his chest, and tangle in his hair.

As he returned to Hawk's side, disbelief and sorrow and a scalding anger rose through his body like fever. He stopped, shaking with it. Hawk watched him silently. At last his locked muscles loosened. He shrugged his pack onto his shoulders, and flexed his hands on his stick.

"Let's go," he said.

They went west, into the scrublands, away from the river. Below them, smoke from the inn's chimney streamed like incense into the still blue day. Despite the late snow, the land was thawing from the winter freeze. Mud sucked at their boots, and beneath the hard brown grass, the soft green of the new growth shone like starlight on water. At the top of a small rise, they halted. Bear looked back toward the inn. Ariana stood outside. Her gown gleamed like blood in the bright morning light.

"Where are we going?"

"Sleeth. It's a small town just below the mountains. We can do it easily in three days."

"You were there? When?"

"A year ago summer. Wolf has—had—a house, and a garden. He traps, and Thea weaves. She made this." She touched her tunic. "Their son was born in October: not this past one, the one before that. Shem, his name is. It means fearless."

With a certain diffidence Bear said, "If you wish—go on. You move quicker than I."

She shook her head. "No. I will stay with you." A traveler watching the hillside, had there been any—but there was none—would have seen the sunshine coalesce and glitter, amber and silver, around the two strangers on the little hill. And then he would have seen a silver-grey hawk lift into the sky with short, powerful wing-beats, while below her a massive red-brown bear crossed the valley and headed north with swift, ground-eating strides.

They kept to the wilderness. They met no humans, save a woodcutter who froze with terror as the huge red-brown bear loped by him. They ate as they traveled. Hawk hunted on the wing. Bear broke river ice and scooped fish from the water. He found the carcass of a moose calf, partially eaten, stuffed under a hedge, and ate most of the rest of it. At night they sheltered in the open: Bear in a copse, Hawk in a tree.

They came to Sleeth just after dawn of the third morning. As Hawk circled down into the meadow, she saw the shapes in the snow, and the animal tracks that ringed them. She changed beneath the drooping birch branches. A west wind thrust across the meadow, spattering her with cool drops. A shadow moved at her back; she whirled, hands fitting arrow to bow and aiming with one indrawn breath. A red-brown bear ambled up from the darkness near the river. Then he changed, into a big, yellow-eyed man.

Kneeling, Bear studied the tracks. "Lynx," he said, his voice husky with pain. "A fox. A boot heel, here." He brushed the snow away from one of the shapes. After a while, he uncovered a woman's bare, brown arm, then her mutilated breasts, then a face. The birds had been at it. "Imarru's balls. What tracks are these?"

Hawk knelt. After a while, she said, "I think, wargs—"

He looked at her as if she had lost her wits. "Wargs? What foolishness is this?"

"Wolf wrote to me. I have the letter in my pack. Just after New Year's Moon, a pack of wargs came out of the north and killed seven people in this province. One, a soldier, was taken on the very walls of Dragon Keep."

Bear said, scowling, "I have rarely heard such nonsense. I have been roaming this country for forty years, and have never seen a warg. Stories to frighten children."

A little wind blew across the stained earth. A dust of snow drifted over Thea's breasts and face. Hawk turned abruptly away.

"Well," Bear said heavily, "you are the scholar. What do you know of wargs?"

"Only that they are creatures of magic."

"And did you see any signs of wizardry while you were here?"

"No. But Wolf told me that Karadur Atani, the Dragon of Chingura, has a wizard brother, who lives far in the north, and that there is some terrible grudge between them. You have heard the rumors. Word has gone out across the north, through Ippa and Issho and into Nakase: *Dragon Keep goes to war in the spring.* There is talk of it even in Ujo."

"I have heard it," Bear said. "You think the Dragon of Chingura intends to take his troops across the mountains, and attack his wizard brother, if, of course, he has one?"

"I would," Hawk said calmly. "If I had a brother, and my brother was sending magical beasts through my land to kill its people, I would not rest until I had my talons in his throat. She pointed through the leafless trees. "Dragon Keep lies that way a few miles, at the foot of a mountain."

"So?"

"Someone has to tell Thea's kin that Thea and Wolf and the boy are dead. It will come easier from a Keep's messenger than from a perfect stranger. And Karadur Atani might find a use for two experienced warriors in his army."

Bear snorted; an insolent woof of sound. "Hah. I have no doubt they could use us. But *I* run with no pack. What do I care for Karadur Atani? The Dragon of Chingura, people call him. But they say he has never taken form. Who knows what he really is?"

"He is Dragon. Wolf said so."

"And what good did that do him? He is dead." He glanced at the bodies. Pain flashed in his yellow eyes.

"I remember when we first met," he said softly. "It was in Selidor. He was young: twenty, twenty-two. He'd been at sea. He had just come round Gate-of-Winds for the first time. He asked me to recommend a tavern. We went to someplace—I can't recall the name—and drank merignac, and ate spiced dumplings, and played dice. He beat me four times out of five. I wanted to go north, to the Green Mountains, I don't remember why. I asked him to come. He was a good traveling companion, you remember?"

"Don't," Hawk said sharply. "Not now. Later, when we are warm and have wine." She knelt again, and brushed the snow back. "Too many prints," she said. "I cannot tell how many beasts there were here, save that there were many. We would lose their tracks in the rocks in any case."

"I will not lose their tracks."

Hawk did not bother to conceal her exasperation. "If you can follow an unknown number of magical beasts across the Grey Peaks into the northern plains, then *you* are the magician."

"If there is a wizard in the far north," he said unexpectedly, "my cousins will know."

"Your *cousins?*"

"My grandparents on my mother's side came from Mitligund. I have cousins there still. Perhaps it is time to go and visit them."

It was not implausible. It was even likely. She had cousins in unlikely places all over Ryoka, and the bear clan was more numerous than her own. "And if there is indeed a wizard in the north?"

"I will kill him."

Hawk swallowed. "Bear, you cannot war on a wizard by yourself."

Bear spun the heavy cudgel till it blurred. "I don't see why not. Magicians die like other mortals." He stared arrogantly at her from his great height. "Do you doubt I can do it?"

Hawk glanced at the sprawled, mangled bodies. The image of Bear marching across the steppes to mount a solitary attack on a wizard seemed idiotic, but she knew well that if anyone could face down a magician alone, it was Bear. Still, it was ridiculous, and dangerous. It was not so, what he had said. Wizards did *not* die like other mortals.

Wolf would have talked him out of it. Wolf would have known what to say. She did not. . . .

"I suppose it will not help for me to argue with you," she said. He raised a tawny eyebrow in disbelief. No one ever won an argument with Bear. "I go to the Keep. But I will meet you there, with or without an army. Wait for me."

"I will try." He changed, in a swirl of crimson light. The sun blazed off his thick pelt. Luminous, tawny eyes stared into hers. He reared, majestic, deadly, massive forepaws bigger than her head. Then, with only the slightest sound, he dropped to all fours and padded into the dappled shadows beside the river.

13

HAWK RODE THE high wind into Dragon Keep.

Spiraling above the ramparts, she saw the Keep laid out below her as its makers might have yearned to see it: gates and towers, stables and forge, barracks, workshops, kitchen, pens, archery range, fighting yards, and riding rings . . . Smoke trickled from a chimney into the indigo sky. The people who lived and worked in the dark granite buildings were invisible, as if some unknown mage had cast a powerful spell.

Folding her wings slightly, she let herself fall in a swift controlled glide to the center of the great courtyard. She changed, and waited: for the boy at the kennels to turn and notice her, for the sentries to see her, and shout warning, for the officer by the well, the bearded pudgy one, talking earnestly to the laughing sloe-eyed kitchen maid, to become aware that the woman in silver-grey with the short dark bow between her hands was not in his company, nor any company of the war band . . . Holding her bow at arm's length, heart drumming through her bones, she waited.

Two women in soft bright clothes, one holding an empty laundry basket, strolled across the wide crowded space. On the west wall, a sentry shouted. Silence grew and spread like ripples in a pond.

Turning, the plump officer said thoughtfully, "Who the hell are you?"

Very slowly, with a watchful eye on the six arrows leveled at her chest, Hawk knelt and laid her bow and quiver on the flagstones. She said, "My name is Terrill Chernico, called Hawk. I live in Ujo. I came to visit my friend Wolf Dahranni and his wife, the weaver Thea. I went to their home this morning, and found them dead in the snow."

. The men looked at one another. The officer said quietly to the man nearest him, "Tell Dragon. He's at the riding ring. Hurry." The man ran. "How did they die?"

"Wargs," Hawk said. "They've been dead for some days."

A stocky man with a square black beard and a gold ring in one ear said, "How do we know she's telling the truth? How do we know she is who she says?"

"Why would she lie?" the officer said. "Besides, Dragon will know." The black-bearded man nodded. The small hairs lifted at the base of Hawk's neck. She heard a horse, coming fast. Two men yanked the postern gate open. A shaggy black gelding pounded through it and came to a stamping halt. A man slid from his back. Sunlight seemed to collect around him, so that she saw through a dazzle a dark, formless presence moving within a column of flame. Then the dazzle dispersed, and she saw clearly a dark-clad man with thick tangled gold hair, and eyes the color of a summer sky. His fair skin was roughened with wind chafe.

I have met the Dragon of Chingura. We met by accident; he nearly put a sword through my throat. He has hair like the sun and eyes like blue fire, and a grip, so I'm told, that can crack stone . . .

"I am Karadur Atani," the man said. His voice was deep, and very clear. "Who are you, and what is this you have come to tell me?"

"My name is Terrill Chernico, my lord. Wolf Dahranni and his wife, Thea, are dead. Wargs killed them."

An incandescent hand closed around the sinews of Hawk's mind. She could neither look away from him nor at him. Her senses spun: the Keep walls evaporated, and she was alone in an infinite space with a being that burned endlessly and was not consumed. She gasped, and felt the link snap free.

"She tells the truth," Karadur said bleakly. "Marek."

"Sir," said the square-bearded man.

"You and Irok are our best trackers. The two of you go, find out what you can: when it happened, and how many wargs. Murgain, where is Tallis?"

The plump man hesitated. An older man, clearly a senior captain, came up on the dragon-lord's right shoulder. He said, "My lord, he is on duty in Chingura." The fair-haired man frowned. "Toby knows the family."

"Does he? Toby." A slender man stepped from the growing crowd of men. "Go to Chingura, and tell Tallis what has happened. Then relieve him at his post." The three soldiers moved; the others in the courtyard made way for them.

The captain said softly, "My lord, someone must inform the weaver's family. Do you wish me to go to Sleeth?"

Karadur shook his head. "No. I will do it." He stood very still: heat, like the blaze of the summer sun, poured from him. It seemed as if he might literally burst into flame. Blue fire shimmered along his arms and hands. Not surprisingly, the captain stepped back. The dragon-lord bent his gaze upon Hawk. She steeled herself for the shock of contact, but the touch, when it came, was surprisingly gentle.

"He was your friend," he said. "I am sorry. Will you stay, until I return? I would like to talk with you." The unexpected, almost tender courtesy brought a prickle of tears to her eyes. She managed a bow.

A lean, dark-haired man limped from the crowd of men. "My lord," he said, "let me come with you." His speech was diffident. Some terrible hurt had been done to his hands: they were scarred and brutally twisted.

Karadur hesitated. Then he said, "All right." He turned to take the reins of his horse.

The man who held them, a comely redhead, said, "My lord—please let me go as well."

Karadur halted as if he had been suddenly turned to stone. Hawk could not see his face. But the impact of the dragon-lord's unbridled rage pulsed through her mind. The agony of it spun her nearly off her feet. It flung the redhead ten feet back and slammed him face-first into a wall. He fell bonelessly to the stone. Karadur mounted; a stableboy cupped his hands, and the man with the crippled hands mounted behind him. Without looking back, Karadur wheeled the big horse toward the postern gate. The grey-haired captain gave concise orders. Men lifted the redhead and carried him away.

The pudgy officer said to Hawk, "You all right? You look a little grey. You want a meal?"

"I want a bed."

"We can do that," he said. "Torik! Take this visitor to one of the guest rooms. If you change your mind about food, let Torik know. There's always something in the kitchens."

The boy brought her to a small cold chamber on the second floor. The curtained windows were narrow and high. A smoke-stained tapestry on one wall showed a scene of an archer shooting at an antlered deer, or perhaps it was a moose. He brought her a basin, a water pitcher, and a cloth, and then left her alone. Wearily she cleaned the grime of Wolf and Thea's death-place from her face and hands.

She drowsed, and finally, despite the discomfort in her head, slept. When the page woke her it was evening. He pointed her to the guard hall. It smelled wonderfully of roast lamb and fresh bread. The pain in her head was a scant grumble. Laying her bow and dagger with the others against the wall, she found a place near a knot of men.

"Orm," said one with a near-shaven scalp. He seemed older than the others. The fresh-faced boy beside him told her gravely that his name was Huw. "Gavin," said another. "Hurin." The servers brought out platters heaped with lamb

chops and bowls of sweet orange potatoes. Hungry men
grabbed for their share. The wine went round.

A body slid in beside her: a lean man with a somewhat
severe face and an officer's emblem sewn to his sleeve. He
reached across her to spear a chop on the point of his knife.

"Herugin Dol, riding-master. Welcome to Dragon Keep."

"Thank you."

"I'm sorry about your friend," he said gently. "I didn't
know him well. We talked, he and I. His loss is a grief to us
all." The men about the table nodded. Shaven-headed Orm
lifted his glass in salute. The others imitated him, and
drank.

Herugin said, "He told me he'd served the Lemininkai."

"So did I. That was how we met."

"Tell me, do they still run horse races in summer down the
avenue beside the castle? I visited Ujo, years ago, when I rode
in Erin diMako's guard. I remember I won ten nobles."

"They still do. And in September, to celebrate the Lemininkai's birthday, they run pig races."

Orm and Huw looked up simultaneously. "Pig races?"
they said in unison.

"It's an old custom. Farmers enter the young boars in the
race: they say it's to celebrate the lord's birthday, but I happen to know that Kalni Leminin was born in January, and
the races are always in September. But after the race the
Lemininkai always pays for a feast, and people wear masks,
and drink wine through the night, and the next day no work
gets done."

"Are they truly races?" Huw asked, fascinated. "I mean,
does someone ride the pig?"

"No one has to ride them. It's always held at the same
place, on a very narrow street, and people stand at one end
and beat on pots, and yell, so that the pigs will always run the
one way. But sometimes the young men, and the girls, if they
dare, try. It's dangerous: if you fall, you can be injured, or even
crushed to death. It's happened. But they put thick leather col-

lars on the pigs, and wind them with ribbons, all of different colors. The riders grip the collars. People bet on the races. I won two nobles on the Yellow Pig, last year. Fools sometimes throw garbage into the street, to try to distract the other pigs so that the one they bet on will win. It rarely works, but it makes the folks who have to clean the streets furious."

"I'd pay to see that," Orm said.

"Would you ride a pig?" Huw asked. "I would. I bet I could ride a winner, too. What do the riders win?"

"The Lemininkai gives a purse to anyone who finishes the race still on top of a pig."

"Which means that no one does, or not often," said Orm.

Marek and a man holding an Isojai bow came into the hall. Karadur entered at their heels. A kitchen girl brought him a cup of wine and a clean plate. The man with the maimed hands moved like a phantom at his back.

"Who is that?" Hawk asked Herugin under her breath.

He followed her gaze. "Azil Aumson. He is"—Herugin hesitated—"he was a singer, and a harpist. He owes his life to your friend. Wolf found him wandering naked in the rocks about six months ago."

"What happened to him?"

"He was imprisoned. He escaped. He doesn't speak of it." The brief answer stirred Hawk's interest, but whatever question she might have asked was never framed. Karadur crossed to their table and sat opposite her. His face was grooved with fatigue, and the sleeves of his shirt were spattered with mud.

The soldiers made a clear space around him. Herugin filled his cup.

He spoke without ceremony, as if he had known her a long time. "We brought the bodies into the house. Thea's family is standing farewell vigil tonight. They'll be buried tomorrow. The men may go if they wish."

"I will tell them," Herugin said.

"We did not find Shem. But there were tracks of lynx

and fox, and fresh ones of bear—and of man. Not your tracks. A big man." He drank, and set his cup aside. "Did you take Wolf's talisman? He wore it on a chain around his neck."

She had not thought to look for it. "My lord, I did not."

"Nor his sword?" She shook her head. "We did not find them."

"A grave robber," Herugin said. "Gods rot his leprous soul."

"When I learn who it was," Karadur said, with terrible precision, "I will stake him in the snow and cut the living heart from his chest. Orm: tomorrow I want you to bring Bessie and Blackie down to hunt for the boy's body."

"I will, my lord."

The Dragon-lord reached within his tunic, and withdrew a folded piece of paper. "We searched the house, looking for the boy. In the back room, behind the kitchen, we found this. It has your name on it." Automatically Hawk took it from his fingers. Someone moved a candle nearer.

She unfolded it. Wolf's clear script leaped from the page.

The wargs have killed nineteen people, but Dragon's bowmen patrol the rocks and roads and have beaten back four attacks, maybe more . . . To tell the truth, I would rather stay . . . I am sure that when Dragon takes his soldiers north, their need will be not for magicians but for warriors . . . I know you would be very welcome . . . This war makes it impossible to plan. Nevertheless, I do. This autumn, once the harvest is in, before the storms start, I hope to bring Thea and Shem south to meet my family. Would you like to travel with us?

Her eyes blurred, and her fingers tightened on the page. Carefully she refolded it, and slipped it within her shirt, next to her heart. "Thank you, my lord."

A server filled her cup. She drank, barely tasting the wine.

"My lord," she said, "have you room in your army for another archer?" The archers stirred. At her side, Herugin nodded once.

Karadur did not immediately answer. Finally he said, "Are you good?"

"I was archery master to Kalni Leminin for six years."

"Why did you leave his service?"

It was a fair question. "I was bored with taking orders. I wanted to work for myself."

"What work do you do now?"

"I make bows," she said. "I have a shop in Lantern Street. The Lemininkai has been generous enough to be a patron."

"Who comes to you? Men of the company?"

"Sometimes. Not often. The garrison has its own bow-makers. But many of the wealthy merchants have their own guard companies, and the folk of the noble houses still like to hunt."

"So do I," he said. "Though the bow is not my weapon. Your offer is appreciated, hunter. But this is not your fight."

"You are wrong," she said. At her elbow, she heard Herugin's swift indrawn breath. "It is my fight. Wolf was my friend. The man who killed him is my enemy. If you have a place for me, I will ride with you; if not, I go alone." His soldiers did not speak to him like this, she knew. She felt his anger, like a fire in her head. But she was changeling, and not some unprotected boy. She set her teeth, and endured it.

He said shortly, "Find me tomorrow. We will speak of it then." He rose, and strode toward the doorway. From where he had been waiting, the maimed harpist moved from the dancing tumult of shadow to walk with him.

As she retrieved her weapons, the grey-haired captain touched her elbow. "Excuse me," he said. "I know you must be tired. But if you have time—" She followed him into an empty room: the sort of room that messengers were brought to, and left in to kick their heels against the walls while pages looked for the right person for them to talk to.

"It's Rogys," the captain said. The candle in the wall sconce threw a fitful, wavering light over his face. "The red-headed lad. You saw him. He's breathing, but he won't wake up. He's got a nasty bruise on his cheek, from hitting the wall. Macallan, our physician, suggested you might know a way to help the boy. It's been said that changelings have the skill to touch a mind, for good or ill."

He was not far; he was in the room next to her sleeping room. Torik lay curled like a cat in the hallway. Besides the unconscious redhead the room held a sandy-haired dapper man, and a pretty, round-faced girl on a stool. She was watching Rogys as a snake might watch a mouse.

"Macallan," said the dapper man. "Thanks for coming. This is Kiala. I've told her to watch him, and send Torik to get me if he so much as flutters an eyelash. He hasn't. Kiala, get up." Macallan moved the candle over the bed. The whole right side of the redhead's face was blue and swollen. His eyes were tightly closed, and there was a white tinge around his mouth.

The physician said, "That swelling's a simple bruise; I've been icing it intermittently. His jaw's intact. His heart's strong, and he can swallow: I got a sweetrose-and-salica mixture down his throat, it's good for internal bleeding, if there is any, and it can't hurt him if there's none."

Hawk nodded. Lightly she laid her palm over the red-haired soldier's heart; not to feel his pulse, but because physical contact lessened the shock of the link. As smoothly as she could, she extended her awareness, like a fisherman spreading a net. She met darkness, over which her own perception spread like a shining silken web, darkness, *fear, grief, confusion*, and then *fire!* searing through synapses, twisting mercilessly through the unprotected mind like a jolt of lightning. It was only memory, but she withdrew quickly, feeling Rogys's pulse race and his limber body tighten under her hand. ". . . Hurts," the boy whispered, and then lay still again.

She looked up to meet anxious eyes. "It's not an injury, I think," she said. "He's caught in a memory of the pain."

Macallan said, "Can you help him?"

She looked down again. "I'll try." She spread her fingers on the boy's chest, and linked again. Slowly, she let her own thought permeate Rogys's defenses. *Let it go*, she soothed, making that inner voice solicitous, warm, loving as a mother's, *let it go, the pain is over, the pain is gone, let it go . . .*

"He's breathing easier," said Macallan.

Hawk sat back. The delicate, unfamiliar effort had made her head ache. She watched the tension leave the muscles around Rogys's mouth. "Let's see what happens now," she said. "He should improve."

Before sleep, she pushed aside the frayed curtain over the window, and cracked the shutter, letting in light and a cool wind. They had given her a brazier. One coal glowed red in the darkness, a one-eyed toad crouched by the bed. Somewhere, on the other side of the tall hills, a red-brown bear was forging steadily north. Ignoring the light headache beating through her temples, she opened her mind, narrowing focus as she had been trained to do, reaching across a white wilderness to locate one familiar mental signature, like a melody within discord. She touched elk and badger, goose and goat, and once a solitary human hunter, but not the mind she sought. Finally she gave up.

She woke in the middle of the night. Someone was weeping. The harsh, broken sound had dragged her from slumber. As she woke, it receded, until she could hear it only at the very edge of her perception. It was not next door: Rogys was asleep, and mending. Not your business, she reminded herself, and thrust her head beneath her pillow. But the weeping did not stop.

She sat up, irritated with herself. Nine years sleeping in

barracks surrounded by a hundred dreaming soldiers: surely she had learned enough to ward off the nightmares of some homesick youngster . . . But this was not a young voice calling in sleep. This was a man's desperate anguish. The image slid into her mind of a lean, still face, framed by dark hair, hardened by some great ordeal: Azil, the harpist, whose hands would never pluck the strings again. Someone had hurt him, deliberately, horribly. She felt a dreadful cold, a miasma of hatred and cruelty that seemed to fill the bedchamber like smutty smoke. A voice whispered across a great distance: *You will never be free, little traitor. I have your soul in my palm; I need only close my hand to crush it . . . You will never be free. You will never be warm.* The perverse light whisper ran like a knife through her bones.

She flung a vehement command to the man in bed: *Wake up!*

The demand jolted him from sleep. He lay shivering, covered with sweat. Shuddering with revulsion and pity, Hawk pulled her awareness back. Kicking free of the quilts, she crossed to the window and flung the shutter back. The frigid night air rushed in. The sky was clear. She gazed at the star patterns, naming them in her mind: the Dagger, the Lantern, the Boat. That one, with two red stars low in the sky, that was the Lizard. She watched the stars until the sickness left her mind. At last the cold and the need for sleep drove her back to her pallet. With a fervent prayer to Sedi, the goddess of dreams, that Azil the singer's nightmares would not return—not that night at any rate—she drew the quilts around her head.

14

IN THE MORNING, as was her custom, Hawk woke early.

For a moment, she did not know where she was. The feel of the air, pure and thin and cold against her skin, was like the feel of the air in Voiana, the town in which she had been born. Eyes closed, she listened for her sister Ana's soft breathing in the nearby bed . . .

Then she opened her eyes, to see cold dark walls, a brazier, a high shuttered window. No, this was not her mother's house. Rising, she dressed. The Keep was still, though sentries moved on the walls. Smoke from the kitchen rose into the grey dawn sky. She cleaned and oiled her weapons. That done, she went to breakfast. The dining hall was filled with the smell of sausage and the clamor of men. As she entered the big hall, an arm waved at her. She went toward it, and found Huw and Orm sitting side by side. Huw made a place for her.

After the meal, she went searching for Karadur Atani. She went first to the tower chamber, where Derry, the blond page, had told her he was certain to be. He was not. She went next to the barracks, and from there back to the dining hall, and lastly the kitchens.

"Gods above," said an ill-tempered, balding man with an apron, "why would he be here? Have you tried the stable?"

She tried the stable, and the fields where yelling men charged their horses at each other. "No," Herugin said, "he hasn't been here this morning. Did you try the tower?"

As she left the stable, Hawk passed a small training ring. In it a solitary rider was taking a broad-back roan gelding through its paces. She recognized Azil Aumson. His gloved hands lay still on the horse's withers, barely touching the reins, as he turned the big horse into figure-eights using knees and thighs, as archers must in order to be free to shoot on the run.

On her way back to the tower, she stopped by the second-floor chamber in which Rogys slept. Though his face was still discolored and swollen, his breathing was even and easy.

"Dragon came in this morning," Kiala replied to her question. "But I haven't seen him since. Did you look in the library? He goes there sometimes."

"I don't know where it is."

"Torik can show you."

The library smelled of books, and of a thousand stories caught within scrolls or between leather covers. Hawk stalked covetously through it. Torik trailed her, unsure whether she should even be there. "No one but Dragon ever comes here," he said nervously.

"I'll wager the physician does," she told him, noting a well-used Guerin's *The Properties of Herbs* on a middle shelf. She found a copy of Netheren's *History of Ryoka*, bound as she had never seen it; a scroll of Lucio's *Journeys* lying loose on a table; a complete, though smudged, copy of Leopoldo's *Annals*—the dusty cover left brown smears on her fingers—and maps, many maps, even star maps. Her fingers itched to unroll them.

Finally she returned to the tower. This time she saw what she had not noticed before: a second door off the little landing. She pushed at it, and it opened.

Sunshine glared off dark stone. She shielded her eyes with one hand. Dark pebbly granite extended into an eternity of sky. Twenty feet away from her, Karadur Atani stood with his back to the door.

He whipped around, blue eyes blazing dangerously, and she braced herself for fire. But he caught it back. "Hawk of Ujo." He surveyed her. "Do you know what this place is?" She shook her head. "You of all people should be able to guess. Come. Look closely." He beckoned. She walked forward. The granite was scarred in regular patterns; a repeating scar of five radiant lines, the clutch and drag of huge, diamond-hard talons.

The hairs lifted on the nape of her neck. "The Dragon's Roost."

"Yes. I was two, I think, when my father first showed me this place. He lifted me between his hands, and held me in the air. I was very small. I remember the blue sky, and the heat of his hands." He shook his shoulders loose, like a man about to lift a heavy weight. His tone changed. "So. Are you still minded to join my war band?"

"I am, my lord."

"Have you met my captain, Lorimir Ness?" She nodded. "Let him know that you have signed on. He will tell you what your duties should be." She bowed. "Hunter."

"My lord?"

For a moment she thought she saw him smile. "You will not find service in my company boring."

Lorimir assigned her to Murgain's troop. The plump man was a fine archer, and a patient teacher, though a little soft with the younger ones, permitting more horseplay than Hawk ever had among her soldiers. But Orm, his sergeant, was not soft, and he missed nothing.

The first three days she trained with the others. Though each of the captains had separate troops, all the soldiers were expected to know how to ride, mount a charge, use a spear on horse or foot, shoot—though some of them, goddess knew, shot very badly indeed—and handle a blade. Hawk had never enjoyed sword practice: the wooden training weapons were always too long for her, and men who accepted that she could, and did, consistently outshoot them, could not endure the thought that they might lose a sword bout to a woman, and came at her with rage. She ended up disarmed, bruised, angry, and, as most of her instructors had gently or caustically pointed out to her, theoretically dead.

The fourth day, Murgain told her at breakfast that she was excused from sword practice. "I want you to teach the short bow." He jerked a thumb toward the men sprawled along the benches. "Take them to the field and let them show you what they can do. Choose the ones with talent, and let me know who they are. I'll send Orm with you, if you wish, to keep them in line."

She said quietly, "I'll keep them in line. I don't need Orm." She pointed: "You, you—get up. Move!" The command snap, which she could summon without raising her voice, made them hop without thinking. "Huw, take some men with you and draw ten Isojai bows, with quivers and arrows for each of them. Meet us at the range."

"Yes, ma'am!" Huw said. He dragged Arnor and Gavin with him.

"Let's go," she said. She looked hard at the others. By the time they reached the range, Huw and his assistants had arrived with the arrows. "Targets. Finle and Stark, set them up close." Stark sauntered toward the round, tied discs of hay. Finle followed, more slowly. With elaborate care, like men in a dream, they rolled the targets against the wood frames. The other men watched her, wondering what she would do.

She waited patiently until the malcontents halted their provocative fussing, and then called, "Finle. Stay there." She strung her bow, and, taking five arrows from her quiver, handed them to Huw, fanning them out as she did so, steel points turned away from her. "Hold them so," she told him. Taking the first of them from him, she nocked her bow, and raised her voice. "You will find the pull on the short bow surprisingly strong. You will want to flex your left elbow—

so. Finle! Lay your hand on the center of the target." She saw him check, and extend his hand. "Splay your fingers." He obeyed. "Don't move them."

She said casually to the entranced observers, "Accuracy and speed are a matter of practice, of course, just as they are with the longbow." She shot the first arrow hissing into the straw beside Finle's thumb. The sweat sprang on his face. The second arrow fell into the gap between his thumb and second finger. Coolly she sent the last three arrows into the straw between his fingers. "Few of you can do that with the longbow." She raised her voice again. "Finle, come in now. Bring the arrows."

She gave Murgain a list of names, fifteen in all. Orm and Huw were both on it. "Finle's not on here," he said, surprised. "He can shoot anything."

"He doesn't want my teaching." Though outwardly docile, he had handled the little bow clumsily, deliberately fumble-fingered, glancing at her sideways to confirm that she'd noted his ineptitude. "What's wrong with him?"

"His friend Garin was killed the first time the wargs attacked. They grew up together, close as brothers." He peered at the list. "Irok's not on here either."

She had watched the little hunter shoot. "There's nothing I can teach *him*."

The fifth afternoon, Rogys returned to barracks. No one commented on his swollen face; his friends, with unexpected delicacy, behaved as if he had never been away. At dinner that night, he laughed and talked, shoulder to shoulder with his fellow horsemen.

After the meal the men pulled the tables back. A troop of four ringed and beribboned jugglers had ridden up from Castria. Bare-chested, shining with sweat in the torchlight, the jugglers tossed plates and knives and lit torches back and forth in a spinning storm. Half-hidden in the shadows, Karadur Atani leaned against a wall to watch them. Azil

Aumson stood near him. Hawk had heard the name the soldiers gave him. They rarely spoke of him: he was Dragon's
business. That night, leaning on the ramparts beneath the
splendid stars, she tried again to find Bear. Still, there was
no answer. She had asked Irok how long it would take a
man to go from Dragon Keep to Mitligund. He had
shrugged. "Clear weather, plenty food, no holes in the
snow, no wolves, no bears, seven, eight days."

A bear loping through drifts of snow moved faster than
any man. But even Bear could be slowed by storm, and he
would need to hunt. "What's the hunting like?"

"Four years, three years ago—good. Elk, deer, goose.
Now terrible."

"Why?"

"Wizard. Makes ice."

Suddenly everything began to happen very quickly. Telchor
Felse, the smith, brought every sword and spear in the ar-
mory into the light, sharpening the dull ones, examining
each for loose rivets and nicks that could weaken a blade
in battle. Upstairs, Macallan did the same with his little
knives.

Hawk took one of her boots to the leather-workers, and
had them replace a loose heel. She sharpened her dagger
and her arrowheads. Ten men were detailed to make
torches, winding pitch-dipped cloth around wood splits.

"What are we going to do with fifty torches?" Huw asked.

"Wait and see," Orm said, stretching. "That's the last of
them. Gods, my back's sore."

The horses were rested, and exercised, and rested again.
Edruyn, riding too fast on slippery ground, lamed one of the
mares. Herugin took him back of the stables and thrashed
him, though not so harshly that the boy could not ride, or
fight. One of the ten pack mules destined to go north sick-
ened, and had to be replaced. Telchor Felse examined the

hooves of fifteen mules and eighty horses, and spent three days replacing worn or ill-fitting shoes.

Two nights before the April full moon, Spring Moon, Karadur ordered a feast. Ambrosial smells floated across the fields all day. The men in the training hall, under Lorimir Ness's stern eye, moved through their swordwork as if drugged, or in love. By sundown, it was impossible to concentrate, or even to think about anything except food. When the dining hall opened, the men swarmed in to find waiting for them a meal fit for a midsummer feast: salmon steaks and roast goose and glazed honeyed ham, onions and beans and bread, sweet potato pie drizzled with sweet cream. They cheered the cook, and ate as if they expected it to be their last meal.

Hawk sat with the archers, a wine cup between her palms. Huw, beside her, was steadily devouring his second — or was it his third? — piece of pie. She closed her eyes, and then opened them, jolted by sudden noise. The men at Dragon's table were pounding on it with fists and empty tankards and the hilts of their daggers.

The hard, strident drumming spread to the other tables. Dragon let the clamor continue for a few minutes. Then he rose, and raised a hand. Pitching his deep voice so that it filled the long hall, he said, "A warrior's trade is war. It is what he studies, and what he longs for."

The drumming hilts responded: *Yes. Yes.*

"In two days' time, your schooling ends. In two days' time, you march north. You have an enemy there: a cruel, ignoble enemy. His wargs have taken life from your comrades and children and friends. You have the right to vengeance, and you will take it utterly.

"Your enemy has a stronghold in Mitligund."

In Mitligund, the daggers cried.

"He calls it the Black Citadel. You will destroy it. He has men who fight for him."

Who fight for him, for him, for him.

"You will kill them. He has wargs who do his bidding. You will hunt them as they have hunted your friends, and you will kill them, too."

The young men sat upright, cheeks flushed, eyes shining. Karadur lowered his voice a tone. "Now I must command a favor of you, a favor which some of you will hate me for." The men sat straighter. "A small force must remain at the Keep, to hold it, and to keep the farmers and villagers vigilant while the war band is gone. Marek Gavrinson. Stand up." At the center table, the bearded man rose. "I wish you to govern this force. As proof of my trust, I promote you to lieutenant, and raise your pay commensurably. I know," the deep voice continued, "that at this moment you would prefer to be a foot soldier in the war band, and that you are damning my wishes to the deepest hell you know. But I also know that you will obey me. The following men will fight in your command. Tallis. Arnor. Rogys. Sigli. Ilain. Wegen." He named twelve altogether. "Into your charge I give my castle and the lives of those who depend on it. Yours is a place of honor. I know you will not fail me."

Marek said firmly, "We will not, my lord."

"The rest of you: in two days we ride to Mitligund. Warriors, make sharp your weapons!"

Men leaped to their feet, shouting jubilantly, and banging on the tables. Servers brought pitchers in, and filled the tankards with sweet foamy beer. Karadur returned to his seat by the hearth. Marek crossed to talk with him.

Herugin, sitting at the next table, had risen to shout with the rest. Hawk called to him, "Your lord gives a good speech."

He elbowed his way from his bench to hers, and joined her. "He does."

"Did you know what he planned to say?"

"No. Oh, I knew some would have to stay behind. I didn't know who. But Marek is the right man. He has a wife and two sons in Castria. Arnor is injured. Sigli and Tallis, too, have families."

Amid the rustle and mutter of voices, one began to sing. The voice was clear and skilled, strong, but with an odd rasp. *"O the red boar, the red boar of Aidu. The red boar ran to the mountains; the red boar ran to the sea; the waves sprang up till they touched the clouds and the thunder rang with a dreadful sound; O the red boar, the red boar of Aidu."*

The singer was the maimed man. Hands still in his lap, he wove the story of the magical beast and the relentless hunters who tracked him across fields and seashore and finally the very firmament. Other voices, less melodious but with admirable energy, joined him to roar the chorus. *"O the red boar, the red boar of Aidu."* At the last mournful, elegiac verse, the others dropped away, leaving Azil to sing alone.

"And the horns rang out as the red boar died; and stars tumbled out of the evening sky; O the red boar, the red boar of Aidu."

"More!" someone shouted.

Touching his throat, Azil shook his head. Karadur filled his own glass with ale and passed it to him. The harsh lines had smoothed from the Dragon-lord's face; for that one moment he looked carefree, serene, and young. In the kitchen, a girl wept: someone's sweetheart, or sister.

Yawning, Herugin pushed the heels of his hands against his eyes. "Gods, I'll never make it through the night," he said mournfully. "I'm watch officer."

His yawn made Hawk yawn as well. "I'm for bed."

"I'll walk with you to barracks."

In the sleeping hall, two men sat by the near fire, their heads bent together. It was Rogys, his cheek still slightly marked, and Finle Haraldson. They rose abruptly as Hawk and Herugin came into the long chamber.

"Sir," said Rogys.

Herugin nodded. "You should be in bed," he said mildly. "Or on watch."

"Yes, sir," Rogys said. "But I—sir, I don't want to stay behind." His low voice was passionate. "You know I don't."

"I know," Herugin said. "Nor does Marek, or Sigli."

"That's different."

"How is it different?"

"Marek has children. Sigli, too. Arnor's hurt, and Wegen is an old man." Wegen was perhaps thirty-five. "Sir, would you speak to him on my behalf? He might listen to you."

But Herugin shook his head. "I'm sorry, Red. I like my head on my neck. This is no time to question his orders. Go to bed, both of you." The young men did not move. He put an edge into his voice. "*Now.*" He put his hands on his hips. "Young idiots."

"You would feel the same," Hawk said. "Wouldn't you?"

✣   ✣   ✣

IN THE STRONGHOLD and prison known as the Black Citadel, Shem sat shivering in a nest of dirty blankets. He was cold. They had taken his clothes, and given him a blanket with holes in it to cover him. His baby face had thinned.

He was alone. Takumik was absent, as he was often: hunting, or standing guard, or digging one of the endless tunnels that made up Koriuji's Lair. The men who had shared the ice cave with him were also gone. A rumor had gone around the castle, of a prince in the south who would soon be coming north with a great army . . . They had tried to leave the castle with gold beneath their shirts. Wargs had gotten one of them, and the white bear the other. Koriuji had released it from its cage, and it stalked the snow around the castle, howling defiance at the open sky—gaunt, dangerous, insane.

Twice, by Koriuji's order, Takumik had brought Shem to the empty high-ceilinged chamber, and held him for the white worm's inspection. The first time Shem simply

wailed in horror. The second time, cajoled dumb by Takumik, he remained mute. The monster leaned close, leering.
"Do you hear me, boy?" it said. "Your mother and father are
dead. You are mine." That night Shem saw the ravaged pale
face hanging in air, frozen in the walls, even burning in the
fire's smoke. He lay whimpering in his blankets, afraid to
close his eyes.

Moving clumsily—his small fingers were stiff—Shem
felt in his nest for his treasure. Cupping it in his hands, he
breathed on it to warm it, then held the spiky-legged figure
to his cheek. It smelled of what it was, bread dough.
"Boppy," he murmured. He drowsed, the dog-figure tucked
in his fist.

A bumping noise in the corridor roused him. He thrust
Boppy out of sight. Takumik stumped in. "Here," the man
said, in his own language. Dropping a lump of cooked meat
into Shem's lap, he bent to the brazier. The dark, dank
chamber warmed and brightened. Takumik sat, and
brought out a larger portion of meat. "It's fresh, a bird." He
mimed eating, lifting hands to mouth. Shem bit into the
stringy flesh. It had little taste, but it was hot.

They chewed companionably, and shared the waterskin
between them. After a while, the man spoke softly, still in his
own tongue. The boy listened curiously to the guttural, grumbling sounds. "The white bear killed another man today. He
was coming from a hunt, and she sprang upon him, and tore
his throat out." Takumik mimed claws. "I was digging today. I
do not understand all this digging. They say it is for gold but
there is no gold, nothing but rocks and dirt." He lowered his
voice. "The guards say that they have been told men are coming, many men whom they will kill. They are thy people,
these southerners. The one who leads them is called *Dragon*."

"Dragon," Shem repeated. The word woke a memory of a
bright-haired giant with blazing eyes and warm, steady hands.

"If they come, this castle will fall to them like butter to
the sun. If they come, there is a place I shall hide thee, until

the killing is over. Thee shall be—" Takumik's grumble stopped. Shem smelled the stink of his fear.

Gorthas crouched in the mouth of the cave. "The little wolfling," he said. "Come here, wolfling." Shem did not move. Takumik shrank away, as the warg-changeling reached contemptuously past him and snatched the boy from his blankets.

Tucking the boy under one arm, he trotted through the twisting slimy passageways to the central hall, where the white worm sprawled on its chair. He tossed the child to the ground. "Here it is, my lord."

Shem looked at the monster on the chair. A decaying human face atop the worm's gross body stared at him blackly, ravenously. "Has it been hurt?" the worm asked.

"Not at all, my lord."

"Good. It must not be, not yet. When this is over, truly over, I shall give it to you, for your play." The snakelike tongue slid out and back. "Ssshem. You underssstand me?"

Gorthas said, "Answer your master, wolfling." Shem's throat was too dry to work. Gorthas cuffed him. "A disobedient wolfling. Shall I make it speak?" A hard hand licked out, gripping unerringly, painfully. "Such a tender little cub." He prodded Shem's ribs, grinning as his fingers found the sore spots. Shem cried out, and tried to wriggle free.

"Enough," the worm said. The warg lifted his hands. "Where is my bear?"

"Outside, baying at the sun."

"Excellent. The army comes soon. Almost they are ready, horses and men. Tell the guards on the walls to remain watchful. Any man caught sssleeping will have his hands chopped off. Tell them ssso."

"I will tell them, my lord."

"The army has a new recruit. A little bird has come to fly beside them: one of the Red Hawk sisters." The worm writhed on its chair. "Wolf, white bear, red bear, hawk, all, all will be mine."

"My lord," the warg-changeling said, "when the army comes, will you let me take the wolfling?"

"Why, what will you do?"

"Build a pyre before the castle gate, and hang the naked cub wriggling and screaming above it." His eyes gleamed like spear points. "And then I will do the same to Azil."

The monster giggled hideously. "Not yet. First we will have a battle, a battle, a battle: battle, betrayal, and death ... Later you may do it. But first it must be taught, as dogs are taught. Has it been collared and brought to heel yet?"

"Not yet, my lord."

"No? Do it!" Again, it giggled. "I will watch."

"As my lord commands." Seizing Shem's hair, the changeling drew the child's head up. He laid his other hand measuringly along the soft skin of the boy's throat. "Shem, stay here," he said as he released his grip. He left the hall. When he returned, he carried a leather dog collar with a metal buckle and a chain leash.

He knelt, and buckled the rough leather around Shem's neck. "Good dog," he said, and clipped the chain to the collar. "Shem, stand."

Shem stared at him. Gorthas jerked the collar. The boy gasped, and felt with both hands for his throat. "Shem, stand."

Shem did not move, and again Gorthas jerked the chain. It took several repetitions before the boy stood at command. "Shem, come."

But at this Shem set his sturdy legs, and would not move. Gorthas's blow tumbled the little boy to the ice. Shem yelled. Gorthas jerked the collar. "Be quiet!" He leaned close, reaching for the child's mouth, and Shem shrank and was still. "Good. It learns. Shem, stand. Shem, walk."

The degrading, ugly lessons went on, interspersed with cuffs. Finally the worm said, "That will do. Take it to its hole."

Almost tenderly, Gorthas unclipped the chain. The

child's cheek was bruised, and there was a raw mark on his neck, under the leather. There was a wild hopelessness in his face that had not been there before. The changeling scooped him off his feet.

"Come, wolfling. Battle, betrayal, and death, and then we will cook you, slowly, so slowly . . ." He glided through the tunnels, and slung the exhausted child into Takumik's arms.

PART
FOUR

15

At dawn two days later, while stars still shone in the western sky, Karadur Atani led his war band north from Dragon Keep.

They rode one after the other, watchful, in close order. *Stay alert and together,* Lorimir had instructed. *Any straggler becomes an easy target for wargs.*

Hawk rode with the archers. Herugin had given her Sunflower, a sure-footed dun mare. They traveled in silence: they had no concern for secrecy—seventy horsemen, ten pack mules dragging sledges, and ten well-laden spare horses, could be concealed from only the dimmest of spies—but Dragon was grim as iron, and the men took their mood from him. Last of all, amid the rearguard, Finle Haraldsen rode with a forbidding face. His fellows left him alone.

They stopped briefly at midmorning to eat, and then pushed on until sunset. They saw no wargs, or other beasts, save a grey fox that watched them suspiciously from a hole in a rock. They camped overnight on the mountainside, huddling against looming rocks in what shelter they could find. Hawk laid her bedroll beside Orm and Huw. The sun's light was gone, except for the last rays lighting the highest peak. The silver moon hung in the sky like a broken coin.

"I don't like this place," Orm said morosely. "I've no wish to fall asleep, and wake to find myself halfway down the cliff."

"We could tether you to a rock, like the horses," Huw said.

They woke into darkness and led the horses up the trail in the predawn silence. By the middle of the morning, they reached the ice. It lay ominous and still before them, a lifeless landscape that seemed to reach forever into distance. A wind swept endlessly north to south. The men cinched their hoods tight around their necks. The sky was pale with cloud.

"Raise the banner," Karadur said. Raudri, the standard-bearer, let the dragon banner unfurl on its pole. The wind whipped it angrily back and forth, and then subsided to an evil, rushing mutter. "Sound the Advance." Lifting his horn, Raudri sent the bright clear music winging across the bleak plain.

Past midday, they came to what had once been a village. Blackened and charred wood spars poked desolately from the frozen ground. Stones that once had belonged to barns and sheds and homes lay tumbled aimlessly about. In a few spots walls rose, seemingly untouched, as if the despoilers had been too lazy or too hurried to pull them down. At the far southern corner of the village stood a stone house, roofless and chimney-less but with walls intact.

"We'll stop here," Lorimir said. "The horses need rest."

Herugin, whose face was drawn with cold, said, "The men could do with hot food, sir."

"All right. But quickly."

It was the archers' turn to cook. They laid wood for a fire in the shelter of the walls, and hammered spits into the frozen ground. Orm sent men to bring meat from the supplies.

Huw grumbled, "I don't like this place. It stinks of wizardry."

"Baby," said Orm. "Your feet stink worse."

Edruyn said, "How does he know where to lead us?"

"Have you never heard of maps?"

"But there are no landmarks." He waved an arm at the white emptiness.

Finle, arms filled with frozen meat, said, "The Hound has been here. I heard him say so." The men fell abruptly silent. "And so have we. This is Ashavik. Dragon brought us here three years ago September. We were hunting elk. They gave us hot bread to eat. Orm, you remember the girl with the braid and the blue kerchief, who smiled at you?"

"How can he remember one girl?" Huw said. "There have been so many girls."

But Orm said, "That was here? Are you sure?" Finle nodded. "Aye, I remember. The well was there. But it was all green . . ." His voice trailed away.

Hawk had just finished her meal when a voice at her elbow said, "Archer? Excuse me." It was Derry, bundled so that only the reddened tips of his ears showed. "Dragon would like to speak with you."

She followed him to the roofless house. Macallan was there, and Azil, and Dragon. He was holding a rolled map loosely between his bare hands. Despite the cold, he wore no furs, only his usual dark clothes, and over them a simple wool cloak. She felt the link between them: she saw it in her mind's eye, gleaming like a rope of fire across darkness.

"My lord. You sent for me."

"I did," he said. "I need your changeling eyes. We have entered our enemy's country. Will you go aloft, and scout for us?"

The request did not surprise her. It was work she knew well. "As you wish, my lord. For what shall I look?"

"I want you to find the mist. You have heard men speak of it? It is a device made by my enemy: a wall of fog, inhabited by nightmare. You will know it when you see it. I want to know where it is, and how long before we reach it. Take care not to enter it."

"I will take care, my lord."

Aloft, she made a pass over the camp, and then swung north northeast. Pale clouds hovered over her, vast and pitiless as the sea. The winds were chill, slippery as oil beneath her wings. She passed a flock of ptarmigan, wheeling and darting in the wind. She flew over a burned village. In the middle of it, surrounded by broken stone, a skinny-sided elk pawed the snow, hunting for some living greenery. Three red foxes worried their kill. Nothing else moved amid the ruins save shadows, and snow-spume.

Quite suddenly, in the moment between wing-beat and wing-beat, the land beneath her vanished under a thick, roiling grey cloud. She slowed her flight, and dropped toward it. The fetid smell made her sneeze. Wisps of rank fog coiled upward to meet her. Fell voices seemed to whisper inside it. She circled lower, straining on the very edge of hearing, but could not distinguish words.

Repelled, she drove upward into the white sky. By the time she reached the war band, it was twilight. She landed, and changed to human form. At first she thought the men had raised their tents amid the ruins of yet another village. Then she realized: what she had first taken for walls were rock formations jutting from the snow. In the grey light, the spires seemed enchanted, a tribe of hunched and hooded old men, caught in the cold and turned to stone. The new camp was well east of where she had left them. Tethered horses stood in the shelter formed by rocks, feed bags on their noses. Their jaws worked steadily.

Nine canvas tents sprouted around a common center. Dragon's tent sported the dragon banner. He was not there, but Lorimir was, and Azil, and the physician. Fire danced in a low-footed brazier; the air smelled of meat cooking.

Lorimir waved her to a cushion. She sat, rubbing her shoulders. Azil handed her a leather-bound flask. "Careful," he said. "It's hot."

The wine eased the ache in her bones. She closed her

eyes, and saw white behind her eyelids. No one spoke to her; she was grateful: her mind was wordless, caught in the white wild soundlessness of the hawk's flight. Lorimir and Macallan talked about a lame horse.

Derry brought her a skewer of cooked, savory meat. She had nearly finished when Karadur came out of the darkness. He gestured her to stay seated, and went himself for meat. Azil gave him a mug. He sat on a cushion. The firelight glinted on his hair.

He said, "What did you see, hunter?"

"Ice," she answered. "Snow. I saw places where men had once lived, but no men. I saw elk, and a flock of birds, and a trio of foxes feeding in the snow."

"Did you find the mist?" She nodded. "How long, do you think, before we reach it?"

"A day, my lord. Two, if we are slow."

"We will not be slow. Thank you, Hawk of Ujo. You have done me good service this day. You must be spent. Go and sleep."

✿ ✿ ✿

"ENEMY IN THE camp! Awake. Awake! The horses! They're killing the horses!"

The horrifying cry lifted through shrill animal screams. Flinging themselves from their bedrolls, fearful men grabbed for weapons and raced bootless and cloakless over snow.

The clouded sky had cleared. Under a vast corona of stars, skeletal warriors on gaunt pale steeds galloped soundlessly through the camp. They wore tall metal helmets, and bore swords, shields, and long spears made of ice. Grinning, they thrust spears at the running men.

Hawk, half-asleep, nocked an arrow and shot at the skull-face beneath the nearest helmet. The fleshless warrior, gazing directly at her through his arched eye-sockets, laughed, and faded. Her arrow flew through him, and buried itself in snow. Other shafts, loosed by other hands, sped through their macabre targets. In the center of the camp, Olav howled, and swung his long-handled ax at a pale warrior's throat. It glided dreamlike through gleaming bone, without hindrance or effect.

Someone shouted in pain. Lorimir's voice rose powerfully above the melee: "Hold! Archers, hold your arrows!"

They froze, breathing hard. Noiselessly, the ghostly warriors rode between the tents, and vanished into smoke. The horses milled in the horse lines. An eerie silence settled over the camp. "Torches," Lorimir said. Half a dozen men brought torches. By their light, all could see the buried arrows, the churned, unbloodied ground. Men on the ground clutching their sides rose, feeling for mortal wounds that were suddenly absent.

One man knelt, swearing, a Keep arrow through his arm. Macallan bent over him. "A flesh wound. Not serious. Help him to my tent," he said briskly. "Any more hit?"

"Gods, they were illusions," someone murmured. The word spread across the camp. "Illusions. Phantoms. Ghosts." A man laughed in astonishment and relief. Murgain shouted at his men to collect their arrows.

Karadur had not joined the fighting. He stood at the mouth of his tent, watching the horse lines. "Herugin," he said, his deep voice carrying across the camp, "report!"

Herugin came jogging into the torchlight. "My lord," he said grimly, "three horses are dead, their throats and bellies torn. Wargs. Three broke free of their tethers, but one has already returned, and the other two will, I think, come back of themselves." He took a slow breath. "Three men are dead, as well." The laughter stopped. "Tonio, Ralf, and Ferlin. They were sleeping among the horses. They were killed in the same manner."

They were all men of Herugin's wing. "Take me to them," Karadur said.

They threaded their way among the nervous horses to the

edge of the camp. The dead men had been wrapped in blankets and laid upwind of the lines. Herugin lit a spill. The dragon-lord knelt beside the first man. Grimly he drew back the blanket. An eyeless face gazed palely into the starry night.

Herugin said, "That is Tonio. He was youngest. You remember, he played the flute so badly . . ."

"I remember." Karadur moved to the second man. "Ferlin. He was my page. He was so proud to be taken into the garrison." He moved to the third man. "Ralf—he has a wife in Chingura, has he not?"

"Her name is Shela. A new baby girl, too."

"This, too, will be paid for." Karadur patted the blanket into place. "When we get home, we will do them honor . . ." He rose. "You know that we must leave them here."

"I know," Herugin said. "They will understand. They would not want us to delay." They returned to the center of camp.

"Lorimir, from now, sentries walk in pairs," the dragon-lord said.

"I have already ordered it, my lord," said the captain.

"It was a clever tactic, to distract us with illusion while the wargs killed. We must not let it happen again."

Footsteps sounded at their backs. "My lord," a voice said. Three men appeared from the direction of the horse lines. The man in the middle, arms held fast in the grip of the other two, was Rogys. "We found him among the horse lines. I have his sword."

"Let him go," Dragon said softly. The men on either side of the redhead drew their hands away. The camp was still, a painful stillness in which only torchlight moved, and snow-spume, blown by the night wind. "Herugin, did you know of this?"

Herugin said tautly, "No, my lord."

"He is in your command, is he not? You should have known. Rogys."

"My lord." The words were scarcely audible.

"I ordered you to Marek's command. I thought you were a warrior. You disobeyed me. Worse. You deserted your post." Rogys was white. The torch-light gleamed on the hard curves of Karadur's face. "Lorimir, what penalty would my father have ordered for desertion?"

Lorimir said, "My lord, your father the Black Dragon would have ordered the deserter's hands severed from his wrists, and he would have been left to bleed to death in the snow."

A shudder went through the listening men. At Murgain's side, Finle dropped to one knee and hid his face in his hands.

Karadur said, "Lorimir, have you aught to say?" Lorimir shook his head. "Murgain?" The archery master was silent. "Herugin."

Herugin said thinly, "My lord, he did not fight or run from capture, although he could have."

Finle lifted his head from his hands. "My lord," he said, "may I speak?"

Murgain said sharply, "Be silent, Finle."

"It was he who first raised the alarm tonight. Had he not been there, and awake, more men might have died."

Karadur said, "Is that true, Red?"

Rogys nodded. Swallowing, he said hoarsely, "I was sleeping with the horses. The ice warriors rode right by me. I tried to stab one of the wargs, but its scales turned the blade." He pointed to the sword in Sandor's hand. The blade was broken.

"I see," said the dragon-lord. Finle's eyes kindled with hope. "Byrnik, how many hours to dawn?"

Byrnik, who always knew, answered, "Seven, my lord."

"Stand back," the dragon-lord said to the watching men. He extended both hands: fire streamed from them, as it had when he kindled the wood. It poured fiercely across the snow. It circled Rogys, glowing, and the hissing snow retreated from it. Then it subsided, making a bright narrow ring in the snow.

"Till dawn, you will not step beyond the fire," Karadur said.

Eyes on his lord's face, Rogys nodded. "I understand, my lord."

"Seven hours. No one is to help him." He turned, crossed the frozen camp and entered his tent. In the silence, the sound of the wind could be plainly heard.

The men of the Atani war band slept fitfully that night. Men slept and woke and slept again. Staring scratchy-eyed at tent poles, they listened to the unquiet wind, as the shocking cold crept through layers of clothes and blankets. *A man trapped in the open in winter needs to move, to keep the blood moving. It is colder out there.* The night crawled. When at last the first light of the new day began to seep across the sky, every man of the camp was out of his tent.

The sky was clear, the air bitter cold. Ice crackled underfoot. Shifting from foot to foot, blowing on their hands, the men watched Karadur's tent.

Huw whispered, "Is he standing?"

Orm said, "Too dark. Wait."

"I see him," Hawk said quietly. "He is standing." She could see Rogys's silhouette: he was upright, head turned to watch the sun. The boundary of fire gleamed, white-gold, around his feet.

Dragon's tent flap was pulled aside. Without haste, Karadur emerged. He strolled across the snow crust. Rogys was shivering convulsively.

"Well, Red?" the dragon-lord said.

Every man in the camp could see the lift of Rogys's head. "My lord," he said hoarsely, "I have obeyed your command."

Their eyes met, and held. Karadur said, "And can you walk?"

"I can walk, my lord." Rogys lurched forward, clearly numb from the knees down.

Hawk held her breath. Don't fall, she thought, and knew every soul in the camp was praying it with her, you witless, lucky, courageous fool, don't fall . . . He didn't. As he stepped across the fire line, he wobbled, but a powerful arm clamped around him, holding him on his feet. Lorimir snapped an order, and four men dashed across the snow to take Rogys from his lord's grasp.

By breakfast, Rogys was walking unsupported. Hobbling to the officers' tent, he said penitently to Lorimir, "Captain, I'm sorry. It was stupid."

"It was," Lorimir said shortly. "But you paid for it. Let's hope Marek has not."

Rogys flinched at that. To Herugin, he said, "Sir, I'm sorry. I couldn't—I *couldn't* stay behind."

Herugin looked coldly at him. Finally he said, "Idiot. If you ever even *think* of doing anything so brainless again, I'll take the skin off you in inches. Get out to the lines. And don't run, or you'll snap an ankle."

"Sir!" Rogys snapped a crisp salute.

They left the dead, both men and horses, behind. Lorimir suggested butchering the horses. "We could use the fresh meat."

But Karadur forbid it. "We eat nothing that has been touched by wargs."

Karadur pushed the army ruthlessly that day. The air was cold, searingly cold, dry and windless, and the sky brilliant, a shimmering iridescent blue. Crusty snow split like glass under the horses' hooves. The frozen landscape glittered, beautiful, deadly. Midday they stopped, to eat hard bread and cheese, and rest and water the horses. Macallan moved through the troop, checking for frostbite and snow-blindness.

As they made ready to leave, Lorimir ordered that the torches be passed out, one to every other man. Huw said, "I heard the captain and Lieutenant Herugin talking in the cook tent. They said we should reach the mist today."

Edruyn said, "They say the men who go through it come out mad." His beardless face was drawn, and not with cold.

Orm said roughly, "Don't trouble yourself, boy. That's Dragon's business. He'll get us through."

They saw the mist before they came to it. Ominous and grey, it loomed ahead of them, taller than the tallest oak: a dense wet wall.

Edruyn whispered, "It looks like fog on the ocean."

Huw scoffed, "When did you ever see the ocean?"

"I never did. But my father's brother Finn went to Skyeggo, and he told me. He said the fog there rises from the waves at dawn, and retreats before the morning sun, and blows in again at sunset."

"I suppose he saw sea-serpents, too."

"If he did, he never said."

As they neared the mist, Lorimir called, "Form columns." The men pulled their horses into lines. The officers, and Dragon, rode forward, until they stood only feet from the roiling fog.

Tendrils of damp, like grey mold, snaked over the snow. Voices like the memory of evil dreams called from the ashen reek. The horses shied, snorting, at the foul odor. "Gods, it stinks," Murgain said morosely.

As if it had heard, the wall of mist churned. Suddenly it tore, and a great yawning fissure, like a monstrous mouth, appeared. At the edge of the mouth flickered rows of sharp tiny teeth. A tongue of mist licked the frigid air. The big black gelding half-reared, and trumpeted defiance.

Lorimir said quietly, "My lord, the men will endure this. But the beasts may not. Fog and fire together—it asks a lot of them."

Karadur said, "Herugin, what do you think?"

Herugin said, "My lord, they know their riders. I think they will suffer it."

"We will try," Karadur said. Turning Smoke to face the company, he pitched his deep voice so all could hear. "Hear me, Atani warriors. We have come to the mist. You've heard the hunters' tales; you know what it is. Within its depths are phantoms, creatures of a vengeful mind. Our enemy intends us to scurry back across the mountains, yelping like whipped dogs."

An angry growl lifted from the throats of the men. "The hell we will!" someone called.

"We will not. Instead, we will attack. Our enemy loathes and fears fire. So, fire will be our shield and our weapon. Lift your torches!" The riders yelled. Karadur raised his hands, fingers spread. Amber fire, unfueled, uncannily silent, blazed from his open palms and streamed through the air to the torches. Pitch flared; dry wood crackled and spat sparks. Like a bright and deadly river the fire whipped across the snow. The mist humped, and recoiled, shrieking at the fire's touch. Raudri raised the banner. The golden dragon's glittering head seemed to arch across the white cloth. The black gelding leaped forward into the fog.

"Follow him! Together! Damn you," Lorimir shouted, "ride together!"

Shouting like vengeful demons, the soldiers thundered into the mist. Knee to knee, like cavalrymen charging a line of swordsmen, they galloped through the fog, brandishing their torches; nightmare voices yammered in rage, and then fell silent, as the mist boiled to nothingness at the assault of flame. As they swept from shadow into sunshine, they saw the dark-cloaked figure waiting on his horse. They surrounded him, exultant, cheering.

Finally the captains quieted them. "Form ranks," Lorimir snapped. They drew the lines into formation.

Ahead of them, the land sloped upward into a snowy ridge. "Sound the Advance!"

Raudri blew the horn. They rode over the ridge, and stopped.

Before them, as far as human eye could see, stretched a lifeless waste of ice. And in the middle of it rose a massive ebony-walled fortress: the Black Citadel.

16

THE FORTRESS DOMINATED the ivory-white plain. A massive edifice of unassailable walls, soaring spires, great smoking chimneys, vast dungeons beneath layers of impenetrable stone, it seemed improbably close, perhaps a mile away, less.

"Heart of the gods," Murgain said softly, "it must be big as a mountain!"

"No," Karadur said. "This is wizardry. The castle is still three days from us, and when we reach it we will find it neither so big nor so fearsome as it appears."

From the ridge the land seemed a featureless waste. But under the smooth deceptive snow drifts, the ground was rucked and rutted. Lorimir sent out double the usual number of scouts. "With *that* on the horizon," he said quietly to the dragon-lord, "the men will find it hard to keep their attention on the ice. I want no accidents, and no surprises."

The riders moved in loose formation, north and east. After an hour's steady progress, one of the scouts came riding back to report an abandoned village ahead of them. Black spars rose like grave markers, mute witness to human cruelty, and human endurance. Just beyond it, a cluster of five elk nosed weakly at the snow. They were mostly bone, and so famished that they did not run or scatter, as normal beasts would, but simply froze, staring with blank hopelessness at the war band.

Lorimir said, "My lord. Fresh meat."

"No," Karadur said, after a moment. "Let them live."

They passed two more burned and gutted villages. In one, the scouts found a mummified body in the snow. The eyeless, desiccated face bared its teeth in a desperate rictus of pain. Four stakes had been driven into the ground. Wind-torn rope showed that the man had been fastened to them, spread-eagled and tied . . . There were rocks all about him.

"He was stoned," Macallan said. He parted the layers of cloth with the tip of his dagger. "See here, and here. His legs were broken, and these three ribs are crushed. There was evidently no one left alive to free him. If the stoning didn't kill him outright, exposure did."

"I wonder what they wanted from him," Herugin said, with distaste. He glanced at the tiny cluster of what had been huts. "It can't have been gold. These are hovels."

"Information?" guessed Murgain.

"Entertainment," said Azil quietly. "Amusement."

Here and there, a great rock jutted like the blade of a knife from the snowy ground. On many of them, a human hand had chipped out a spiral. The men filed through them silently.

Suddenly, from within the moving files of men, a terrible, inhuman scream pierced the white silence of the ice. The horsemen seized spears and bows and moved swiftly, automatically, to battle stations. Then the screaming stopped. A mule had tumbled into an ice crevasse and broken a leg. Someone had shot it.

"Can we get it out?" Karadur asked.

"We think so, my lord."

"Good. Lorimir, call a rest. Tell the men to drag that mule up and butcher it."

They halted where they stood. Chance, or some minor

god's mercy, had stopped them on the side of a gentle slope. The contour of the land effectively rendered the Citadel invisible. Without that inimical, forbidding structure squatting on the horizon, the soldiers' spirits and voices lifted. The horses, grateful for the rest, stood stolidly, while the dead mule was roped and hauled it from its hole. A corps of enthusiastic butchers, under Macallan's caustic supervision, skinned the beast, scraped the hide, quartered, disjointed, and packed the carcass. Those not lured by carnage slept, or took advantage of the halt to make the necessary, time-wasting repairs to weapons, harnesses, cloaks, boots, and cooking pots that are the bane of all armies. Sentries sat their horses, hands on their bows, eyes watchful.

Hawk cleaned and oiled her weapons. Then, sitting in the shelter of one of the tall rocks, she rested her head in her hands and called across the miles to Bear. The silence made a faint roaring sound in her mind, like the turmoil of a far-off sea. Suddenly she sensed him . . . *Bear!* she called. But swiftly as the sensation of contact had come, it vanished.

She looked up, discouraged and with a headache. Karadur Atani was sitting on a scrap of hide, watching her. She had not felt him, which surprised her. She *should* have felt him; they were only feet apart. Then she felt his effort, and realized that he was shielding her, crudely, but effectively, from his own power.

He said, "What were you doing?"

"Listening." She pulled her cloak more closely around her stiff shoulders. The dragon-lord sat at ease, with only a light cloak thrown across his back. His face, as ever, was unreadable. She wondered where he had learned that impassivity, and at what price.

"For what do you listen?"

"Other minds," she said.

"Animals?"

"Animals, yes. And changelings, and men."

"Are you a physician, as well as a tracker?"

"My knowledge of healing is minimal, my lord."

"Yet you were able to help Rogys. Macallan told me. You were taught these skills?"

"Yes. My mother taught them to me, as she learned them from her mother."

"Do all changeling folk have such faculties?"

"I don't know," she said. "Power differs from species to species, as well as mind to mind. Hawk and Cat have strong clear abilities. Wolf has some. Bear and Shark have almost none. Whale and Serpent have numerous abilities, but strange ones, I was told."

"And Dragon?"

"Your power is enormous, my lord. You must know that."

"I do know it," he said, with an uncharacteristic diffidence. "I can see in the dark. I can call fire out of the air. I can find a lie in a man's mind. But I am untrained." The wind stirred his hair. "It was not my intention to injure Rogys."

"The dragon temper," she said.

"Yes. I have so much more to learn."

The admission made her realize, for the first time, how young he truly was. The Black Dragon had died twenty years ago. But changelings, as she well knew, came early to their strengths. She herself had been full-grown at fourteen.

"Surely one of your kinsfolk, my lord, can instruct you in the use of your powers."

His hard still face did not change, but his eyes did. She looked away from him. *Dear Mother, what did I say . . . ?* But when she faced him again, that appalling blaze of anguish had vanished behind his potent self-control.

They rode on. In the illusive distance, the Black Citadel gleamed evilly. Just past noon they encountered a second, more brutal reminder of their adversary's savagery: the mummified corpses of three children. They sprawled half on top of each other, as if even in the last moments of life they had tried to help or defend each other, or at least to stay together. The smallest, a little girl, was very small indeed, no more than three or four years old.

Azil said, "They were hunted. Forced to run, and slowly chased, until they dropped from exhaustion. Probably the parents were made to watch, before they too were killed or enslaved. There will be a village nearby, and other bodies."

Herugin, voice grating as if his throat hurt, said, "How do you know?"

Azil answered tonelessly, "I watched it."

Just before sunset, Hawk felt the pressure against her mind.

Elated and relieved, she reined Sunflower to a stop. *Cousin, where are you? . . .* She heard no response. She tried again, and heard nothing, or perhaps something, a teasing echo . . . *Bear!*

Cousin, the whisper came, *you called me . . . ?* Evil laughter scraped her thought. Her vision swam with sickness. The mind behind the laughter was savage, foul as an opened grave.

"Hoy," said Finle at her elbow, "are you all right?"

"No," she snarled at him. She wheeled her horse and cantered back to the line. "My lord," she said, guiding Sunflower alongside the black gelding, "you had best halt the advance. Something is out there."

Raudri had the horn against his lips before she had finished speaking. The scouts pulled in. Karadur said, "What sort of something, my hunter?"

She shook her head. She did not want to approach it further. "A mind," she said. "An evil mind."

"Animal, human, or warg?"

"Not animal." She shivered. "It called me cousin."

She saw Azil Aumson's face change. "Gorthas," said the singer.

Karadur said curtly, "He shall not touch you." He glanced at the sky. "Lorimir, we camp here. Whatever is out there can come to us." He issued quick, pointed orders. Behind a bulwark of sledges and wood barricades, the men set a bristling hedge of spears. Bonfires blazed at the corners of the barricades. Lorimir doubled the watch. The dark came quickly. As if to torment them, a wind blew up. It ripped at the tents, and troubled the horses. The air seemed charged with a distant, ominous booming.

In the archers' tent, the men talked little. Hawk lay on her bedroll between Edruyn and Huw. Her legs were twitching. Edruyn was asleep: she could hear his regular, shallow breathing at her ear. Huw, half-awake, was caught in night thoughts. She stretched a little. Her mind would not settle. Finally she sat up, and with a muttered apology, yanked on her boots and left the tent. Clouds scudded overhead, and shredded into starlit wrack. She went to the latrine pit, and then walked toward the eastern barricade. Gingerly, she let her changeling-sense extend into the wintry darkness, half-expecting to hear that brutish, vicious whisper . . . But it did not come. The threat had withdrawn. Some animal lurked out there, some fearful, famished predator, a lone bear, hunting across the ensorceled landscape, or perhaps a starved, angry wolf.

She heard a step, and turned swiftly. It was Rogys. He held a long spear in both his hands. While his fellows had been butchering the mule, he had begged the whetstones from Telchor Felse's keeping, and sharpened the spearhead until its edge would shave a hair, or part a strand of wind-blown wool. He nodded to her.

"I couldn't sleep," she said, looking into the darkness. The wind knifed at her bones. Sparks from the bonfires swirled hissing into the crusty snow. "Have you seen or heard—anything? Wargs, or ice warriors?"

Rogys shook his head. "No wargs, no ice warriors. Just shadows."

❦　❦　❦

OUTSIDE THE CAMP, a bear crouched in a snowdrift. It was hungry and it was angry. Its head was filled with rage, like a gritty smoke.

At its back, the Black Place whispered, soft malevolent terrible noises that the bear could not understand. Ahead of it lay the human camp. The men had food, but they also had weapons, and tall yellow fires. The bear feared the Black Place, and it feared the fire. In the very deepest part of itself, where the noises could not reach, it remembered warmth, and healing laughter, and human fellowship. But the foul smoke filled its mind, and remembrance retreated before its desperate anger. It gazed balefully at the leaping yellow flames, and, growling softly, it bit the snow.

❦　❦　❦

THE NIGHT WIND had chased the clouds: the sky was a bright cold blue. They rode in formation: pack mules in the center, officers and a picked band of men in front, archers forming a deceptively loose line in vanguard, sides and rear. Their shadows paced behind them, edges sharp as razors. Ahead stretched snow, pale as the belly fleece of new-sheared sheep. Hawk, Orm, Finle, and Edruyn rode in the vanguard. Directly in their path, ominous and sinister, the spires and ramparts of the windowless fortress gleamed like toothy lumps of coal.

Suddenly Finle halted. "Hoy!" His voice was sharp with excitement. Hawk rode a little ways toward him. Arrow on the string, he gazed to his left. "You see it?" he said softly. He pointed with his head. "In the tall drift. An animal. Perhaps a wolf—"

She smelled it then. It was not a wolf. The great red-brown bear rose suddenly out of the snowbank, its amber eyes glaring. Standing on its hind legs, it roared, a deafening, awesome sound. Finle's mare screamed, rearing in terror, and Finle's arrow went wide.

Sunflower's muscles bunched. Hawk leaped from her back, as the yellow horse bounded away, reins trailing.

"Shoot it!" Finle shouted, fighting the bay mare as she danced and curvetted and tried to run. Rapid hoofbeats, coming fast, drummed over the ground behind her.

The bear dropped to all fours. Head lowered, weaving slightly, it stared dangerously at Hawk. Finle shouted at her again, urging her to kill. Out of the corner of her eye she could see the riders of the war band forming a wide circle about them. The archers had their arrows poised. Fur stood up like hedgehog quills on the great bear's humped back. It crouched, ears back.

She called, "In the Mother's name, don't shoot!"

Dragon's deep voice said, "No one will shoot."

He was at her left elbow. "Tell them to keep back." She heard him give the orders. "Bear," she said. "Don't worry, my friend, we'll free you from this." The bear regarded her fixedly. There was no sign of human sapience in the flat, feral, yellow stare.

Gently she touched the defended mind; felt fury, fear, and a vast confusion.

The dragon-lord said softly, "This is a friend of yours, I take it?"

"Yes. His true name is Ogier Inisson. But no one calls him that. He is Bear. He is friend to me and to Wolf Dahranni." Again she touched Bear's mind. She encountered bone-deep torpor, the fatigue of a beast hunted nearly to death. She reached beyond the miasma of fear and anger into human memory. *A fire in darkness, a flash of gold, the feel of coins in a palm, a woman's musky scent, the welcome warmth of bare skin against bare skin, the tangy taste of wine on the tongue . . .*

Bear, she said silently, *come back. You are with friends. Come back.*

A crimson mist seemed to float across the sunshine. The big bear became a bronze-haired, bearded man. He took a step, and folded full length on his face in the soft snow.

Kneeling, Hawk rolled him over and slid her hands beneath his shirt and jerkin, looking for blood. She touched his face. It was warm, but not hot. He was not wounded, not feverish. His eyes were closed. He mumbled, and moved one hirsute hand. Karadur knelt beside her. "He was the bear whose tracks Marek saw," he said slowly. "And also the man?"

"Yes. We traveled together from Ujo, he and I. But he goes his own way; he always has. I would not leave Wolf and Thea unburied. I asked him to wait for me, but he would not. He is very stubborn."

"He has pursued us all this time?"

"No, my lord. He went ahead of us. He crossed the mountains before we did."

"You should have told me this before we left the Keep." The words were mild enough. But beneath them the dragon temper smoldered. She waited, kneeling in snow, while sweat trickled down her sides and from her scalp. Finally she felt his anger dissipate. "Can you wake him?"

"I can try."

She laid her palm over Bear's heart. His thought was a jumble of sense and images: *a swirl of fetid grey fog, a red-eyed wolf crouched to spring, a corrosive whispering voice that burned like acid, a golden dragon . . .* She felt him wake, then. "Ungh!" His yellow eyes opened. She jumped back, as he surged to his feet in a great ursine rush. "Hawk?" He swayed, big-knuckled hands opening and closing on nothing. Then his shoulders lifted; she saw him take in the encircling riders, and, silent beside her, the big man in the dark cloak.

He drew a deep lungful of air. "Gods, I'm hungry."

*   *   *

Karadur ordered a halt. They camped in the open, beside a huge weathered stone. The dragon-lord touched nothingness to flame, and Bear devoured three half-cooked mule steaks and drank a skinful of red wine with the air of a man who had not eaten for days. "I do not know when last I had a meal," he explained apologetically. "I remember a day and night in which I ate nothing. I *think* I remember. I was almost wholly bear, then."

"Tell us what happened to you," Karadur said. There were six of them at the fire: Hawk, Bear, Macallan, Lorimir, the dragon-lord, and Azil Aumson. Sentries prowled the camp's perimeter.

"It was the mist." Bear lifted his hands, looked at them, laid them again in his lap. "I lost my stick," he added sadly. "It must have fallen into the snow."

"The mist," Hawk prompted.

"Yes. I had heard stories of it, but I have heard many stories, and I have seen some sorcery—" He hesitated. "Tricks and fripperies, most of it. So I walked into the mist, cursing its stink, but unafraid, only a little troubled, for it was thick, and I thought that in the murk I might miss a step, and tumble into a crevasse. I kept my stick in front of me." He mimed a man stabbing at the snow with a pole.

Karadur said, "What did you see in the mist?"

"Lights, and shadows. Bizarre faces; illusions. I saw a scaly, fanged beast, but I swung at it with my stick, and it disappeared, so I knew it was not real. Once I saw my mother's face, as I knew it when I was a child. She has been dead over ten years . . ." He wiped the matted tangle of his beard. "Then the beast returned, and attacked me. It smelled foul, like something long dead."

"Warg," said Azil Aumson softly.

"I suppose. I changed, and we fought. It was a long fight. Peculiar. It clawed me, and I did not feel it, and the gashes it gave me did not bleed. And the beast, too, did not seem to feel its wounds, and it had many. At last I grappled with it, and broke its back. The body blew away in the mist. So I knew that it had been an illusion, though it had sounded and smelt and felt real. The killing seemed to make the mist angry. It muttered and hissed at me, in a language I could not understand. You know how it is in dreams? Someone speaks a language you do not know, and you almost understand it. It was like that. I continued north and east—"

Lorimir interrupted. "How did you know?"

"Know what?"

"Your direction. Hunters have told of wandering in circles in the mist for hours, even days."

Bear smiled a little. "I always know where the sun is." He reached for the wine, and drank. "Then the wolf appeared. I thought at first it was Wolf, alive again, as in a dream. It looked like Wolf, and it even smelled like him, a little. But its eyes were mad, and red, as the warg's eyes had been red. It challenged me, crouching and growling. I fought it, too. Fighting the wolf was like fighting the warg, except that the battle went on much longer. I grew tired, but the wolf did not. But at last I broke its back. And as the wolf faded it grew to look more and more like my friend, until at the end it seemed wholly so, and it wrung my heart. That made me very angry at the mist, and I cursed at it, and clawed at it as if I could make *it* bleed. I walked for hours. It was still day, but night was coming. The mist muttered and grumbled at me, in that language I was almost able to understand. I tried to change, and realized that I had forgotten how. No, not forgotten; it was as if the way to change was in that other language, the one the mist was speaking, and I could not understand it." He glanced at Hawk. "I should have stopped, then. But I did not. Then the dragon came." Lorimir exclaimed softly. "It towered over me, three times my height. Its eyes were red, too. It glowed, like a star. It was gold, and breathed fire. It bellowed at me, a sound so thunderous I thought the mist would freeze and crack open like a shell. The dragon sprang at me like a great cat, with splayed curved claws, and so I fought it. I tore at its soft belly with my teeth and claws. I swiped at its head as it stooped, and blinded it. It tried to bite me, and I evaded its jaws, and finally I leaped upon it, and wound my arms about its huge head, and forced it back, and bit its throat, and its blood ran into my mouth. Its blood was honey-sweet, and hot. And it died.

"I was wholly animal, then. The mist voices taunted me, and I bit and clawed it. I walked northeast, but with no sense of purpose, other than to escape the mist. When at last I came out from it, it was dawn, and I was trapped in an evil wind. I dug a hole in a snowbank, and stayed there, with snow piling over me, and slept. When I woke, I was starved, and my mind was filled with the taste of blood, and the lust to kill." His heavy face was drawn. "I did not know that I was more than an animal. Had you not found me, I might be bear still."

For a little while, no one spoke.

Hawk said quietly, "I tried to find you. You did not hear me?"

"I heard the voices of the mist, and my own heartbeat." Bear looked doubtfully at his hands. "I feel odd, without my staff. I feel as if a piece of me was left behind, in the mist." He nodded toward the men and horses spread across the snow. "This is a fine little army you have here. With so many, men, horses, mules, how did *you* avoid the mist?"

"We burned it," Karadur said. "It does not like fire."

"Ah. I will remember that. I shall be more wary of wizards' tricks in the future." Bear shook his massive shoulders loose. "I owe you a debt for my rescue, my lord."

"You were Wolf's friend," the dragon-lord said. "I count no debt." For a moment, his eyes gleamed humor. "Besides, my soldiers nearly shot you."

"But they did not. And in recompense I have eaten your steaks. You are generous."

"I have reason to be so. My enemy obviously fears you, or he would not have expended himself so to trap you."

"Where do you go now?" Lorimir asked.

"To that ugly black castle we see in the distance. It appears impregnable, but I suspect that is illusion, like the illusions in the mist. When I reach it, I will hunt a wizard, and when I find him, I will do my very best to kill him. Unless you and your fine little army are before me."

Karadur said, "We will be pleased to have you travel with us. You know our direction: it is the same as your own. You are welcome to share our food, and our fire. We may even be able to find a stick to your liking."

"Join your army?" Bear lifted his brows. The small hairs stirred along the back of Hawk's neck. "Our direction may be the same, my lord. But I am not certain that we share a common goal. Wolf Dahranni was dearer to me than my own brother."

Be careful, my friend, Hawk thought at Bear, *Oh, be careful.* She could not tell if he heard her.

Karadur said, "I do not doubt it." For a moment, the dragon-lord met Bear's eyes directly, without restraint. Hawk, watching, saw Bear's face tighten at the touch of flame. "You knew him many years. He lived in my domain under four years. We met three times."

He rose. A hot breeze swirled for a moment along the cold ground, and ground fog rose suddenly from the snow-covered earth. The fire winked out. Karadur strode swiftly away, Lorimir beside him. Macallan and Azil Aumson followed, more slowly.

All that day, the war band rode across seemingly endless ice toward the castle. It loomed before them, clothed in illusion, immense, hostile. The indifferent sun moved lazily across a sapphire sky. Behind the lines of soldiers, behind the rearguard, came Bear. Just before sunset, they halted. The odor of meat bubbling in the cook-pots spread among the tents. Hawk ate a hasty meal, and then prowled to the edge of the camp, where Irok and Olav stood sentry.

"Have you seen any sign of my friend?" she asked.

"I smell woodsmoke in the west," the northern hunter said.

Hawk gazed westward, calling on her changeling sight. She saw a flickering light that might be a fire, and a hunched shadow that might be a seated man.

Irok said softly, "He should not be out there. Is not safe."

"Why? What have you seen?"

"Seen nothing. Heard nothing. But he should not be alone."

She metamorphosed: human form to hawk. The air shimmered, like moonlight seen through smoke. The west wind danced under her wing-feathers. She flung herself across the distance. Bear sat on a rock, a skewer of meat, rabbit, perhaps, in one huge hand.

"I thought you might like company," she said. And then she stepped forward. His face was drawn, made old with an expression of hopelessness and despair that she had never thought to see it wear . . . "Bear, what is it? What has happened?"

His voice was almost indifferent as he answered. "I cannot change."

Hawk laid a hand on his arm. She could feel his dread through his skin; it shocked her. She had never known him to panic. "You are tired. That's all it is. You need rest, and a sleep with no dreams to crowd you."

He gazed at her blankly. She was not sure he saw her. "No." He dug one hand into a pocket, pulled out a figure carved in red-gold amber. He held it out to her. The little bear was chill as a corpse, and mottled with an eerie serpentine darkness. "It is enspelled," he said quietly. "Or I am. I cannot tell."

They did not speak after that. She sat with him while the fire burned. At last he lay down. She rolled into her cloak, her knife, as always in enemy country, under her hand. They lay back to back, sharing warmth. After a while his breathing deepened. When she was sure that he slept, Hawk rose, and changed, and made her solitary flight back to the war band.

17

IN THE MORNING, the black castle seemed to fill the eastern horizon.

The war band spread out across the snow in two great wings. With outriders on the flanks, they rode steadily toward the castle. The day was warm; the tall towers seemed to float in a mist. After a little while, a rumor traveled along the lines: the castle had changed. It looked farther away, and since that was patently impossible, that meant that it was smaller.

"It's shrinking," Huw said in wonder. He pushed his furred hood back. "Maybe it'll shrink to nothing. Maybe it's not there at all."

"Baby," Orm said. "It's there. It's showing us its true size, that's all."

But the sense of malice and threat emanating from the castle did not shrink. Men fingered weapons and looked warily left and right, and even over their shoulders, as if expecting to see fell, magical beasts tracking them across the tundra.

Suddenly, on the right ride of the line, a scout yipped, then shouted. Three of them converged. In a moment, Sandor came racing toward the head of the line. He looked extremely happy.

"My lord, we found a man! Jon spotted him crouched beside a rock."

"Bring him to me," Karadur said.

The scouts herded their find in front of Karadur's horse. His leather armor was shabby and patched. His tattered black surcoat was torn along one shoulder, where a badge might once have been sewn. The scouts had taken his sword. The short blade was notched and rust-spotted.

At the sight of Karadur on his tall black horse, he fell to his knees.

Karadur glanced at Azil, riding as usual at his left hand. "Do you know him?" Azil shook his head. "Get up, man," Karadur said. A scout prodded the sprawling fugitive to his feet. He wore a small stained pack on his back. "Tell me, have you seen this banner before?" The man cringed. He had a thin face, fringed by a straggly blond beard. "I see that you have. If you lie, I will know, and my men will cut your hands off, and we will leave you to the wolves. Tell me your name."

"S-Sori."

"Where do you come from? Who is your lord?"

"I—I have no lord. I come from Coll's Ridge."

Karadur nodded. "I know it. It lies northeast of Chingura. The tor's shaped like an arrowhead, and there's a river near it, the Windle." The fugitive's jaw dropped. "It is mine. I know my land, even the piece that Reo Unamira holds for me. You were not born there, though."

"No. I was born in Kameni."

"I thought so. Were you outlawed?" The thin man did not answer. Rogys leaned the point of his spear against the soldier's scrawny throat. "Answer."

"Yes! Yes."

"For what were you outlawed?"

"I hit a man, and took his purse."

"Did he die?" Sori nodded. "So you are a murderer and a thief. Just the sort of man that Reo Unamira finds useful. You are Reo Unamira's man now, are you not? What brought you so far from Coll's Ridge?"

"Gold," the man said sullenly. "I was promised payment in gold."

"Payment for what?"

"Service, to the lord of the black castle."

"And did you get your gold?"

"Yes. But I gave it to Gog at the little gate, that he might let me through, and not betray me." The aggrieved whine in his voice might almost have been funny. But no one smiled.

"How did you learn of the black castle?"

Sori looked blank. "Nittri Parducci, Nittri the Ear. He told me."

"And what did Reo Unamira think of your desire to change masters? Did he give you leave to go? Or did you neglect to ask him?" The outlaw shrugged. "I see. Who is lord of the black castle?"

"Koriuji."

"Who is Koriuji? What does he look like?"

Sori said, "Koriuji is not a *he*. Koriuji is an *it*. Koriuji is a monster." The horror in his voice was unfeigned. "A white worm, with a human face."

Karadur looked at Azil. The maimed man shook his head slightly. The dragon-lord said, "You have seen this monster with your own eyes? Does it speak?"

"Assuredly I have seen it. It speaks to Gorthas, may he rot in hell."

"So you know Gorthas," said Karadur. "What is he to Koriuji?"

"Gorthas is Koriuji's captain." The man shuddered. "They are both monsters."

"When did you come to the castle? How long ago?"

"Seven months. Since September last."

"How many soldiers defend that castle?"

"When I came, there were fifty. But now there are under twenty in the garrison. Some have died, and of the rest— most chose to run."

"Like you. How many horses?"

"None. They break their legs against their tethers rather than serve the monster."

"Wise beasts. How many wargs?"

"Three, now, and Gorthas. There were more before."

Lorimir leaned forward. "Why did the soldiers leave? Why did *you* leave? You said you were paid."

Sori licked his lips. "I was paid. But, that place—from here it looks strong, but from within it is all dust and darkness. It is always cold. The air smells like mud. The walls reek of misery, and of hatreds, old, old hatreds . . ." He hugged himself with both skinny arms. "I wish to gods I had never seen it."

There was a small silence. Karadur said, "Has the worm other creatures that serve it?"

"Just the white bear. Gorthas released it four nights ago. It gallops in circles around the castle, and howls at the sun like a mad thing."

Karadur looked at Azil Aumson. The singer shook his head. "I know of no white bear."

The dragon-lord said, "Listen to me, Sori. I am looking for a man. He would be about my height, fair as I am, yellow-haired, with a white scar along one cheekbone. He would wear fine clothes, silks, furs, jeweled rings. Have you seen such a man within the black castle?"

"No."

"You are certain?" The man nodded.

Olav kneed his horse to Karadur's side. "My lord, my ax is thirsty. This man is a thief and murderer. Let me kill him." He glared at the hapless captive.

Sori fell to his knees. "Please, my lord, let me go. I mean you no harm. I want only to be gone from this hideous place. If you release me I will go south, where no man knows me, and you will never hear word of me again. I swear it." His whining voice firmed with a sudden, desperate courage.

Karadur said thoughtfully, "I agree, he is a knave. But he cannot hurt us." He turned back to the deserter. "Take off your boots."

"My boots?" The scrawny man looked horrified. "Merciful lord, if you take my boots, my feet will freeze! I'll die!"

"Then die." Four men bore the scrawny soldier to the ground. With distaste, Rogys yanked his boots off. "Give him his sword, and let him run." Finle flung Sori's sword spinning. The thin man scrambled for it, arms and legs milling like a spider's.

They rode onwards. "What do you think?" Karadur asked Lorimir.

Lorimir raked a hand through his beard. "It is good to know he has so few men, and that the castle is weaker than it looks. If it is truly undefended, it will be easy to take." He hesitated, then said, in a lowered tone, "Of course, it may be a trick. I know you would recognize a lie, if a man were to tell it—but what if he truly did not know he was lying? The castle might be stronger than he knows. He might have been permitted to escape, in hopes that he would cross our path."

Karadur said, "It is possible."

At noon, they stopped to eat and care for the horses. The scouts had found a wonder, a rare sight: a copse of green spruce trees. Bent and twisted though they were, their color and scent in the bleak, barren landscape were achingly dear and familiar.

Hawk, sitting with the archers, was unsurprised to see Derry coming for her. She followed him. Karadur stood at the perimeter of the camp.

"I need your eyes again, hunter," he said. "I need you to see what waits for us between here and the black castle. Can you do that?"

With steady, powerful strokes, she drove upward, and then hung, wings spread, letting the high warm wind hold her in its palm. Below her the company, small as insects, moved over the snow.

She circled higher, and soared east, toward the black castle. From this height she could see its true size. It was large, but no larger than Kalni Leminin's big red palace. It seemed oddly empty. Such an edifice required servants and soldiers, but she saw no living thing about the fortress, except two sentries, one on the battlement, the other at the gate, and four stubby-legged dogs, who ran in a tireless, ground-eating trot toward the war band.

Dropping lower, she saw that they were not dogs, but wargs. A malevolent whisper rasped against her mind. *Cousin, I come. It will be pleasant to make your acquaintance. Tell your master . . .* She hissed with a hawk's fierce rage.

When she landed, Karadur was waiting for her. "Well?" he said.

"Wargs, my lord. Four of them, coming this way."

Karadur ranged his army to meet them in a half-circle, with himself and his officers on foot in the center, and the archers on the wings. The wargs were fanged, snouted, and small-eyed like pigs, and they stank. They halted, just outside the range of a thrown spear. Three of them crouched into the snow. The fourth jogged a few feet more toward the war band, and stopped.

Then there were not four wargs, but three wargs and a hairless, grinning man, with a face like a skull, and red glowing eyes. He bore a long pole, on which flew a white flag, the flag of truce, the herald's flag. He wore a black cloak over black armor, and the device on it was a white spiral on a black field. The wargs settled onto their scaly bellies, like dogs waiting for a master.

His bow toward Karadur was a mockery of courtesy. "Karadur Atani, lord of Dragon Keep! I am Gorthas, herald of the Black Citadel. Welcome to my master's country." His voice rasped like metal over rock. "Ah, I see a friend among the dour faces! Azil, prince of thieves and traitors. I am glad you did not die on the ice. You afforded me much entertainment. I look forward to renewing our acquaintance. I have much still to teach you about pain."

He grinned horribly. The watching men stirred. Hands tightened hard on weapons.

Karadur said flatly, "My warriors want very badly to kill you, monster. Tell me why they should not."

Gorthas chuckled. "Oh, assuredly they should not. Not until they, and you, have seen what fine toys I carry. First, this." He drew his sword from its sheath. "A Chuyo blade, in a fine leather sheath. Does anyone know it?"

There was a small stir in the ranks. Then Rogys said, "I know it. It was Wolf Dahranni's blade."

"Good, good." The envoy brought something glittery and small into the light. "There is this, also. Pretty thing it is."

Hawk said, "That is Wolf's talisman."

Gorthas peered at her. "Ah, there you are, cousin!" He tossed the silver chain and its pendant into the air, caught it, and tucked it away. "This toy is mine now, since its wearer has no need of it. And lastly—" He reached inside the black cloak and withdrew what appeared to be soiled scraps of blue cloth. He pitched them to the snow. "You may find these interesting, my lord Dragon."

"Rogys," Karadur said, "bring them to me."

Dismounting, Rogys stepped slowly from his place at Karadur's back. Stiffly he knelt to gather up the bits of cloth. Karadur took them on his palms.

"A child's shirt," said Gorthas gleefully. "A child's pants, lovingly woven and sewn by his dear departed mother. A little wolfling's clothes. Perhaps someone here knows them."

"I know them," the dragon-lord said. "Why do you have them?"

"As evidence, my lord Dragon. The little wolfling, unlike his parents, is not dead. He is in Mitligund, in the castle of Koriuji. He is cold, and frightened and hungry. My master has no fondness for children. But he will survive—for a while. How long is entirely your choice." Gorthas's hideous voice was soft with delighted malice. "My master has known for months that you planned to attack him this spring. If you wish the child to live, he says, you will halt this invasion. If you refuse, the boy will die in slow torment, as prolonged and agonizing as can be contrived. I leave it to your imagination to consider how."

The soldiers stirred, horror and raw repugnance on their faces. But Karadur's impassive gaze did not waver. He said, "Why should I hold the life of one child so dear as to agree to that? You and your beasts have entered my domain and murdered my people."

Gorthas shrugged. "Like yourselves, my lord, we are hunters. Your men hunt moose and elk and deer over the steppe; why should my wargs and I not enjoy such privileges in your domain? My master grieves that you begrudge my companions and myself our forays."

Karadur said, "My men and I hunt for food."

"Or pleasure. Or to keep sharp your weapon skills. My wargs do not eat, but I do. Come, this is wasting time. What say you, my lord? Children can be so easily hurt. Does the babe live, or die? It is your choice." He folded his arms. The men, except for Finle, watched Karadur.

The dragon-lord sat as if he had been turned to stone. Finally he said, softly, "Lorimir. My lord?"

"You knew him well. Tell me: what would my father do now, were he in my place? Would he turn tail, and ride home?"

Uncharacteristically, the captain hesitated. Then he said, "My lord, were he here, your father the Black Dragon would utterly reject this commerce. He would burn that castle and everything in it, including the child's bones, to bare white ash."

For a moment, caught in a common dream, they all saw it. *Wings spread wide, floating like a giant leaf, the great*

*black dragon stooped low over the gleaming castle. White
fire, relentless and searing as the wind from the sun, streamed
from his open mouth. Black towers blazed like new-lit
torches. Stone walls crisped and curled like paper . . .*

Even Gorthas saw it. His crimson eyes lost their triumphant glitter.

Karadur nodded. Pitching his voice so that all his men
could hear, he said, "Monster, I will not dishonor the dead.
Nor will I turn back. Instead, I will make a compact with
your master.

"I challenge him, or his champion if he so prefers, to single combat: a battle to the death. If I win, the child he has
taken captive will be released to me unharmed, and you
and your wargs will forever cease to hunt in my land.

"If I lose, your master takes my castle and my domain for
his own."

Lorimir said, under his breath, "Dear gods. My lord—
what—" Karadur waved him silent. The soldiers looked at
one another.

Gorthas said smoothly, "It's an interesting proposition,
my lord Dragon. Where and when do you suggest this fight
occur, and with what weapons?"

Karadur shrugged. "As I am challenger, that is your master's choice."

"I see." The warg-changeling yawned. "I will convey
your proposal to my master."

"No." Karadur signaled as he spoke. On a single indrawn
breath, the archers of the company laid arrow to bowstring.
"You will accept or reject it, now."

Gorthas stiffened. He said, voice rasping like a rusty file,
"If you kill me now, you doom the wolfling to a miserable
death."

"I will grieve to the depths of my soul," said the dragon-
lord. "But you will be dead, and your master soon after."

"You cannot kill my master."

"I think I can."

"You know nothing. You think he is a sorcerer, a little apprentice wizard, whom you once knew." Gorthas's voice hissed with malevolence. "He is darkness and destruction. He is the devourer of light, the emperor of despair. Warriors and princes and wizards bow before him. His name rings through centuries. You will learn it, before you die."

Despite themselves, the listening soldiers responded with a roar of disbelief and defiance. The wargs roused, snarling. When the clamor ended, Karadur said, "You speak well for your master. Will he save you, do you think, from my archers' arrows? Do we have a bargain? Or do you and your wargs die?"

Gorthas snarled. "I tell you, I cannot—"

Karadur said, "Archers, spare the monster. But kill the wargs."

Bowstrings hummed in deadly concert. The three wargs yowled, and convulsed, each with ten trefoil-barbed arrows embedded in it. A terrible stench, of rot and decay and corruption, came from the corpses. Gorthas crouched, frozen. The staff in his hand trembled with impotent rage.

"Monster, you may live, or not. Speak now. Do we have a bargain? Yes or no."

"Yes!" The word was a bestial howl.

Leaning forward, Karadur said searingly, "If, when I arrive, the boy has been harmed, I will burn the castle, and everything in it, down to its very heart. Monster, you are dismissed."

For a moment, nothing happened. Then grey smoke stained the day. Gorthas the man vanished. A solitary warg clashed its jaws together, and raced over the snow.

18

After dinner, when the camp was still, Hawk went first to speak to Murgain, and then to Karadur's tent. Rogys stood sentry before the entrance. "Ask him if he will see me," she said.

The tent was bright with candles, and, after the crowding of her own tent, seemed spacious: it held two pallets, and a brazier for warmth, a stool, and a wooden chest.

Azil Aumson sat cross-legged on the second pallet, his face in shadow. Karadur sat on the stool. He was holding a bound book.

"My lord, forgive me for disturbing you. I have a request."

"You are not disturbing me." He set the book down and swung to face her. She felt the link between them tighten. Muscles moved fluidly beneath his shirt. His skin gleamed like polished metal in the light. "What is it?"

"My lord, I have been—*listening*—for my friend Bear all afternoon and evening. I have not been able to find him. I wish to leave the camp to search for him, and, when I find him, I would like your permission to tell him what has happened today."

"You have left camp before without my permission, hunter." She did not answer. "Very well. Go, and tell your friend the Bear what you think he needs to know. And tell him, too, that my offer to him is still open."

"I will, my lord. Thank you."

Karadur let the book drop open again. Then he said, "Hunter. What do the men say about what happened today?"

She had thought he might ask. "My lord, they are happy to have killed the wargs. They are angry on behalf of the child. They would like to storm the castle, especially since they believe it is unprotected. But they trust your judgment, and they believe, with all their hearts, that you would never place your domain at risk. They believe you cannot be beaten."

She saw the two men exchange glances. "Any man can be beaten," the dragon-lord said dryly. "Thank you. Go. Safe journey."

She stepped from the tent. The night was clouded, but the camp was as usual ringed by torches; their glow would guide her back. She changed, and spiraled into the night, plunging upwards in a sudden hunger to be free of everything except wind and sky and the smell of the earth. She flew for a time, until her heart eased.

Then, cautiously, she opened her mind and called her friend's name. He might hear her, and answer. He might hear her and not respond. With a spell-sickness on him, his perceptions might be dulled: he might not hear:

Bear, she called. *Don't hide from me.* She repeated it, stretching her thought to its limit. But she could not feel him. She flew in circles, lower and lower, looking for the spark of his fire to the west of the war band's camp. Once she thought she saw it, and arrowed downwards, but it was nothing, a star glinting off the ice . . . Finally she gave up. She climbed steadily upward, hunting for a thermal, a rising wind on which to stretch her wings and ride, but the wind had changed; it blew fitfully, coming now from the west, now from the east. The camp was *there:* eastward across the steppe. Laboriously she beat her way toward it, cursing the refractory winds.

After a long, long time, she knew that she was lost.

Her wings felt sticky. She could not see the ground. The stars swung in unfamiliar circles. They made patterns, the patterns had names, but she could not remember the names, nor why she needed to know them. She was flying through a thick close fog: it had drifted slowly around her, tendril by tendril, but now it was everywhere, coating her feathers with foul ash. It was the mist. Summoning her strength, she beat furiously against it, forcing herself above it; but it slowed her, and dragged her down, tangling her in subtle, confusing strands.

Then she struck the ground. Because she was in hawk form, and therefore light-boned, the fall did not kill her. But it drove the sense from her mind and the breath from her lungs. When at last consciousness returned, she opened her eyes to find herself in human form. Brightness seared her vision: the flames of a torch, held near her head. Her hands were bound behind her back.

A rasping voice snapped an order, and the man holding the torch retreated. Then a grinning hairless man bent over her, where she lay on her side in the snow. "Well met, cousin." He kicked her in the ribs. It hurt. "Get her up."

Human hands closed urgently round her arms and jerked her swaying to her feet. Her head ached. She smelled human fear. She pulled against the thick ropes on her wrists, but the knots were taut and secure. Her weapons—bow, knife—were gone. Her vision blurred, then steadied. She counted five men, and Gorthas. He wore Wolf's sword at his belt. He smelled of dead things.

He held his hand out, showing her the silver hair-clip with the arched hawk-wings. "Is this what you miss, archer?"

She would not acknowledge his victory. "I was looking for my knife."

He hit her in the face. It rocked her head back, and

blurred her vision again. "Don't talk," he said. "You speak only by permission."

She waited until she could see again, and then said, "You asked me a question."

He hit her again, with his fist. Agony drummed through her skull, and the strength went out of her legs. She sagged. The silent men kept her standing. The fear-smell was theirs.

Gorthas waited until she could hear him, and then said genially, "I will hit you if you speak again. Do you know where you are?" He gestured. The man with the torch lifted it so that she could see. Before her, the earth was pitted and torn as if monster talons had clawed it. Beyond the savaged ground rose a great square darkness: the Black Citadel. A frosty breeze blew from its open gate. "Bring her in. And douse that torch, you fool!"

They made her walk. Head pounding, she stumbled through a maze of icy hallways. She tried to map them but her aching mind could not hold the patterns; they slid from her. Suddenly they halted. Gorthas pushed her to her knees. Winding his hand in her hair, he forced her head up. She saw an icy chair, elaborate as a throne. On it coiled a monstrous white worm. A human head topped its glistening body. The face seemed young—and then something shifted, and it looked old, a hundred years old. Horribly, impossibly, the pallid features seemed familiar.

A small boy, clothed in rags, crouched beside the chair. He had a collar around his neck; it appeared to be attached to a chain. He had Wolf's narrow face, and Thea's hazel eyes.

"Hello, Shem," she said, forcing the words through her body's weakness. "Do you remember me?"

Gorthas hit her. The child did not look at her: he watched Gorthas. The worm swayed toward her. "Ssso," the inhuman throat hissed, "my missst has netted a bird. You thought it burned, didn't you? Fools. My mist is not destroyed so easily. What shall we do with her, warg? Shall we kill her now? Not yet, eh? Too quick. She must sssuffer. They mussst all sssuffer." Dark, mad eyes probed gleefully into hers. This was the mind whose malice she had touched in flight, the mind which had tortured Azil the singer, which still tormented him.

"Warg! You have the talisman?" Gorthas opened his hand. The worm bent its grotesque head, opened its human mouth in a way no human jaw could move, and swallowed the clip. "Mine, now. Your power is mine, little hawk. What shall we take first, warg? Her handss? Her eyess? Yesss, but not yet. Break her arm, warg. Just one."

Hawk struggled, but they threw her easily to the ground and spread her right arm across the ice. Gorthas lifted a club, and slammed it down across her upper arm, and a second time below her elbow. She felt the bones shatter. Two men hauled her up, and walked her through a labyrinth, to a sunless chamber filled with empty cages. Gorthas pointed to a tall, narrow cage. The soldiers opened the door and flung her in.

Her numb right arm dangled uselessly; she could feel it swelling. Nausea rocked her: she retched. Dazed with pain, she lost her balance, fell against the icy bars. Gorthas laughed. "Don't struggle, little bird. A pretty cage for a broken bird. Does your wing hurt? Don't worry. You will cease to feel it, soon."

☙ ☙ ☙

AZIL AUMSON WAS dreaming.

He knew that he was dreaming, but the knowledge did not help: he was trapped. In his dream he watched a man stumble through knee-high snow. It was night, and cold. Somewhere a child was crying, a high, wretched, sobbing sound. Shadows snapped at the running man's heels: red-eyed shadows, wargs, three, no, four of them, grinning as they herded their hapless, gasping prey in ever smaller circles. The face of the running man was his own. He fell. His leg snapped on a rock. Painfully, without hope, he began to crawl.

Run, little traitor, hissed a soft, malevolent, familiar voice. *You cannot escape, you can never escape. Your mind is mine* . . . He came from sleep screaming. Someone's greater weight was restraining him, hands on his shoulders. He blinked upward, into shadow, and a glint of gold.

Karadur said, "You were making a noise."

He lifted his hands, and moved lightly to the other side of the tent. Azil sat up. His head ached. "Sorry. Bad dreams." The tent was cold: the wood in the brazier long since burned to ash. A fat fist of a candle threw light across the small enclosure.

Derry slept at the foot of his lord's pallet, snoring lustily, his whole head tucked beneath his quilt. "Derry." Karadur nudged the sleeping page with the toe of one boot. "Breakfast. Get up."

"My lord?" Derry rose sleepily from his blankets. "Oh. I'm sorry, my lord." Yawning, he knuckled his eyes. Azil swung his legs to the floor. He felt drained, as if he had not slept.

A second candle near the washbasin ignited with a sputter. Shadows bloomed across the tent walls. Azil fumbled for his boots. Slowly, clumsily, he worked the stiff lacings through the metal eyelets. Within their leather sheathing, his hands hurt: a steady, angry burning, like hot iron in flesh. "When did you last take those gloves off?" Karadur asked.

"I don't remember."

"Do it now."

"They're fine, my lord."

"*Do it.*" Breathing hard, Azil forced the thick gloves from his fingers. "Are they festered? Show me."

Azil extended his hands. The red scars were crusty with dried blood.

Karadur swore. Striding to pitcher and basin, he filled the basin and brought it to the pallet. "Put your hands in the water." Cold as snow, the water numbed the pain. "Where's the jar of ointment Macallan gave you? Derry, find me that jar." Derry rooted in his pack.

"I have it, my lord."

"Give it to me. Azil, let me see your right hand." Azil obeyed. With gentle ruthlessness, Karadur worked the cooling ointment into the wounds of each twisted hand.

The burning eased. "Better?"

"Yes."

"Derry, go get us some breakfast," the dragon-lord said, over his shoulder.

Derry ducked from the tent. Azil's heart hammered. Karadur put both hands delicately on either side of his face a moment. His palms were warm as summer.

"My lord," Derry called from outside the tent, "Captain Murgain would speak with you."

The dragon-lord lifted his hands, and moved back, until there was a clear space between them. "Murgain, come in."

The archery master entered. He had lost weight on this journey: his tunic hung loosely on his belly. "My lord, I have what I think is bad news." There was a flicker of fear in his eyes. "Hawk of Ujo is not with us. I know you let her leave the camp last night, to seek her friend. She has not returned. The men are troubled. So am I."

"Tell them not to be concerned. It is probable that she met her friend the Bear, and is traveling with him. I gave her permission to do so."

Murgain's face lightened. "Ah. I did not know that, my lord." He left the tent.

After a moment, Azil said, "Do you think he believed you?" It had taken him that moment to bring his breath under control.

"It doesn't matter, as long as he can persuade his archers that it's true." Karadur picked up his sword from its place beside his pallet. "It may even be true." He balanced the long sword on his palms.

He said, "The morning Tenjiro took my talisman, he said to me that he did not think he could kill me. Whatever he sends against me—whatever illusion or monster of wizardry he conjures up—I believe I can defeat it."

"So does the army," Azil said. "So do I."

"But it may be that we are all wrong. If we are—if Tenjiro's champion kills me—whatever ensues, you will not fall again into his hands. I have given orders—" Karadur halted, and looked up.

Azil said peacefully, "I have my knife."

"You might not have the chance to use it. So I thought."

"Finle?" Azil said.

Karadur nodded. "I will withdraw the order, if you wish."

Azil reached for his gloves. "No," he said. "Let it stand."

☙ ☙ ☙

THE MIST OF the day before had vanished; the day was bright and almost warm. They rode in their usual loose formation, scouts fanning out ahead and to the sides, swordsmen in the middle, archers at the sides and rearguard. Ahead of them the castle's dimensions had entirely diminished to a normal size. They would reach it by nightfall. The horses, even the usually stolid geldings, caught the fey mood. They pranced like colts under the pale blue sky.

Raudri said, "My lord, look." He pointed south.

"What is it?" Lorimir muttered, squinting into the sun.

"A bird," said Herugin. "A big one."

Karadur said, "A hawk?"

"I think not." Herugin lifted both hands to shade his eyes. "I think—it's an eagle, a white eagle. What is it doing so far from the mountains?" As he spoke, the great bird came steadily nearer. It soared above them, graceful wings spread wide, its talons curled deceptively beneath its body. Its feathers were so white as to seem iridescent.

Karadur said, "You cannot tell from here, but there is

another mountain range, far north of us, taller than our own. This land lies in a great valley between them. I have seen it in maps." He gazed with a curious hunger at the great eagle.

A few miles from the castle, the ground changed: it was riddled with rents and pits, flanked by piles of slag. The riders picked their way carefully through the patternless rubble. A scout—it was Finle—shouted, and waved. The men halted. Karadur and Lorimir rode forward to investigate.

Wordlessly, Finle pointed downward. At the bottom of a ditch sprawled the half-eaten body of a man. All about it, in the scarred earth, and in the white powdery snow that lay over the scars like netting on a woman's hair, were huge splayed tracks.

"Those are bear tracks," Lorimir said. His horse, scenting bear, or else the corpse, tossed its head and tried to retreat. He held it with a heavy hand. "Easy, now. What a horror."

Finle said, "The mined ground ends where Irok is standing." He pointed forward, to where the small archer sat on his horse. "After that all is level again."

"Any sign from the castle?" Lorimir asked.

"Sir, they don't even seem to know we're here."

The captain gazed at the castle. "My lord, I don't like this," he said to Karadur. "We are too close to the walls, and this ground is treacherous. They may be plotting an ambush. We should camp in a field of our choosing, not his."

"Do what you wish."

Lorimir lifted his voice. "Company, attention! We fall back. Four-hour watches. If you see a white bear, kill it. Herugin! As many sentries as you think necessary to guard the horse lines and the supplies."

"Captain," said Finle. He jerked a thumb toward the sky. "Look at that."

A massive cloud was bubbling out of the northeastern sky. It was grey-green at the edges, and black at the center. Lorimir shouted, "Light fires, big fires. It will be dark soon."

He lowered his voice. "Gods. That's one hell of a storm. How the hell did it blow up so quickly?" Like a monstrous claw, the cloud groped for the sun.

"Maybe it's not a storm," Karadur said quietly. "Maybe it is simply—darkness."

The ominous cloud blew inescapably toward them. Within an hour, the leading edge of the cloud was overhead. Lightning blazed randomly through its roiling core; it smelled wet and brassy, like a rain cloud, but no rain fell from it, not a single drop. There was no thunder.

Karadur sat motionless beside the fire, gaze fixed on the dancing flames.

Lorimir said, "It looks like a tempest over the Kameni plains."

Macallan said hopefully, "Perhaps it's an illusion."

"No," said Herugin and Lorimir together. The younger man had come in briefly from the horse lines to eat and get warm. "No," Lorimir said. "I don't believe it."

Slowly the immense cloud covered them, thick as night, swallowing the sun. Derry yawned and yawned, jaws cracking. "Boy," Lorimir said, "get yourself a blanket, and go find a place to sleep. You'll have us falling on our faces in a minute. And you," he said to Herugin, who was pacing round the fire, "you're making me dizzy. Go back to the lines."

Herugin grinned bleakly, and obeyed. Murgain limped out of the dark, glanced at the dragon-lord's set, withdrawn face, and made his report to Lorimir. At last Karadur shifted, and loosened his shoulders. His face was drawn with weariness.

Azil handed him a cup of hot wine. "What were you doing?"

"Listening."

At that moment, silent as the distant lightning, the white eagle dropped from the sky.

Karadur leaped to his feet. The fire roared upwards: a

pillar of fire blazed into the night. The eagle vanished. In its place stood a silver-haired woman holding a black staff. Lorimir drew his sword and leveled it at her breast. She smiled. A bright green vine twined along Lorimir's sword blade. A violet-blue trumpet-flower bloomed impossibly at its tip. A sweet fragrance wafted from the blossom.

"Let your sword drop, Lorimir Ness," she said. "I am not your enemy."

Lorimir opened his unnerved hand. The sword fell to the earth. The woman picked it up, brushed the pliant vine from the steel, and handed it to him. She wore a man's leather breeches, and a scarlet cloak lined with fur over a silvery tunic. Her feet were bare. She nodded to Karadur. "Good evening, my lord Dragon."

"Who are you?" Karadur said.

The woman said, "I am a mage." Her eyes blazed like green lamps in her weathered bronze face. "Some call me the Last Mage."

"What is your name?"

"You know my name, my lord," the woman said tranquilly. "It is inscribed on your heart. I assure you, my lord, I am not from the black castle. I find the place as loathsome as you do; perhaps more so, since I know more of its past, and of the being that inhabits it. I have traveled over great distances to help you, from Ippa all the way to Nalantira Island, and back to this place. Do you know your enemy's true name, and nature? I do. It is not what you think. Will it please you to sit, and hear me? I mean you only good."

"My lord—" Lorimir began, and stopped. Karadur had lifted a hand. The blazing, burning column sank to its bed. Far above their heads, the vast dark cloud spat lightning.

"I will hear," Karadur said.

19

"ONCE, IN A far gone time, there lived a man. His given and family names are lost, but we know that he came from that part of Ryoka that we call Kameni, and that he was blessed with a strong spirit and a keen and flexible intelligence."

It was the oddest occurrence of the ride, so far; stranger even than the sudden appearance of the Bear: not the apparition of the mage, but the effortlessness with which she drew and held their attention.

"At the time of this story, magic thrived in Kameni. Throw a stone, hit a sorcerer, the saying went. And as it happened, this man was a sorcerer, celebrated throughout Kameni for his spell-working. But in his heart, the sorcerer was dissatisfied with the incantations and illusions of sorcery. He desired more than enchantment and artifice: he desired to be a mage."

Karadur said, "A mage is greater than a sorcerer?"

"The province of sorcery, fundamentally, is spell-working. Most spell-working is trickery, fantasy, illusion." The mage scooped up a pebble, and threw it into the fire. A red rose bloomed within the fiery amber heart. Leaning forward, she reached into the flames, plucked the rose, and handed it to Karadur. As his fingers closed on the thorny stem, the flower dissolved into thousands of tiny ruby fragments. Like scarlet sand grains, they ran glittering from his hands.

"A spell can be countered, can be changed, or undone. Magery is knowledge. The first true knowing a mage is granted, whether he wants it or not, is the knowledge of the place and time and manner of his own death." The pleasant voice remained composed. She might have been describing the weather. "Some cannot endure this learning: they leave all magery behind, and exhaust life running from their own deaths. Some turn magic inside out, searching frantically through their arts for the means to avoid it.

"This man was one of those. There are spells that can extend life. He found them. There are spells to guard and to protect against injury and illness: he used them to render himself invulnerable. Death and its workings became the center of his attention. And as his attention constricted, so also shrank the nature of the man, until nothing remained of him but hunger and terror: hunger for life and terror of his own death."

"Because bodies die, he discarded his. Because lovers and friends and kinsmen die, he abandoned human ties. The manipulation of death became his instrument. Evil men employed him for their own designs. He took their money, did their bidding, and outlived them. He seduced lesser magicians to him, and devoured them. As his knowledge grew, it pleased him to use it to frighten and torment, until he had divested himself of all human qualities, save those nourished by darkness. He became known as Ankoku, the Hollow One, the Dark Mage." Karadur stirred. "You know the name, my lord?"

"I have read it."

"Then you know, perhaps, what happened next. The great wizards of Ryoka cried, Enough. They brought their own magic against Ankoku's foul spells." She paused, a hand to her throat. "Forgive me," she said huskily. "I am not used to long speech."

Rising from the fire, Azil walked toward the nearest circle of men. He mimed drinking. They shoved a wineskin into his gloved hands. He brought it to the fire, and offered it to her.

"Thank you," the mage said. She drank, and gave it back to him.

"Ankoku built a stronghold in the north. He called it the Black Citadel. Historians name this struggle the Mage Wars, but that miscalls them, makes them sound as if the combatants all were sorcerers and magicians. But it was not so. Battles raged over the northern plains. Men and women fought in these battles, and died, and rose again. The green fields of Kameni became a battleground for wraiths." The fire flared. The mage spoke softly to it. It turned white, green, blue, amber, and for an instant, black.

"At last, putting forth all strength, the magi broke the Dark Mage's power. He was defeated, and captured. But his might was such that his conquerors, though they had beaten him, could not destroy him. They brought him to the Hill of Anor, in Kameni. Once it was the center of the great city, and home to kings. Later, it became known as the Place of Stones. On its crown, in a time so lost to us that we cannot name it, the ancients erected a great henge. The stones are broken now, or hidden under the earth, but in Ankoku's day they stood, tall and silent, and a deep magic flowed through them.

"The magi set the Empty One within that circle, and made spells far beyond the province of ordinary magic. They built a prison, not of stone walls, but of enchantment, a magic so complex and so powerful that nothing would ever counter or change or undo it."

Karadur said, "Then the Dark Mage still lives?"

"He does. He has no human body, no eyes, no ears, no tongue. But he survives, and even imprisoned as he is, and bodiless, he is capable of terrible mischief. But to make it, he must be summoned, by one who knows the Calling Spells, and has the will to say them, and to pay the price."

"What is the price?" Karadur asked.

"Enslavement. Emptiness. Death."

Lorimir said, "Why would any man or woman choose to do that?"

"A good question, Captain. But few who call Ankoku know what waits for them. The mages died, you see, all but one, and with them died their memories." The mage's voice was soft and sad. "And even if they did know, most would not turn aside from what he offers them."

"Which is?" the dragon-lord said.

"Power," the silver-haired woman answered. "Wealth beyond their dreams, mastery of magic, even immortality. It is a lie, of course. But they do not know that."

Azil said, "But—the mages died. How did those who call Ankoku learn what to say?"

"Knowledge is never destroyed. And there is a place in Ryoka where all is remembered. Your brother Tenjiro, my lord"—she nodded at the dragon-lord—"came to that place, one still summer day. Turgos, its guardian and keeper, saw him and knew him. A *neat lad, glittery as a sunflower*. He came seeking power; not the power already in him, but a greater gift, which he did not have, and had no right to. He did not find it.

"But he found its shadow."

"Is he dead?" Karadur asked.

"No. He is *changed*. He is no longer Tenjiro Atani: he is Koriuji, the Winter Worm. He woke Ankoku from his sleep, and now he himself has become Ankoku, the Empty One, who must devour others to live. Ask your friend, my lord. He knows."

Karadur said, "*Why?* There are men who would sell their children for what he was born to: grace, wealth, nobility . . ." The mage did not answer. The dragon-lord took a long breath. Like an actor donning a mask, the terrible control returned to his face.

He said, "Who is Gorthas? Do you know?"

"Gorthas is a warg-changeling. Once he was human, a fearsome warrior, and Ankoku's most trusted captain. Long ago he pledged himself wholly into the Dark Mage's service. Like the wargs and the Citadel itself, he lives when his master calls him."

"Can he die? I have promised myself his death."

The mage said, "He can be killed. I do not know if he can die."

A deep vibration, like the tremble of a mountain before it falls, boomed from the clouds. Lightning slashed across the sky; thunder broke over the suddenly unsettled camp like a wave tumbling toward shore. Horses bugled in terror; voices shouted from the horse lines. Rising, Lorimir raised his strong voice above the clamor. "Rogys, go help Herugin with the horses. Orm, Irok, Finle, Lurri, keep your eyes on the black castle! You others, raise the tents, quickly!" Lorimir turned. "With your permission, my lord—"

"Go," Karadur said, not looking at him. Lorimir strode into the darkness. A man's shirt fluttered by them, flung by the driven wind. They heard the stutter of hoofbeats: a panicked mule cantered past them, tether trailing. Two men on horseback followed it.

Karadur lifted his head. "And my brother?" he asked harshly. "Can he die?"

"I do not know," said the mage gently. "But whatever he has done to you, pity him, if you can, my lord. His fate is terrible. Ankoku has consumed him. He is bound to the darkness. And in the end, Ankoku will betray him."

The dragon-lord said, "He killed my people. He threatens my land. I cannot pity him." A wind, hot and dry as the

Nakase khamsin, swirled over the barren ground. A feral incandescence began to play beneath Karadur's skin. "I believe I know your name, mage."

"Do you, my lord?" She rose, facing him as if she faced a judgment.

"I believe you are Senmet of Mako, who killed my father. Tell me I am mistaken."

"No, my lord. You are not mistaken." She leaned heavily on her staff. "Shall I tell you how it was? Kojiro Atani, the Black Dragon . . . I had never seen anything quite so beautiful. A running horse or a soaring eagle or a dolphin leaping from the sea is beautiful, until you see a dragon in flight. His scales were obsidian. A brilliant scarlet crest adorned the arch of his head. His wings were wide as a field. His fire was white, not blue, or yellow, or red, as is earth's fire: it was white, and hot as the fire that burns at the core of a star. That is what dragonfire is.

"He soared across forests, and scorched them with his white breath, and they burned; he flew over the river, and breathed fire upon it, and it hissed away into steam. Barges burned, and docks, and bridges fell apart like toys made of twigs. People on the bridges tumbled into the rising steam, and screamed as they died.

"I made a storm, thunder, lightning, rain, hail. I hoped it might drive him away. But the Black Dragon roared—and there is no sound on earth like a dragon's roar—and soared through the storm, and when lightning struck near him, he opened his jaws and swallowed it.

"I made an illusion of a second dragon, a brilliant golden-scaled dragon, and sent it into the sky, hoping that it would distract the Black Dragon from the city. But the Black Dragon roared again. Every window, bowl, and mirror in the city cracked. He breathed upon the golden dragon, and it shriveled into silver lace. Fiery rain fell upon the buildings. They burned.

"So I extended thought, as magicians are taught to do. I touched the dragon's mind. I showed Kojiro Atani the blazing buildings, and the river rising into steam, and people, all the people, dying. He faltered in flight, and in confusion and remorse, he changed.

"He fell from a great height, into fire."

"So that was why they never found his body," Karadur said. The fire beneath his skin was fading. He rose, and faced the mage. "I hunted for you for two years, all the time I was in Mako. I wanted to kill you. Finally I was informed that you were dead."

She raised silvered eyebrows. "Who told you so?"

"Erin diMako."

She shook her head. "If he said so, then he lied. But I do not think Erin diMako would lie to you, my lord. I do not think he could. What exactly did you ask him, and what did he say?"

"I asked him what had become of Senmet of Mako. He said only another wizard could truly say what had happened to you. He said, *There are no wizards in Mako.*"

"Ah." Her wide mouth quirked. "It was truth, if not all the truth. For years I traveled dazed and silent through city streets, begging food from passersby, sleeping in gardens and stables and in the doorway of a brothel. I did not know my name, nor even that I had once been a wizard."

Pure astonishment moved across Karadur's face. "Gods. Why?"

"It is no light thing," Senmet said softly, "to destroy a dragon. I was within Kojiro Atani's mind when he fell."

Thunder cracked overhead, impossibly loud. The air smelled of heated iron. "What woke you?" the dragon-lord asked.

"Ankoku." A violet rose bloomed at the tip of the mage's staff. It blackened, and the petals turned to ash and blew away in the wind. "The mind of the Empty One, moving across my city. He brought me from sleep."

"I wonder that you dared to come here," Karadur said.

Senmet bowed her head briefly. "The Dark One chose this arena, not I. But"—she looked up, and smiled, and mischief flickered in her emerald eyes—"did you not hear me say that the first true knowing a mage is granted is the knowledge of the place and time and manner of her own death? I know when and how I am to die, my lord Dragon, and it is not here, and not now, and not at your hands."

A horse barreled toward them. It slowed; Edruyn dropped from its back nearly into the fire.

"My lord, the gate has opened. Gorthas and six soldiers are coming this way, across the mined lands, under truce flag. My lord, the child is with him."

"Find Lorimir and tell him. Raudri!" Karadur's voice rolled over the camp. "Sound the Assembly." He turned to Senmet. "Wizard, can you do anything about this racket? Or is simple weather-working beneath the dignity of mages?"

Senmet pointed her staff at the black, growling sky. The thunder muted. The dense, dark clouds began to slowly draw away from one another. Raudri blew the trumpet. The soldiers dashed for the horse lines.

Mail gleaming, dragon pennant rippling in the wind, the company assembled in crescent formation. Archers sat with arrows taut against their bowstrings. The triple-barbed tips glittered.

Gorthas came steadily onward across the mined land. Six unkempt and sullen armored men marched at his back. One held a torch. A second carried the flag of truce.

Beside and a little behind Gorthas trotted a barefoot, nearly naked, very dirty child. He wore a broad, stiff leather collar around his neck, with a chain clipped to it.

"Come, Shem," said Gorthas, and snapped the chain.

He moved forward. The child followed. "Sit, Shem," Gorthas said, and snapped the chain again. Shem stumbled, glanced at him, and crouched, doglike, on the cold ground.

20

"MY LORD DRAGON." Gorthas sketched a jaunty bow. "My master sends you greetings." The changeling jerked the chain. "As you see, I have brought the little wolfling with me. Shem, stand!"

The little boy rose, his vacant face turned toward Gorthas. Beneath his scanty rags, he was trembling with cold.

"He is unhurt: eyes, ears, tongue, arms and legs present and undamaged. He has learned to stand, to sit, and heel, and to keep silence unless given leave to speak. My master believes that speech is a privilege, and that children should be silent in the presence of their elders. Shem, sit." The child obeyed.

Karadur did not speak, but his eyes were burning. The soldiers slouching at Gorthas's back shifted uneasily under that formidable gaze.

A watery shaft of light pierced the dense grey clouds. It glinted off mail and fittings and harness buckles, and touched the mage's hair to shining white. Gorthas's eyes narrowed. "Is your land so bare of fighting men, that you needs ask your old women to fight for you, my lord Dragon?"

Karadur said, "She is not your business, monster."

The changeling bristled. "I am Koriuji's captain; all that moves within my master's territory is my business. Who are you, old one?" His voice rasped with contempt. "Some senile hedge-witch, traveling with the army to mix simples?" Senmet leaned silently on her staff. Her weathered face was thoughtful, and a little sad.

Gorthas made a dismissive gesture. "I smell magery upon her. But all the mages of Ryoka could not destroy my master. My lord Dragon, my master directs me to say to you: he accepts your offer to fight his champion. He agrees to your terms. If you win, the child is yours, and my wargs and I will find other prey. If my master's champion wins, your castle, your domain, and your men are my master's." *And mine*, said his eyes. "The battle will take place tomorrow, at dawn, in the field in front of the Black Castle. As for weapons"—he paused—"my master will allow you what weapons you have brought with you, no others. Sword, knife, spear. No ax, halberd, mace, or morgenstern."

"I will need my horse," Karadur said. "I am a cavalry officer."

"Very well. My master agrees to that. Shem, stand!" The child stood slowly, too slowly to please his tormentor. Gorthas cuffed him. The boy staggered. A sigh like an indrawn breath went through the ranks of the soldiers. Finle, at the end of the line, silently lifted his bow.

Gorthas said genially, "Children must be disciplined." He spat in the dirt, and grinned like a skull. "Alas, he is frail. I anticipate little sport from him—later. Would you like him now?"

"You would release him?"

"I would exchange him."

"For what?"

"For my friend, your traitor, Azil." Gorthas's foul voice bubbled with joyful malice. "It would be a fair exchange, my lord. I cannot imagine he is much use to you. Consider, before you refuse. The boy is trained: he can fetch your wine, and clean your boots, warm your bed. The man is broken. You have his body, but his mind and soul are my master's. You can smell it on him, the lovely stink of darkness. Even his nightmares are not his own."

A hot wind blew across the frozen ground. Karadur said, "You speak riddles, monster."

Gorthas put his hands on his hips. "You wish me to be plain?" He raised his voice. "Azil Aumson is Koriuji's spy, my lord. Whatever he sees, my master sees. Whatever he knows, my master knows. The dreams are the channel; the dreams are the way by which my master knows his mind, and through his, your own. For this purpose he was returned to you. I perceive you doubt me. It is known that the Dragon of Chingura can see a lie in a man's mind. Do you see it in mine?" His voice rang challenge. Karadur did not reply. "Were he my servant, I would flay him, and hang him living in the noon sun over a slow fire. But since you choose to keep him, I will prepare that delight for my little puppy, my wolfling. Come, Shem!"

He turned crisply. Shem trotted at his heels. His escort split to let him lead, and then closed behind him. The iron gate rose; from within the castle, a horn brayed, a mockery of sound.

Karadur's face looked as if it had been cut from flint. He said to the mage, "I have heard that such a thing was possible. I did not know it could be done without the dreamer's knowledge."

"If it can be done, the Empty One could do it, and would. He delights in betrayal."

Karadur turned toward Azil. The singer's face was bloodless. He set his shoulders, as a man might brace himself to receive the force of a powerful wind. The dragon-lord said, his voice curiously gentle, "Captain Lorimir. Azil Aumson is to be disarmed, and kept under light guard until I am free to consider this charge."

"It shall be done, my lord." Lorimir gave quiet orders. Olav and Irok guided their horses to bracket Azil's roan between them. Sliding one hand within his cloak, the singer brought out a small sheathed knife. He extended it, not looking, to Olav.

✤   ✤   ✤

THEY CLEARED A tent for him and furnished it roughly with a stool and a pallet. Lorimir set guards about the tent. Olav brought him food, and wine. He drank the wine. He was not afraid, not really, but the pain in his heart made it hard to eat.

Lorimir came in twice. The second time, he brought a candle.

"Are you comfortable?" the captain asked.

Azil shrugged. He was not particularly comfortable: it was dark in the tent. *Traitor, little traitor. I have your mind in my hand. You will never be free.* The bitter, monotonous words raced through his head like the refrain of a song.

Lorimir said, "Do you need anything? Are you cold?" Azil looked at the candle. "I will leave it for you."

"Thank you," Azil said.

As the captain left the tent, he turned not toward his own tent but toward the dragon standard. Lurri stood guard beside it. "Ask Dragon if he'll see me," Lorimir said. Lurri ducked his head into the tent, murmured, and then held the flap wide.

Derry, brush in one hand, cloth in the other, was cleaning a helmet. Karadur, on his pallet, held a naked longsword across his knees. He had unpegged the hilt. Firelight gleamed like water along the tempered, polished steel.

"My lord," Lorimir said. Derry set the helmet aside and brought Lorimir a cup of wine. "Thank you. My lord, may we be private?"

Karadur said, "Derry, go." Seizing his cloak, the page exited the tent. The dragon-lord fit the sword hilt back on its tang. The heavy cavalry sword was meant to be swung two-handed, but Karadur handled it as though it had the weight of a much slighter weapon. He reached for the rosin ball. "Well?"

Lorimir said, "My lord, Azil Aumson is secure, as you commanded."

The dragon-lord's face was in shadow. He tapped the powder ball down one and the other side of the blade. "Did he say anything to you?"

"He thanked me for a candle."

Karadur picked up the cleaning cloth. His hand moved steadily along the sword-blade. After a while he said pensively, "You are my counselor as well as my captain. You heard the charge. You tell me. Was it treason?"

"Was it true?" the captain asked.

"It was true."

Lorimir raked fingers through his beard. Finally he said, "I am no scholar, my lord. That is a question for magistrates to argue. I can tell you: every man, woman, and child in your realm knows that Azil Aumson would cut his own heart out with a rusty knife rather than do you hurt."

"Rogys disobeyed my order, and left his post to follow the war band. I know as well as you that it was love for me, not fear of battle, that moved him. Should I have left him unpunished?"

"It is a different case," Lorimir said. "Rogys is young, strong, well able to endure a night in the open. Azil is not."

"I know very well what he is," Karadur said evenly. He oiled the blade, and, reaching for the black sheath, slid the longsword home. *Feed me*, it said in a lethal whisper. After a moment he said, "I also know what my father would have done, if a man of his had betrayed the secrets of his councils to his enemy."

"Do you?" said Lorimir. "What?"

"He would have had his soldiers bring that man to the Keep. He would have ordered the bones in the man's arms and legs and pelvis broken, publicly, and decreed that he be chained by his neck to a stake in the Keep's courtyard, and left, unsheltered, without food, without water, to suffer and starve and slowly die."

Lorimir nodded. "It is possible he would have done that." He moved a candle stub from the stool, and sat. "My lord, I am a soldier. My calling is war, not law or justice. But if you will hear me, I have a story to tell you."

"A story?" The blue eyes flicked to his face.

"It is a story I have never told to anyone else, my lord, nor ever would." Lorimir kept his voice at a measured pace. "For six months during the years she was your father's wife, your mother Hana and I were lovers."

There was a long silence. Karadur brought the sheathed longsword across his knees. "Go on," the dragon-lord said.

"I will tell you how it was. We traveled from Nakase, from her father's hall. She was sixteen, and lonely. I was twenty-four, and leader of the escort. It was my first command. Nain Diamori had charged me to bring his daughter safely to Ippa, and I would gladly have died in her service — for honor, and because I thought she was beautiful. We rode together, over the long miles, and she confided in me: she told me how frightened she was, of the journey, and of her husband-to-be. She even feared the mountains. *There is not enough green in this place,* she said. *Will they let me have a garden, Loren?*

"We came to Atani Castle, and she married the Black Dragon. You know what he was. He was dragon, and he had a dragon's temper. He was never cruel to Hana, but there was only a little tenderness in him, and he did not dispense it freely. So Hana turned to me, and I, idiot that I was, gave her what she needed: tenderness. It was difficult for us to meet; she was surrounded by women, and I had guard duties. But we managed, somehow. I suppose it was a kind of madness. It was summer. We met in the old buttery by the abandoned well, and we told each other each time we met that this would be the last time. We knew if Kojiro Atani ever learned that his wife was cuckolding him with one of his guards, the best either of us could hope for would be a quick death."

His throat was dry. He found the wine, weak as it was, and filled his cup. "That first winter, Durach Muire, the swordmaster, fell ill. Dragon named me as his lieutenant. I barely saw her then: my duties doubled. In late spring a band of Isojai came over the western canyons, over the ancient Wall, and attacked western Issho. Rako Talvela asked Pohja Leminin, Kalni Leminin's father, for aid, and the old man called on us to fight.

"I was wounded in that campaign. It was a sword-stick in the shoulder, no great hurt, but I caught a fever, and ended up flat on my back. Old Durach was still sick. Jon Ivarson of Chingura took my command, and I fretted, fighting weakness, until Lirith—you remember Lirith—threatened to tie me to the bed. Your mother came and sat with me. She had cool hands, and her clothes smelled of lavender.

"When at last I was well enough to walk, she walked with me, in the kitchen garden, and into the fields, and to the old stone well. And whatever those stones saw, they told no one.

"Finally my shoulder healed, and I went back to my duties.

"Then Hana discovered that she was pregnant. She feared—it was just possible—she feared the child was mine. She begged me to leave. But I could not leave her to face that fear alone. And I knew that if the child, once born, was recognized as mine, there was no place in Ryoka to which I could escape. The Dragon of Chingura would find me. So I did not leave.

"And you and your brother were born, and Hana died.

"I thought then, in my grief, *I can go home. Nothing holds me here.* But I had sworn an oath to your father. So I stayed. I did my work. And after a while I met a girl. She lived in Chingura; her name was Miranda. I did not marry her, but we suited each other well enough without that . . ."

Karadur said, "I remember her. She died of lung-fever, while I was in Mako."

"Yes. But she was well then, and gentle-hearted, and her smile reminded me of Hana's, and so I stayed.

"In January, on a cold morning, the year you were four, your father summoned me to his chamber. I polished my boots and weapons, and went to him. He told his page to leave, and invited me to sit, and himself poured wine. He told me he intended to name me swordmaster in Durach's stead, for the old man had continued sick, and it was clear that he would not recover enough to resume even the lightest of his duties. He asked me if I would do it.

"I said I would. He asked me if I missed my home. I said I had once, but that I had made Ippa my home, and had no wish to leave it."

"He said, *I know it was hard for you to travel so far, to serve so severe a master. I honor your courage.*

"I thought: It was not you I came to serve. But I said, and it was true: *My lord, you have only been generous to me.*

"He smiled then, like the shimmer of light on a sword as it springs from the sheath. I felt that smile into my very bones. He had never looked at me that way before. And I realized that he knew that Hana and I had loved each other, and that we had betrayed him. Perhaps he had known all along. Perhaps he had just that moment taken the truth from my mind.

"But he said nothing, only held me with his eyes. I sat trembling.

"Then he said, *And so I will continue to be. But you must promise me a thing, Lorimir Ness. You must swear to serve my sons when I die.*

"I made that promise. I could not do otherwise. Within seven months he was dead. I wondered later if he had had some foreknowledge of his death. He could have killed me: he was my lord, and I had betrayed his trust, and broken my oath. But he only smiled like a sword, and dismissed me."

Lorimir's face was wet; he wiped it with a gloved hand, glad that after all these years he could still weep for Hana. "Excuse me, my lord," he said, rising. Without waiting to be dismissed, he stepped from the tent.

✣ ✣ ✣

Within the fastness of the Citadel, Hawk leaned against the bars of her prison, and waited for the dawn.

She was uncertain how long she had been there. There was no natural light in the room, only the flickering wer-light; it, and the pain from her head and arm, confounded her senses. Her broken arm throbbed painfully. From shoulder to elbow it was swollen and hot. She had tried to fashion a sling from her cloak, so that at least it did not dangle, but had not been able to manage it. She had heard Karadur's mind, searching for her through the storm: but the poisonous miasma of spite that filled every cranny of the Citadel would not allow her to answer him. She had half-slept, and dreamed, hideous tormenting dreams, from which she had awakened sick and shaking. Some time ago a skinny man in rags, probably a slave, had brought her a cup filled with water, and a hunk of dry brown bread. She forced herself to eat it.

"Is it day or night?" she asked him.

He shrugged, and opened his mouth to show the mutilated stump of his tongue.

"Did Gorthas do that?" she asked. "There's an army outside this castle. Gorthas will be dead soon." He looked at her with disbelieving eyes, and then backed from her as if her words were dangerous. The wer-light made her head ache. She shielded her eyes from it. For a moment desperation threatened to overwhelm her. She could not change. *She could not change.*

Methodically she felt along the icy bars with her good hand, from where they joined the frozen ground to as high as she could reach. They seemed solid. She kicked at the place she had seen the cage door open, but the blows had no effect, and the jar against her injured arm made her head spin. She yearned for a pry bar, even a stout stick.

An image rose in her thought: Bear. She saw him, hairy, huge, vengeful, crouched in the shelter of a jagged stone, watching the castle. Truth or illusion? She did not know.

Bear, I am here, she sent into the waning night . . . *I am here. Come and find me.* He did not answer. Wolf would have answered; Wolf would have heard her. But Bear had not heard, could not hear her, and Wolf was dead. She leaned against the bars, fighting hopelessness.

From a pain-filled drowse she heard the tramp of boots, and jerked awake.

Gorthas leered outside the cage. "Good morning, cousin," he said.

The door opened, and three men dragged her out. She elbowed one in the throat and kicked another in the knee, tumbling him cursing to the floor, but then they had her. Gorthas's hideous face gleamed with an evil joy. One of the men was smiling too, but the others moved like automatons as they half-carried, half-dragged her to the chamber with the throne.

The worm swayed in the strange half-light. Shem lay curled on a filthy blanket at the foot of the icy chair. Gorthas said, "My lord, I have brought the changeling as you commanded."

"Excellent," the serpent said. "Resstrain her." Its features seemed to shift and change: from someone young, fair-skinned, with pale blue eyes, to someone else, something else, something barely human, and old, horribly old.

The men looped coils of rope around her legs and arms and chest and tied her to a pillar. She smelled smoke.

"Ssso," the worm hissed. "Do you fear pain, little bird?" She saw the brazier heaped with coals, and the heating skewers. "You cannot escape. Do not think your commander will rescue you. He believes you are a traitor. He believes that you deserted him, as his friend Azil, his dear, treacherous friend, deserted him."

Rancor dripped like acid against the walls of her mind. The worm threw its protean head back, hissing with grotesque laughter.

"Bear," it said, "Bear, come and find me. Your friend Bear cannot hear you, little bird. He lies in the sssnow, bleeding, with an arrow in his gutsss."

"You lie," Hawk said.

"How do you know?" said the worm. "You cannot know. Your power is gone, little bird. I ate it." It yawned, showing her its crimson gullet. "Do it," it said to Gorthas.

Gorthas picked up a pair of gloves. "My lord, shall I take both eyes?"

"No," the worm said. It arched over her. "Not yet. Take just one. Do it ssslowly."

"Hold her head," Gorthas said to the soldiers. They wound their hands in her hair and slammed her head back against the pillar. Gorthas twirled a skewer in the coals, then lifted it. Hawk felt the heat on her cheek. She struggled savagely to turn her head, to rip her own hair out by its roots. The men only gripped more tightly.

"Scream, cousin," Gorthas rasped. "They say it helps, if you scream."

The blunt, glowing point, a piercing spark of agony, teased her right eyelid, and withdrew. And again. And again.

Her mind was screaming, but she would not scream.

She did not scream, as the red-hot skewer seared bit by slow bit through her eyelid and into her eye.

21

BEFORE DAWN, BEAR Inisson stood in a hollow against the western wall of the castle.

A narrow wooden door barred his way inside. The lock housing was broken, and the upper hinge was loose. The wall which from a distance had appeared so massive was flimsy as a wooden fence. Friable as sandstone, it crumbled under his hands.

On the other side of the door, a man was standing guard. Bear had heard his footsteps, and then his snores. No sentries walked the battlements. Ravens roosting on the towers slept, heads tucked under wings. Far aloft, at an unimaginable distance, the stars wrought intricate designs across the face of night.

Bear scraped the sharpened tip of his cudgel softly, rhythmically, over the door planks. The snores stopped. Bear waited. The door opened. Bear waited. It opened wider. Moving into the door's mouth, the man peered into the boundless darkness. Mercilessly, Bear rammed the butt of the cudgel into the guard's chest and just as ruthlessly into his face. He doubled soundlessly to the ground. Stepping inside, Bear closed the useless door. The passageway was barely tall enough for his head. A sickly greenish light made a patchwork lattice along the rough cold walls.

Somewhere a man's voice grumbled, but the words bounced off the walls, so distorted that he could not tell from where they came, or even how many men were speaking. Rage drove through him like lust. He hated them. He wanted to hunt them, to surprise them and kill them, one after the other. But he had come for the wizard. Gripping his cudgel, Bear glided in a predator's soundless stalk along the narrow, fetid corridor.

Behind him, the guard, eyes bulging, lay strangling on his own blood.

☥   ☥   ☥

THE WAR BAND roused before dawn.

Azil sat solitary in his tent. The candle had long since burned out: the enclosure was chill and lightless. The camp woke. Horses whickered; sledges hissed and bumped along the frozen ground. Swords rattled in their sheaths. He smelled woodsmoke, and the excrement of horse and mule and men, and his own stink.

His fingers ached; they were locked with cramp. He closed and opened them until they worked. He had sat all night in his clothes. He had not dreamed; but then, he had not slept.

Olav and Irok came to get him. Olav helped him with his boots. They brought him water with which to wash, and escorted him to the latrine. The sky was pearl-grey, like the inside of a shell. A quicksilver line of light trembled on the eastern horizon. He noted, with detached amusement, who among the men he passed looked at him, and who would not, and what their faces said. As he returned to the center of the camp, he heard the beat of wings. A white shape wheeled overhead. He wondered if the mage had spent the night in eagle-shape, and if so, where she had slept. There were no trees, no cliffs to roost upon. But a mage could take any form. She could have been a stone, or fire, or the wind itself.

"I would like some light," he said. They brought him a candle, and then, though he not asked for it, a brazier. He stood over the heat. Then he heard the step he had been waiting for, and a deep voice, and turned. The tent flap parted. The candle flared.

Karadur had bound his hair with a gold cord. His sword hung down his back. He was wearing a chain-mail shirt; the steel rings glittered beneath his dark cloak.

"I dismissed the guards," he said. "You are free to go where you wish." He held something out. Instinctively Azil took it.

It was his knife.

His throat was dry as dust. Now when he most needed it, his voice had deserted him. "Thank you," he managed. He slid the knife into his shirt. And then, because some things had to be said, he asked, "Am I to be punished?"

"For dreaming?" said the dragon-lord. He moved nearer the light, and Azil could see, by the deep grooves in his face, that Karadur had not slept either. He wondered if any-one had.

Four steps separated them. Only four steps.

Lorimir Ness spoke from the other side of the tent. "My lord, it's almost time."

"A moment," the dragon-lord said. He took one step forward. The candlelight fell fully on his face. "Azil. I never asked you. I may not have a chance to, later. You knew, years ago, how much my brother hated me. *Why did you agree to help him?*"

Azil said, "He told me that you were in danger. He said"—it was amazingly difficult to say the words—"that be-fore you took the form you should sire children, to safe-guard the line."

Astonishingly, he saw the dragon-lord's brief half-smile. "Yes. He told me that, too. He was probably right. Was there more?"

He did not want to say it. But it would be dawn soon; the army was waiting. The thing in the castle, the consumed, degraded being that had been Tenjiro Atani, might win the coming battle. They might never speak again.

He answered, through the thunder of his own heartbeat, "Tenjiro said that you would change. That once you took the form, you would change so much that I would not know you, nor you me. He said you might go mad, like the Black Dragon; that you might fly into the sun, like the dragon-king Lyr. I believed him."

The dragon-lord bowed his head. Then he said levelly, "Had I known you were alive, I would have come to find you." The candle flared, lighting his face. There were tears on his cheeks. "He said to me, when he left: *I will punish him for you. I will care for him with the exact tenderness that you have used toward me.* I thought you were dead."

Azil said, "I knew that."

"I would know you from the heart of the sun. I would know you even if I were mad. I will know you always, whatever form I wear. I swear it."

"My lord," Lorimir called again.

Understanding, like a breaking wave, swept suddenly across Karadur's face. "Your hands—it was Tenjiro who crippled them. Not Gorthas." Azil nodded. "He wanted to destroy your music. Why would he do that?"

"I think—revenge. He so wanted me to speak to him—to beg, to ask for mercy. I would not."

"Not at all?"

"I did not speak for three years. It was all I could do."

"Tell me."

He could not tell the story standing. He sat, and locked his hands together, so they would not shake. "The second time I escaped from Mitligund, I was very weak. I didn't get very far from the castle. The wargs found me, and held me, until men came from the castle, and dragged me inside.

"Gorthas was waiting for me. This time he did not beat me. Instead, he told me he would blind me. He described how an eyeball sizzles and melts when hot iron bores into it. The men tied me to a pillar, and brought a brazier, and iron skewers. He heated them in front of me, until they were red-hot.

"Then Tenjiro came, and stopped it. He said I was a fool; if I were to enter your domain you would hunt me like an animal. He said he would show me what Dragon's justice was like. He went away, and came back with the black box. Your talisman lay in it; it was unchanged, brilliant, hot as a star. I thought it would be dulled, but it was not. He told Gorthas to free my hands, and ordered me to lift it from the box. I tried not to obey. My hands moved anyway. It burned. He would not permit me to lose consciousness. He made me hold the band in both hands, until it seared flesh to bone, and then ate the bone. Ultimately I could not grip it, or anything. Gorthas put me back in the cage."

Outside the tent, the men were waiting. Derry stood in front of Karadur's tent. He hugged a beaked helmet of gilded, polished steel. The side guards of the helmet were fashioned to resemble wings. Rogys led the black gelding to his master's side. Smoke wore thick leather pads at chest and cheeks. His harness had been burnished till it shone. The men assembled as they had the day before, in crescent formation, officers in the center. Karadur brought Smoke to face them.

"Well, companions, we have come a long way together." Soft as the words seemed, they carried easily to the second line. "It is no small feat, to have crossed the ice from Dragon Keep to Mitligund in five days, against the will of a wizard. Never will it be said that the warriors of Dragon's country arrived late to a battle . . ."

"Now comes the harder task. I know I have your swords." A dry twig skittered under Smoke's hooves; he shied. Karadur's gloved hands tightened on the reins. "Give me your heart's pledge, that you will honor the covenant you heard me make. You must stand, and watch me fight, and not interfere, unless and until your captains otherwise instruct you." He glanced at Lorimir. "Do I have your promise?"

They did not shout, or pound their shields. They nodded, and gripped the hilts of their swords. "Raudri, sound the Advance." He turned Smoke's head toward the light. Raudri, beside Lorimir, blew a light trill on the horn, and raised the dragon banner. In slow procession they crossed the torn, pitted land. The eagle soared above them. As they rode, the sky changed from pale grey to violet to mauve. The riders formed a half-circle facing the Citadel's iron gate. Karadur took his helmet from Derry, and held it on his saddlebow. Raudri blew the Challenge.

The great gate groaned as it lifted. Gorthas sauntered forward. Shem, collared and chained, crouched at his heel. Six men stood at his back. One bore a pennant: the white spiral on a black field. Gorthas wore armor, and his cloak showed the same device.

"You are punctual, my lord. My master bids you welcome once again. He regrets that it will be necessary for you to die here." He scanned the line of silent men. "I have a message for your company. My master bids me say: if any of you would live, lay down your arms, here, now, and kneel at his feet. He is merciful, he will spare your lives — except for the little traitor, Azil. He is *mine*." The sky turned ivory-white. No one moved. Karadur lifted the helmet, and settled it on his head. A cloud of ravens rose screeching from the battlements. Sunlight brushed the Citadel's spires.

A massive shape rose over the castle's roof. Sable wings unfurled like silken sails. The underside of the wings glittered in the morning sun. Horned and fanged head arched in triumph, the great beast flung itself into the sky. Its talons shone like razored steel. It was twenty-five feet from great fanged head to whiplike tail.

It hurtled toward the man on the black horse. Despite all discipline, the horses fought their bits and plunged in terror. "Mother of us all. A dragon!" said Lorimir. Wheeling

Smoke swiftly from the path of the dragon's deadly dive, Karadur drew his sword, and swung at the slicing claw. The dragon soared evasively into the sky, and drove downward. Its black, faceted eyes, big as a man's fist, glowed with a pulsing, alien light.

Again Karadur guided Smoke out of its path, slashing at the dragon's forelegs with the long, sharp sword. On the third advance, the dragon bellowed. An icy liquid spattered from the sky. It burned what it touched, like acid. The dragon circled like a wrestler looking for an opening. Again it dived, and again retreated from Karadur's slashing blade. It swooped again. Smoke reared, whinnying wildly in pain. The dragon's trailing claw had laid the horse open from flank to tail. Karadur leaped from the gelding's back. The tip of the dragon's talon snatched his sword from his grasp and sent it spinning across the pebbly ground.

Herugin seized Smoke's trailing reins. Edruyn scooped the sword from the dirt. Whirling, Karadur held out his gloved hand. "Rogys!" Darting forward, Rogys slapped his spear into Karadur's palm as a runner passes the baton.

Like spectators at a race, the soldiers cheered. Screaming fury, the dragon drove downward, talons spread to hold and rend. Bracing himself against the immense weight, Karadur thrust upward with the long spear into a soft place between foreleg and body. Tearing free, the beast climbed upward again. Its left foreleg hung freakishly. White blood dripped from the wound. It circled, then pounced. Karadur slipped the oustretched talons with astonishing speed and slashed at the dragon's wing. The damaged membrane folded on it-self. The dragon shrieked, and fell to earth. It landed toad-like on three legs, great muscles bunching. Opening its black mouth, it howled in rage. A fetid smoke spilled from its throat. It leaped forward, slashing at the dragon-lord with its fangs. He slipped the blow and swung the spear. The scales turned it. The beast snapped at him, and again he stabbed at the neck. This time the blow connected, driving deeply into the dragon's flesh.

The beast shuddered and yowled. Its eyes closed spasmodically. Karadur hurled himself upward. Like a giant cat, he swarmed up the dragon's scaly side and landed just behind the great arched head. His dagger blurred as he drove it to the hilt in the dragon's throat.

Pale blood sprayed into the sun. He wrenched the dagger out and struck a second, and a third time. The horned, obsidian head tossed and twisted in agony. The long body fell, shuddering. Soldiers yanked their horses out of the path of the lashing tail.

Karadur leaped to the ground, bringing the spear with him. He waited, weapon poised. The dragon's spiny tail twitched. A shiver rolled along the twenty-foot frame. Then the dragon's body quivered, split, and opened like the unfurling halves of a chrysalis.

A great white worm uncoiled from the carrion reek. It flung itself across the dragon's body, fangs snapping at the dragon-lord. Karadur met the charge with a blow from a mailed fist. The worm recoiled, then lunged again, and this time the fangs bit a tearing wound in Karadur's right forearm. Blood streamed down his sleeve. The worm hissed like an adder.

Lorimir said quietly, "Archers. Take aim."

Forty archers swung their bows up. The barbs glittered in the sunlight. Herugin, at Lorimir's elbow, said hoarsely, "Captain. Don't do it."

Lorimir said, "Would you let him die?" The worm whipped its body forward again. Karadur stepped back. As the great ringed trunk extended, he brought the razor-sharp spearhead slashing across its tender belly, and in the same strike brought it over his head and down in a terrible lunge. It speared the worm through. Karadur leaned into the spear. Venom smoked along the worm's ivory fangs; it thrashed and bit the air. Blood, pale as the dragon's blood had been, trickled from the gaping wound.

Then the worm's glistening integument seemed to peel away in translucent, papery sheets. Impaled by the spear, a fair-haired man, gasping in pain, lay on the stony ground.

Karadur took off his helmet. His hair was soaked with sweat. He knelt. Tenjiro's face was ravaged with pain. He lifted a feeble hand to grasp the shaft of the spear.

"Kaji. Pull it out."

Karadur said, "If I do, you'll die."

The gaunt face twisted. "No. I won't die. He will not let me. You will see. Pull it out."

"No."

The ravaged face changed. Like an empty jar into which water is poured, it filled with malice. Hollow, inhuman eyes glared into Karadur's.

"Curse you, then, dragon brother. May your victory turn to ash and dust." The reaching hand clawed for the dragon-lord's throat. "You will never be free of me. My spirit will live, it will follow you, and doom you. I promise it."

Karadur said, "Your threats are empty, Ankoku. When this body dies, you shall sleep."

Again, Tenjiro Atani's voice whispered, "Pull it out. Pull out the spear."

"No." Karadur touched his brother's drawn forehead with his gloved fingers. "Tenjo, it need not have been like this."

"You lie. You always hated me. In the womb you tried to kill me."

Karadur leaned forward. "Tell me where my talisman is."

Tenjiro Atani smiled. "Ah. Can you beg for it, brother dear? No, I see that you cannot. It is hidden. You will never find it. Damn you, Kaji. *I* should have been lord of the realm. *I* should have been Dragon." The emaciated body arched in pain. "Ah, it hurts!"

"You were dragon," Karadur said softly. Something eased in the haggard, racked face. Karadur's steel-mesh glove pulled back. They heard, rather than saw, the hammering blow.

The towers of the Citadel seemed to waver like smoke in the wind. A deep rushing wail arose from the stone. Gorthas and Shem were nowhere to be seen. The soldiers ranged before the gate looked stunned. Karadur wrenched the spear from the corpse. He stood, balancing it on his palms, then whirled, and flung the spear at them. They scattered.

"Kill them!" the dragon-lord said.

Forty archers released their arrows. The men died. The ground beneath the castle shook; stones tumbled from the quivering walls. The air boiled with dust. The portcullis creaked, then roared like a live thing, and fell, iron spikes digging deep into the ground.

Karadur, head bent, stood over the body of his brother. Herugin raced to him. "My lord," he said, "we must go. The castle is falling."

Karadur said, unmoving, "I know. But we must take him with us."

The castle's south wall tottered. Herugin said, "There is no time." Karadur seemed oblivious. Herugin laid a hand on his lord's shoulder. "My lord, the men will not move to safety unless you do."

Karadur looked slowly up. Then he seemed to hear the words. The castle's east wall rocked on its foundation. He took a step toward the line. Horn notes floated cold and clear in the golden morning. The Atani war band fell back, as the walls of the Black Citadel rocked and slid and crumbled into ruin. Armed men, and others, clad in rags, clawed wildly through falling stones to escape the destruction.

"My lord," Herugin called, "do we spare them?"

The dragon-lord shook his head. "No!" Coldly, swiftly, Finle and Orm and Edruyn and Huw aimed and loosed their arrows.

Suddenly Lorimir shouted, "Hold arrows!"

A huge, bearded man in dark leather struggled coughing out of the dust. His arms were filled with a human burden. The bearded man picked his way through the slag-heaps toward them. His yellow eyes glowed fiercely through the ashen tangle of hair.

Huw spread a cloak on the ground. Macallan brushed the long dark hair back from Hawk's face. Her face was discolored, lips bruised and swollen. Her right eye-socket was empty, and scored with fire.

Bear said, "I found her in a cage. I was looking for the wizard."

The physician ran knowledgeable hands along Hawk's right arm and side. She flinched, and grunted. He moved her head. She winced. "You were hit?"

"Yes."

"Can you say how long ago?"

"Not sure. In cage." Hawk's left eye opened. "Wizard dead?"

"Yes," Azil said. "Dragon killed him."

Her mouth curved in a small smile. "Thirsty," she said. "Water."

"Give it to her," said the physician. "Slowly."

Bear cupped a careful hand under Hawk's head. Azil Aumson pushed forward. He held a waterskin between his ungloved hands. He tilted the skin to Hawk's swollen, dust-filmed lips. She sipped slowly. "How long were *you* in a cage?" she whispered.

"Three years."

She closed her eye. "Shem. Saw him in the castle. Is he safe?"

"Hiding," the singer said. "Don't worry. We'll find him."

Macallan said, "That's enough speech." He slid back, just a little. Karadur knelt beside him. "The right elbow is smashed," he murmured. "Arm broken. Two ribs cracked."

The dragon-lord laid one gloved hand lightly on Hawk's uninjured shoulder. "Who did this to you, hunter?"

"Gorthas."

Soundlessly the white eagle glided from the sky and landed in the dust. It cocked its bird head, and then became the mage. She leaned on her staff.

Karadur rose. "Lorimir, set a guard around that castle. The gods alone know what is hidden in that place. But if a mouse runs from beneath those stones, I want to know of it."

Lorimir said doubtfully, "There can be nothing alive in that desolation." The dust swirled around the stones of the broken castle. Only the spire with the banner, unsupported by walls, remained unfallen.

"Then bring me the bodies of Gorthas and the child."

"We will search the ruins for them."

"Do it. Whatever the men find—buttons, old shoes, dry bones—I want it dragged into the light."

"Tell them to take care," said the mage. "There is old evil in this place. If they find any books, warn them not to open them, and if they come across an unbroken mirror, let them cover the glass with cloth before touching it."

"And if they find a box, a small, cold, black box"—the dragon-lord framed it in both hands—"they are not to move it. Make sure they understand that."

"I will," Lorimir said firmly.

Karadur glanced at Hawk. "Macallan, what can you do for her?"

"Strap the ribs. Bind the arm. Salve the eye, and cover it. I would ordinarily give poppy, for the pain. But I am afraid, if she were to sleep, she might not wake. It can happen if the head is injured. It would be best if someone were to sit beside her, and keep watch."

"I will stay with her," Bear said.

"No," Hawk said. "Don't want you. You stay." She caught Azil Aumson's sleeve in her good hand.

With a loud crack, a piece of the standing spire broke from its place. Thick dust laddered the air. Delicate as a coiled rope falling out of the sky, the remainder of the tower closed slowly in upon itself, and crashed to the ground.

At last, when the dust had come to rest, Herugin and Orm lifted Tenjiro Atani's wasted body out of the dry, parchment-like coils of the worm's epidermis, laid it on a litter of crossed poles, and bore it across the slag-heaps to the camp. The dragon, its sail-like wings stiffening in the brightening day, lay where it had fallen.

At Lorimir's order, the men, in groups of three or four, combed through the fallen stones. The sun climbed higher in the pale blue sky.

After an hour, Murgain limped to where Karadur was sitting beside the physician's tent. "My lord, we have been twice through the ruins. We have found no sign of Gorthas or Shem."

"What have you found?"

"Dust," Murgain said. "Bodies: they were trapped in corridors when the walls fell. None of them is Gorthas, or Shem. Rusted cooking pots, a brazier, a shattered knife, a wooden bowl—we have a small pile of such things. No black box."

"Show me," Karadur said grimly.

Murgain brought him to where they had laid out what had come from the wreckage. He said, "We can widen our search to the land beyond the castle. There must be half a hundred holes and ditches, maybe even tunnels, where a patient man might lie hidden."

A worn triple-thonged whip lay on top of the meager pile. Frowning, the dragon-lord flung it violently across the ground. Rogys appeared at his elbow. "My lord," he said breathlessly, "we've found something. We don't know what it is."

It was a column of mist: a white, hovering, opaque mist.

It twisted in the sunlight, leaping and falling and rising again in a slow serpentine pattern.

Rogys said, "Byrnik found it, my lord. He touched it, and look." Byrnik extended both hands. His palms were white and blistered.

Karadur knelt, and passed a hand through the swirling mist. "It's ice-cold," he said softly. "Cold as the heart of the Void . . . Ruil, find the mage. Ask her to come here." Ruil raced off. "Byrnik, let Macallan see to your hands."

"Yes, my lord, I will," said Byrnik. But he did not move.

Senmet of Mako came up to them.

Karadur said, "Wizard, do you know what this is?"

The mage leaned thoughtfully on her staff. "I know what it looks like."

"It is immeasurably cold," Karadur said. "Colder than it can be, and still be vapor, not snow or sleet or ice. No natural fog can be this cold."

"I see," the wizard said. "Well . . ." She pointed her staff at the mist, and spoke. Nothing happened. She repeated it. The mist thickened. "No. That's not what I want to do," she muttered. "Ah." She aimed the staff again.

"Let all objects and beings seen and unseen now manifest and be made visible . . ."

Like snow-spume blown by a playful wind, the white mist blew away. A small black box lay in a hollow of earth. Karadur knelt, and rose with the box in one hand. He thumbed the lid back. A white radiance burst from the cavity. He turned the box, and held it upside-down.

The dragon armband slid into his cupped palm.

22

Karadur's fingers closed lightly on the glittering arm-band. The lines of weariness and strain smoothed from his face; it seemed to fill with wonder. Ruil bent to pick up the box. "Leave it," Karadur said sharply. The boy stepped back. "Would you take it?" the dragon-lord said to the mage.

"I will, my lord Dragon." She touched his arm, and pointed southward. "Go that way," she suggested. "You'll need the space."

He did, winding his way past ditches and gravel-pits and heaps of piled stones. The land dipped slightly: he disappeared, then reappeared. Finally he stopped. Rogys said, "What is it? What is he doing?"

"Watch," said the mage.

A crystalline dazzle shimmered like a curtain across the face of day.

When it dissipated, the man was gone. The dragon towered over them. His sleek, diamond-shaped scales gleamed like molten gold in the sunlight. Barbed spikes, delicate as feathers, formed his mane. He was immense: lean and long, over fifty feet from graceful arching head to the barb on the end of his whiplike spiky tail. Opening his fanged mouth, he roared, a crackling throaty trumpet of triumph and power. His wings unfolded like fans.

Muscles bunching, he leaped aloft. The great wings beat, and caught the air. He circled once above them, and cried a second time. Then, with prodigious grace, the sinuous body straightened and sped like an arrow shaft, straight toward the sun.

The horses, not surprisingly, went mad.

Plunging and thrashing, they snapped their leather tethers like bits of straw. Stakes, pulled wholly from their mooring, bobbled and clattered along the ground. Those not tethered simply ran, carrying hapless riders with them. Even the mules, who had been chosen for endurance and sturdiness of temperament, fought their pickets and charged in different directions, taking with them whatever gear they carried. Herugin Dol sank to his knees and hid his face in both hands, shaking. Orm bent over him.

"Vaikennen's balls! You all right?"

The dark-haired officer lifted his head. He was laughing, through tears. "Yes. Oh gods. It will take us hours to get them back."

Orm stared at him, and shook his head. "Sandor!" he shouted. "Take the captain somewhere he can sit down." He pointed to where Hawk of Ujo rested on a pallet. Azil Aumson was with her. Sandor obeyed. As he lowered Herugin to the ground beside the injured archer, a string of frantic horses galloped past them. Herugin was paper-white. Sandor pressed the wineskin into Herugin's hands. The cavalry master raised the skin. He had to do it twice: half his first attempt went down his shirt. But the second attempt succeeded: color returned to his face, and his shakes diminished.

"Sorry," he said.

"Nothing to be sorry about," said Bear, looming suddenly over the pallet. He grinned, and clapped Herugin gently on the shoulder. "That sound—if I were a horse I'd have run, too.

"I saw his father," he said unexpectedly. "Kojiro the Black. I was roaming through the Nakase hills in summer, near to Yarrow, heading for a little vineyard I know of, when he flew over my head, flying low. It must have been twenty-four, twenty-five years ago. He was jet-black, except for a scarlet crest that ran between his eyes and over his head, and part way down his back. He spoke to me. He said, *Well met, cousin Bear. How goes the hunting?* And I called back, not aloud, but in the way changelings can sometimes speak to each other, *It goes well enough, cousin. And yours?* He didn't answer, but he laughed, the way a thunderstorm might laugh, if it could. It rang in my head for days."

The slow steady voice had brought a measure of calm to Herugin's face.

"Yes," he said ruefully. "It felt like that. Like thunder tearing through my head." He lifted the wineskin to his lips and drank a long draught. "I was eleven when Kojiro Atani burned Mako to the ground. I remember white rain falling, and burning in the air, and my mother's terror. But I don't remember the dragon." He squared his shoulders, and got to his feet. "I'd better get to work," he said.

Bear watched him walk away. "Your Dragon has some good men about him," he commented. "*He'll* be all right. He's stretched a bit tight, that's all."

Hawk sat slowly up. Macallan had bound her arm to her side, and contrived a patch for the exposed, raw eye socket. She stared into the azure sky.

"I hate him," she said harshly.

"Who?" Azil said. His eyes stung with the dust.

"Your Dragon."

Huw the archer trotted up to them. He was dusty, as they all were, and had a scarf wound about his arm. "Captain wants to move back to the camp."

"What about the horses?" Azil asked.

"He says they'll find us when they calm down." He stooped. A little shyly, he said, "Hawk, can I help you?"

"I can do it," she said. She rose stiffly, and very slowly, so as not to jar the strapped arm. "Are you hurt?"

"It's nothing. A graze, when the tower fell." Huw glanced about. "Your bow—"

"Gone," she said. Bear moved to help her walk. She glared at him. "I am not crippled!"

"You helped me," he said mildly.

Hawk's lips tightened. She said, "I could use an arm." He crooked his elbow, and let her hold him, matching her very much smaller stride with his.

A shadow of disappointment passed behind Huw's eyes. He turned.

Azil caught the boy's sleeve. "They're old friends," he said softly. "Sometimes it is easier to share one's pain with those who have seen it before."

Huw blinked, and then nodded. Azil opened his hand, and let him go.

Senmet of Mako, six feet away, caught his eye. She held, in both hands, a small black box. "I believe you know this box," she said.

"I helped to make it."

"Your lord asked me to take care of it." She smiled at the expression on his face. "Do you fear it will corrupt me?"

"Should I?"

"No. Though it is kind of you to think so. They want us to move," she said. "Will you walk with me? The footing grows treacherous further on, and I am an old woman."

"I would be happy to walk with you," Azil said gravely, "but only if you promise not to outrun me. You are no more an old woman than I am."

They had just reached the edge of the pitted land when Gorthas, eyes gleaming crimson, surged out of a cavity, almost at their feet. He was holding Shem beneath one arm. His free hand was clenched around a broad-bladed knife.

"My friend Azil. How fortuitous." He smiled with dreadful malice at the singer. "I hoped you would pass by. I will rip his intestines out through his rib cage, as I did his father's, and you will watch me do it. My master hates you, singer, do you know that?"

Azil said, "Your master sleeps."

Gorthas's eyes glowed with fury. "Yes. But he will wake. Did you not hear me say he is deathless? I will send your soul to serve him."

Pebbles rattled on the icy ground. Finle, thirty feet away, reached for his bow.

Gorthas's head snapped toward him. "Archer, if you touch your weapon, the child dies." Finle went still. The warg-changeling grinned viciously.

"Finle Haraldsen, it was I who met your friend Garin on the wall that night. I ate his tongue and his eyes. You cannot know what pleasure it gave me."

Rage and horror chased across Finle's face. Gorthas set the tip of his knife against Shem's belly. His fingers tightened on the knife. "Now, wolfling."

"No," said Senmet. "I will not allow this." She spoke one sinuous, sibilant phrase. Azil's hair stood on end. The knife in Gorthas's hand became a wriggling black snake. He dropped it with a startled oath. A cry rang across the blistered earth: not a human sound, but a deep bestial bellow of fury. A gaunt white bear hurtled out of a hole toward the changeling and lunged for his throat.

Gorthas, with astonishing agility, spun away from the lunge and into the slag-heaps. The bear roared again, and followed, snapping at his heels. Finle leaped backwards. From everywhere, it seemed, men shouted, and ran toward them, weapons in hand.

"Don't kill it!" Finle shouted. "The warg is here, and he has the boy. Let it flush him!"

Gorthas had vanished. The bear turned in a circle, head down, growling softly. Its ears were mutilated stumps on its pale head. Its eye sockets were scarred and empty.

"Stand still," Senmet said softly to Azil. "It cannot see nor hear; it hunts by scent."

The great head swung from side to side. Senmet spoke in the wizard's tongue. The wind blew suddenly, strongly, out of the north. The bear raised its head, and howled. It leaped a ditch and flung itself up a pebbly bank, claws scrabbling for purchase.

Gorthas hurled Shem, wrapped in his cloak, into the bear's path.

Finle loosed an arrow. It missed, and spun into a slag-heap. Grey smoke fouled the air: Gorthas the man vanished. A snouted, iron-colored warg crouched motionless among the slag-heaps. The archers released their arrows, but before any of the shafts hit, the warg disappeared from sight.

The white bear rumbled, deep in its throat. Its long head quested back and forth. It dropped to all fours, and started toward Shem.

"Hoy!" Finle shouted desperately. He waved his arms. "Here, look, look!" But the white bear ignored the noise.

A second, deeper rumble arose at the white bear's back. A red-brown bear with amber eyes loped with deceptive speed across the pitted land. The white bear raised its muzzle, and turned stiff-legged to face this new challenge. The hair on its neck stood straight up. It opened its jaws and clashed its teeth together warningly. The huge cinnamon-colored bear imitated the gesture. They faced each other, heads lowered. White Bear charged. Red Bear braced for the attack. They roared, and locked jaws. White Bear, disengaging, slashed its teeth along Red Bear's chest. Bellowing, Red Bear crashed into White Bear, knocking it off balance and exposing its flank. Lunging, he struck two slashing blows. Blood trickled down White Bear's sides, staining the pale fur.

With six long strides, Finle reached Shem, scooped him from the path, and raced from danger. The oblivious combatants circled, roaring, and closed again. They slashed terrifyingly at each other, broke apart and plunged forward again, rising to their hind feet. Red Bear's jaws closed massively in White Bear's throat. White Bear yelped, and staggered.

Red Bear, its great jaws marked with blood, released it. White Bear slumped. A film of silver-blue rain shimmered in the blue air.

A haggard, naked woman sprawled in the dirt at their feet.

Blond-white hair streamed along her long body nearly to her knees. Her prominent ribs were scored with claw marks. Blood pumped from a great rent in her throat.

Bear Inisson, breathing in great gasps, sank to his knees beside her. His chest dripped blood. The woman's hands clenched in the dirt, and then opened. The bright red river slowed, and stopped. "I tried to reach her," Bear said hoarsely. "She could not hear me. Is the boy safe?"

"I have him," said Finle.

Hawk of Ujo came up beside him. "Gorthas," she said hoarsely. "Where is he?"

"Gone. Escaped unhurt: we never touched him, damn his monster soul." Finle pointed. "If we had horses, we could try to catch him—" Far to the north, an iron-colored shape loped easily along a snowy ridge.

Bear struggled to rise. "I can't," he said hopelessly.

Hawk's dark eye burned with rage. She flung her head back, glaring into the brilliant sunshine, and screamed. It was not a human sound. High on the ridge, the warg halted. It changed. The hairless man grinned from the safety of his distance, and waved.

Like a star falling to earth, the golden dragon plunged out of the azure sky. He roared; that terrible crackling sound. Gorthas screamed as the terrible, scimitar-shaped claws closed. With powerful strokes of his sun-bright wings, the dragon soared aloft. Then his claws opened. A motionless, torn thing plummeted into the snow. Slowly, very slowly, the dragon glided to earth. He landed on the plain from which he had first risen, and settled like a resting cat on the steppe-land. Heat steamed from his nostrils. He yawned, showing teeth like spear heads, and a curling black tongue. Then, glittering wings folded down upon his back, he gazed at his human companions with alien eyes.

Azil Aumson moved. With steady strides he walked toward the great golden beast until he stood in front of it. He knelt. The huge narrow head arced down. The dragon nosed him lightly. A crystalline dazzle ricocheted across the sky. Karadur Atani stood before his friend. He reached a hand to touch Azil's face. They seemed to speak for a moment. Then the dragon-lord put one hand on Azil's shoulder, and brought him to his feet.

They strolled together toward the motionless war band.

A faint dust of gold, like pollen, gleamed on Karadur Atani's skin. Not a few of his men stepped involuntarily back. Lorimir Ness walked to meet him.

"My lord," he said, with only the slightest tremor in his steady tone, "welcome back."

The dragon-lord smiled at the older man. "I have no words to thank you," he said quietly. He looked at the body of the white-haired woman. "Tell me about this."

Lorimir said, "This is—was—the white bear, my lord. She was hiding somewhere in the diggings. So was Gorthas. She pursued him, and to escape her he flung the child in her path. The Bear"—he gestured at the kneeling, russet-haired man—"stopped her."

Bear said, "She was blind, and he wrapped the child in his cloak. It was clever. I didn't want to kill her. But she was mad. Her mind was filled with Gorthas; she wanted only to kill him." He smoothed the matted, dirty hair back from the mutilated face. "This was her country, once. I would like to bury her here. But the ground is hard."

"There are stones," Lorimir said. "We will build a cairn."

Karadur said, "Where is Shem?"

Finle said breathlessly, "I have him, my lord."

Karadur took the boy between his hands, and knelt.

Shem's hair was stiff with dirt, and his soft child's skin was filthy; he looked worn with terror, tired beyond thought. The stiff leather collar ringing his small neck had raised an ugly welt. Karadur snapped it. It crisped to ash between his fingers.

"Shem," he said gently, "thou art going home now. The man who hurt thee is gone, gone forever. Thou will ride a horse, and will have enough to eat, and clean clothes, and no one will touch thee." Shem looked blankly at him. Patiently Karadur repeated it.

Comprehension stirred in the boy's long-lashed hazel eyes. He whispered, "Shem go home?"

"Yes," Karadur said. He ruffled the little boy's hair. "Finle, have you a younger brother?"

Puzzled, Finle said, "No, my lord."

"Find me someone who does."

Finle looked blank.

Someone said, "My lord, Huw the archer has brothers." Half a dozen hands pushed Huw forward.

"How old is your brother?" the dragon-lord asked.

Huw said, "My lord, I have three brothers. Legh is sixteen, Gowan twelve, and Rauri nine."

"Were they placed often in your charge, when you were still at home?" Huw nodded. "Good. Huw, this is Shem Wolfson. He is—perhaps two?"

Hawk said softly, "He is not even two. Changeling children grow quickly."

"Shem, this is Huw. I place thee into his charge. He will find thee a bath, and clothes, and food, and then he will bring thee back to me. He will not hurt thee. Treat him carefully," he said to Huw.

Huw lifted the boy expertly onto his hip. "Hey, little fellow," he said, "you want to help me find my horse?" He started to turn. Shem grabbed frantically at Karadur's fingers.

"Wait," the dragon-lord said. Blue flames danced along his palms and up his arms. "Dost remember this play? All is well, cub. Be easy, now. Thou art safe." Finally Shem's taut grip eased. Huw took him away. "Lorimir, there is a small herd of elk south of here. Some of them have heft on their bones. Send out a hunting party. We'll need fresh meat for the journey home." The men looked at one another. "Unless you think the men are too weary to hunt . . ."

Lorimir said carefully, "My lord, as to that, we have a small problem."

It took nearly six hours for the horses to return to camp.

They wandered in, footsore and skittish. "Four are lame," Herugin reported, "and one of the mules has a gashed leg. She must have fallen. As for the others—give them a night's rest, and they'll be fine."

During those six hours, the men had not been idle. The dead of the castle had been dragged into a pile and left for the crows. Bear Inisson, with Finle and some of the other scouts, had raised a cairn over the body of the dead changeling.

Huw bathed Shem in a camp kettle, and dressed him by pouring him into the folds of a borrowed tunic and cinching it with a twist of rope. "It's all I could find," he said, as he handed the boy to Karadur. "At least it's clean."

"It will serve," said the dragon-lord lightly. "All right, cub?" The pinched, terrorized look had left the child's face, but it was thin, and very wary. He regarded the dragon-lord steadily, unspeaking. The ring of Telchor Felse's hammer sounded like a bell in the bright air. There was mending to be done before the homeward journey: shoes for the horses, a patch on a kettle, an edge on a sword. There was always mending to be done.

"Herugin: my brother's body goes with us. I place it in your charge."

"My lord," Herugin said crisply, bowing.

Hawk of Ujo, with Azil Aumson beside her, sat outside a tent to watch the men of the war band work. Her face was taut with pain. She showed no inclination to sleep, which Macallan said was a good sign. With them sat Senmet of Mako. Karadur, still carrying Shem in his arms, came to the tent. He had taken off his mail, and Macallan had bandaged his torn forearm. "Hunter," he said, "Macallan tells me your head is not so injured as he had first feared. But he says your ribs and your arm need rest. I hope you will stay in Dragon Keep until you are fit to travel."

Hawk said tightly, "Thank you, my lord."

"Shem," said the dragon-lord, "dost know this person? She is called Hawk. She comes from Ujo, a big, beautiful city, which thou wilt someday visit. She is thy friend."

Shem frowned slightly. "Hawk?" he said questioningly. "Hawk fly?"

"Not now," Karadur said, very gently. He pointed to the singer. "Dost know this person? This is Azil. He is *my* friend." He lowered the boy to the ground. "Wilt stay with these folk a moment? I shall be close by, I promise."

The boy looked at the one-eyed woman for a long moment. She beckoned. "Come, Shem," she said softly. "I know I look strange, but I will not hurt thee." Silently the child took two steps toward her.

Karadur said, "May we speak, mage?" The barefoot mage rose, staff in hand. They walked a little ways from the tent. "Wizard, is there any gift I may make you, any thanks for what you have done?"

Senmet shook her head. "I have no use for gold, my lord. And indeed, you have already given me something: a little black box. I will take it to Mako, and study it."

"What do you hope it will tell you?"

"What it is. What it does." A scarlet rose bloomed at the end of her staff. It turned into a miniature scarlet dragon, which spread its wings and flew away. "My lord, I think I shall leave you soon. My work here is complete."

"Shall I see you again?"

Her lips curved. "Does that mean you no longer wish to kill me?" She sobered. "We will meet again, my lord. We are bound, mage and dragon. I cannot see the pattern's shape, not yet, but I feel its presence."

He nodded. "Do you return to Mako?"

"I do."

"Tell Erin diMako our war is over, and our enemies slain."

"He will be glad to know it."

"And if ever you have need of me, call me," he said. "I will come."

That night, a gold and crimson sunset spread like a benediction across a cobalt sky. The men built bonfires; the rich scent of roasting meat steamed into the air. Lorimir, with a stern warning as to what would happen to anyone who drank too much, sent the wineskins round twice, and then a third time. The moon rose. They toasted it. They toasted Lorimir, and Herugin, and Murgain. Dice came out from knapsacks: Rogys and Orm wrestled, and Rogys, who had had too much to drink, got his face rubbed in the snow. At the archers' fire, Murgain sang 'The Lay of Helos and Nell,' a mournful love song. Olav sang a song in his own language which no one understood, but everyone liked; it had a conspicuous rhythm, and a rollicking, polysyllabic, incomprehensible chorus, which they thundered back to him.

Karadur sat apart from the celebration. Shem, wrapped in the dragon-lord's cloak, sat curled in his lap. The little boy watched silently as blue sparks floated from the dragon-lord's fingers along his bare arms until they wreathed his head.

Finally the dark, still figure sitting beside the one-eyed archer rose. Firelight glinted off his scarred hands. The company fell silent.

Slowly, he began to sing. They knew the song well: it told of intrigue, and bloody ambush, and of seven men, chosen by an ancient king, to ride through dangerous country to bring his loyal army back to him. But the errand was betrayed, the messengers pursued and slain, all but Dorian, shining Dorian, who survived and led the army to his king's rescue. It was the celebration of a hero's journey. But Azil did not sing it so. He sang it as a lament, and the beloved refrain — *"Riders at the gate! There are riders at the gate!"* — became a song of mourning. *"We fall that you may ride,"* he sang. *"Remember . . ."*

Around the guttering fires, the soldiers bent their heads, remembering their dead left in the snow, or buried in fields or under stone. Lorimir sat gazing into the distance, and the look on his face was one that none of them had ever seen before. Finle wept openly.

It ended. No one clapped. Rogys poured wine with an overly steady hand, and held the cup out to the singer. Azil did not take it. Instead, he walked to the dark-cloaked figure who had sat apart from the revelry. Lifting the little boy from Karadur's lap, he brought the child to Huw the archer. Lorimir spoke softly. Men drifted yawning to their blankets.

Azil waited.

Finally Karadur rose. He caught Azil's wrist in one hand, and pulled him to his feet. The tent was warm, and empty. A glimmer of moonlight, delicate as the rain on a sea bird's wings, shone through the tent flap. Ductile shadows flowed over the canvas walls.

Sitting on the edge of his pallet, Azil took off his boots. His breathing, he noted with an odd detachment, had entirely escaped his control. He took off his shirt. He heard the rustle of cloth. A finger touched his lips in silent command.

The sure searching caress seemed to strip the skin from his body. He cried out once, as fire permeated his senses, and he thought his bones would melt.

23

THE NEXT MORNING, as the Atani warriors came from their bedrolls to greet the rising sun, they found a different land.

Stepping from their tents into the buttery sunlight, the men gazed in disbelief. The sharp stark whiteness of snow had vanished. A matrix of orange poppies and fiery-blue lobelia dappled the ground. A pale green haze lay over the steppe. Picketed horses snatched eagerly at new grass. "What happened to the ice?" Edruyn asked.

"Who cares!" said Huw happily. He lifted Shem to his shoulders. "Look at this, cub. The ice has gone away. See the colors? What d'you think of that? Beautiful, eh?"

"Boof," Shem whispered.

In the tent she shared with Bear, Hawk sat motionless on her bedroll. Bear had gone to the cook-tent. Changelings heal quickly; already the wounds in Bear's throat and side had begun to knit. Hawk's head was fine, though it felt strange. She had cropped her hair severely: it sprang from her head in black and silver spikes. She clenched and released the fingers of her right hand, as Macallan had told her she had to do if she wished it to keep any strength. Her ribs had ceased to hurt. If she tried to move quickly, they would. The space where her right eye had been throbbed beneath its patch, but only slightly. Macallan had salved the raw place with a potion from one of his little jars.

The deeper pain was not amenable to Macallan's potions.

She mostly wanted solitude: a place to hide. But one could not hide in the middle of a war band. Someone scratched at the tent.

"Come in," she said, expecting Macallan with his jars.

It was not Macallan; it was Huw. "I thought you might need something," he said.

"I'm all right." She squinted at him. "Your face looks different."

He flushed. "Got tired of scraping myself raw every other day."

The faint brown stubble was barely visible. "I like it. It makes you look older." He grinned. "Where's your charge?"

"With Dragon. Have you seen?" He waved an arm. "Everything's changing!" His enthusiasm was moving. Hawk followed him from the tent. The air, which had been icy for so long, was sweet with the promise of spring. On the near horizon, an elk, ribs showing, meandered westward. Its spindly legs seemed impossibly frail and long.

A flock of grey geese, honking in rhythm, soared over the camp. "Those are the first geese I've seen in this gods-forsaken land," Huw said.

Bear appeared. He carried two skewers of meat and a cloth heaped with pan-bread. He held out one of the skewers. "Elk," he said. Hawk took it. Manipulating the skewer with her left hand was idiotically difficult. Huw, suddenly turned shy, muttered something and withdrew.

Bear shoveled hot bread into his mouth. "That boy's in love with you, you know."

She frowned. "Huw? He's almost a child."

"He's young," the yellow-eyed man said blandly. "So what? I doubt he's a virgin. Once you heal, you can allow yourself a little fun, surely." He grinned at her expression. "Do you want this bread, or do I finish it?"

"I want it," she said, scooping the last hotcake out of the grease-soaked cloth.

Raudri, by the officers' tent, lifted his horn to his lips, and sounded the trill that signaled Break Camp. The men scattered the fires and hauled briskly at the tents, impatient to be gone from this eerie place. Not very far away, bodies sprawled: the servants of the Citadel, cut down by the Atani war band's arrows. Hawk ducked into the tent to retrieve her belongings. They were few: a leather pack, which had belonged to a dead man, a spare shirt, lent by Irok, socks, a bedroll. Bear tied the bedroll to the pack and helped her strap both to her back. He looked ready to march. The bandages around his clawed chest lay concealed beneath his vest.

"You'll have to ride one of the spare horses," she said.

"I'm not coming with you," he said. "I go east, into Nakase, and Kameni, if need be." He opened his hand. A small, cloudy-white quartz bear sat in the hollow of his palm.

"It was my cousin's. I took it from her corpse," he said bleakly. "I go to find her family. I will give them this, and tell them how she died. From there I will return to Sogda. Though when Ariana sees me she'll probably throw crockery at my head."

It was pointless to argue. "You are hurt," Hawk said finally.

"Scratches." He scowled at her, and put both arms about her, careful not to press against her shattered arm. She laid her cheek against his massive chest. "Nothing troubles Bear, remember? You are not to worry about *me.*"

Together they went to tell Karadur Atani that Bear Inisson would not be journeying south with the war band. They found him in the horse lines, with Shem tucked into the circle of his arm. The little boy was stroking the nose of a big red gelding.

"This is Gambler," the dragon-lord said. "He is not so clever a horse as Smoke, but he is very well-behaved. We shall ride him today, thou and I." Gambler laid his ears back. The dragon-lord caught his bridle with a firm hand. "Oy, my beauty, what is it?" He turned toward the changelings. "Cub, dost remember Hawk? I told thee yesterday, she is thy friend. This man is Bear. He is also thy friend." Karadur's face was still closed: habit did not change so quickly, and there were marks of grief along his mouth. But through the secret link that bound her to him, Hawk felt the steadfast current of joy.

Shem's hazel eyes, so like Thea's, gazed into hers. "Hawk." He had held her hand the day before. "Hawk not fly."

It hurt. It would always hurt.

The dragon-lord said, "You look better. Both of you."

Hawk said, "I am healing, my lord."

"And you, Bear Inisson?"

Hawk said, "My lord, he comes to say farewell."

The blue gaze sharpened. "You are leaving us?" Bear explained. Karadur Atani nodded slowly. "I understand. Take what supplies you need from our stores. Do you need a horse?"

Bear shook his head. "I don't like horses, nor they me." He looked at the small boy. "Shem Wolfson," he said gently. "I knew thy father well. I hope we meet again, thou and I. Safe journey."

"Safe journey," the dragon-lord said.

Within an hour, the company left Mitligund.

At Macallan's request, they traveled slowly; the black gelding, though mending, required frequent rests, and Hawk could not yet endure a quick pace. Sunflower, as if mindful of her rider's weakness, paced smoothly along the uneven ground. Huw rode at Hawk's right. It was evident, from his expression, and the way he twitched every time she lifted her rein, that he expected her to fall. She told him curtly to relax.

"I'm an archer. I can ride with no hands, if I have to."

Behind them, a mule pulled the sledge that bore Tenjiro Atani's body. It was flanked by three men: one on each side and a third to ride behind it. Edruyn said softly, "Too bad we can't just drop that thing in a ditch. It makes my skin crawl." Irok, riding behind him, grunted agreement.

But Orm said, "Best shut your mouth if you want to keep your precious skin. That *thing*, whatever else it may have been, was once your lord's twin brother."

For two days, they followed the emblems of their own passage: the black cicatrices of bonfires, scorched like brands into the earth. The grass grew at a stunning pace. By the morning of the second day it was fetlock high. More elk appeared, nosing at the marvelous grass, and skinny, starved deer. The second night, they camped beside a copse of trees.

"I know this place. This is where we killed the wargs," said Huw.

That night, Hawk dreamed. She was running through a high snowdrift. She could not change. She could see, and in the dream she had two good arms, but it did not matter, whatever shambled after her was coming nearer. It would, she knew, catch her . . . Her breath burned in her throat. Skin seared with cold, snarling in cornered rage, she turned, to face a misshapen, twisted, red-eyed horror. *Ah, cousin*, it rasped, *there you are* . . . It leaped for her throat.

She woke sweating and shaking. The tent stank of smoke and salt. Huw's voice, over and over, whispered her name. He was holding her, very lightly, careful not to jar her arm.

He felt her wake, and started to move.

"It's all right," she said. "Stay."

The morning of the fourth day, Karadur left them. He spoke briefly with the captains. Then he walked past the perimeter of the camp, and changed. He lifted into the pale blue sky with an impossible bound, soared thrice over the camp, circling higher and higher each time, and then shot southward. Shem, sitting on Huw's shoulder, lifted his small face to the sun. "Dragon gone," he said solemnly.

All that day, they watched the sky, but saw only grey geese and ptarmigan, and once, a pair of golden eagles. At their midday rest, Hawk was leaning against a rock in the sunlight when she heard a step. She looked up, into Azil Aumson's dark gaze. "Can you find him?" the singer asked.

She had not tried. As she had before, alone in the Keep, she opened her mind, reaching for a signature of fire somewhere in the distance. Other minds, some human, some animal, brushed hers, but she ignored them. Once she thought she touched Bear's mind . . . She rubbed her aching temples. "I can't reach him. He's too far away."

At sunset, they halted. Shem, toddling through the camp with his fingers tightly clasped in Huw's, pointed southward. "Dragon coming."

"Are you sure?" Huw asked curiously. "I don't see him."

"Shem sure," the boy said confidently. "Dragon come." They waited. The great golden form swept silently over the savanna. The sun ran like molten copper along the vast sweep of his wings. He landed and changed. His men greeted him with a certain shyness, mindful of the immense, alien presence that shimmered behind his eyes.

That night, most of the men chose to do without tents. Karadur and Azil sat side by side in front of a fire. The sky, clear as water, was hung from edge to edge with stars.

A heavy footfall made them turn their heads. It was Huw, with Shem in his arms. "Excuse me, my lord," the archer said. "He is fretful. He would not sleep before he had seen you."

Karadur held up his big hands, and Huw set Shem between them. "So, cub, here am I," the dragon-lord said gravely. "What is it? Art frightened? Art cold?"

The child shook his head. "Shem warm." He had begun to speak more readily, now. "Dragon gone. Where dragon go?"

"Dragon goes far away, cub." Karadur ran a finger through the boy's now-shining hair. It fell nearly to his shoulders. "But I will come back, always."

The little boy pressed confidingly against the dark-cloaked man's shoulder. "Dragon go," he said firmly. "Find Papa."

The three men exchanged quick glances. Karadur said softly, "I am sorry, Shem. I cannot bring thy father to thee, cub. He has gone far away, farther than even a dragon flies." The child's face whitened. "Leave him with me," the dragon-lord said to the archer. Karadur wrapped his cloak around the child. "Listen, cub. Shall I tell thee of the place we are going? It is a big house, Dragon's house. Thou hast seen it before. Thou madst friends with the cooks, and slept in a big kettle. Dost remember this?" Light, wide eyes stared into his. Softly Karadur told the tense, silent child about the stables, the dogs, the eating hall with its bright tall fires, the kitchens filled with wonderful things to eat . . . Shem's eyelids closed, and his rigid muscles relaxed.

But in the middle of the night, Shem woke. The cloak that wrapped him was warm, and warmer still was the man beside him, the deep-voiced, shining man with fire in his hands: *Dragon*. It was night, but bright fires burned nearby. Overhead the stars made a great white arch like the line of Huw's bow. But there was an empty space inside him, as if the cold had crept inside him. Mama was gone. The red-eyed monster who had hurt him had hurt her, too, and made it so that she would not get up again. He had seen her lying in the snow. But his father had fought them, and his father was strong, stronger than any monster . . .

But his father was gone. He felt the empty place inside him swell and swell until he thought he might crack.

The following morning, the fields around the camp were burnished with apricot-colored butterflies. "Look," Karadur said to the hollow-eyed child. He swung the boy to his shoulder and strode toward the field. The butterflies fluttered upward, surrounding man and boy in a great orange cloud. Where they had been, thousands and thousands of tiny white flowers spread over the earth like lace.

All that day, Shem was withdrawn and silent. "He needs to weep," Azil said.

But Shem would not weep.

Late that day, they came upon a scene they had encountered before: the sprawled bodies of three children. Karadur called a halt, and sent men out with shovels. They dug a grave, and gently lifted the rigid bodies into the softened earth.

The following day they halted in a burned village. The blackened spars were limned with green: clusters of meadow rue and fireweed had taken root everywhere. Here, too, they had a burial to attend to. South of them, jagged mountains rose above the plains, with three tall peaks clearly higher than the rest: Whitethorn, Brambletor, and tallest of all, Dragon's Eye, its crown shadowed in cloud. All day they rode toward the mountains. At last they halted, in Ashavik, the village in which their dead waited. The horses had been ravaged, but the wrapped human bodies lay almost undisturbed. Grim-faced, the men of Herugin's wing set to with shovels.

That night, Azil sang: no dirge, but an old song: it told how Tirion the archer went hunting on the night of Spring Moon, and came upon a great black buck, the finest and most majestic animal he had ever seen. Calling his dogs, he stalked it and each time he thought he had trapped it, it escaped, and fled from him.

> And Tirion vowed, "I will take the black buck,
>   before the night is done.
> "But the buck ran free, O the buck ran free; the
>   buck ran free as the wind is free!"

And so Tirion stalked it. Far, far it ran, across fields, hills and rivers, and spring turned to summer, and summer to fall, and fall to winter, and still the buck eluded him. But Tirion's heart burned, and he would not turn back. And on the night of Spring Moon, a whole year from when his hunt began, the dogs brought the black buck to bay against the side of a hill. Full squarely Tirion shot; but his shaft turned to flame as it flew, and his arrows turned to flame in their quiver, and the great buck turned into a great horned man, who fixed the archer with eyes of flame.

And Tirion fell to his knees, for he knew then that the buck he had been chasing was really Imarru the Hunter, to whom all hunters owe fealty. And laughing, Imarru forgave him.

> "*For never has man pursued me with such a*
> *faithful heart.*
> "*And the buck ran free, the buck ran free; the buck*
> *ran free as the wind is free!*"

The next day, they crossed the pass into Ippa.

It was hard, this climb; harder than it had seemed when they started out, two short weeks before. It was warmer, but the rocks were slick, and the winds harassed them mercilessly. "At least there are no wargs," Edruyn said. The beasts, relieved of the heaviest load—that of the wood, which had kept them from freezing through wintry nights—moved eagerly up the narrow trail. The men moved more slowly. Hawk cursed steadily under her breath. Huw had cut her a staff from a tent pole. It helped, but the strapped arm and the adjustment which she had not fully managed to make in her sight made her struggle for balance with almost every step.

Just before the highest crossing, Karadur called Herugin to his side.

"I want to give my brother's body to the winds," he said quietly. "Will you help me?"

They lifted Tenjiro Atani's bier between them. A small track led away from the place they had slept. They followed it away from the main trail. It veered east, then snaked south again, and finally ended in five broad flat steps. "Up," Karadur said. They climbed the stairway and squeezed between two huge rocks to a small, grassy plateau. "This is good," the dragon-lord said. Kneeling, he raised Tenjiro Atani's fragile, wrapped body from the bier, carried it across the small sward, and laid it in a bracken-filled hollow.

The wind, like some invisible giant, slapped its palms against the rock. The mountain seemed to shake. High above them, death's outrider, the black condor, sailed in slow circles. Herugin said diffidently, "My lord, perhaps we should build a cairn."

"No," Karadur said. He rose. "No cairn. Let the birds come, and rain, and wind and sunlight, until even his bones are scoured clean."

They slept that night on the cliff side.

It took most of the day to descend the pass. They reached Atani Castle at sunset. The sentries had seen them coming: the dark square castle blazed with light. Torches lined the walls, and lamps and candles burned at every window. Horn music, lilting and joyful in the crisp air, filled the valley. Shem, from his place on Karadur's saddlebow, poked his head through the slit in the dragon-lord's cloak. "House," the little boy said. "Big house."

Karadur tousled the child's dark silky hair. "It is as I told thee, cub, remember? This is Dragon's house."

Faces peered from the battlements: guards, cooks, kitchen maids. "Welcome, my lord!" someone called from the ramparts, and Karadur lifted an acknowledging hand. The horns called again, echoing down the hillside into the valley. Bareheaded, sword at his side, Marek Gavrinson stood unaccompanied just inside the gate. He knelt, and rising, reached to hold Karadur's stirrup. He saw Shem. His eyes widened with astonishment.

"Well, Marek Gavrinson," Karadur said gravely, "how fares my land?"

The question was ceremonial. Marek said, his tone measured and formal, "My lord, your land is at peace, and as secure as you left it. It waits to welcome you back." He signaled: a horse-boy ran from the shelter of the outside wall to snatch Gambler's rein. "How fared your campaign, my lord?"

The folk on the wall hushed, and leaned to listen. Raising his voice, Karadur said, "Our war is ended, and our enemies slain."

And suddenly they were all shouting, to him, and to the hardened, weary men who followed him. The cheers swelled and echoed, a wild jubilant reverberation that echoed into the hills, and down the sloping fields toward the villages nestled in the lowlands. Women waved their aprons, calling wild welcome to husbands, brothers, sons. Karadur dismounted. Men—the men they had left, and many more, from fields and farms and villages—swarmed from the postern gates to seize the horses' reins and guide them to the stables. The dogs penned on the other side of the wall barked furious greeting. A mule brayed; the horses whickered and tugged on their reins, scenting the familiar smells that meant rest, food, warmth, journey's end.

The portcullis lifted. Liam Dubhain emerged from the gate, and clapped Lorimir on the shoulder. Murgain lifted Sinnea off her feet and into his arms. A spare, quiet, ageless woman, her girdle laced with keys, came through the narrow doorway. Azil Aumson slipped from his horse to embrace her. Nestled in the crook of Karadur's arm, Shem gazed at the excited men and women.

"Dragon coming," he observed serenely.

Wraith-silent, colorless, weightless as shadow, the

shadow-dragon seemed to coalesce out of the dark grey walls. The shadowy head loomed higher than the iron gate. Its eyes glittered like chips of rainbow. A woman gasped, a high indrawn breath of fear and wonder. Marek, face white as chalk, stepped back from it. His mouth opened, but no sound emerged.

"Don't be afraid. It will not harm you," the dragon-lord said. He lifted the child to his shoulder. "We are home, cub." He stepped beneath the iron gate. Silent as the starlight, the shadow-dragon bent its supple neck, and followed him into the torchlit castle.

PART
FIVE

24

THERE WAS LITTLE space for privacy in a castle.

You would think it would be easy, Hawk reflected, to find a place to be alone. Dragon Keep was big, with empty rooms, unused attics, dusty silent chambers that could be entered at odd times, like the middle of the afternoon, when no one would be looking . . . But somebody was always looking. Maids and pages, guards and grooms, everyone knew everyone else's business.

A bee droned past her ear, searching for nectar amid the bright heart of the daisies. Her back was stiff. She shifted in the soft crushed bracken. This place—it had once been a buttery—was better than the castle, anyhow. It was secluded, fragrant with daisies and the blowzy yellow roses that twined up the inside of the broken walls and dropped petals everywhere. Bryony Maw, the Keep's laundry mistress, had told her of it. The roof had gone, and most of the inner walls. But the outer walls were still solid after who knew how many decades.

Huw's head lay heavy on her breast. She stroked his face. "Mmm." Opening his eyes, he nuzzled at her neck. The October sun fell across his bare brown skin. He was sweating; they both were. Even in the shade of the wall, the day was hot.

"Gods, you're beautiful."

Hawk smiled. She was not beautiful: she was lean as a hound, weathered as a post, and eighteen years older than he was. But he liked saying nonsense like that, and she did not try to dissuade him.

"We've been here two hours," she said.

He kissed her nipple. "I don't care. I want to stay here forever."

There was little likelihood of anyone disturbing them. Half the men were down in the villages, working in the farms. "You know we can't. Get up." He moved. Hawk sat up, hunting her clothes. She found her underclothes and breeches, and worked her shirt over her head.

They strolled to the castle. The courtyard was hung with drying laundry. It smelled of soap. Edruyn came out of the barracks. He had filled out, since spring, and had lost the puppy look over which he had taken so much teasing.

"Hey. I was looking for you," he said to Huw. "Elief and I put the targets up. Want to shoot?"

Huw shrugged. "I'll get my bow." They walked off toward the barracks. Hawk no longer slept in barracks; she had a room to herself, the same small chamber she had slept in when first she came to the Keep. She had found it cold. It was cold no longer; it was hers: her pack on the table, her cloak on the bed. She washed at the basin. A warm breeze touched her face. The window shutter was open, curtains wide. It was still light. She flexed her right arm, feeling the joint tighten and tighten until it no longer moved. She had written to Tiko in June: *I must be in the north a little while longer . . .* Karadur Atani had said to her, a week after their return from the ice: *There is a place for you here, if you want it.* She had not answered; her wounds were too deep, the place of her despair too raw and tender. Since that conversation, she had barely seen him. Once, during the worst time, right after the injury, she had felt the link between them flare to life. *Get well, hunter,* the dragon-lord's thought said. *I have need of you.* But he had mostly left her alone, to find her own healing.

Dinner in the hall that night was festive. The men, those not staying with family on farms, had returned from the villages. The harvest was in: "Corn twice as high as your head, and pumpkins *this* big!" The food came around: venison, buttered yams, crisp red potatoes, brown bread firm and rich as cake.

At the end of the meal, the servants cleared the tables. Sigli and Wegen pulled out a keph board. The young men, in high spirits, thrust the tables back to wrestle. There were new, young faces in the hall: many of the men who had ridden north that spring had left Dragon's service to return to farms and families, and the summer levy had brought maybe twenty bright-eyed, supple youngsters to the Keep, eager to learn to shoot and ride and wield a sword.

Hawk brought her wineglass to Herugin's table. He was acting captain. Lorimir, for the first time in many years, was gone from the Keep. He had left in September to visit his family in Averra. Huw made room for her beside him. Rogys and Finle, seated across from each other, were arguing hotly over the best way to train deerhounds. Beneath their raised voices, Herugin said softly in her ear, "Did you hear the news? Murgain and Sinnea are to be married."

She had not heard. "When?"

"Next month. Not many people know. There's more. He plans to leave the Keep."

"Leave his position?"

"Even so. He wants to try his hand at farming. Dragon has agreed."

Suddenly Rogys said, in a tone of delight, "Hoy. Look!" He waved his arms.

Marek Gavrinson threaded his way down the long room to their table. He had left the Keep, though not Dragon's service: he was living in Castria now, charged with watching the roads and ordering the guard on the market and village gates.

"You're fat," Orm said to him.

Marek grinned. "Care to wrestle? Bet I can still put you on your back." He tossed his riding gloves to the table. "Gods, I stink like a goat, and I'm thirstier than anyone has a right to be." Huw pushed a glass into his hands. He tipped his head back. "Ah, that's good. The traders are here; it's mad in the market. You all look very pleased with life. Done any hunting?"

"Some," said Finle, who had. Rogys, who had not, feigned a punch at him.

Herugin said, "Marek, most of us have been grubbing in the fields for the last ten days. Drink your wine, and tell us what you hear from the traders."

Marek sank to the bench. "Ah, the traders. Well, the traders tell the most amazing stories. It seems that Karadur Atani led an army of his men into the frozen wasteland north of the Grey Peaks this summer to storm a wizard's castle, and capture the enchanter's treasure chests."

Rogys said, "I don't recall any treasure chests."

"Do you recall an army of goblins? The giant wolves? The standing stones that sang alluringly in women's voices?"

"I missed those," Orm said, with mock regret. Finle laughed.

Rogys said, "Does no one know what truly happened?"

Marek said wryly, "Would you want them to know it? All of it?" Rogys went red. "Some do, I suppose. Men talk to their wives, or to their friends. In Chingura and Sleeth and Castria, they know."

Finle asked, "Do they know what he did? Do they know what he is?"

Marek said, "They have seen him." The words, and the wonderment behind them, silenced even Rogys. Hawk saw him then in her mind, as she had seen him in the sky at sunset or at dawn, rising from the Dragon's Roost, with fire in his eyes, and sunlight clinging like liquid gold to the membranous weave of his spread wings . . .

Herugin said, "You seem well. I suppose all is serene in Castria?"

"All is very well. I left Arnor in charge. I came to make my report, that's all. Larys, on the gate, said Dragon was gone."

"He is," Herugin said. "He should be back by dawn."

"Can you find me a bed tonight?"

"You can always sleep in the stable," Rogys said. "What other lies are the traders telling?"

"There's a story going round about a bull."

"What bull?"

"Some bull belonging to a farmer near Yarrow. Remember last month's lightning storms?"

"Gods, yes," said Orm feelingly. "I spent a week, it seemed, pulling cows out of mud wallows and picking up flattened fences."

"Well, this farmer's bull—his name is Bjorn, the farmer not the bull—Bjorn's bull trampled his fence and went helter-skelter into the fields, chased by the farmer's dogs and the men and boys from two villages. They flushed it from a copse, and then no one knew what to do. Finally someone got a bright idea: they soaked a cloth in grape mash—this bull, it seems, has an unconquerable yearning for grape mash—and tied the cloth on a pole, and used it to lure him back to the corral."

Orm said pensively, "I knew a girl in Yarrow once—"

Rogys asked, "Did she like grape mash?"

Through the laughter Herugin said, "What other news have you heard? Is all well in Mako?"

"As far as I know. Let's see. Gerris Hal, the old lord of Serrenhold, has the wasting sickness: he's not expected to live out the year. The Chuyo lords are fighting again. The grape harvest in Merigny is reputed to be particularly good this season. Oh, and the Lemininkai's daughter is betrothed."

Hawk asked, "To whom?" She remembered Kalni Leminin's daughter, Selena, as a grave girl whose sweet smile and calm demeanor masked a wickedly mischievous bent. She had once spent an otherwise tedious afternoon in the Lemininkai's palace by catching grasshoppers and filling the boots of all her father's visitors with them.

"Some Kameni prince."

"Prince?" Finle said. "We don't have princes in Ryoka."

Hawk said, "We did once."

Herugin lifted his head. "Listen."

A rushing, thunderous murmur shook the Keep. They heard the great wings beating, and the drag of razored claws across stone. The young men stilled. Soft-footed, they ceased their contests and drifted from the hall toward the barracks.

In a little while, the dragon-lord entered the dining hall. He walked through the shadowy, silent room to their table. They rose.

"My lord," said Marek. "I came to make my report." They waited for the dragon-lord to sit before resuming their seats.

One of the serving-girls brought him food. His windblown hair was crusted with salt. The dragon armband glittered on his sinewy forearm. The door at the back of the hall opened; Azil Aumson strolled into the hall. Karadur looked up, and smiled. Azil seated himself at Karadur's left shoulder. Herugin slid a glass of wine in front of him.

"So," the dragon-lord said. "How is it in Castria?"

"All's well, my lord. The traders are here. The harvest is mostly in and I think your steward will tell you when the accounts are made that it is one of the best in years. The men have worked hard. Some sheep were taken from Miri Halleck's farm."

"How many, and by whom?"

"A ram and two ewes. No one knows who was responsible. A shepherd saw two of Reo Unamira's men riding near her land the day before, but there was no proof."

Karadur said, "Let her know that the Keep will recompense her for them. What else?"

"A wax trader from Firense had his purse stolen. The thief was a peddler from Derrenhold. He was lashed and branded."

Hawk rose to leave. Fire brushed her mind. *Hunter, stay.* She sat, heart beating faster than it needed to. She filled her own glass with sweet wine, and drank it off quickly. The candlelight glinted in the dragon-lord's hair. She watched him under lowered lids. Pots clanged in the kitchen; a woman laughed, a high lilting sound, like the refrain of a song.

The door from the kitchen opened. A child's voice, defiant and passionate, said, "I know he's here. Let me go!" A small body squirmed through the narrow opening and flung itself unhesitatingly across the shadowy hall.

As he neared the bench where the dragon-lord sat, the boy slowed, and halted. His tunic was streaked with dirt. A purple bruise puffed his left cheek.

Karadur gazed at him impassively. Then he said, "Well, cub. What's amiss?"

Shem said, "Simon hit me." His baby speech had gone. He was two, but had the height and heft of a child of four. His face had changed: the hollow thinness of deprivation had been replaced by a lean beauty. He looked very much like Wolf.

"Why did he hit you?"

"I bit him. He said he would put Turtle in the pot."

"What do you want me to do about this?"

Shem said, "I want you to punish Simon."

"For hitting you?" The boy nodded. "How hard did you bite him?"

"Hard," the boy said, with pride. "He's bleeding."

"How hard did he hit you?"

Shem started to answer, and then stopped. He touched the swollen cheekbone. "Not so hard," he said grudgingly. "But if he puts Turtle in the pot I will *kill* him!"

"Yes?" said Karadur. The boy looked at him. "Come here, Shem." Shem edged forward. His shoulders were very straight. Karadur reached out a hand, and pulled him close.

"You will not kill Simon," the dragon-lord said firmly. "It would be hard for you to do, he is bigger than you. But you will not do it, because Simon is my servant. I do not allow anyone to hurt my servants unless I order it to be done. Do you understand that?"

"Yes," Shem said earnestly. "But—"

"I know. You don't want Simon to put Turtle in the pot. He will not. I promise it. But you must keep your puppy out of the kitchen during mealtime, when the cooks and servers are busy."

"But Turtle is the smallest of all the puppies. He gets lonely."

Man and boy regarded each other. The listening men smiled. Karadur said gently, "Say what you want, cub."

Shem said staunchly, "It is cold at night now. I want Turtle to stay with me at night, in my bed. But Kiala says no."

"Ah. I see. Tell Kiala you have my permission to let Turtle into your bed. But if he makes a mess, *you* shall clean it up, not Kiala. Is that clear?" Karadur flicked a finger against Shem's unbruised cheek. "Good night, cub. Rogys, will you see he gets safely to his bed?"

"I will, my lord," Rogys said, rising. He held out a hand. "Come on, cub."

Finle rose. "With your permission, my lord—" The two of them walked with the child to the door.

Marek said softly, "He has grown so . . . I will never forget the sight of him on your saddlebow, the night you came down from the mountains. Do you mean to keep him?"

Karadur said, "I do."

"Does he know that this is his home?"

"He knows that it is his home now, but in his deepest heart, home is a house by the river, with two people he loves, whom he saw killed."

Hawk saw, in her mind, the small, empty house under the birch trees. The meadow where Wolf and Thea had died was thick with grass. The river sang plangent lament beneath the birch trees. The moon shone through the high window into the room where Thea had worked on her loom. . . .

Silent as night, the dragon-wraith emerged out of nothingness. Folding its dark wings, it coiled at Karadur Atani's feet like a dog.

"Hunter," Karadur said, "how is your arm?"

The small hairs rose on the back of Hawk's neck. She said, "It is healed, my lord, as much as it will be."

"And what is it in your mind to do now?" he mused. "Shall you return to Ujo, to Lantern Street, and make bows?"

"I think not." Around them the men had fallen silent.

"Then stay here."

She folded her arms. Her right elbow tightened and pulled where the torn tendons had scarred. "What would I do in Dragon Keep?"

"Murgain's position will be open soon."

"I cannot draw a bow," she pointed out tartly. "Besides, Orm has earned that post. I will not take it from him." Orm, at the other end of the table, went red as a poppy.

Karadur leaned forward. His eyes blazed blue fire, brighter than the torchlight. "Then stay as my councilor, as my teacher—as my friend. We are bound, hunter. You know this, you whose rage called me from the sky."

She did know it; she could feel it, burning between them. Dragons whirled before her inner eyes: golden, silver, black, azure, red, white, one the color of iron, another the color of stone. Wings furled, wings spread, they tumbled through her mind, through blue skies, through moon-light, through a waste of snow, through a black and starless silence, through the blazing heart of the sun. . . .

She could not move. At his back, the men were watching her.

There were words she could say. She had heard others say them, to other men. *I swear fealty to Karadur Atani, lord of Dragon Keep. At his bidding I will come and go: my knife to his hand, in war and peace, in speech and silence, until he release me, or my life fails, or the world ends.* They were words only. She did not need them. She held her hands out, across the table and felt his huge, warm ones close around them lightly.

She said, "I will stay, my lord."

When she left the hall, the Hunter's Moon was glowing in the autumn sky, plump and yellow as a Kameni apple. The mingled scents of honeysuckle and rosemary drifted from the kitchen garden. Walking into the courtyard, she found a bench, and sat.

After a while, a man strolled quietly across the moonlit night. She had thought it would be Huw, or Herugin, but it was not: it was Azil. She nodded. He seated himself on the other end of the bench. A yellow-eyed owl, white wings spread, glided overhead.

He said, "He is wholly Dragon now. Do you feel it?"

"I feel it," she said shortly.

"He holds back, with everyone. Almost everyone."

"With you?"

"No."

"Do you find it hard to sustain?"

"Sometimes." *Do not lose yourself in Dragon's Country. It is perilous to know and love the dragon-kind . . .* "I am glad you chose to stay."

She said, "I will teach him everything I can. But it may not be what he wants."

"Do you know what he most wants?"

She shook her head.

"He wants to find his kin. For six months he has flown the length and breadth of Ryoka, hunting for them."

"Why?"

"Because he is alone," Azil said. "He has no father, save in memory, no mother, no brother, no one like him in or out of Ryoko. He is the Dragon of Chingura; there are no others. Can you imagine it?"

She could not. Her mother lived still in Voiana; the women she called her sisters were scattered across Ryoka: dark-haired, keen-eyed women whom she had mostly never met, but whom she would know at once, from the way her blood would sing when she saw them . . . "No." The granite at her feet sparkled with the moonlight. The owl swooped suddenly downward. A mouse screamed thinly, and then was still. "What if he does not find them?"

Azil said, "If he does not find them, then he will look for a woman who will wed him, and bear his children."

"Do you mind?"

He smiled. He said reflectively, "I won't know, until it happens. It will change him. But I can sustain that."

They returned to the hall. Dragon had gone, but Huw and Herugin and Orm were still there. Orm had taken out his dice. Huw leaned back, resting his head against her belly. She let her hand stroke his hair. Azil drifted from the hall. She knew where he was going. She bent, and blew in Huw's ear.

"Come on," she whispered. "Let's go to my room."

Hawk woke to hear the horn blowing.

Arise, arise and come!

She lifted on her elbow. For a moment she did not know where she was: it was cold, and moonlight shone around her, and the sound, blowing through darkness, reminded her of waking to fire and arrows on the ice. Huw had gone.

He had left the window shutter open; the curtains were whipping like sails in a breeze. Below, the dogs penned in the courtyard howled like demons. The horn was still calling, *Arise, arise and come!*

She flung her clothes on, and hurried to the hall. Every torch and lamp and candle in the place was burning. Dragon was there, and a woman, holding a riding whip. She wore a man's breeches and a leather tunic like a soldier's, and her face was smeared with mud beneath a crown of thick gray hair. It was clear that she had once been very beautiful. Hawk had never seen her before. The room was filling with whispering, grim-faced men. Hawk looked for Huw.

"Who is she? What has happened?"

He said tensely, "Mellia Amdur. Thorin Amdur's wife."

The woman was speaking. "Hern rode after them. He was hurt, but he rode anyway."

"Who were they?" Dragon asked.

"I could not see: they wore kerchiefs on their faces. But they came from Coll's Ridge. There must have been twenty of them. They were drunk, and laughing. They did not burn the barn. I left Leanna and the children inside it, with the girls and the grooms." Her voice broke, then steadied.

Dragon laid a hand briefly on her shoulder. "We will find them," he said. "Herugin, I want thirty men horsed and armed. Mellia, did they see you?"

"They saw me. Three of them came after me, but I was riding Melody, she is the swiftest of the mares, and I know the trails. I lost them in the woodlands."

Azil Aumson spoke from his place against the wall. "They will not know she is here. They will expect her to have gone to Chingura. They will be watching the east road."

"Then we will come on them from the north." He raised his voice. "Listen, all." The room went silent. "Twenty men, possibly from Reo Unamira's land, burned Thorin

Amdur's house tonight and drove off the stock. Thorin and Garth are dead. The children and servants are in the barn. We ride first to the farm, and then in pursuit of the killers. Is Macallan awake?"

"I am here, my lord," said the physician calmly.

"We shall need you. Marek, the command here is yours. Orm, you direct the archers this night. Hunter." The dragon-fury burned inside her mind. "There may be a wounded man somewhere on our path. Can you find him for me?"

She fought free of him. "I can do it," she said.

25

THEY TOOK NO road out of Dragon Keep. They cut north and east across the fields and into the forested hills below the mountains, racing through the narrow trails.

Mellia Amdur rode at Dragon's back. She had refused to stay behind. *My house, my husband,* she said. Her horse was badly winded; Herugin gave her Falcon, and she rode as if she had been born in the saddle, whispering to the spotted mare as a man might croon to a lover. Speed was vital now, not secrecy. Still, they were as silent as thirty armed riders and their horses can be along a woodland trail. There was no shouting, and few words: only the jingle and snap of metal, the hard breathing of horses, and the sound of hooves striking the ground.

They climbed one hill, galloped for a time along a barren ridge top, and then went down, into a forested valley. As they came from under the trees, Hawk smelled burning. Her long sight showed her the silhouettes of barn, stables, and sheds. Red fire flickered through fallen timbers. Beyond the curve of the valley, Coll's Ridge lifted lightless and bare against the majestic scrolling of the stars.

At Karadur's signal, they halted. He wheeled his horse to Hawk's side. "What say you, hunter? Are they watching the house?"

She reached into the darkness. There were no watchers on the hillside. "No, my lord." They rode across the fields.

Mellia went to the barn, calling softly through the doors. A woman came out, followed by three children. The boy glared fiercely at the shadowy strangers. The two little girls huddled in her skirts. Macallan trotted by her, carrying his instrument bag. The men lit torches. They combed the buildings.

"My lord," someone said, "we have found him." Three men moved from the darkness, carrying a man's body between them. They laid him at Dragon's feet. The dead man's clothes were stained scarlet from a wound in his chest. His hair was ruddy, his beard nearly white.

"Who is he?" Hawk whispered to Herugin.

"Thorin Amdur, Mellia's husband. He was cavalry master to Kojiro Atani. He was at the Keep when I arrived. I served under him for a year. His eldest son, Dennis, is head of the first cavalry wing in Ujo. He's red-haired, like Thorin. He's got a scar on his neck." Herugin drew his thumb along the side of his throat.

Hawk said, "Rides a bay stallion with a silver bridle? I remember him." He was affable, clever, and a competent officer. But then, Kalni Leminin did not promote incompetent officers.

A second body had been found. Sandor and Rogys laid it beside the first. "Garth," Herugin said. "The second son. Hern is the third son, and Ellis the baby. Ellis is not here; he is in Mako, serving in Erin diMako's guard. But Hern—"

"Hern may still be alive," Karadur said. "Herugin, leave five men here, and designate five more to take Mellia, Leanna, the children and the servants to Castria. Hurry."

With ten fewer men, they rode up the ridge. The splendid moon made the ridge top seem nearly bright as day. Hawk gazed down the slope of the sleeping forest, feeling the watchful thought of the night creatures, crouched in burrows or perched on tree limbs or curled in the shadow of rocks . . . "There," she said.

Hern Amdur lay beneath a fir tree, his dead horse beside him. Dazed with pain, he stared with evident confusion at this crop-haired stranger with an eye-patch standing above him, saying his name. Then Dragon bent over him.

The wounded man said, "Sir? My lord?"

"Yes. Lie still," Karadur said. He laid a light hand on the boy's head. "Where are you hurt?"

"My leg. A blow from a club. They shot my horse." He struggled to rise. "Sir—my father and my brother Garth—they're dead."

"I know. We came from the farm," Karadur said. "But your mother lives, and Leanna, and your brother's children." He slid an arm around the boy's lean shoulders, and eased him to a sitting position. "Who were they, Hern? Could you tell?"

"They were Unamira's men, sir. I recognized them."

"Your mother said they masked their faces."

"They did. But I knew them from their riding. The one who killed my father is named Edan. He's big and dark-haired; I've seen him before. But the one who gave the orders is a stranger to me."

Macallan knelt, and ran his hands along Hern Amdur's leg. He said calmly, "The leg is broken, and needs to be set."

"There's no time," the dragon-lord said. "Strap it so that he can ride as far as Castria."

Hern said, "No! Not Castria." He caught Karadur's arm. "My lord, I can ride—"

"No. You are going to Castria," said the dragon-lord, with finality.

"I need to straighten the leg, and then splint it." Macallan took a flat piece of wood from his bag. "Give him some brandy." Someone passed up a leather flask. "It will not take long, if you stay still. If we could have someone to hold him—"

"I will do that," the dragon-lord said. He shifted his position so that Hern could lean against him, and wrapped his arms around the slighter man. "Scream if you must," he said. But Hern did not scream, nor did he move, though he did groan once, as Macallan straightened the fractured leg, cushioned the splint with soft cloth, and bound all together with twine.

"Done," the physician said to his patient. "You did very well. You can have some more brandy, now."

Hern fumbled the flask to his lips. His face, in the shimmering moonlight, looked very white. He said faintly, "Dennis will be so angry at me. I told him I would keep them safe."

Karadur said, "Your brother may spend his anger on me. It is my charge to keep your family safe, and I failed it. Let us see if you can stand." He put an arm around the boy's slender back, and heaved him upright. "Arn, give him your spear. Hern, you will go to Castria. I shall send two men to ride with you. You are to rest, to heal, and to care for your mother. That is all you have to do, now."

☫   ☫   ☫

IN THE HOUSE on Coll's Ridge, the men were placing bets.

"A penny on the cat," Blaine yelled.

Nils, who had helped to trap the cat, threw a shoe at Blaine. It missed. One of the hounds leaped on it and carried it away to chew. "A penny? Blaine, you chiseler. Ten pennies."

"Twenty on the cock," offered Edan. He had to raise his voice to be heard. It had been Edan's idea to put the feral cat and the red fighting cock together in the barrel. Two men had been badly scratched, and the cock had nearly pecked Edan's eye out.

The noise was astonishing. In a moment the old man would come lurching down from his rooms, and shout at them. Someday, Treion Unamira decided, someday he would rip the old sot's throat out, as he had no doubt the cat was now doing to the bewildered cock. The cock had sharp spurs and a wicked beak, but the cat had teeth and claws and night vision and a deadly hunter's instinct. Were he willing to bet, he would bet on the cat. He lifted his wineskin. It held merignac, that liqueur of the gods. It tasted like honeyed fire. His grandfather's cellars contained six jeraboams of merignac; five now. He smiled, remembering the night's work. It was only a beginning, but still, they had done well. The old sot, his grandfather, had never done more than steal sheep and harry unwary merchants while Karadur Atani's back was turned. There was no future in sheep-stealing, and no fun in it either. But now, with the horses, his little tribe of brigands could do more. They had all of Ippa to range in—no, all of Ryoka. They would grow. He saw himself riding at the head of an outlaw band a hundred strong . . . The Bastard's Company, men would call it. He would like that.

He had originally intended only to steal the horses, not to kill, but the arrogance of the old horseman, coming at him with a sword, had enraged him. Firing the house had been an afterthought. Still, it had given him pleasure to watch it. He had always liked fire.

The uproar from the barrel was becoming tiresome.

"Stop it," he said to Edan. "Let them out." The men looked at him in stupefaction. Edan started to argue, thought better of it, and kicked Edric in the side.

"Get up. We're letting them go."

Warily they pried the top from the barrel. The cat staggered out, sneezing, bloodied. Nils whooped, and stuck his hands out. "Pay me!" he yelled. They squabbled about the winnings.

"Shut up," Treion said. He didn't raise his voice, but the place grew still. They were all learning, except the habitual drunks and the stupid ones, and unfortunately as long they could ride and shoot, he needed even the stupid ones. At least they had learned not to lie to him. He loathed lies—

they made him sick, literally. He had warned his grand-father's men—curs, who lied as easily as they breathed—the very first week of his arrival at the house, how much he hated it when people lied to him, and that if they did it, he would know. They had not believed him, of course. But they did now.

Edan, without being told, went out to make sure that the sentries were still there, still sober, and looking in the right direction. That was good. The stolen horses were hidden in the woods, picketed and guarded by two men he trusted; at least, he trusted them to need money, and now that he had finally deduced where the old sot kept his purse, he had money. That was also good. In another month he would have this motley miscellany of ruffians licked into shape, or dead. It troubled him that the woman had gotten away, but he was sure she had not recognized them. He had made it absolutely clear to his men that he would cut the throat of anyone who thought to ride without a mask. No one had challenged him.

Edan came back inside. Treion raised an eyebrow in question. Edan nodded.

Then the men with the swords came in.

❦ ❦ ❦

IT WAS NOT a fight. They found the men who had been left on guard—half-drunk, no trouble to subdue—and bound them, and entered the house. They disarmed the drunken outlaws. One man, more abstemious and agile than the rest, heard them coming and vanished out the back. Another— big, dark-haired—tried to fight, and got his head cracked for his pains.

The archers herded them outside, into the clearing before the manor house, where a pack of half-trained, hungry hounds skulked, growling and making angry rushes at the horses. Finle shot two of the dogs, and the rest fled. The manor house was scarcely more than farmhouse, with a long hall added on to it, in which the outlaws slept. The inside of the hall was littered with animal feces and half-eaten food and soiled rags that had once been someone's clothes. A bloodied cat lay panting in a corner.

"Gods," Rogys said, looking about, one hand on his knife, "this place is a dung-heap."

"I want Reo Unamira," Dragon said coldly. "Find him. Bring him to me." He turned, and walked to the clearing, where Orm's archers held their bows on the sodden outlaws. The Hunter's Moon burned fiercely overhead.

Herugin, sword in hand, took Orm and Lurri and went upstairs to the sleeping chambers. A man yelled: a vivid stream of invective, abruptly silenced. Then an old white-haired man, with Herugin behind him, walked through the doorway of the house. He wore a bedraggled night-robe. Herugin's sword point was in the small of his back.

The old man put his hands on his hips, ignoring the sword. "What damnable insolence is this?" he demanded grandly. "Who dares to interrupt my resht—rest?"

Karadur Atani looked at him. "You know who I am."

"Do I?" The old man squinted. "Ah. Yes. My overlord comes to visit me. Had I known you were coming, my lord, I would have prepared a prop—a proper welcome." He weaved down the front steps, staggering a little at the final, broken step. Herugin sheathed his sword. "Iva," the old man called into the moonlight, flinging his arms wide, "Iva, we have guests! Bring wine." He tottered. "Shorry. No more wine." He peered at the archers, and at his sullen, sobering men. "Wassis? Whassamatter?"

Karadur said, "Do you know where your band of cutthroats went tonight, old man? To Thorin Amdur's farm. They stole the horses. They killed Thorin and his son Garth. They fired the house and left everyone in it to burn."

"Ri-ridiculous," Unamira said. "Why would they do such a thing? I did not tell them to do that." But fear flickered at the corner of his eyes.

"They did it. And you must answer for it," the dragon-lord said.

Reo Unamira drew himself up, a parody of offended dignity. "You should not speak so to me, my lord. I served your father with honor. I saved his life in battle."

"I know it," Karadur Atani said. "You have traded on that service for thirty years. I grant you one day's grace. By sunset tomorrow you and your family must be gone from my domain."

"What of them?" the old man demanded. He waved an unsteady hand at the bandits.

Karadur said flatly, "They killed my people. Their lives are forfeit." He gazed at the sweating bandits. Their faces shone in the moonlight. "Which of you is Edan?"

No one answered. But two of the outlaws turned their heads. Karadur pointed to a broad-shouldered, dark-haired man. "You. Step forward." The man so addressed lifted his head slowly, and slouched one step toward the center of the clearing. "I think you are he. Finle. Kill him."

Finle's bow hummed. Edan jerked, and reeled backwards, hands plucking helplessly at the feathered shaft protruding from his chest. He fell.

The old man's seamed face twisted with malice. He scowled, and spat in the dirt. "So much for the gratitude of the dragon-kind." He raised his cracked voice. "Iva! Iva, we are leaving. Our gracious liege is dispossessing us from our home. Maia! Treion!"

The house door opened. A tall woman in a blue gown descended the damaged steps into the moonlight. Two lean, yellow-eyed wolfhounds, one coal black, the other silver-grey, paced at her side. "Treion is gone, Grandfather," she said.

"Gone . . ." The old man looked at her fretfully. "Gone. I don't understand. Where is Iva?"

She sighed wearily. "Iva is not here, Grandfather." She turned to face the dragon-lord. "My lord," she said, "as you can see, my grandfather drinks more than he should. It makes him say foolish things." Her gown, though patched and worn, was clean. She wore her long brown hair up and back on her head, Nakase fashion.

Karadur said, "Who are you?"

She gazed at him gravely. The wolfhounds stood like statues under her hand. "I beg your pardon. I am Maia diSorvino. My mother was Iva Unamira."

Reo Unamira leered. "You were supposed to marry her, boy! Your father and I had that all planned. But then he went mad. Mad Dragon." He tugged at his disheveled hair.

Karadur said slowly, "I remember. Your father sent a letter . . . That must have been five years ago. But I thought you were younger."

She smiled slightly. "I was younger. Five years ago I was thirteen."

"You are from Nakase?"

"I was born in Nakase, in Sorvino. My father is Marion diSorvino. I lived in his house as a child. My mother and I returned here six years ago."

The old man said airily, "You like the look of her, m'lord? I'll sell her to you. Twenty nobles. I'll even throw in the dogs." He snapped his fingers in the direction of the impassive archers. "You there. Get me some wine."

"Your mother—"

"Is dead, my lord. She died in January last year. She had been sick for many months."

"I am sorry."

"Why should you be? You never knew her."

The old man whined, "I want a drink. Treion took my merignac. Little bastard. She would never say who he was, no matter how I beat her." He cackled. "I knew, though. I saw them meeting in the woods." His words trailed into mumblings.

Maia diSorvino said quietly, "My lord, I beg you, ignore him. He has been like this since before my mother's death.

Thorin Amdur's death was not his doing. My brother Treion planned and led that raid. Ask any of his cohorts, if any are sober enough to talk. They will tell you." She flicked a contemptuous look at the outlaws.

A cheerful voice said, "My loving sister is quite right. I do not deny it." A man with hair the color of honey sauntered into the clearing. He was stylishly, elegantly dressed, in a manner wholly different from the outlaws' haphazard garments. "However, I must correct her assertion that I ran away. I did not run away. I merely moved faster than these cretins." His glance at the men he led was a duplicate of his sister's. "I am Treion Unamira. They call me the bastard." The sword in his right hand looked serviceable and quite sharp.

Karadur said coldly, "I have no interest in your parentage. Was it indeed you who led tonight's raid?"

"It was. Though I did not kill the old man. Edan did that." He nodded toward the dead man. "I see he has paid for it."

"You are a thief and a murderer," Karadur said. "Herugin, take him."

"Certainly, my lord." Herugin, drawing his sword, walked confidently toward the fair-haired man. Treion Unamira stepped forward, a lazy, seemingly artless step, but there was nothing torpid about his sword-arm. His blade licked the air like a slash of fire. Herugin's sword tumbled from his hand. Treion's sword point flew to the cavalry officer's throat.

"I am not to be taken so easily, my lord," the fair-haired man said. "Tell your men to lay their arrows in the dirt. Otherwise he dies."

No one moved. Herugin looked at Karadur. The dragonlord said stonily, "Do it." The archers let their arrows roll onto the ground.

"You drunken, stupid pigs," Treion Unamira said scathingly to the outlaws. "Find your weapons and meet me where we left the horses. Go." The freed men scrambled to obey. "My lord, as you have ordained, we will leave. You will not see us again, though you may hear of us. I intend that you shall hear of us. I will take your officer with me, however; he shall be my safe-conduct till I leave your land. Edric, get a long rope. Tie his wrists together in front." An outlaw came forward, fumbling with a length of cord. He wrapped the cord around Herugin's wrist. The end of the rope trailed in the dirt. "Good. Now get me a horse. One of theirs. Excellent. The rest of you, take their horses. Hurry." The outlaws obeyed. "Edric, tie the other end of the rope to the saddle." The tip of Treion's sword did not move an inch.

He waited until the rope had been secured, and then mounted. "I understand you brand brigands in this country." The sword point slashed at wicked speed across Herugin's face, and returned immediately to his throat. Blood dripped from a shallow cut on his left cheek.

"My brand," Treion said.

He prodded Herugin lightly in the center of the chest. The sky lightened. From the high branches, the summer birds were calling down the dawn. A fiery pattern played beneath Karadur's skin. He said tightly, "If he dies, make no mistake: I will find you."

"I wouldn't want you to do that," Treion Unamira agreed helpfully. "So I suppose I shall keep him alive. Farewell, Grandfather." He gazed coldly at the old man. "You are a vicious old drunk. I hope your death finds you soon. Farewell, sister dear. Walk, you." He urged the horse into the trees. Herugin, unable to resist, trotted at his side.

The old man collapsed onto the steps of the decaying house.

"That bastard. Iva's little bastard," he whined morosely. "It was my idea to name him Treion. It means treasure. I meant it as a joke. The joke's on me. He took my treasure. Stole my soldiers. Drank my merignac." He grinned crazily, showing yellow crooked teeth. "Bad dragon. Mad dragon. Mad as your father."

"Old man, be quiet," Finle said.

"Mad dragon. They say you killed your brother for his treasure. Chests of gold and jewels." He waggled his fingers in the air. "Poof! I had chests of gold and jewels once. Dragon's gold. Your father gave it to me. I told him he should marry her, but no, he wouldn't do it, not my daughter, the lovely slut.

"He fucked her, though. I saw them, I saw them meeting. I knew the Diamori girl would never satisfy him."

All color fled from Karadur's face. His cobalt eyes glittered: alien, unbearable, remote.

The farmhouse exploded. A terrible crackling heat engulfed the building, the ground, the trees. A hot wind roared across the valley. Reo Unamira's mouth opened in an O of helpless astonishment. Then he was burning. The morning blazed with lightning. A shadow fell over them. The Golden Dragon sprang into the air, spread wings beating the sky. He soared above the burning farmhouse, cobalt eyes glittering with rage. Blue-white fire streamed from his open mouth.

Fire licked at them with a thousand hungry tongues. "Run!" Finle cried. Hawk's vision filled with flame. Maia diSorvino raced ahead of her, hair loose in the wind. The black wolfhound loped at her side. The dragon's inhuman, furious bellow split the sky. A searing silver rain fell from the brilliant air. The fir trees blazed like candles. A pungent smoke blew across the hillside. There was no place to go. Hawk stumbled. The smoke was thickening. She gasped for breath.

A hand grasped her arm. It was Orm. "The stream—this way." Her single eye stinging with tears, choking, nearly blind, she followed him. Someone shrieked, a hopeless, wordless cry of pain. The air itself was burning.

They fell into the water, and held each other, while the air dripped fire.

"Pray," Orm whispered.

Hawk prayed that the firestorm would not find them, that the dragon would remember that he was human, and that below him were other humans, some his friends who loved him, and whom he also loved. . . .

The fire stopped on the ridge top. The bare rock would not burn.

The men from Dragon Keep, and Hawk, gathered on the north side of the hill. She and Orm, Finle, Rogys, and half a dozen others had found shelter in the stream. The rest—ten men, including Macallan and Elief, and Huw—were dead.

Orm had lost his hair. Finle and Rogys were burned. Their horses were gone: the outlaws had taken most of them, and those not taken by the outlaws had fled before the dragon's roar. Like their riders, they lay black and foul on the hillside, trapped and killed by the relentless flames. Two horses—Finle's bay mare, and Smoke—had survived. Finle, despite the bad burns on his arms and hands, had chased and caught the bay. Smoke, though seemingly unhurt, hovered at a distance, refusing to come to Rogys's steady calling.

On the south side of the hill, Coll's Ridge was ash. The Unamira house was gone as if it had never been. The Golden Dragon was gone: vanished into the sky.

Maia diSorvino had survived the firestorm. They found her, grey with smoke as they all were, and with one whole side of her gown charred, sitting on a rock, looking down at the place where the house had been. There was no sign of the grey wolfhound, but the black dog lay panting at her feet.

Orm, after an awkward pause, walked toward her. The

black wolfhound lifted its head and growled. She spoke softly to it, and it stilled.

"Are you all right?" Orm asked. "Do you have a place you can go? Neighbors? Friends you can stay with?"

The brown-haired woman smiled wryly. "The grand-daughter of Reo Unamira? What do you think?"

"You need shelter," he said. "Come with us."

"To Dragon Keep? Karadur Atani might not like that. I will be all right. I have lived on this ridge for six years: I know it well. Morga can hunt for me." The black wolfhound's tail thumped; she bent, and stroked its neck. "You need not trouble about me." It was evident she would not change her mind.

They discussed, briefly, what to do. Orm said, "I say we go back."

Rogys said, "What about Herugin?"

Orm said, "He might be dead. We don't know. There's nothing we can do for him as we are." There was no argument. Leading the weary horse, they turned north along the ridge top. Hawk trudged in Orm's footsteps. Her clothes stank of river mud. Her skin felt hot all over, and her lungs ached with each breath.

Her mind ached, too, and her heart. Huw was dead, his bones melted in the earth.

Birds, shocked mute by the dragon's roar, had started to sing again. A curious chipmunk popped its head out of its hole.

Hunter . . .

Hawk stopped. Rogys, behind her, lost his balance, slipped, and swore. The sound seemed shockingly loud.

"What is it?" asked Orm.

"Dragon," she said. She gazed upward, and pointed. "There."

The golden beast fell slowly toward them, floating like a leaf in the wind. He landed, and changed. They waited, un-certain, as he walked to them across the blackened ground.

His shirt was shredded, his golden hair tangled. He looked unutterably weary.

He did not speak, nor did they.

But his eyes, his eyes were human.

EPILOGUE

———◆◆———

THERE WAS A beehive in the hollow log.

He had not seen it at first, but then the bees had come zooming over to buzz about the primroses he was lying in. Being curious, he had watched them, and seen them drink from the delicate purple flowers, and then vanish, pif-poof.

He sat by the log while bees trickled in and out, and told them his name, and that he had no interest in their honey or their babies. Lauren, the Keep's beekeeper, had told him to do that whenever he met strange bees, and indeed, it worked: the bees seemed barely to notice him.

Lauren had told him that bees were lucky, and that if you were kind to them, and did not trouble them, they would lend you some of their luck. *What's luck?* he asked. The beekeeper had laughed. *You'll find out when you lose it,* she said.

He sat with the bees for a while. Then he went back to the secret place he had found. It was a flawless hiding place. The great boulder jutted out from the slope of the hill so as to make a wonderful shadow, and the tall, flame-colored flowers—fireweed, Hawk called them—that grew down-slope from the boulder made a brilliant spiky fence, behind which a small, patient boy could lie and remain entirely unseen.

The sky was unbelievably blue. Far to the west lay a line of feather clouds, harbingers of rain to come, but rain too held its wonders, such as the reappearance of frogs and newts and dusky purple lizards that hid in the rocks, and ventured out at twilight. It had not rained for days. Finches bobbed in the tall dry grass, hunting seeds and insects, calling to one another. The shadowed ground was dry, a little cool, but he had brought his cloak to lie on. There was bread and a hunk of cheese in his pocket, and, wrapped in cloth, a piece of hard dry smoked beef for Morga.

He had hidden his pony near the stream, among the birches. The spindly trees shifted and trembled, but the pony, a placid beast, never moved. The grass beneath the birches was green and thick, delicious if you were a pony. He had eaten grass once, just to see what it tasted like. It had made him sick. The pony was grey and white, mostly white; he had named her Bella, after the white flowers that opened in early spring and looked like upside-down bells.

A cold friendly nose poked into his ear. "Morga!" He rolled on his side. Morga licked him happily. He hugged her.

"Lie down," he whispered, patting the dirt. She lay down immediately. She was the biggest dog he had ever seen, much bigger than Turtle, bigger even than Savage, the great bull-headed, scar-faced leader of the Dragon Keep hounds. Her lean body was solid with muscle.

He butted his head companionably against her furred flank. "Big dog," he said softly, "you big old dog." He dug into his shirt and brought out the strip of meat. Her tail thumped.

"Don't grab," he admonished her sternly. Morga took the meat from his fingertips with terrible delicacy. Her immense, triangular teeth were sharp as swords.

He rolled on his back, and stared at the cerulean sky. No one—except Morga—knew he was here. That had taken some cunning. Turtle, usually his constant companion, was tussling with his brothers in the dog pen, under the watchful gaze of Luga the dog-boy. Kiala thought he had gone

with Devin to play in the buttery. Devin thought he was in
the stable. Rogys, who had helped him saddle the pony,
thought he had gone for a sedate, permitted trot to the training ground. Devin would not tell; even though he was
eight, and Shem nearly six, they were the same weight, and
the last time they had wrestled, Shem had won. Kiala would
not tell; she liked it when he was gone; it meant she had less
to do. Rogys *would* tell, if he went to the training ground,
and Shem was not there. *Listen, cub,* Rogys had said, *ride
carefully! If you're hurt, Herugin'll skin me.* Shem had
promised to be careful. He meant to keep that promise; he
did not want Herugin to skin Rogys. He was nervous of
Herugin, who was extremely strict, and more than a little
frightening to look at, with that long red scar on his face.
Shem had once asked him where it came from. Herugin
had told him that a bad man had put it there, and that he,
Herugin, would someday find that man and kill him.

Hawk had told him that there had been a terrible fire on
this hill, many years ago. He had been a baby, then, too
small even for a pony. He was older now, old enough,
surely, to ride alone, even this far from the Keep. It *was*
quite far; he knew that. But he was a good rider. And nothing could happen to him here. This was Dragon's country,
all of it, from the tall dark mountains where the condors
lived, to places that were farther than he could ride even if
he rode all day.

He rolled on his stomach, and peered down at the little
stone house in the holly thicket. When first he had seen it,
riding behind Hawk on her horse's back, it had seemed familiar, as if he had seen it before. He thought he must have
dreamed it. When a tall, slender woman with long brown
hair came from the cottage, she had looked familiar too.

He had said to Hawk, *She was in my dream.*

Hawk had said, *What dream was that, cub?*

But he had not been able to answer her. And then it
seemed to him that he was wrong, and that he did not know

the brown-haired woman. A strange sadness had come over him. It made his face all prickly and hot. From that moment, the little house seemed to him to hold a mystery. Thrice now he had come here, alone, and stretched himself in the tall brown grass, and watched, unnoticed by any but the ebullient finches and the big black dog.

Then he heard the drumming.

He thought at first it was the bees, roused to rage by something invisible. Then he felt it, through his skin. He laid his ear to the ground. It was horses: no, not horses— one horse. Morga had heard it too; her body quivered; her lean head lifted, ears turning to track the sound.

He craned his head around to watch the ridge top. He saw the shadow, and then the big black horse came over the ridge. He knew that horse, and the fair-haired, dark-clad man who rode it. Swiftly he crunched himself small, and thrust himself deep under the lip of the boulder, where the shadow was deepest. Morga barked, a high flat yelp of welcome. She dashed up the slope, ears pricked, head erect, tail waving like a flag.

Shem held his breath. Bella knew the black horse, too. Bella might whinny. If Bella whinnied, she would be discovered, and so would he . . . If he was found, Kiala would be beaten, and Herugin might indeed skin Rogys. And Dragon, the fair-haired man, the most important person in all the world, would be angry with him, for riding so far alone, for pretending to be where he was not, and most of all for doing what he knew would mean that others would be punished . . . He felt cold. *Don't let it happen,* he whispered silently to the friendly bees.

The fair-haired man brought the horse to the trough to drink. Morga sidled up to him, and he gentled her ears, and scratched her under the chin the way she loved. Bella did not whinny. Shem breathed again.

The cottage door opened. The brown-haired woman came out. She was wearing blue. She called Morga. The wolfhound trotted to her instantly. The woman petted her and told her something which made the dog's ears flatten and her tail sag in disappointment. Then she went and lay down beside the door.

Dragon tied Smoke's reins to the gatepost. He did not hurry.

The woman waited, her face still and bright and warm as sunlight.

Taken by that stillness, the boy beside the rock watched as the man walked down the path. The woman held her hand out. Their fingers laced together. They passed beneath the holly that grew over the door, and, silent as the figures in a long-forgotten dream, entered the little house.